*Spoils of War* is Peter
in London, grew up i
for the past seventeen
complex and intriguing thrillers, *The Wacy Conspiracy*,
was made into a successful feature film and established
his reputation as an international bestselling author.

*Also by Peter Driscoll*

SECRETS OF STATE

*and published by Corgi Books*

# SPOILS OF WAR

## Peter Driscoll

**CORGI BOOKS**

**SPOILS OF WAR**
**A CORGI BOOK : 0 552 13827 4**

Originally published in Great Britain by Bantam Press,
a division of Transworld Publishers Ltd

PRINTING HISTORY
Bantam Press edition published 1994
Corgi edition published 1995

Set in 10/11.5pt Plantin by Photoprint, Torquay, Devon

Corgi Books are published by Transworld Publishers Ltd,
61–63 Uxbridge Road, Ealing, London W5 5SA,
in Australia by Transworld Publishers (Australia) Pty Ltd,
15–25 Helles Avenue, Moorebank, NSW 2170,
and in New Zealand by Transworld Publishers (NZ) Ltd,
3 William Pickering Drive, Albany, Auckland.

Reproduced, printed and bound in Great Britain by
Cox & Wyman Ltd, Reading, Berks.

*For Bruce Hunter. And with thanks to
several friends whose knowledge of the
Middle East, offered generously but
anonymously, has contributed to
the writing of this book.*

# Prologue

Waiting by the window, Noura was the first to see the car arrive. The glare of its headlights suddenly filled the gap between the gateposts a hundred metres away, throwing shadows towards the house from the date palms along the drive.

The car stopped in the gateway. Noura was in no doubt who the visitor was, for only his kind were free to move about during the curfew. The hut once occupied by security guards was caught in the beams of light and she saw the figures of two soldiers shambling out of it. Flip and Flop, her imbecile protectors, half asleep as usual. They bent beside the driver's window and then straightened up and saluted, pantomiming alertness after their dazed vigil. The car nosed forward down the drive.

Noura turned to her companion. 'It's him!' she whispered excitedly. 'He's come for me, Dale.'

She found her hands shaking as she fumbled in the darkened room for the small bag she had packed. Fear had eroded her confidence. The weeks of uncertainty, the horror stories from beyond the gates, had made her unwilling even until this minute to leave the precarious safety within the compound walls; but suddenly she was impatient to go.

Her excitement turned to guilt as she faced her friend again.

'I hate just leaving you here, Dale.'

'I'll be fine,' the older woman said. 'You've already helped all you could.'

'But you helped *me*,' Noura protested. 'I could ask him if he can do something for you.'

'Don't complicate things. He doesn't know I exist.'

'He might be able to take you out as well.'

'He might decide to arrest me instead. Forget it.'

The faint hum of air-conditioning filled the silence, masking any sounds that might have entered the room from the desert night. Noura did not argue further. The other woman had a quiet determination that she didn't know quite how to cope with. She had also once been Noura's college teacher, although to look at the two of them now – almost identically clothed in colourless *fustaan* frocks, cheap sandals and black *abayas* – they might have been sisters playing at dressing up.

The lights of the car swept towards them. Its driver knew the layout of the compound, turning away from the main house and down the secondary drive towards the newer buildings. All were deserted except this one and the servants' quarters at the back, inhabited now by only three or four frightened Indians and Filipinos.

'I'd better go,' said Noura.

They went to the front door together and kissed and hugged each other. Their close confinement here had produced an intensity of feeling between them that brought the pricking of tears to Noura's eyes. She said: 'What are you going to do, Dale?'

'I told you, I have other friends. You just take care of yourself.' Dale paused. 'You are sure you can trust this man, aren't you?'

'I think so. I must, really.'

'Good luck, then. *Tawasal bis-salaama*.'

'You too. Goodbye, Dale.'

Noura gave her a final hug and opened the door.

Stepping out of the air-conditioned house was like walking into a furnace; though it was close to midnight, the blast of dry summer heat carried on the *shamal* wind was so fierce it made her gasp. She watched the car gliding quietly into the courtyard, its driver dousing the lights as it stopped a few metres in front of her. It was a big, pale-grey Mercedes, probably stolen like everything else they were using.

The driver's door opened and the Iraqi officer got out.

He was in civilian dress, as he had been on the other occasions when he'd come to the house: a dark suit, a white shirt and a narrow tie. He didn't greet her, but stood and studied her critically under the starlight as she approached.

'Is it safe to leave?' she ventured. She'd been frightened of him at first, and his manner still made her feel awkward. Him. He had never told her his name.

He ignored the question but eyed the bag she was clutching. 'You've brought nothing that will identify you?'

'No.'

'Listen carefully. The plane is waiting. There are certain things you must remember in case you are asked. You will travel as my wife. For tonight my name is Ghani and you are *sayida* Al-Falaki. Given name, Fatma.'

'Al-Falaki?'

'Remember it,' he emphasized. He seemed edgy and preoccupied. 'Conduct yourself as a married woman. Say nothing unless you are spoken to. Put on your *hijab*. And wear this.'

He held up something between his thumb and forefinger. She took it and saw that it was a wedding ring. With some misgiving she slipped it on her finger, then drew up the veil to cover the lower half of her face. Aware that the front door was still open, that Dale was probably watching from the shadows, she glanced involuntarily back at the house.

He detected the movement. 'Who's in there?' he demanded.

'Only a servant.' Noura surprised herself with the swiftness of the lie. 'She knows nothing.'

He looked at her disapprovingly. 'You people and your servants,' he said with mild disgust.

He turned towards the car and she followed. She made

11

for the front passenger door but he stopped her and opened the one behind.

'In here,' he said. 'It is expected. You are a wife now.'

The soldiers grinned and saluted again as the car passed through the gate. His own soldiers, hand-picked to be her watchdogs, too peasant-ignorant to wonder why they'd been told to guard the daughter and the house of one rich man while their comrades raped and looted all the others; unaware of how long the arm of a rich man could be.

The Mercedes moved past the gates and between the high walls of other great houses, dark and abandoned. It felt strange to be out on the streets after the weeks of confinement, stranger still to find them deserted under the clamp of the curfew. The Iraqi drove cautiously, alert no doubt for roadblocks manned by his trigger-happy countrymen. Think of him as Ghani, she told herself. Although she hadn't the courage to say it, Noura thought he might treat her with more respect. He knew who her father was, and surely he was being well rewarded for what he was doing. He naturally hadn't told her anything but the barest details of his plans; but he had hinted gruffly that he had enemies of his own to contend with.

Perhaps to help calm his nerves he picked a tape from the shelf beneath the dashboard and put it on the deck. Melancholy *f'jeri* music filled the car, the work songs of pearl fishermen echoing the romantic version of their past that Noura's people clung to. Some of them hypocritically, she considered. Like her father, who could buy almost anything and anyone, regretting the way that wealth had corrupted the old values. Shaking his head over his daughter's independent ways after sending her to spend half her life in the West. Still, this was no time to find fault with him. Her father was a worker of miracles. In spite of her defiance in the matter of her marriage, he had found a way to rescue her from this nightmare.

Noura wished Dale could have come with her. During

12

the dilemma over her betrothal she had grown to depend on the older woman's calmness and good advice, a reliance that had grown after the invasion when her former tutor had come to her in a predicament of her own. It had never crossed Noura's mind to refuse her refuge, though she knew her father would never have permitted her to shelter a foreigner wanted by the invaders.

She stared at the back of Ghani's neck as he guided the car out of the residential area, on to the Fifth Ring and then the airport motorway. There were only a few military vehicles about, their drivers showing no interest in the civilian car, and there was still no sign of any roadblocks. It was as though the city had been evacuated, not occupied, and yet a sense of nameless evil hung over it.

The suburbs fell behind them and soon the lights of the airport came into view across a flat expanse of desert. The Mercedes began to slow down and a few moments later Noura saw the barricade ahead, barrels drawn across the exit road and flashlight beams dancing in the hands of soldiers. She sat rigid with tension as the Iraqi brought the car to a halt, lowering his window, letting in a gush of hot air.

A young officer sauntered over. Ghani held out an identity document, and at the sight of it the soldier stiffened to attention.

'*Estikhbarat*?' he said. 'My apologies for troubling you. And the lady . . .?'

Ghani answered for her. 'My wife. We are travelling privately to Baghdad.' He had another document ready, presumably the *shahadat*, the paper of Iraqi citizenship he had said he would procure for her. The officer gave it only a cursory glance.

'Thank you. God give you a safe journey, *ya-ustaz*.'

The car moved forward. Ghani passed by the main terminal buildings and took a side road running parallel to a long wire fence. Behind this were signs of tremendous

13

activity. Big transport planes were parked under floodlights at the edge of the airfield; trailers laden with cargo were being hauled into sheds and warehouses, or offloaded into waiting trucks. All this in the middle of the night, presumably to avoid the daytime scrutiny of American reconnaissance planes.

At the end of the fence was a gate guarded by more troops. Another brief inspection of their documents got them through, apparently into some section of the airport reserved for military use. Soldiers swarmed everywhere, and Noura had a sense of having penetrated some forbidden nerve centre of the occupation.

Ghani swung onto an unmarked route behind a long line of buildings, away from the lights and the bustle. Noura had lost all sense of direction but guessed they were heading towards an outer edge of the airfield. Off to one side she could see a section of runway, a black stripe flanked by rows of lights disappearing across the desert.

The car made another turn as it reached the last of the buildings. The Iraqi drove a short way down a strip of concrete paving and stopped. He switched off the engine and the lights, letting darkness envelop them. He opened the glove box, and by the dim lamp inside it she saw him take out a heavy pistol. He cocked it, engaged the safety catch and slipped it into his pocket.

'We walk from here,' he said.

They got out of the car and, in spite of the heat, Noura felt a shiver of apprehension. This place seemed utterly deserted, vaguely sinister. The building they were parked beside was a huge, windowless structure, at least a hundred metres square and made of dark-painted corrugated iron. She took it to be an aircraft hangar. To the other side was a fenced-off area containing fuel storage tanks; beyond that was nothing but desert.

Ghani led her to the wall of the building and they moved along beside it. In the shadow that it had cast the darkness seemed absolute. When they reached the corner he paused and held up his hand, cautioning silence.

The front of the hangar faced out on to a concrete apron. The building had high steel doors arranged in movable sections, some of which had been folded back to make an opening a few metres wide. A light from inside was thrown across the apron to where a plane was parked.

Her heart lifted at the sight of the plane. It was a private jet, its smooth, pale shape similar to that of her father's Lear, but bigger. Two engines were mounted to the rear of its fuselage. A door just behind the cockpit was open and a ramp led up to it. The cabin lights were on but there was no sign of anyone in or near it.

A noise came from within the hangar. It was a low, rumbling sound as if something heavy was being rolled across the floor. It stopped after a few seconds and then she heard a brief, incoherent murmur of men's voices.

Ghani did not seem to share Noura's relief. If anything he was more uneasy than ever. He was looking furtively around and she realized that he smelt of nervous sweat.

'Go to the plane,' he whispered suddenly.

Noura began to ask why but he cut her short with an angry mutter. 'Go there. Wait for me.'

She was reluctant to leave the protection of the darkness but she stepped forward. In her rubber-soled sandals she walked silently out onto the apron.

The aircraft was about thirty metres away. As she approached it she saw that the ramp leading to the door had no steps, only metal rollers for loading cargo. She scrambled awkwardly up it and ducked in through the door.

It was hotter than ever in the airless cabin, but what she saw made her forget her discomfort. Apart from the pilot's seat and the one beside it, there was room for six or eight passenger seats. All but two of these seemed to have been removed. Wooden pallets were spread out on the open deck space, three layers of them on which rows of curious yellow slabs had been placed, the size and shape of small bricks. There was something familiar about the look of them – their texture, the way they reflected the dim cabin lights with a soft metallic glow – that she couldn't quite call to mind.

She glanced uncertainly back towards the hangar. If Ghani was still at the corner he was invisible in the darkness. A shadow crossed the lighted opening in the building and Noura instinctively flinched back from the doorway, moving further into the cabin.

Her way was blocked by the stack of yellow bricks. She bent down and pressed her palm to one on the top row. It had a cold, smooth, slightly soapy feel. It was small enough to allow her fingers to grip it, but when she tried to pick it up it seemed stuck to the pallet. She realized it was too heavy for her hand to lift.

In a moment of insight she understood what it was. A few years ago a jewellery firm on a promotional visit from New York had put a bar of pure gold on display in a glass case in the lobby of the Phoenicia Hotel. It had been the same size and shape as these bricks, and according to the explanatory notice it had been worth a hundred and fifty thousand American dollars. In this plane there were several dozen of them at least, possibly hundreds. There were more of them to come, for extra pallets were stacked against a bulkhead to the rear.

She felt faintly dizzy and questions crowded her mind. If this was the aircraft that was to fly them to safety, why had it been loaded with this cargo? And did Ghani know about it?

Faintly, the odd rumbling sound she had heard through the hangar wall reached her again. Glancing out through a porthole, she saw a man silhouetted against the opening, manoeuvring a contraption out of it, a two-handled trolley with metal wheels which he trundled noisily across the concrete. There was just enough light for her to see the gleam of gold bars on the trolley. He was bringing another load of them to the plane.

Noura dropped to the floor, out of sight through the porthole. Bewilderment had given way to fear. Where was Ghani? If he'd explained what was going on she would not have felt so helpless. She knew so little of Ghani – not even who he really was – that it was impossible to guess at his intentions.

She heard the trolley draw closer. Though she did not understand what was happening, she felt sure now that she had not been meant to be a part of these proceedings, that they had nothing to do with Ghani's obligations to her father, and yet that her fate was bound up in them. Her friend, Dale, had been right to question the trust she had put in the man.

The trolley stopped beside the plane. She heard the man grunt with effort as he lifted the first of the new batch of gold bars on to the ramp. Then she heard his exclamation of surprise.

Light flooded into the cabin through the portholes and the doorway. Bright, glaring shafts of it, overlapping each other. The headlights of cars racing onto the apron, their beams sweeping around like searchlights. The discordant roar of engines shattered the silence. Tyres shrieked, doors slammed; there came the sounds of men shouting and running, from close by and from some distance away.

And then, shooting.

Two or three hard bangs somewhere near the plane. Half a dozen more echoing explosively inside the hangar. More confused shouting, more milling around.

Noura hadn't dared lift her head. She lay face-down on the deck of the plane, hearing her breath coming in quick, stifled gasps through her veil. Excited voices reached her from beyond the doorway, and then there were men stumbling up the ramp, over the metal rollers. Two or three of them bulking against the cabin lights, smelling of sweat and tobacco, one of them pulling her roughly to her feet and propelling her forward. Dazedly she recognized the blue overalls that

17

were the uniform of the *Mukhabarat*, the Iraqi special police.

They manhandled her to the cabin door and flung her down the ramp.

She was pitched head-first down the rollers and landed in a heap at the bottom, breaking her fall with her hands but grazing them searingly on the Tarmac. She was seized and lifted again, half-dragged between two men. She felt a strange tackiness on her face and her burning hands, and realized she had fallen in a patch of blood. It had formed beside the body of another blue-uniformed man who lay on the ground, his trolley of gold bars overturned beside him.

The *Mukhabarat* pushed her to the door of the hangar. Of the three or four cars that were parked around it the closest was a black Cadillac, polished to a bright sheen, its chromework gleaming in the reflection of its own headlights. A pennant hung from a post on its wing and a man in a pale uniform and a dark beret sat in the back. Inside the building, lamps set among the high steel girders shone down on a squat, heavy van. It was an armoured security vehicle of the sort used for transporting money, but painted in desert-coloured military camouflage. Through the open rear doors more gold bars were visible, stacked on pallets like loaves in a baker's van.

Beside the vehicle, two more men were sprawled. Blood stained their blue overalls and had run in rivulets from beneath their bodies to mix and begin congealing in a single large pool. Beyond any sense of horror now, Noura thought: It's their own people they've been killing.

The men backed her up against the iron wall of the hangar. They let her slump against it, dazed with shock, and stood on either side of her. There were three or four other Iraqis moving about the building, but there was no sign of Ghani.

After a minute another man came through the doorway. He was the one who'd been sitting in the Cadillac. The shoulderboards of his uniform were smothered in gold braid and he carried a short cane bound in leather. He looked Noura up and down, then reached out and pulled off her *hijab*, making her flinch. He took her by the chin and turned her face into the light, studying her features dispassionately through dark, heavy-lidded eyes. He said calmly: '*Ya-aanisa*, you had better tell me exactly what your part has been in this.'

She wanted to reply. There was something so cold and forbidding about this man that her instinct was to placate him, to spill out the truth. Besides, she owed no loyalty to Ghani now; but fear had brought a choking sensation to her throat and she couldn't find the words. The man went on watching her, slapping his palm with the cane once or twice in a studied show of impatience. Then, without warning, he lashed out with it at her face. It struck her hard across the left cheek, slamming her head sideways. The pain was immediate and agonizing, making her cry out.

'So you do have a tongue in your mouth,' the man said. 'At least that is established. In time you will use it to explain why you were stealing gold from the Iraqi state treasury.'

Noura stared at him incredulously through tear-filled eyes. She could feel her face swelling, her left eye starting to close. She found her voice at last.

'I know nothing of this. Please believe me. Find the man who brought me here. Ask him.'

'What man?'

'He's one of you. I don't know his real name. Tonight he calls himself Ghani. He was to help me leave the country.'

The Iraqi looked around him in mock surprise. 'And where is this Ghani now?'

'I don't know. I think he ran away.'

'You don't know his name, and you don't know where he is.' There was a trace of amusement in the Iraqi's voice. He paused for a moment. 'Well, that's what happens when

19

you put your trust in a thief. Whatever he told you, that plane is so heavy with gold that I doubt there would have been room for you.'

'Let Ghani answer to you,' Noura said.

'I wish he could. It might save me a lot of trouble.' The man sounded almost playful now. 'You see, Ghani is *my* name. Your friend is evidently someone else.'

Noura was speechless again. She had thought she was escaping from a nightmare, but now she knew it had only just begun.

*Part One*

# 1

When Jack Rushton told Alison he was thinking of going back to Kuwait for a few days, she made one of her faces. It was a play of features that he had once found quite appealing but that now vaguely irritated him, a slight upward twisting of one side of her mouth that seemed to express scepticism and disapproval at once.

'What for?' she said.

'To get our money out. You know the banks have just reopened.'

'They won't let you have very much.' Alison read the newspapers just as avidly as he did. 'They said they'd only be releasing a few thousand dinars to begin with.'

'That's better than nothing, isn't it? Nearly everything we've got left is still out there.'

'Don't I know it? You could arrange to have it sent by post, surely?'

'That could take weeks. Maybe months. Things still seem pretty chaotic. If I'm on the spot perhaps I can find a loophole in these new regulations.'

'We can't afford the air fare, Jack. Not for something that isn't essential.'

'I thought you might be glad to get rid of me,' he said flippantly, then qualified the statement with a gesture around the sitting room. 'After eight months of being cooped up with me.'

They didn't argue any further. They'd become frightened of arguments, which had a way these days of suddenly turning personal and nasty. They also upset the twins, who were getting just old enough to sense an unpleasant atmosphere without understanding it. Jack went ahead with his plans, though not without a certain sense of guilt. Alison had been right: his journey wasn't really necessary. It was an expensive excuse for getting away.

Kuwait airport still wasn't taking any commercial traffic so he would have to travel via Saudi Arabia. It took a few days to renew his visas and he left London on Good Friday, 29 March, one month and a day after Operation Desert Storm had driven the Iraqis out of Kuwait. He flew to Riyadh and then on to Dhahran, where he stayed overnight with his friends Eric and Sylvia Patley.

The banks in Kuwait City had been open for only a few days and apparently were still being besieged by their customers. Over dinner he made a joke out of the purpose of his journey, telling the Patleys he'd never expected to have to stand in a queue to collect his life savings. Eric took him seriously though, insisting there was no need for that, offering to lend him whatever he needed. Eric was one of those spontaneously generous people you found among the long-term expatriate community. He and Sylvia were a childless Canadian couple in their sixties who shared a splendid penthouse with eight or ten tiny dogs. They had befriended Jack and Alison during a holiday weekend in Bahrain and ever since had doted like surrogate grandparents on their twin girls. Apart from that there was nothing sentimental about Eric, who had knocked about the Middle East for thirty years, quietly making a fortune in a number of slightly dubious financial enterprises. Eventually, with the blessing of Aramco, the Saudi-American oil giant, he had set up in Dhahran as a freelance investment broker, finding good homes for the tens of millions of surplus dollars that the company's foreign employees saved every year from their tax-free earnings.

Jack refused the offer. He wasn't broke, at least not yet; and perhaps an uneasy sense had grown in him lately that he wasn't the right kind of person to lend money to. However, he did accept Sylvia's invitation to borrow her car for a couple of days and save the cost of hiring one.

He set off at five the next morning, with daylight just creeping in over the placid waters of the Gulf. The artificial garden city that was Dhahran quickly gave way to desert; almost the only feature along the level, monotonous road to the north was the Tapline oil pipe that kept it company for a hundred and fifty kilometres before turning off to travel to the Mediterranean. The road was already busy with military traffic, though, and he had to stop at half a dozen checkpoints – the Saudi soldiers seeming not quite sure who or what they were supposed to be checking – so it was nearly nine o'clock before he reached the border.

Well before that he had seen the smoke from the burning oil wells, thick black pillars of it, already familiar from the television pictures, rising hundreds of feet above the desert ahead before thinning out and drifting towards the coast on the light westerly breeze.

A long convoy of American military vehicles was being waved through the border post at Al-Nuwaisib, but for him there was the usual wait while the Saudi immigration and customs officials argued languidly with each other over the validity of his visa and the documents of the borrowed Ford Granada. They got done with him eventually and he passed through the arched concrete gateways on the Kuwaiti side, where the formal arrangements seemed to have broken down. There were no passport officials in sight, just a military detail beside the customs office and an animated crowd of soldiers who surrounded the car, ignoring his proffered passport and asking if he had cigarettes to spare. They weren't begging, they were willing to pay for them, showing him fistfuls of five- and ten-dinar notes, explaining that the Iraqis had stolen the cigarette stocks along with everything else.

Jack shook his head, regretting that he hadn't had the foresight to bring a few cartons to distribute. It was Ramadan, when tobacco was supposedly forbidden, but

25

many Muslims smoked to ease the hunger pangs of their dawn-to-dusk fast. The soldiers didn't seem to mind. They were Bedouin, the stateless Arabs whom the Kuwaitis relied upon to fill the ranks of their army.

'Liberation, but no cigarettes, no nothing,' a corporal grinned. He had a lapel badge of President Bush stuck in his beret. 'You American?'

'British.'

'Reporter?'

'No, businessman. I was living here.'

'Coming back now? Good. *Mabruk*. I congratulate you.'

'*Mabruk* on your liberation,' Jack said, sidestepping the question.

'Go in God's protection.'

He drove on. Past Al-Nuwaisib village the smoke was thicker, floating across from the Wafra oilfield and hanging in the air like a greasy fog. Through it there was just an occasional glimpse of a pale, lemon-drop sun. In the distance the fires started by the Iraqis burned with fierce orange flames against the empty landscape, giving the bizarre impression of an industrial disaster visited upon a wilderness. Already their toxins had begun discolouring the spring flush of grass in the yellow-grey desert beside the road. Here, too, were the first signs of the destruction the allies had wrought on the invaders: the carcasses of a pair of tanks, scorched by high explosive to a reddish-brown colour so they looked as though they'd lain rusting here for years.

Soon he caught up with the vast American convoy, petrol and water tankers and big Mack trucks laden with food cartons, hospital equipment, pumps and generators, a whole life-support system for a sick city. Steadily overtaking the vehicles, passing the turn-off to the beach resort at Al-Khiran, he was seized by a sudden feeling of despondency.

It had nothing to do with the present condition of the country in which he had lived for five years. At least, not directly. Jack didn't know whether to consider himself lucky or not that he and his family had been back in England last August when the Iraqi tanks had rolled into Kuwait City. Relieved that Alison and the twins were safe, but not so sure about himself. Conscious that friends and fellow-expatriates were facing mortal dangers, taking risks for each other, while he mooned about the house in Banstead contemplating the failure of his company and the shaky state of his marriage. Gentlemen in England now abed. Guilt and frustration in equal measure.

At least he had known more or less what to expect when he came back. Like everyone else he had followed the war and its aftermath obsessively on television and in the newspapers. He had gone through the usual catalogue of responses, from amazement to anger to dismay, and yet had discovered that he was experiencing these things at a distance that was more than physical. He wasn't detached from them; he simply had no passionate involvement in them. Lacking the sense of affinity that old Gulf hands like Eric Patley had, Jack sensed that Kuwait had become part of his past. He had enjoyed his life here, but had not grown to love the place for itself.

The feeling that afflicted him now was more personal. However, he had shaken it off by the time he reached Umm-al-Haiman, where the road swung towards the coast and met up with the Fahaheel Expressway. There was more evidence here of the one-sided conflict that Saddam Hussein had called the Mother of All Battles: abandoned troop carriers bulldozed into the sand, and the wreckage of coastal artillery, blown out of its concrete emplacements, twisted into bizarre shapes and scattered along the beach like displays of metal sculpture. The sky was growing darker. A canopy of smoke hung over the Gulf and new, thicker clouds of it were rising from the Burgan and Al-Ahmadi fields to the west. The sulphurous fumes seeped in through the car's ventilators, catching in his throat. From Al-Misila, most of Kuwait City could normally be seen; all that was visible now above a vast grey smudge were the great, minaret-shaped water towers on the promontory and the tops of the taller office blocks.

In the suburbs, in Jabriya and Hawalli, the only people he glimpsed on the streets were gathered, with plastic buckets and bowls, around the American water tankers. By half-past ten he was in the city centre, driving round Safat Square in an eerie twilight with his headlights on. There wasn't much damage immediately visible, but the atmosphere suggested a place that had been struck by the plague. Uncollected rubbish was piled in the streets beneath withered palms and orange trees. What few electric lights there were shone from the bigger commercial buildings that had been provided with generators. Soldiers lounged at every corner and civilians drifted about in a dazed and aimless way, the men in their pale *dishdashas* looking like ghosts wandering in the dark.

There was a more purposeful air, however, about the people who stood in long queues outside the banks. With their reopening, a new currency had been issued to replace the old dinars that had been looted in their hundreds of millions by the Iraqis. Jack guessed he was in for a long wait. He considered putting off his business and going to see what had become of his apartment, but decided that would be too unpleasant a beginning.

His own branch of the Gulf Bank of Commerce was in Abdulla Al-Salim Street, across from the warren of little alleys that comprised the Gold Market. He parked the car and walked back, passing a noticeboard outside the bank where a crowd of merchants stood with sheafs of currency, anxiously comparing the serial numbers with those listed as stolen. Behind them the queue reached halfway up the street. Rather self-consciously he went and joined it.

The dim flickering light of oil lamps came from a few of the shops in the Gold Market, but most of them seemed closed. The adjacent Souq-al-Harem, where black-robed market women had crouched over their stocks of mysterious herbal medicines, was quite deserted. It seemed unbelievable that for more than a month this great bazaar of a city had been without currency, without anything to buy or sell.

His thoughts went back to the strange surge of depression that had afflicted him as he drove here. He knew it had been set off by the sight of the road leading to Al-Khiran.

In their first years in Kuwait, when the girls had been babies, Alison and he had spent some of their best times there. They would drive down from the city to a rented chalet at weekends to swim or fish in the Gulf, or just to laze about in the heat. Sometimes they travelled with friends but more often they were alone. They seemed to have been content with each other's company then, long before the destructive arguments over money had begun, the heavy silences, the diminishing of common interests to the point where almost all they could talk about was the children. One day not long ago he had woken up to the realization that he was living with a stranger.

To friends in England, and to Eric and Sylvia last night, he had repeated what he had told Alison about coming back for the money that had been frozen in his bank account since the invasion. The other reasons were not entirely clear even to him. He was forty years old. He was a business consultant whose business had folded, which was a bit outlandish when you thought about it. Possibly in getting away from Alison he was hoping to find out if he could live without her. Perhaps, with a chequered career behind him and an uncertain future ahead, he was trying to take stock of his life.

It was an hour before he made it through the doors into the opulent marbled interior of the bank. A generator hummed in the background and the strong electric light made him blink after the darkness of the street. There was air-conditioning as well, providing instant relief from the fug of oil smoke. The queue ended at a roped-off barrier, and at every counter customers were arguing with harassed clerks who endeavoured to explain the state of their accounts and the regulations governing the exchange of new dinars for old.

Mr Latif, the assistant manager, was in attendance at one of the counters. He spotted Jack and welcomed him with an astonished grin and a vigorous handshake.

'It's good to see you, sir! How are you?'

'I'm all right. But how have you been?'

'Oh, I've survived. That is something to be thankful for. I'm glad to be back at work, but, as you see, it's chaos here, absolute chaos.' Mr Latif gestured hopelessly at the crowd. He was a small, busy Palestinian, gossipy and always anxious to please. His manner seemed more nervous than usual, perhaps because of the hostility his people were encountering over the way some of them had collaborated with the Iraqis. Jack could not see Mr Latif in this role. He had lived here for more than twenty years and seemed quite uninterested in politics. He dressed nattily in business suits and took a flattering interest in his Western customers.

'You've just come back, Mr Rushton?'

'Only temporarily, I'm afraid.'

'Oh, dear, that is a pity.' Mr Latif had handled Jack's business account as well as his personal ones, and was well aware of the problems he'd been facing. 'No chance that you could start up again? KIC wouldn't take you back as a partner?'

'I don't think so.' Under Kuwaiti law a foreign business could hold only a minority stake in a local one. The Kuwait Investment Company, fifty per cent government-owned, had been in partnership with Jack's firm until it had pulled out of the arrangement last July. 'If they didn't want me then, I can't see them wanting me now.'

'Somebody else, then?'

'Frankly, I can't afford to hang around waiting to see.'

'Then what can I do for you?'

'I'm afraid I have to close my private accounts.'

Mr Latif disappeared into a back room and returned with printouts of Jack's statements. They showed roughly what he had expected. He had just over eight thousand dinars on deposit and seven hundred in his current account. That made a total of about fifteen and a half thousand pounds sterling. Together with the five or six thousand he had in London, it was his total cash worth after the winding up of his company. It wasn't much to show for five years' work.

'There's some interest still to be computed on that,' said Mr Latif. 'Unfortunately, under the new regulations, I can't let you have it all at once. You're allowed to withdraw only four thousand dinars immediately – about seven thousand pounds. I can probably manage to give you a sterling draft later today, if you wish. After that you're restricted to withdrawing four thousand dinars a month, so it will be another two months before you have it all.'

'Isn't there any way around that?'

'I'm afraid they're enforcing these rules very strictly.'

'Then I suppose I'll have to live with it.'

'Four thousand today, then, and the rest to be transferred later to an account in the UK? Unless I can persuade you to keep some of it on deposit here? We'll be offering good new rates soon. Tax-free as always.'

'I'm looking for something back at home. I'll need all the money I can get my hands on.'

The Palestinian leaned confidingly over the counter. 'There's a huge job of reconstruction to be done here, Mr Rushton. Apart from the damage to the oil industry, the whole economy will have to be rebuilt almost from scratch. New businesses will be opening up all over the place. So many of the Westerners who have left here won't be coming back. It would be a pity for a man like you to miss such an opportunity: a man who knows the Gulf, who already has contacts . . .'

Jack was shaking his head. 'It's a nice idea, but I don't think so.'

'If it's a question of finding a new Kuwaiti partner, I could make some enquiries for you.'

'Thank you. But it's more than that, really. I need a new start, maybe in a completely different field. Besides, I don't think my wife wants to come back here.'

'I understand,' said Mr Latif.

Jack arranged to return for his bank draft at three o'clock. Back outside, heading for his car in the poisonous artificial twilight, he knew he could no longer postpone his visit to the apartment.

He drove towards the Qibla district, past the municipal park that had been turned into a gigantic American army bivouac. On the road surfaces there were strange parallel sets of corrugations which he suddenly realized had been made by the tracks of tanks. The old Bristol Hotel was still closed; so was the Meridien, with the pool in which he had begun teaching the twins to swim, just a stroll across the street from his apartment in the Muthanna complex. Its entrance was boarded up and it looked badly scorched by fire. There had always been something superficial and unreal about this city, slapped down as it had been on the site of an ancient Arab port, thrown together on the proceeds of oil revenues in the space of twenty years. Now, strangely, the devastation it had endured seemed to give it a character it had lacked. Returning to it was like visiting a relative stricken in your absence by some memory-distorting illness.

The entrance to the Muthanna's underground car park was open and unattended. Within the dark basement there were only three or four cars, all looking dusty and abandoned. Piles of bulging refuse sacks stood in the corners; when he got out of the Ford he heard a rustling that suggested rats.

Not unexpectedly, the lifts were dead. Luckily his apartment was on only the fifth of the building's thirteen storeys and he made his way blindly up the unlit staircase.

The entire floor seemed deserted. It smelt of dust and stale air. By the thin light from the windows along the corridor he saw that all the apartment doors were closed and apparently intact; but, oddly, their handles had been removed. He went to his own door and tried the key. The Yale lock responded but without the handle the lower latch wouldn't budge. He bent down and peeped through the hole where the spindle had been. He saw only a fragment of white-painted wall.

He was startled by a noise from behind, a creak and then a footfall. He straightened up, staring into the gloom. A door had opened down the corridor and a light from behind it threw the shadow of a figure towards him. The figure of a lean, wiry man, his stance threatening but somehow familiar.

'Who's that?' Jack called.

The man relaxed. He reached back for something behind him and then stepped out of the apartment. He was carrying a length of metal pipe in one hand and, in the other, a door handle which he held out to Jack.

'Is this what you were looking for?' he said.

'Vincent! Jesus, you gave me a scare!'

'Likewise,' said Vincent Hand drily, emerging into the half-light, smiling through his beard. He flourished the piece of plumber's pipe. 'You might have been an Iraqi soldier. There are still some of them on the run.'

# 2

They had been neighbours, never close friends, but now they hugged each other like brothers. Vincent Hand was an Irish veterinary surgeon employed at the Kuwait Zoo. Like most of the Western men who'd been present at the time of the invasion he had been trapped there until he was allowed to leave last December. Now, it seemed, he had been among the first to return.

'My animals,' he explained. 'I had to get back to them. You should see what they did to the animals, Jack. But you'll want to get into your apartment. Here.' He gave Jack the door handle. 'A primitive security measure, but effective. The determined thieves got what they wanted, but it kept the casual ones out. I more or less appointed myself the caretaker of the building. The only foreigner in it who was free to move around, you see.'

'You mean you've looked after my stuff?' Jack said.

'Uh-oh,' Vincent cautioned him. 'I couldn't stop them taking your stereo or television, anything like that, but I think you'll find the rest of it is more or less intact. A lot of other places were stripped clean, down to the light bulbs and the wall sockets.'

Jack felt grateful but still a little bewildered. He fitted the handle loosely to the door, locking the spindle into place, turned it and entered the apartment. It had a faintly sour smell and the chilly feel of a home long unoccupied. The big L-shaped living room looked bare but only, he realized, for lack of the more obvious consumer goods: the television set, the video recorder and the stereo. Hell, though: the Isfahan carpet had gone as well, his one real treasure. They'd known enough to roll that up and take it

34

away. The bookshelves and paintings remained untouched, however, and the furniture was all in place.

The kitchen had been stripped of everything electrical, from the refrigerator and washing-machine down to the toaster. From his and Alison's bedroom only the radio alarm clock had gone, and the twins' room looked undisturbed, with fluffy toys still piled on their beds. Of the clothing that the family hadn't taken with them to England, little if any seemed to be missing.

It was all a bit laughable. It was pathetic, in fact. Apart from the carpet, the things they had taken were the artefacts that they imagined represented Western wealth. They had stolen the symbols of lifestyle that television and advertising had conditioned them to crave.

There was no electricity and no running water. The telephone was still in place in the hallway, but when he lifted the receiver it was dead.

Jack went to find Vincent Hand, who had made a tactful withdrawal to his own apartment. He was sitting in an armchair in the gloom, eating a sandwich and reading a book by the light of a gas pressure lamp.

'You're in time for some lunch,' he said. 'A bit simple, but I'm still living like a troglodyte. Help yourself.'

His kitchen was as bare as Jack's but he had some provisions, mainly scrounged from the American civil aid workers who were helping him at the zoo. There was a loaf of sliced bread, a can of tuna, a packet of cheese slices and some bottles of mineral water. It wasn't hard to imagine Vincent getting by on such thin fare at the best of times. He had the makings of an ascetic, a neatly bearded, middle-aged polymath bachelor, passionate about his profession, who spent his leisure hours improving his mind. He loved music and reading, and his bookshelves were laden with serious works. He was a self-sufficient man, better equipped than most to stand the rigours of occupation.

Jack made himself a sandwich and joined Vincent in the living room. He, too, had had his possessions plundered. Half of one wall, now bare, had once been occupied by a complicated stereo system. Across the room, a glass cabinet that had contained a collection of jewel-handled Arabian daggers had been smashed and emptied.

They sat in silence for a while and looked out of the window at the smoke-blurred view, over rooftops with their shiny spherical water tanks, towards the harbour. There were a thousand questions Jack wanted to ask but he thought they would all sound naïve. He left it to Vincent to open the conversation.

The Irishman finished his sandwich and brushed crumbs reflectively off his beard.

' "Come, thick night," ' he quoted, ' "and pall me in the dunnest smoke of hell." Lady Macbeth,' he explained. 'Only difference is it's like this all the time – morning, noon and night. Preferable to having the Iraqis here, anyway. You were lucky to be out of it.'

'I suppose so.'

'When I got home to Dublin,' Vincent said, 'just before Christmas, I found I couldn't talk to anyone about it. People were sympathetic, but they weren't equipped to understand. I'd start telling them about some of the atrocities and soon I could sense them thinking I must be exaggerating.

'Try this: back in October I was driving home from the zoo when I came across the aftermath of a traffic accident. It was at an interchange out on the Fifth Ring. This guy, a little vegetable farmer from down near Wafra, had had the bad luck to bump his pickup truck into a Buick full of Iraqi secret policemen.

'He didn't do much damage, just crumpled the wing of the car. It probably wasn't even his fault, but the Iraqis decided to teach him a lesson. They were the people who called themselves the *Mukhabarat*, the worst bastards of the lot. There were some ordinary soldiers digging a foxhole

36

across the road, and one of these cops got a shovel off them and used it to cut the guy's leg off. Just got him down on the ground and hacked away with the shovel blade until the leg was gone below the knee. Broke right through the tibia and, of course, severed all the arteries. Then they left him there to die.

'They were just driving off when I arrived. I did what I could to clamp the arteries, keep his heart going, bundled him into my car and screamed off to the Farwaniya Hospital, but he'd already lost too much blood. He was dead before I got there.'

'Some lesson,' Jack said.

'The Buick wasn't even theirs. Stolen, like everything else.'

Vincent paused. 'They also killed a lot of animals at the zoo. I couldn't stop them; they'd have killed me as well. Mostly it was the army conscripts, who were basically just dumb peasant boys. They shot the gazelles and the zebras and skinned them and ate them. They were running short of rations by then, they were hungry, so in a way I can't blame them that much. But they also shot an elephant, for no reason at all. Four or five rounds from a Kalashnikov: I've taken two bullets out of her shoulder and I'm going to try for the rest this afternoon. They shot a bear, but I think she'll live as well. A three-star Iraqi general drove all the way out there for the pleasure of shooting a baboon in its cage. Now that *was* calculated cruelty.'

As Vincent recounted these atrocities Jack wondered fleetingly whether he was trying to work on his neighbour's guilt about not having been here, about experiencing none of this. But the Irishman's tone did not seem pointed. He spoke in a quiet, matter-of-fact way, as though he needed a listener but didn't much care what sort of impression he was making.

'That's how it was, Jack, all the way through. A mixture of sadism and vandalism, some of it planned, some of it spontaneous. The raping, for instance: it started as a kind of reward to the troops, a day or two after the invasion. They began with the Asians, the Filipino maids and the Thai factory workers. They declared them *halal*, you know, permissible, while Arab women remained *haram*, forbidden. But that changed as well. They were soon raping Kuwaiti women too.

'The torturing and the executions were deliberate, of course. They were part of the campaign to suppress the resistance. The secret police would turn up at a house, very polite, very reassuring. One of the sons would be asked to go with them and answer some questions. Sometimes he'd just disappear. More often he'd be dumped at the front door a few days later with a bullet through his head. Maybe with his fingernails pulled out as well, and scorch marks on his skin, from electrodes. The family would be told to leave him there, as an example to others. Some of those young men were in the resistance, it's true. They were trying to gather intelligence, but they weren't going round killing Iraqis. A lot of the time they were just trying to help their own communities, organizing food supplies, that sort of thing.

'Then there was the looting. Even more systematic, above a certain level. The flip-flops took whatever was handy. The others—'

'Flip-flops?'

'We called the ordinary conscripts that. They had plastic sandals, no boots. Within a few days they're all strutting around in Reeboks and Nike Airs, lifted from the shops. But that was the small stuff. The peasant boys didn't know what to look for. The organized thieving was done by the secret police and the regular army. It was more than an invasion, Jack, it was like the sacking of Rome. They didn't try to justify it, they just said, "This isn't Kuwait any longer, this is the nineteenth province of Iraq, this stuff is ours." But I'm talking too much.'

'No. Please go on.'

'Well, there was a pecking order. The regular soldiers would get the things like your fridge and your washing-machine. The Republican Guard officers took the televisions and VCRs. In this building they got the master keys off the caretaker and went through every apartment. Anything they didn't want themselves they sold to the carpetbaggers, second-hand merchants who brought fleets of trucks down from Baghdad.

'The secret police, though, the *Mukhabarat*, they got the real pickings. They went through the Gold Market, took everything they could lay their hands on. You remember all those little shops, crammed with twenty-two carat jewellery? All of it gone. And the Central Bank, across there?' Vincent pointed vaguely over the rooftops. 'Well, you can't see it now, but I watched them from up here one morning, calling in a tank to blow the front doors open, going in and taking the gold bullion and the currency reserves out of the vaults.'

Being an Irish citizen, Vincent hadn't been interned along with the British, American and other Western nationals. Though his movements had been restricted, he'd been better placed than most foreigners to know what was going on. He'd also become quite an accomplished thief himself. He talked about how he and his fellow-Irish had kept themselves fed by making dawn raids on a frozen-food storehouse at Subhan, a place whose existence the Iraqis never caught on to. He spoke of supplying the resistance from the same source with food for hundreds of Kuwaiti families, and of stealing video recorders from another warehouse and bartering them for feed for the zoo's animals.

This reminded him that he was due back there. Jack, who had lost track of the time as he listened, also realized he had to return to the bank for his draft.

'I'll catch you later,' Vincent said. 'I'll see if I can pick up a few bits and pieces for you.'

*     *     *

39

If Jack had been inclined to self-pity he might have started thinking that fate had conspired against him over the past few months. As it happened, he was not much of a believer in fate. Pondering the events of that period, he could only conclude that he had been the victim of a couple of quite unrelated coincidences.

It was merely by chance that the Kuwait Investment Company had chosen to announce that it would not be renewing its partnership contract with Jack's firm, Kilrush Business Consultants, just a few days before the invasion. The news reached him while he was in England on leave: KIC was setting up its own consultancy division and no longer needed the services of Kilrush. Jack had been ready to hurry back and try to set up a new arrangement with some other firm, but the arrival of the Iraqis had put paid to that idea. It was also a coincidence that the blow had fallen at the worst possible time for the company. The London end of the business, which was managed by his partner Reg Kilmartin, had been losing money for the past two years. The British economy had just begun a dive into deep recession, leaving Reg in an impossible position. At the time these things had seemed bound up with each other; and although the downhill slide in Jack's marriage had begun much earlier, they had certainly helped to accelerate it.

As it was, he was forced to recognize that when business was bad, nothing was more superfluous than a business consultant. Back in the mid-eighties, when he and Reg had left their jobs with Hellig Associates, the financial intelligence firm, to set up on their own, the future had looked promising enough. They were both in their early thirties then, both with ambitions that stretched beyond helping other people to make money. With hindsight, they had probably been victims of the prevailing enterprise culture, the go-for-it philosophy that held out a promise of riches to anyone bold enough to make the big leap into self-employment.

It had worked well enough at first, but in the final two or three years the Kilrush office in London had ridden on the back of the profitable Kuwaiti operation that Jack had established and run from the headquarters of KIC. He and Reg had already taken cuts in their salaries in an effort to reduce the overheads. Suddenly, instead of having two strings to their bow, they had found themselves with none and had been forced to dissolve the company.

Reg had gone cap-in-hand to Hellig's and asked for his old job back. Resisting pressure from Alison to do the same, Jack was still determined to find a way of setting up again on his own. So far he had had little encouragement from the banks he had approached in search of a loan.

One paradox in all this was that Reg had put far more of his heart into the business than Jack had, and consequently suffered more from its demise. Reg, too, had had a varied career, including a spell in the Army before going on to study economics, and had been determined to make a go of things. Another revelation was how badly Alison had taken the news. It was she who'd succumbed to visions of a bigger house, expensive holidays, a second home in France, things that he could never quite believe in. It wasn't that she was greedy; if these desires reflected anything it was a craving for security and status. Her father had been a gambler and she should never have married another one. Marriage to Jack had given her a precarious self-respect, and she'd become terribly conscious of her role as the wife of a successful businessman; but when the business began to fail she started seeing him in a different light. It seemed almost to prove something disappointing about him that she'd suspected all along.

In contrast, Jack had discovered that he could conduct his life quite easily without letting it be ruled by the need for money. He might worry about feeding and clothing his family, but he was not going to become bitter about the disappearance of a dream.

★    ★    ★

He got to the bank at a few minutes after three. It was less crowded than before and he found Mr Latif hovering expectantly behind the counter. He was also looking anxious again, and Jack wondered if he had bad news to impart.

'Any problem with my sterling draft?'

'None at all. Quite the contrary. Everything in order.'

In earnest of this Mr Latif handed him a plain white envelope. 'A draft for seven thousand pounds, almost to the penny,' he said. 'And the balance still due will be forwarded to your bank in England. Unless you've reconsidered my suggestion about keeping it here?'

'I'm afraid not.'

'Very well. It's just that, with reference to our discussion earlier, about new business opportunities here, about finding you something . . . well, I took the liberty of mentioning your case to a certain gentleman.'

Jack stared at Mr Latif. He didn't recall actually discussing these things, merely responding to a few casual remarks.

'What gentleman?' he said.

'I spoke to him in the strictest confidence, I assure you. He is from an old and respected Kuwaiti family. He is also a director of the bank and has been paying us a visit. As a matter of fact he is still here,' Mr Latif added diffidently. 'He said that if you had a few minutes to spare, he would very much like to meet you.'

'I don't follow. To talk about an investment, do you mean? A partnership?'

'He didn't explain what he had in mind. Perhaps only a general discussion.'

'Mr Latif . . .' Jack tried not to sound exasperated. 'It's very kind of you to try to help, but perhaps you're under a misapprehension. The money in my accounts here is almost all the money I've got. And I need it in England. There isn't any more salted away. I don't have anything that would interest a high-powered banker.'

'Without breaking any confidences, Mr Rushton, I gave him a rough idea of your financial status. I don't think it matters to him. You will not be wasting your time talking to him. He is a wise and interesting man, although at present you may find him rather . . . serious. He has suffered a grievous loss. His daughter died here during the occupation.'

Now Jack thought he understood the source of the Palestinian's uneasiness. He felt that he himself was being placed under a moral obligation, and while this irritated him vaguely he could not help being intrigued.

He shrugged and said, 'I suppose I'd better meet him.'

Mr Latif smiled with relief. He raised a flap in the counter, ushered Jack through and led him across the open work area to a private door in the rear. They climbed a flight of marble stairs and walked along a carpeted corridor to an imposing pair of panelled doors at the end.

Latif paused in front of the doors. He seemed to hold his breath in anticipation for a few moments before he gave a gentle, almost reverential knock. A listless-sounding voice invited them to enter.

# 3

The room that Jack and Latif stepped into was designed
not as an office but as a place for receiving guests. It
had no desks or telephones. It was somebody's idea of a
Western-style VIP lounge or corporate hospitality room
with a few, not very successful, Middle-Eastern touches.
The low couches arranged around the walls were smothered
in embroidered cushions. The fitted carpet was a drab shade
of grey, relieved by three or four colourful Persian rugs.
Glass-topped coffee-tables and a few brass ornaments were
the only other furnishings.

A wide window looked out on what might have been
a pleasant view of Sief Harbour and the bay. Now the oil
smoke lay so thickly across the scene that almost nothing
was visible beyond the Ports and Customs building on the
waterfront. The man who stood by the window, however,
looked as though he'd been staring out of it for some
time. A few seconds passed before he turned, almost
absent-mindedly, to face his visitors.

He was tall and extremely thin, his leanness not disguised
even by the flowing skirts of his *dishdasha*. His face was
long and narrow, with a large beaked nose and a black,
trowel-shaped beard. A Western cartoonist's caricature of
an Arab sheikh, with the difference that his eyes were not
deep-set and piercing but wide and liquid brown, almost
doe-like. Together with the folds of the traditional *gutra*
head-dress that framed his features, they gave him the
dark, dispirited look of a Byzantine Christ.

Jack knew the face but for a moment couldn't place it.

'May I introduce,' Latif said with eager formality, 'Mr
Jack Rushton to Dr Mustapha Sultan Hamadi? Mr Rushton

is the English gentleman whose name I mentioned to you, Doctor. And as I explained to you, Mr Rushton, we in the bank are honoured to have Dr Hamadi on our board of directors.'

As he looked at Jack, Dr Hamadi's expression seemed to show only the slightest flicker of interest. But he reached out a slender, gold-ringed hand and gave Jack's a delicate shake.

'How do you do,' he said. He held Jack's gaze for only a moment before addressing the Palestinian. 'What refreshment have we to offer, Latif? Coffee? Tea?'

'Only the vilest American coffee, sir. But I believe there is mint tea.'

'Do you care for mint tea, Mr Rushton? I apologize for the lack of choice.'

'Please don't.'

Mr Latif bustled out of the room. Dr Hamadi, with a polite but rather weary gesture, showed Jack to a seat.

They settled at either end of a couch across from the window. In spite of his instinctive Arab courtesy Hamadi's manner seemed almost indifferent, and Jack wondered if he had been talked into this meeting by the enthusiastic assistant manager. But that would have been absurd. Jack had instantly recognized the name – and then, of course, the face, from a thousand photographs over the years in the *Kuwait Times* – of Dr Mustapha Sultan Hamadi.

He was not just from an old Kuwaiti family, as Latif had described him, he was head of one of *the* families, the half-dozen or so important clans who held most of the emirate's affairs in their grasp. He was not merely a director of this bank; through his holding company, the Hamadi Finance Corporation, he controlled, or had a major stake in, at least ten or twelve of the country's biggest enterprises. He was also on the boards of several official bodies responsible for awarding contracts and investing Kuwaiti oil revenues and other assets overseas. As with so much else there, his personal and corporate fortunes were intertwined with those of the state.

In short, Dr Hamadi was rich beyond fantasy. And he wanted to talk business with a man who possessed twenty thousand pounds and a four-bedroomed house in Surrey?

The doctor's melancholy gaze roved about the room before settling on Jack. He smoothed down his dark winter *dishdasha*, which was tailor-made from fine English worsted. The *agal* that held his head-dress in place had four spherical clasps of solid gold, each the size of a golf ball. He seemed in no hurry to start the conversation and Jack knew better than to take the lead. All the same, he had an urge to suggest right away that his position was being misunderstood. Remembering what Latif had said about Hamadi's daughter having died, he thought the man might still be in shock, his judgement affected by grief. Jack felt that he ought to have offered his condolences, but he didn't know whether Latif had been indiscreet in mentioning the fact.

'I believe,' said Hamadi suddenly, 'that you are back here only temporarily. You intend to return to England soon?'

'Within the next few days.'

'But you have no immediate commitments there?'

'I'm out of a job, is another way of putting it.'

The doctor ignored this levity. 'The reason I ask,' he said, 'is that when Latif told me of your background and present circumstances, it occurred to me that you and I might perhaps be useful to each other.'

Jack waited for more. When it didn't come he said, 'Latif may have been overselling me. I'm just a business consultant, and actually I'm not a very good advertisement for my profession. I don't have much money . . .'

'It's not an investment I have in mind, Mr Rushton, but something more in the nature of a commission. Tell me about the business you were in here.'

'My firm was in partnership with the Kuwait Investment

Company until they decided they could save money by doing my job for themselves. They started a programme some years ago of providing investment for small- to medium-sized Kuwaiti businesses. My job was to look these firms over and make sure they were run efficiently so that KIC wouldn't be pouring their money down the drain.'

'What did that involve?'

'Mainly it was a matter of financial control. You'd get some little guy who used to sell carpets in the *souq*, and now he was turning over ten million dinars a year importing luxury goods, but still running his business like a market stall. Not quite keeping the money under his mattress, perhaps, but almost. Refusing to delegate, doing his own bookkeeping, getting overwhelmed by details. My job was to see that his operation was streamlined . . .'

There was a knock on the door and Latif led in a pair of Pakistani servants bearing the impedimenta of tea-making. He fussed about them as they arranged the silver kettle and burner on a table and set out a plate of sweet almond cakes, procured God knew where. Mint tea was poured into a tiny cup for Jack but neither food nor drink was offered to Hamadi. To his embarrassment, Jack had forgotten it was Ramadan. The hospitality was for him alone.

Hamadi had lapsed into a dreamy silence again, leaning back on the cushions behind the couch. Studying him more closely, Jack put his age at barely a few years ahead of his own, and yet his manner seemed to separate them by a generation at least. He was one of those men who seem never to have been young, though his perfect and barely accented English suggested a boyhood banishment to Eton or Winchester. The doctorate was probably an honorary one bestowed by some university grateful for an endowment.

He stirred himself once the others had gone. He said: 'I was thinking, Mr Rushton, of asking you to act on my

47

behalf in a small financial matter. It might tie in with your return to Europe. Initially it would mean searching out some information of the sort that you may be equipped to find. I understand that before you came here you had some experience in the sphere of financial intelligence?'

The question surprised Jack. Then he recalled talking to Latif once, it must have been years ago, about his previous job; it was just the kind of thing the busybody Palestinian would remember.

'In a small way, yes.'

'Tell me about it.'

Jack felt as though he were reciting his CV. 'I was with a firm in the City of London,' he said, 'that carried out confidential research for clients. It was called Hellig Associates. We would enquire into the ownership and the financial state of companies, sometimes on behalf of banks or creditors, more often because a purchase or merger was being considered. We were also business brokers; we'd identify a firm that looked like a good take-over prospect for a client and get a finder's fee if the deal went through. We'd do our own investigation of the company first, naturally. It was detective work, of a sort.

'Did you ever catch any crooks?'

Although Hamadi didn't smile, the question contained the first dry hint that he might have a sense of humour. His manner was also sharper now, and it was easier to get a sense of the considerable power that he wielded.

'Crooks weren't our department. We did sometimes stumble across a clear breach of the law, and then we'd usually find a way of tipping off the police or the Serious Fraud Office without getting ourselves involved. There were grey areas, of course, especially when it came to firms working out of offshore tax havens, or disguised by foreign ownership or holding companies. As a rule, the more layers of management, the more they had to keep quiet about.

'Generally, though, Hellig's job was just to establish their strengths and weaknesses. As you know, the books of a business rarely tell the whole story about it. A company could be quite innocently undervaluing its own assets. Another one might be much less vulnerable than it looks because the purse strings are held by some wealthy backer who's determined to keep it afloat. A lot of it comes down to personalities.'

'Indeed. And were you able to investigate the private circumstances of such people? The sources of their wealth?'

Jack had been wondering what direction Hamadi wanted the conversation to take. Was this it? He had also concluded that there'd been nothing at all coincidental about the way this meeting had been set up. Busy tycoons like Hamadi were rarely found hanging about by chance in branch offices of their empires.

'Occasionally,' Jack said, 'it was worth greasing a few palms to get a look at banking records and that sort of thing. But there are other ways, signs that you learn to look for. We were a bit more sophisticated than a credit-checking agency, although sometimes that's what it felt like.'

'You mean you didn't enjoy it?'

Jack sipped mint tea and considered his reply. Would a man in Hamadi's position, from his background, understand anything of this? 'I did at first. In fact, I think I was quite good at it. I could be . . . plausible, which is a useful quality. But what we were doing, what it mostly amounted to, was helping some people to screw other people. Often that meant helping wealthy people, the ones who could afford our fees, to get the better of the less wealthy.

'I suppose you could say that's what capitalism is all about. But this was the early eighties. There was something, well, distasteful about the whole business climate then. It encouraged the worst kind of greed. Some of Hellig's clients specialized in asset-stripping. They'd get us to find publicly quoted companies that had capital tied up in assets – land or plant, say – that were worth far more than the total market value of their shares, and they'd buy

49

control of them. These were often little firms that were getting by all right, that actually produced things and employed people, that didn't just shift paper around; but the asset-strippers weren't interested in taking them over as functioning concerns, only in what they were sitting on.

'I didn't like a lot of those people, Dr Hamadi. As a matter of fact I rather despised them. Sometimes our clients would ignore our advice, or refuse to believe what we told them. To tell the truth, I'd find myself quite enjoying it if some big faceless corporation burned its fingers trying to buy out a competitor. Obviously my instincts were wrong. I wasn't in the right job. That's one reason I left.'

'Interesting,' said Hamadi. 'A capitalist and also a subversive.'

'Perhaps what I'm trying to say is that I wasn't all that good at what I was doing. I let my feelings get in the way.'

'What I have in mind need not trouble your conscience,' Hamadi said easily. 'And you do seem quite well qualified for it. You also know this society. You understand what we have been through.'

Again Jack waited before supplying his own cue. He set down his teacup. 'What does it involve?'

'It's a matter of enquiring about some funds that were deposited in a bank account in Europe, with a view to arranging for their release. The transaction took place during the Iraqi occupation here, and as a result there are some technical difficulties involved. For various reasons I am prevented from concerning myself directly. I need an agent to act on my behalf, in a circumspect way.'

'Can you be any more specific?'

'Not at present. If you are interested in what you have heard so far we can take it further.'

Jack shrugged. 'I have to say frankly that there are people better equipped than I am for that sort of thing. People with more resources, like Hellig's themselves. There's also a company called Kroll Associates in New York—'

'Too big and too impersonal,' Hamadi said firmly. 'I would prefer to deal with someone who has a closer understanding of the background.'

'A lawyer, then?'

'If I had wanted a lawyer, Mr Rushton, I could have telephoned one in any of a dozen countries. Lawyers' enquiries have to be formal. This is a delicate matter, one that concerns my family. For the present, it is merely a case of what you call financial detective work. It may sound rather a trivial job, but I believe I can offer you satisfactory terms. In the meantime, in appreciation for your giving me your time this afternoon, I'll arrange to advance you a sum equivalent to the balance that is blocked in your accounts here. In other words, you are free to take all your money back to England whether you accept my proposal or not. Latif will take care of the details.'

Jack began to protest but Hamadi interrupted by reaching into a pocket of his robe and thrusting out a card. It was printed in Arabic on one side, English on the other.

'I don't propose to say anything more at the moment, Mr Rushton.' He was all business now. 'Think carefully about what I have told you. If you are interested, please attend the *diwania* at my home at six o'clock this evening. If you don't turn up I will understand. I will know to look elsewhere.'

Vincent Hand was back from the zoo when Jack returned to the Muthanna. Vincent said he had operated successfully on the elephant and was still hoping to save the bear. Somehow he had also found time to procure some extra rations and a small gas lamp for Jack's apartment, as well as a flashlight to help him find his way up and down the stairs.

As they sat together again staring out at the smoke-shrouded city, Jack found himself ungratefully thinking that the one thing he would like above everything else was a drink. He had got used to alcohol during his eight months at home, perhaps a bit too used to it; but it would never occur to Vincent to keep bootleg whisky in his house, much less any of the toxic home-made concoctions that went under the name of 'flash'.

'I rather envy you your job,' Jack said.

'I can't imagine why. There's not much money in it.'

'It's honest work. It satisfies you. Anyway, after twenty years of playing with other people's money I haven't got much of my own to show for it.'

'What's the point of all those qualifications of yours, then? You took a degree in economics, didn't you?'

'And a diploma in accountancy,' Jack said. 'It's just that I've begun to wonder lately whether I've always been in the wrong line of work.'

He would have found it hard to explain his feelings to Vincent. Content with his animals, his books and his music, the Irishman had a way of assuming that anyone involved in the making of money must be obsessed by it. Jack knew this to be true only in an abstract way. In spite of his own training in the theory and management of money he had never learned to think about it with the right degree of . . . well, detachment on the one hand, reverence on the other. To a true professional it had a metaphysical quality, it was something to be dealt with symbolically, through the sacred runes of a balance sheet. To people who were seriously rich it had even less reality; it was just there, the way water was there when you turned on a tap. Once you were beyond any actual need of it, once you were in the league of Dr Mustapha Sultan Hamadi, say, it represented only intangible things: privacy, power, the capacity to manipulate people.

Without going into details, Jack told his neighbour about his encounter with Dr Hamadi and the invitation to visit his house that evening. Vincent said wryly: 'Well, you've fallen on your feet. You've got straight into the right social circles.'

'You know Hamadi?'

'Of course not. But I know about his family. They were one of the original clans of the Anaiza tribe, the people who came from the Arabian interior and virtually created Kuwait early in the eighteenth century. Gave up roaming the desert and settled down to making money. Earned their first fortune out of pearl fishing and their second out of trading – and then, of course, God knows how many billions after oil was discovered. Did you hear about his daughter?'

'I was told she died recently.'

Vincent turned and stared at him. 'She didn't just die, Jack. She was tortured and murdered by the Iraqis.'

'Jesus Christ!'

'And raped, I believe. But that was par for the course.'

'What happened?'

'All I know is what I heard on the grapevine, mostly from a friend of hers who used to be her tutor at the university. Her name was Noura. A girl of twenty-two or three. She was unlucky to be here at all. Her people were out of the country for the summer, like most of the wealthy families, but I gather she came back because she was due to get married. The arrangement fell through, as it happened, but the upshot was that she was trapped here after the invasion.

'A few weeks later she was arrested by the *Mukhabarat*. They accused her of helping the resistance to try to smuggle gold out of the country. A pretty pathetic excuse: she was a rich man's pampered daughter, and you know what that means out here. Surrounded by servants, never having to lift a finger. She probably didn't know how to boil a kettle, never mind smuggling. It was probably done out of envy or spite.

'Anyway, she was taken to the Nayef Palace – you know, the police headquarters, just down the road from here, which the Iraqis had turned into a torture and interrogation centre. And like a lot of others she never

53

came out. Her body was dug up from under the basement a couple of days after the liberation.'

'It doesn't make any sense,' Jack said.

'A lot of things don't.' Vincent gestured through the window at the swirling oil smoke. 'Like setting fire to the wells. Stealing light bulbs. Shooting my elephant. I stopped looking for sensible reasons after a while. Do you want to know what it was really like here, Jack? It was like living in a country that had been taken over by drunken children.'

# 4

The address on Dr Hamadi's card was in Salamiya, off the smart end of Salem-al-Mubarak Street. To anyone who knew Kuwait the address told its own story: the district was a designer suburb, an enclave for the super-rich of the emirate, a place of staggering affluence set on a peninsula that jutted out into the Gulf ten kilometres or so from the city centre. Apart from the Emir and his family in their various palaces, most people who really mattered lived in Salamiya, and everything that money could buy was to be found there. Jack was curious to see how it had fared under the occupation.

It had the feeling of an oasis, its wide, quiet streets lined with palms and flanked by verges of grass grown on imported soil. Most of this vegetation had gone untended since late last summer. A lot of it had died, and now the oil smoke had begun to turn the rest an unhealthy shade of yellow.

The smoke was hastening the approach of dusk when Jack stopped the Ford Granada opposite the entrance to Hamadi's house. Like the rest of the mansions hereabouts it was hidden behind high walls, set well back from a broad sidewalk on which no-one ever walked. The wrought-iron security gates were open, however, and he could see down a length of paved driveway to a curious set of yellowish conical structures.

A uniformed private guard stood outside a hut by the gates, packing a holstered pistol and a two-way radio and suspiciously eyeing the Granada. Jack had arrived at the appointed time but had not yet decided whether to go inside. Although he had dressed for the occasion, exchanging his travelling clothes for a grey pinstriped suit, he had told himself he would make up his mind on the way. Now he still wasn't sure. Caught between curiosity and a vague apprehension, he didn't know how far he wanted to get involved in the affairs of a man like Hamadi.

In spite of the casual nature of the invitation, Jack knew that he was under something of an obligation to turn up. Accepting Hamadi's promise to advance him the money he was owed by the Gulf Bank of Commerce had placed him at a disadvantage. But the doubts he had felt that afternoon had returned. Why did Hamadi need someone like Jack Rushton to dig out information for him? And why couldn't the job be entrusted in confidence to one of his international army of lawyers? Because it was illegal? Had that been the point of his little joke about catching crooks?

One phrase the doctor had used stood out in Jack's mind. *A delicate matter, one that concerns my family.* For an Arab that had to be a very delicate matter indeed, and something to which no outsider – above all a *nasrani*, a non-believer and a virtual stranger – would normally be privy.

Two cars were coming down the street, headlights probing through the smoke. They slowed as they approached Hamadi's gateway and Jack saw that they were both Rolls-Royces. The first one turned into the entrance and halted, its liveried driver lowering his window to talk to the security guard. Then both of them swept into the drive. Through the rear windows Jack caught sight of the pale *gutras* of their male passengers and felt reassured. He wouldn't be the only guest, then; Hamadi had meant what he'd said about the *diwania*.

He swung the Granada across the road and stopped in front of the gates. He gave his name to the guard, who jabbered briefly into his walkie-talkie before waving him through. Fifty metres down the palm-fringed driveway another security man tried to direct him to the front of the house. There was a moment's confusion before the man realized this was not another chauffeur-driven limo and pointed him instead to a spacious car park beneath some mimosa trees.

Jack left the Ford like a poor relation among a dozen Rollers and Cadillacs and walked along a cobbled pathway to the house.

Now that he was close to it he understood its architecture. Kuwaitis loved to remind themselves of their desert origins, and this place had been designed around the notion of a nomad's camp, a compound of interconnected tent shapes of different sizes, each with a steeply pitched roof sheathed in copper and painted the colour of sand. The lesser buildings attached to the main house were meant to accommodate the siblings and children and in-laws of an extended family. Long vertical windows in the roofs showed lights provided by a generator. It was a bold conceit; the house that formed the centre-piece was very large but gave an impression of delicacy and airiness.

The front door was set behind an archway in one of the smaller tents. An Indian manservant answered the bell and admitted Jack into a circular entrance hall, bare of furniture but with a beautiful mosaic floor. A tiled fountain in the middle was dry and had had its centre-piece ripped out. The servant showed Jack down a corridor to a doorway from which came a murmur of male voices.

He had been to many *diwanias* and knew what to expect. They were at the centre of Kuwaiti social and business life, and the name described both the venue and the occasion: a kind of cross between a club and a cocktail party without the alcohol, a forum for news, gossip, argument and the exchanging of favours. Men of note in the community held a *diwania* at a fixed time once or twice a week, often in a room set aside for the purpose, as this one evidently was.

It was another tent-shaped room, perhaps ten metres in diameter, with another lifeless fountain at its centre. The ceiling rose to about six metres at its vertex. Not only the floor but the walls, to above head height, were encrusted by tile mosaics with intricate floral designs, gleaming in the light reflected from bracket lamps. Cushions were set all around the walls except on the far side where wide glass doors looked out on a courtyard. The atmosphere was fresh; the air-conditioning was working. It seemed the house had not suffered badly from Iraqi vandalism.

A couple of dozen men were in the room, some of them sitting cross-legged on cushions but most gathered around a table where food was set out, relieving their hunger after the day's fast. Dr Hamadi saw Jack hovering in the doorway and came over at once.

'I'm glad you could join us. Come and meet some of my friends.'

Hamadi allowed himself a smile, apparently more at ease than he had been that afternoon. He had changed into a white *dishdasha* and an embroidered waistcoat. He led Jack to the table and urged him to select from platters of date tarts and dried figs, and baklava and konafa pastries oozing syrup. He snapped his fingers and a hovering servant offered a choice of coffee or fresh orange juice. Jack could not imagine where it had all come from but felt it would be undignified to express his surprise.

The doctor also introduced him to the nearest of his guests, affable middle-aged men stuffing themselves like schoolboys with sweetmeats. They had surnames like Al-Sabah and Mutawa and Bahar, men from the foremost Kuwaiti families, all of them connected in one way or another with its richest enterprises. They greeted Jack with courtesy, switching into polished English to include him in their conversation. They were exchanging stories about the occupation which, it became quickly apparent, none of them had endured at first hand.

'In my office, I'm told, these peasant Iraqi boys arrived with orders to strip the place, and they said to the clerks, "You have a great life, all you have to do is sit around watching television all day." They were talking about the computer screens. They'd never seen one before. Can you believe that?'

'That's nothing. A crowd of these people, these stall-holders from Baghdad, showed up at my brother's house and cleaned it out. They left only one room untouched, and do you know what was in that? Four paintings by Turner, some things he picked up at Sotheby's two years ago, the most valuable items in the house!'

Jack listened politely. He seemed to have little to contribute, reckoning that the theft of his Isfahan carpet hardly rated a mention in this company. After eight months away he also found the absence of women strange. No doubt there were female members of Dr Hamadi's household, but they were staying well out of sight.

There was one other guest who looked out of place as well, a dark-skinned, stocky man standing at the edge of the crowd. Jack was about to step over and introduce himself when Dr Hamadi took him by the arm and steered him away.

'Let me show you my garden,' he said.

Hamadi led him out through one of the sliding glass doors. Though it was almost fully dark now, enough light was shed from the house to illuminate the paved courtyard that it enclosed. Its centre-piece was a shallow tiled pool, again without water, surrounded by a rectangular pattern of pathways, fountains, shrubs and ornamental trees covering perhaps half an acre. An Arab's garden was meant to be an oasis, a cool and secret refuge from the heat of the desert summer. A small replica of heaven, even: all that stuff in the Koran about gardens watered by running streams. On this dark evening, with a smell of rank vegetation underlying the reek of oil smoke, it seemed a neglected and melancholy place.

They strolled around the pool, Hamadi staring at the ground, his hands clasped reflectively behind his back.

'By coming here,' he said, 'you have honoured me by expressing further interest in what we were discussing. It is understood that we now speak in absolute confidence?'

'Yes.'

'And even if you should decide that this is something you don't want to deal with, what I have to say will remain entirely between us?'

'Of course.'

'I liked what I saw of you today, Mr Rushton. I believe I can trust you. In a moment I will explain further why I have approached you with this proposal. But tell me this first: are you familiar with the banking laws of Switzerland?'

Jack shrugged. 'Not especially. I know they're a lot tougher than they used to be.'

'And about to become more so. The famous numbered accounts that criminals and dictators used to hide behind were abolished some years ago, but it has still been possible to preserve anonymity by opening an account through an intermediary. A Swiss lawyer or a trust administrator, say. These are the so-called Form B accounts. The system is still open to being used by the wrong people, and so that arrangement is shortly to be changed as well. Intermediaries will have to declare the names of their clients. A register of account holders is to be drawn up, starting in July. You can imagine that this has the potential to embarrass a good many people.'

'I can,' said Jack neutrally.

'One of these Form B accounts was involved in the transaction I mentioned to you earlier. To put it simply, Mr Rushton, I paid a sizeable sum of money into this account in return for something I didn't get.

'There was nothing illegal about it as far as I am aware, but there would be serious harm to me if the details became known.' Hamadi paused and looked up. 'I want to say, however, that I do not regret my involvement. In similar circumstances I would probably do exactly the same thing again. I was trying to save the life of my daughter.'

Jack said nothing. Hamadi was still watching him but his face was in shadow between the hems of his *gutra*.

'I make no apology for being a wealthy man, Mr Rushton. What is the point of wealth if one can't use it in circumstances like those? But there are others who would see things differently.' He turned and began to walk again, leaving Jack to catch up. They went once more around the pool before he said, 'Do you know what happened to my daughter?'

'I heard about it. Not in any detail.'

Hamadi was tugging something out of a pocket of his *dishdasha*. It was a large leather wallet, from which he extracted a postcard-sized photograph and handed it silently to Jack. Angling it towards the light from the house, he saw that it was a portrait of an astonishingly pretty girl. She wore a Western dress or blouse with a wide, frilled neck. Black hair fell in ringlets down either side of an oval face with delicate features and limpid dark eyes. She smiled at the camera in a way that seemed both shy and inviting.

'That was my Noura,' said Hamadi grimly. 'I still curse the day that she returned here. We were spending the summer as usual at my house on the Cote d'Azur. She was to be married soon after we got back here, early in October. Her husband-to-be was a man name Ahmed Khalid, a member of a prominent family from Abu Dhabi, whom she met while studying at the university here. I was having a house built for them, in this compound' – he gestured across the garden – 'and she wanted to be present to supervise its decoration and furnishing.

'I suppose that surprises you? Noura was a modern girl, not at all bound by tradition. From the age of ten she was educated in England. She did not wear the veil. She knew her own mind, and I respected that. The marriage was not an arranged one, but a matter of her own choice.'

Jack offered the photograph back but he said: 'Keep it. You may find it useful. I have always considered myself

61

a realist, Mr Rushton. I know it is no longer possible to follow all of the old family ways, but perhaps with hindsight I did her a disservice by allowing her so much freedom. I did not realize quite how strongly her attitudes had been affected by her upbringing, by the influence of people without respect for our traditions. She came back here in the middle of July and ten days later she phoned me to say she had changed her mind. She did not want to go ahead with the marriage. The reasons she gave were, to my mind, frivolous ones – but they're of no importance now. I could not force her to marry. I could only urge her to reconsider, to think of the humiliation this would bring to her family. I asked her to come back to France and discuss it with me, but I think she was afraid to face me.

'For more than a week we argued every day on the telephone. And then, on the second of August, the Iraqis invaded. Communications with the outside were cut off. All I knew was that Noura was alone here, with no protection apart from a few helpless servants. I had a good idea what might happen to an attractive young woman at the hands of the Iraqis. I began at once investigating ways to have her brought out.'

When Hamadi paused in his walk again the light caught his face, giving prominence to the big, mournful eyes. He was speaking matter-of-factly now, making it hard to gauge his feelings.

'You've lived long enough around here, Mr Rushton, to understand the meaning of the term *wasta*. Influence. Power. What the Americans call "clout". I have my share of *wasta*, not only here but in other parts of the Arab world. The Iraqis are as susceptible as anyone else to bribery: it's only a question of finding the right person and offering the right price.

'Indirectly, I was put in touch with a senior officer of the occupation forces here, a man who had the power to arrange for Noura to leave the country. In the middle of

August he travelled to Jordan and I went there to meet him.

'The name of this man is Ibrahim Faysal Jalloul, a colonel of the Iraqi military intelligence. It had been explained to me that he was one of many such people who were out of favour with the leadership in Baghdad. He feared for his future under Saddam Hussein and might be open to an opportunity of absconding, provided he was well enough rewarded.

'We met in secret, in Amman, and we came to an agreement. Colonel Jalloul would provide Noura with the papers of an Iraqi citizen and the means of allowing her to travel to Baghdad and then on to Jordan. He told me all this would take time to organize. Others would have to be bribed in turn for their help. In the meantime he would supply protection to this house and to my daughter, ensuring that no harm came to her.'

Hamadi paused. 'We agreed on a payment – a ransom, if you like – of two million dollars, to be paid into a bank account in Switzerland. He insisted that the first half be made available at once, unconditionally. The rest would be due once Noura was safely back with her family. I had no choice but to agree.

'We met again in Amman towards the end of that month and finalized the arrangements that I had set in motion in Switzerland. He told me that his own plans were well in hand and Noura would be free to leave Kuwait the following week.'

Dr Hamadi sighed. 'That was a false promise, Mr Rushton. On the night she was due to leave she was arrested, taken to the Nayef Palace, held on a ridiculous pretext. My first thought was that Colonel Jalloul had grown greedy, that soon he would be trying to raise his price. But no message came from him. When I had enquiries made I learned that he was no longer in Kuwait. He had disappeared.'

'Taking the first half of the ransom money?' said Jack.

'Yes. And leaving Noura to her death. Strangely enough, in spite of the distasteful nature of our dealings, I thought of him as a man of his word. My anxiety must have clouded my judgement. I should not have expected anything but the worst from an Iraqi.'

'He didn't actually . . . kill her himself?'

'Evidently not. When they found her body, in the basement of the Nayef Palace' – Hamadi spoke with difficulty now, threatened by emotions he had been choking back – 'they estimated that she had been dead about a month. They had to check her dental records to be sure of her identity. Jalloul had vanished four months earlier. But I have no doubt that he abandoned her to her fate at the hands of the secret police, the *Mukhabarat*, which amounts to the same thing.

'However, I do not wish to burden you with my personal feelings. Noura is dead, *in'sh Allah*. She cannot be brought back. The reason you need to know all this is because her death has left me in a further predicament.'

Jack waited for an explanation. When Hamadi gave it he spoke in the same tone of weary detachment he had used that afternoon.

'There is a new climate here since the liberation. There are people who want to change our ways, so-called reformers who would interpret my actions as proof of their own belief that the rich and privileged are a law unto themselves. They would also accuse me of trucking with my country's enemies. You know something of my status here. These people could destroy my personal reputation, and that in turn could have repercussions of a business and even a political nature. That is, if they were to find evidence of my dealings with Jalloul.'

Hamadi looked at Jack significantly. 'Unfortunately, such evidence does exist,' he said. 'The money itself was of no great importance to me, but I needed some guarantee that Jalloul would keep his word. I attached conditions to the arrangement, which was made through an intermediary in Zurich. I wanted Jalloul's name linked with mine, in case he should attempt to cheat me. I had a covenant drawn up allowing this nominee to open a bank account – in effect, an anonymous account – on behalf of us both. It was a condition that any withdrawal or transfer of funds would require both our signatures. The details need not concern you for the moment: it is enough for you to understand that I deposited two million dollars in the account, transferred half of it immediately to Jalloul and left the rest to await completion of his part of the agreement. It seemed a reasonable safeguard at the time. It never occurred to me that he would simply take half the money and disappear.

'Now here is the real problem: that account, at the Handelsbank Bauer in Zurich, remains open. The nominee who has charge of it is unable to close it, or to obtain the release of the remaining one million dollars without the agreement of Jalloul. And where is Jalloul? Nobody knows.

'Furthermore, when these new Swiss regulations come into effect in July, the nominee will be forced to disclose both our names to the Federal Banking Commission. The account will no longer be anonymous, and anyone who cares to try hard enough will be able to link my name with Jalloul's. He, in turn, has copies of the documentation which implicate me in the arrangement. Wherever he is, possibly without even realizing it, Jalloul is holding a gun to my head. And there are other people, here in Kuwait, who would be more than happy to pull the trigger.'

Hamadi was staring earnestly at his guest in the feeble light. When he spoke again it was in a tone of entreaty that did not seem at all characteristic. 'I want you to help me prevent that, Jack. For the sake of my family's honour. For the memory of my daughter.'

Faintly embarrassed, Jack said: 'I don't quite see what you expect me to do.'

'Go to Switzerland. Find some way around this difficulty. Settle the agreement and close the account. And eliminate all evidence that the transaction ever took place.'

'But that would mean—'

'In return for your endeavours,' Hamadi said quickly, 'I am willing to pay you one hundred thousand dollars. If you succeed in releasing the one million dollars from the account you are welcome to whatever portion of it you can negotiate for yourself. As I have said, the money is of no real consequence to me. It is nothing compared to the harm it could do.'

'The only way I can see of doing any of that is—'

'I know,' said Hamadi fervently. 'I don't like the idea either. But it may be necessary for you to trace Colonel Jalloul. And do a deal with him.'

# 5

For several moments Jack didn't speak. The darkness, the quiet that surrounded them and the fog of oil smoke hanging over the decayed garden suddenly gave him a sense of unreality, as though he had strayed into a dream. Dr Hamadi hovered in front of him like an anxious pale ghost, and what he had said seemed just as fantastical.

When Jack found his voice he said the first thing that came into his head: 'I can't do it.'

'Why not?'

'I just can't. You say you don't like the idea. Neither do I.'

'What's wrong with it?' said Hamadi. 'Doesn't the money attract you?'

'It's not that.' Oddly, the money was not uppermost in Jack's thoughts. The figures seemed too absurd to be taken seriously. 'It's . . . well, one minute you're talking about a simple financial investigation, and the next you're asking me to find an Iraqi blackmailer and talk him into negotiating with me. It's out of my league. I'm just not equipped to do it.'

'I doubt that you would need to have any personal dealings with him,' Hamadi said calmly. 'Assuming he can be traced, it should be possible to approach him through the bank or the intermediary that we used. But you must realize now why I can't risk doing so myself, or entrust the task to any of my countrymen.'

'Let me see if I've got this right, Dr Hamadi. This is the man who cheated you out of a million dollars and abandoned your daughter to be murdered. And you are willing to do a deal with him? You're prepared to pay him even more money if necessary, just for the sake of concealing what happened between you?'

'There is an Arabic saying that you may not have heard, Jack: Kiss the hand that you dare not bite.' It was all Jack now; perhaps in token of the new intimacy forced on them by these revelations, Hamadi reached out and gave his shoulder a brotherly squeeze. 'But it's not simply a matter of how it would look. It has to do with bigger things, involving the whole structure of this society. You know our history. It's nearly two hundred and fifty years now since my forebears and those of five or six of the other leading families elected one of the Al-Sabah clan as their ruler. They gave political leadership to the Al-Sabahs in exchange for the stability that would allow commerce to flourish in the hands of the others.

'It's been so ever since. It's a system that has served everyone, rich and poor, very well. There are no poor people to speak of now, yet there are those who wish to end the system overnight. Who want to destroy the only traditions we've got. With the misguided encouragement of some of our foreign friends they preach democracy to people for whom the word has no meaning. They talk of redistributing wealth, when history has shown that that only makes everyone poorer.

'In the hands of these people, what I did would be grossly misrepresented. It would be used not only to harm me, but to undermine the position of all the families who have made Kuwait what it is. Of course there is sympathy for anyone who has lost a close relative to the Iraqis; but that applies to so many, most of whom haven't got the resources to do what I did. I would be accused of abusing my position and my wealth. Perhaps the criticism would be valid, but I ask you to think what you would have done in my position.'

Jack had been thinking quite hard, in fact, throughout this little speech. What he would want in Hamadi's place now was justice, even revenge, for the murder of his daughter. But then he wasn't a billionaire or a member of a privileged élite that felt its interests threatened. The rich were different, all right.

He said: 'I really don't think you've got the right man, Doctor.'

'What exactly is your objection?'

'For one thing, I'd hardly know where to begin. All I've ever done is work with pieces of paper. Balance sheets, reports, cash-flow projections. Even when I was an investigator with Hellig's, poking my nose into other people's business, I was only dealing with abstractions. What you need is someone a bit more streetwise. A real detective.'

'And one also with an understanding of high-level finance? I think you're being hard on yourself, Jack. Or is it really a question of ethics?'

'Why should it be?'

'I'm remembering those asset-strippers that you talked about. People you didn't like dealing with. Perhaps you have the same feelings about me?'

'I hadn't got round to thinking about it.'

'Or Jalloul? Technically I suppose he counts as a war criminal. But, as I said, it's most unlikely that you would have to confront him directly. In any case, at present only he and I know of the true nature of the arrangement that we came to. He is in hiding, obviously, but only from the Iraqi authorities. As far as I know he is not wanted by the police of any other country. Probably he is living quietly in Switzerland, or France, or perhaps even England. Some place where he can enjoy his money but remain anonymous. He'll be on the defensive. He won't be dangerous.'

The idea of danger somehow hadn't crossed Jack's mind until now; the risks they had been talking about were not physical ones. But Jalloul had a lot more than money to lose. Who could say for sure what his response would be? Was that why Hamadi was prepared to pay so much to have someone else approach him?

'The hundred thousand dollars you mentioned,' Jack said, 'how would it be paid?'

'Half of it at once, the other half when the deal was successfully negotiated.'

'That's very trusting of you. What if I did a runner without delivering, like Jalloul?'

Hamadi's smile was just visible in the darkness. 'I was wrong about Jalloul because he is an unpredictable Iraqi. Usually I can estimate the price of a man's reliability. Fifty thousand isn't enough to tempt you, Jack. Not when you have a good chance of doubling that and even making much more. Now I must return to my *diwania*. What's your answer? Yes or no?'

'I'd still like a while to think about it.'

'Very well. But time is short. As a start, there's someone here I want you to meet, a man who has some limited knowledge of what happened and who can give you background information on Jalloul. He knows nothing about the ransom, but I've told him you're a financial investigator and he'll help you as a favour to me. You can have complete confidence in his discretion. He will answer your questions but will ask none of his own.'

Most of the Kuwaitis were still gathered round the table, eating and talking complacently about the trials of the occupation. The man Hamadi took Jack to meet, however, was the one he had spotted earlier, standing on his own to one side of the room. He watched without expression as the other two approached him; when Hamadi introduced him to Jack he shook hands firmly but did not smile.

'Mr Jack Rushton, a former resident here,' said the doctor. 'This is Major Abdullah Al-Shaheb.'

Major Al-Shaheb was of medium height, heavily built and unusually dark-skinned. Almost certainly the blood of African slaves from an earlier century ran in his veins. He had a rigid military bearing that seemed unsuited to the loose, flowing lines of the black *dishdasha* and white head-dress that he wore. He held a small glass of orange juice enveloped in a large brown fist.

'The major is one of the quiet heroes of the occupation,' Hamadi said. 'He was transferred from the army to the police security division some years ago, and is responsible, among other things, for the personal safety of the Emir and his family. He arranged their escape to Bahrain on the day of the invasion and remained with them in Saudi Arabia. From there he helped to direct the activities of the resistance and collected information that assisted the allies in the planning of their attack. Abdullah, I have told Mr Rushton you have interesting stories to tell.'

Jack felt uncomfortably put on the spot. He said to the policeman, tritely: 'You must have had some scary moments last August.'

'It was all in the line of duty,' Al-Shaheb said brusquely. 'My job is to prepare for the worst. One day we may come to see the occupation as a blessing. Too many people here had grown used to the good life, as you must know. They were accustomed to having things done for them. They did not know how to fend for themselves, to make sacrifices in order to survive. Some of them still don't.'

Was that the ghost of a disparaging glance that he threw towards the men wolfing down pastries at the table? If so, Dr Hamadi did not appear to consider himself included in the criticism. He gave a hearty laugh and said: 'You're right, Abdullah. There are lessons for us all in that. Well, I'll let you two talk.'

He turned away to join his other guests, leaving Jack and the major staring at each other. Al-Shaheb's features had a sternness that did not encourage small talk. Jack had thought of him at first as looking awkward in this company, unsure of his welcome if he attempted to join a conversation; now he realized there was hostility or even contempt in his manner.

His bright, dark eyes scanned Jack's face as though he were comparing it to those of a list of suspects he had mentally stored away.

'You understand, Mr Rushton,' he said suddenly, 'that I was asked here especially to meet you? I am not a regular attender at this *diwania*, but when Dr Hamadi requests one's presence it is advisable to accept. He told me that you might be making some enquiries outside the country on his behalf, arising out of things that took place here during the occupation. He asked me to assist you in any way I could.'

'Thank you. But actually I haven't yet agreed to what he's proposing . . .'

'I don't know what that is, and it's not my concern. Insofar as it remains confidential and does not conflict with my duties, I am at your disposal.'

This was *wasta* at work, Jack reflected. In spite of his self-assurance, Al-Shaheb with his slave blood was undoubtedly from a humble background. Soldiering and police work were not professions that appealed to the upper or even the middle classes of Kuwait society; to advance his career, to progress to the position of the Emir's personal security chief, he would have needed the patronage of a powerful man. Hamadi was Al-Shaheb's patron: both of them had as good as said so. The major would do the doctor's bidding without asking awkward questions.

Jack said cautiously: 'It's to do with the arrest of Dr Hamadi's daughter. He suggested you might know something about an Iraqi officer she had some dealings with, who also later disappeared. A man named Colonel Jalloul?'

The major grimaced knowingly. 'Of course. There is information on him in our files. We were able to take most of them with us to Saudi.'

Jack was surprised. 'You knew about Jalloul before the invasion?'

Al-Shaheb gave him a look that stopped just short of being condescending. 'The history of our various disputes with Iraq goes back many years before that. It has always been in our interests to learn as much as we could about the members of their military and security services. Do you read Arabic, Mr Rushton?'

'I'm afraid not.'

'Then I will have to translate the files for you.' The major glanced at his watch and said, 'Come to my office and let's make a start.'

'You mean now?'

'Why not? I have an hour to spare, if you do.'

Just like that. Instinctively cautious, Jack was caught off his guard by this abrupt invitation. His mind floundered for an excuse, and then he thought: Why not, indeed? He had not committed himself to anything yet, and he might find it easier to make a decision if he knew a little more about what he could be getting into.

He lingered only for long enough to thank Dr Hamadi for his hospitality, to be handed another card with a business number on it, and to promise to phone him with a decision the next day. Then he left the house with Major Al-Shaheb. The policeman had a Range Rover parked under the mimosas and he set off in it at terrific speed, leaving Jack to follow in the Granada as best he could along lightless roads and through the swirling oil smoke. They turned on to the Al-Istiqlal Expressway and raced towards the city centre. At the Al-Sabah roundabout they picked up the Al-Soor Street dual carriageway that ran beside the few preserved remnants of the old city walls. They turned again beside the Al-Shamiya Gate and passed by the towers of the radio and television complex. The major hadn't said what their destination was, but when Jack realized they were driving up Abdulla Al-Salim Street, not far from his own apartment building, he knew with foreboding that they were heading for the Nayef Palace.

Al-Shaheb swung into a gateway in the whitewashed wall and halted briefly to speak to the soldiers slouching behind piles of sandbags. Then he drove through, waving an arm out of the car in a signal for Jack to follow.

They parked side by side in a big courtyard, empty but for a few other vehicles and surrounded by a variety of nondescript buildings. Lights showed behind some of the windows but most were in darkness. There was a strange sense of hidden activity going on behind this lifelessness, though Jack wondered how much of it was due to his imagination. These buildings had been the headquarters and main barracks of the Kuwait City police, and Vincent Hand had told him something of the horrors enacted in the cells and living quarters after the Iraqis had taken them over. Men, women and young boys given electric shocks, beaten with clubs, burned with cigarettes, strangled, stabbed, mutilated. The women repeatedly raped by the soldiers and secret police quartered in the barracks. Late at night, Vincent said, the screams could be heard from their own apartment block hundreds of metres away.

When the liberating forces had arrived they'd found implements of torture left lying casually about like so much dirty cutlery. They had also dug up the body of Noura Hamadi, among a dozen others, from beneath the flagstones in one of the basements.

Major Al-Shaheb strutted purposefully ahead of Jack across the quiet courtyard, up some steps to an open walkway and into a lighted room. Three uniformed policemen engaged in desultory conversation around a desk leaped to their feet and saluted. The major barked a guttural order at them, then opened a door into another office and ushered Jack through.

The room contained a battered desk, two chairs, a steel locker and a table stacked with brown file covers, each boldly marked in ink with a line of Arabic characters. Beside the single window was a framed photograph of the

Emir that seemed new as well; possibly it had displaced one of Saddam Hussein.

Al-Shaheb showed Jack to a seat. Instead of joining him he went to the locker and opened it. He carefully removed his *gutra* and put it on a shelf at the top, then pulled the *dishdasha* off over his head and placed it on a hanger. Beneath the robe he wore dark slacks and a blue shirt and tie. His head was revealed to be narrow and bullet-shaped, the black hair woolly and tinged with grey. When he finally sat down behind his desk he seemed transformed in character as well as looks. He was a tough cop, back in his own world and comfortable with it.

Sensing Jack's thoughts, he smiled for the first time since they had met, giving a flash of gold pre-molars.

'A disguise I wear for the more traditional social occasions,' he said. 'It also helps to keep me anonymous.' The smile went as quickly as it had appeared. 'Now, what exactly do you want to know?'

On the way here Jack had thought about the awkwardness of asking questions without being able to explain their purpose. It was easy for Hamadi to say that Al-Shaheb would not want to know; but the man was clearly smart enough to draw his own conclusions. For the moment he was saved from answering by a knock on the door. Two of the policemen from the outer office came in, one of them carrying a couple of folders, the other with a tray holding cups of mint tea. All were placed with great care in front of Al-Shaheb before the men saluted and left.

'I'd like you to tell me whatever you can about Colonel Jalloul: his background, and his disappearance. But first it might be useful to know how Noura Hamadi came to be arrested.'

'Of course. Her father finds it too painful to talk about. Not that there is much to tell. There was an arrangement for Jalloul to collect the girl at the house on the night of the third of September. We know from the servants that he did arrive and that they left together, apparently to go to the airport where he would have a private plane waiting to take them to Baghdad. From there she would travel to Amman on a scheduled flight, carrying the papers of an Iraqi citizen.

'What happened after that is not clear, but we know that she never caught the plane. There were rumours of some kind of shooting incident at the airport that night, but it's impossible to know if there was any connection. Noura, anyway, was arrested at some point and brought here. After that, nothing was heard of her until her body was found.

'As for Jalloul, he was an officer of the *Estikhbarat* – that is, the Iraqi Military Intelligence. He was, at the time, in charge of military security in the western sector of Kuwait City.' The major flipped open one of the folders and at once began in a steady monotone to translate what he read. 'Ibrahim Faysal Jalloul. Born in December nineteen fifty in the village of Jalibah, in south-eastern Iraq. A man of humble origins: his father was imam of a small Shi'a mosque. Joined the army in nineteen sixty-eight and graduated four years later from the Military Academy at Ar-Rustamiyah. Married a woman of the Takriti clan, which no doubt helped his career. Perhaps you want to write some of this down?' From a drawer of the desk he took a pad of lined paper and passed it to Jack, together with one of the cups of tea. 'He was a captain by the time the Iran–Iraq war broke out, and . . . yes, this may interest you: just at that time he was attending a course at the British Army Staff College at Camberley, which he passed with honours. And here he is, looking quite pleased at his achievements.'

Al-Shaheb turned the open file around. For the second time that evening, and with unwilling fascination, Jack found himself studying a photograph. It was a group picture of a dozen men in the uniforms of different armies, taken against a background of sweeping lawns and distant, imposing buildings. One of the faces in the second row had been ringed in ink, a lean, rather handsome Arab face with a trim moustache and a forced smile.

'Could you give me a copy of that?' Jack asked.

'Our copying machines were all stolen. But doubtless we have other prints elsewhere. I don't see why you shouldn't have this one.'

Al-Shaheb slid the picture across the desk. As he retrieved the folder and continued to read from it, Jack caught a glimpse of some photocopied pages of typing that might have been in English.

'Jalloul was promoted to major soon afterwards. He commanded a company on the Iranian front for four years before transferring to the *Estikhbarat* and moving to their headquarters in Baghdad. Another promotion went with that. But these formal details tell only part of the story. Jalloul was a professional soldier and one of their more capable officers, not merely a Ba'athist lackey like so many of them. He was also a Shi'a Muslim from the south of the country, not one of the Sunni clique that surrounds Saddam. For all these reasons he was not entirely trusted. Is all this of some help to you?'

'I'm impressed by how much you know,' Jack said evasively.

'There are reasons for that.' The major closed the file and sipped some tea. 'Before I became a policemen I was with Military Intelligence myself. We kept a close eye on people like Jalloul – that is, on officers who were disaffected, who as they rose in rank might represent a threat to Saddam Hussein, or at least be seen as such. One day he might have been useful to us.'

'You mean . . . as a spy?'

'Perhaps, but more likely as a client, a friend. An agent of influence or a fifth columnist . . . whatever you care to call it. All armies, all intelligence services, seek out such people among the ranks of their enemies. In his case, the opportunity to try out his loyalty never arose.'

'I heard that the Iraqis had accused Noura of trying to smuggle gold out of the country.'

'That was rubbish. Another rumour, one that they put about themselves to try to discredit the resistance. They were the ones who stole our gold—'

There was suddenly a commotion outside the room. From the walkway that led past the windows they heard pounding footsteps and a shout of alarm, followed by a series of scuffling noises and incoherent grunts. Major Al-Shaheb sprang to his feet. From the outer office came the noise of the policemen scrambling for the door, and on the walkway there was more excited yelling and then a thump as though someone had fallen heavily to the ground.

Al-Shaheb had a grimly knowing look on his face. 'Excuse me,' he said, and stalked out of the room.

Jack had stood up as well. The shouting and bumping had stopped and now there came a cry of pain, repeated at length and punctuated by the unmistakable sound of violent blows. He went quietly to the window and peered out.

At the edge of the courtyard the three policemen from the office, and two or three others, stood surrounding a man who lay curled up on the ground. Even by the thin light that fell from the windows it could be seen that he was completely naked and was flinching from the beating he was being given. The policemen were taking turns at it, raising their truncheons high and whacking down at whatever part of the squirming body was nearest. Beside them Major Al-Shaheb stood impassively watching.

Jack felt shock and revulsion at once. An instinct arose in him to protest at what he was witnessing, but at that moment Al-Shaheb gave an order and the beating stopped. Two of the cops dragged the man to his feet and Jack saw that his wrists were handcuffed in front of him. He was a young man. Blood gleamed on his face and his eyes were wide with terror. The policemen turned him around and frog-marched him away.

When Al-Shaheb returned to the office Jack was sitting back at the desk again, but his expression must have told the major he had seen something.

'Some trouble with a prisoner,' Al-Shaheb said equably. He sat down and spread his hands in a gesture of helplessness. 'One of our Palestinian collaborator friends. Tried to make a run for it as he was being taken from his cell for interrogation. Without clothes, and in handcuffs!' The major laughed at the absurdity of the idea. 'Now, Mr Rushton, what else can I tell you?'

# 6

Vincent Hand had got hold of a radio with a short-wave band from somewhere, and batteries to power it, and when Jack joined him for breakfast the next morning he was twiddling the tuning knob in search of the BBC World Service. Surprisingly, he was also wearing a jacket and tie. It was Easter Sunday, he reminded Jack; although it was a normal working day here, he was taking the morning off and going to mass at the small Catholic church by the Al-Maqsab Gate.

'By the way,' he said, 'did you know the phones were working again?'

'They are?'

'Well, mine is. It rang a few minutes ago. I hardly recognized the sound.'

They ate bread and cheese again, this time with the refinement of pickled cucumbers from a jar. Vincent said his American colleagues had promised him a Sterno stove to boil water on, and a supply of tea-bags and instant coffee. He announced this with the simple pleasure of an old lag who has won an unexpected privilege; Jack decided not to diminish his enjoyment by mentioning the feast that had been laid out at Dr Hamadi's house the night before.

They listened through a storm of static to the news on the World Service, still dominated by events in the Gulf. There was a brief mention that more than five hundred oil wells were still burning in Kuwait. The focus, however, had long ago shifted to Iraq and the civil wars that Saddam Hussein was fighting on two fronts, against the Kurds in the north of the country and the Shi'a rebels in the south. Although the details were sketchy, the general impression was that his forces were gaining the upper hand. Thousands of Kurdish civilians were fleeing into the mountains bordering Turkey. It seemed unbelievable that the man whose army had suffered such a devastating defeat barely a month ago was not only still in power, but capable of crushing two separate rebellions.

'Surely somebody will overthrow him soon,' Jack remarked, remembering what Al-Shaheb had said about disaffected officers.

'Wishful thinking, I'm afraid,' Vincent said. 'I don't think many people understand how tightly he's got that country sewn up. He's worked his relatives and cronies into all the key positions. And he's careful to eliminate any officer who shows signs of becoming too ambitious. He topped a lot of the generals who'd carried on the war against Iran for him, you know, just in case they started getting notions about themselves. The result is he's got a pretty mediocre army, but one that isn't likely to turn against him. And the secret police answer to him personally. But listen to this . . .'

There was a supplementary report on the radio about claims that Saddam and some of those same cronies had been milking their own government's treasury. Western governments, the newsreader said, were investigating allegations that the Iraqi leader and his close associates had transferred billions of pounds of the country's oil revenues and contract commissions to private bank accounts in Europe and the United States.

A reporter elaborated on the story. It seemed that the exiled Kuwaiti government had commissioned private financial investigators in New York and London to track down hidden Iraqi assets abroad. The Kuwaitis' interest lay in the hope that the money would be paid over as part of the reparations due for the invasion. The investigators had had the help of political opponents of Saddam, now living in Europe. What the inquiry had uncovered was that over a number of years as much as five per cent of the country's oil earnings had been diverted for the private use of Saddam Hussein, his family and his political friends in Baghdad. The money had been diverted into bank accounts abroad and much of it had been reinvested through nominees in American, French and German companies.

Jack said: 'I wouldn't mind betting that my old firm, Hellig's, were involved in that. It's just their kind of thing. But doesn't it rather disprove what you were saying? The father of the nation turns out to be just another cheap crook. Why would he salt away money like that unless he foresaw the possibility of losing power?'

'All it shows is that he's more of a realist than we've been led to believe,' said Vincent. 'He keeps the people he trusts sweet by lining their pockets, and gives them a guarantee of a gold-plated bolthole if times get tough. The only question is how many generals and party officials he can afford to go on paying.'

Jack found the report vaguely disturbing. Although it had no apparent bearing on what Hamadi had told him last night, it did have parallels – corrupt officials, laundered money, secret accounts, the familiar vocabulary of financial sleaze – that suggested something of the morass into which he might be stepping by accepting the doctor's proposal.

And if he did accept it, what would his motives be? The idea of having fifty thousand dollars dropped in his lap was certainly attractive. It would go a long way towards rehabilitating him financially; but that wasn't everything. He didn't mind helping Hamadi out of a personal mess, but he had no instinctive sympathy for him and his kind, or for propping up the position of near-feudal privilege they enjoyed. If he said yes, it would be because the job seemed to offer him something to focus his energies on; if nothing else, it promised him a temporary way out of the confusion surrounding his own life.

He had no particular plans for the day. When he got back to his own apartment he picked up the telephone receiver and was gratified to hear the dialling tone. It was too early to phone Alison in England, though, and he couldn't think of anyone else to call. Instead he went down to the water tanker that was parked in front of the Meridien Hotel and fetched back two bucketfuls, one for himself and one for Vincent. He did his best to shave and wash himself in cold water, then put on a clean shirt and slacks. He noticed that the smell of oil smoke had worked its way into the fabric of the suit he had worn last night and he wondered if a faint odour of the Nayef Palace wasn't there as well, the reek of carbolic not quite disguising something less pleasant.

A feeling of strain had entered his conversation with Major Al-Shaheb after the incident involving the Palestinian prisoner. On reflection, he wasn't disturbed so much at seeing the man being beaten as at the way the major had stood there letting it happen. And the sight of the blood pouring down the man's face had seemed less shocking than the fact that he'd been naked when he had tried to run from the guards. Clearly he was being questioned in circumstances that were degrading and humiliating, and possibly worse.

Al-Shaheb, guessing his thoughts, had said: 'I would not like you to waste your sympathy on a man like that, Mr Rushton. He's a traitor. I'm like most people here, I believe in the cause of the Palestinians, but it's a fact that many of them co-operated with the Iraqis. They betrayed members of the resistance. They helped in the looting. Even since the liberation some of the pigs, like that one, have given shelter to their soldiers and secret police who are still on the run.'

The policeman's look was challenging. Jack couldn't argue with him, sensing the futility of comparing what had happened just now to what the Iraqis themselves had done in this place. He decided to revert to the matter that had brought him here.

'What do you think happened to Colonel Jalloul?' he asked carefully. 'How did he disappear?'

Al-Shaheb shrugged. 'My only information was what came to me in the reports smuggled out by the resistance. In order to plan the liberation it was necessary to have all possible tactical intelligence from inside Kuwait. We asked our people to identify as many senior Iraqi officers as they could, to establish what their jobs were and where they were posted. Jalloul had his headquarters at the air base of Ali al Salem. One day he was there, the next day not. After that he was of no interest to us.'

'What do you imagine *might* have happened to him?'

'You're asking me to guess? It's possible that he was summoned back to Baghdad, maybe for a date with the firing squad.' The major smirked. 'Myself, I doubt that. Jalloul was a good survivor, like anyone in his position. It may be that the *Mukhabarat* were keeping an eye on him, making sure of his loyalty. It may also be that he was aware of it and ready to get out ahead of them.'

'But if he was an intelligence officer himself, in a position of trust, wasn't his loyalty considered beyond question?'

'Of course not.' Al-Shaheb had rolled up his sleeves and sat, in a self-satisfied way, with meaty brown forearms crossed over his chest. 'In Iraq everything is political. An army officer does not just fight for his country; he must show his belief in the ideology of the Ba'ath Party. He must be an Arab socialist, an anti-imperialist, an anti-Zionist. All the same, there are different loyalties, religious disagreements, rivalries between the services. You must not confuse the *Estikhbarat*, the military intelligence, with the *Mukhabarat*, which is more or less an agency of the Ba'ath. They spy on everyone, including the military. They were responsible for most of the atrocities here. They are Saddam Hussein's Gestapo. He is just like Hitler, you see, the way he surrounds himself with different secret groups, each one afraid of the others so that nobody trusts anyone else.

'Take this matter of the gold that you mentioned. Forty tonnes of gold bars, stolen from our Central Bank.

They bring ten special trucks down here to transport it to Baghdad. Already when they get here one has broken down, so only nine go back.' The major seemed to be enjoying giving this little lecture. 'The army gets it out of the bank, but that's all they are allowed to do. The commander of the *Mukhabarat*, a general named Malik, is put in charge of removing it to Baghdad. But even he is not trusted enough to do the job alone; he has to have an escort arranged by the *Estikhbarat* to guard it. Even then, some of it is supposed to have gone missing. They cannot take the blame for that themselves, so they concoct some story about the Kuwaiti resistance stealing it!'

Al-Shaheb shook his head. He had spoken in the same tone of condescending amusement with which Dr Hamadi's guests had discussed the antics of other Iraqis.

'Anyway, our friend Jalloul they do not consider too politically reliable. In his position, I would have made preparations for my future. He was free to travel abroad and he probably had access to false papers. Perhaps he had also put money aside. Even then, he would have to be careful. The *Mukhabarat* has a long arm. It is active in many countries. Its agents spread dissent and fear among the opponents of Saddam; it has assassinated many of them. It's my guess, since you ask me to guess, that our friend heard of some plan to liquidate him, and got out ahead of the liquidators.'

'Could you put me on to anyone who might know more about the immediate circumstances? Your informants in the resistance?'

'Well, that may not be so easy.' For a man so brusquely certain of himself, Al-Shaheb sounded suddenly vague. 'The resistance is disbanded, and it is difficult after all this time to be sure about the origin of any particular piece of information.'

'I couldn't help noticing,' Jack said, 'that part of that file on Jalloul is written in English. Is there any significance in that?'

The major looked at him suspiciously for a moment, then smiled again. 'None at all. We receive our intelligence from a variety of sources, and naturally I am not free to disclose them to you. But I will make what enquiries I can. If I hear anything at all that I think may be helpful, I will let you know.'

Looking back on the conversation, Jack felt he had hardly been enlightened by it. The details of Noura Hamadi's betrayal and arrest were sketchy; the biographical notes on Colonel Jalloul were no more than that; and by speculating on a possible political dimension to the Iraqi's disappearance, Major Al-Shaheb had merely added further confusion to events that were already far from clear. Whatever the reason for it, Jalloul's departure from the scene had been the starting point of the whole business. If Jack was to take on the job of tracing him, it seemed important to have a better understanding of the circumstances; yet Al-Shaheb had seemed oddly dismissive of the one area of enquiry that might have yielded something more.

Jack waited until he heard Vincent returning from mass and waylaid him in the corridor. He said he wanted something to read and was invited into the apartment to help himself from the bookshelves. Standing beside them, perusing a volume on alternative medicine, he said casually: 'You talked a bit about helping the resistance during the occupation. How much did you actually have to do with them?'

Vincent had emerged from his bedroom after changing into his workaday sweatshirt and jeans. He put a finger to the side of his nose. 'Officially, nothing. I'm a citizen of a neutral state, remember.'

'Unofficially, then?'

'I knew who some of them were. I did what I could for them, but as indirectly as possible. Why are you asking?'

Without quite knowing why, Jack had expected the subject to be sensitive. He said: 'I can't go into details, but this bit of work I've been offered has to do with an incident that happened during the occupation. The trouble is, the only information I've been given has come from people who weren't actually here at the time. I'd like to hear another side of it. I need guidance.'

'The truth about a lot of things that happened here is already quite muddy,' Vincent said with a frown. 'Since the liberation, everybody seems to have been a hero of the resistance. From what I saw, the Kuwaitis weren't all saints and the Iraqis weren't all demons. And the Palestinians were not the only collaborators. It just happens to suit everyone's book to see them that way.

'Anyway, I don't know that I can tell you much. As I said, I kept my involvement indirect. My greatest asset was my freedom to move around. If I'd been arrested I'd have been no use to anyone. Besides, I had a fairly tough job of my own to do, trying to keep the animals alive. I located supplies for the resistance to distribute – those frozen-food warehouses I told you about. And sometimes I acted as a courier, taking messages to and from the British and Americans who'd stayed on in hiding. It was all done through friends of friends. I didn't want to know what else they were getting up to, or anything about their leadership or organization. Others got more involved.'

'What others?'

'You won't find many of them keen to talk to you, if that's what you're thinking. You see, the real resisters, not the ones who are boasting about it now, also happen to be in the forefront of the movement for greater democracy here. Wars and conquests do that: they throw up patriotic movements that become a force for change, that refuse to accept a return to the *status quo*. Some of the foreigners who helped these people got caught up in the same enthusiasms. Well, with the Emir and his entourage back in their palaces and their government offices, the very people who helped restore them are now a threat to them. They're talking about ending all those privileges that the ruling families enjoy.

About a wider franchise and a parliament that actually has some power. About votes for women, for heaven's sake! That's nothing less than revolutionary talk around here, and the ruling classes are going to do whatever it takes to stop it.

'Quite a lot of these dissidents are vulnerable to pressure. They're mostly young and middle class, dependent on the government one way or another for their livelihood. Others aren't even Kuwaiti citizens, and they could lose their residence permits, their jobs, their homes. So naturally they're keeping a low profile, at least until things settle down.'

Jack said: 'All I need is to talk quietly to someone. It needn't go any further.'

'All right,' Vincent sighed. 'Your best bet is to go and see Dale Griggs.'

'Who's he?'

'She, Jack. She's a woman. American. As a matter of fact I mentioned her to you yesterday. She used to tutor Dr Hamadi's daughter. I believe she was one of the last people to see the girl before the Iraqis got her.'

'And she's still here?' Jack said in surprise.

'She is – was, anyway – a lecturer in sociology, I think, at the university. And something of an athlete in her time. She stayed on right through the occupation, in hiding. She gave the resistance a lot of help and even managed to send out intelligence to the Americans.'

'Where can I find her?'

'She moves around a lot. All I've got is a contact address out at Al-Adeliya. Try it. Tell her I sent you – but be warned, she may not be co-operative.'

'Scared of losing her job?'

'In her case it's more complicated. She was married to a Kuwaiti, and technically she lost the right of residence when they were divorced. But actually I don't think she's scared of very much. She had to stay on here even after the rest of the Westerners were allowed to go, because the

Iraqis had put a price on her head. Probably she'd have stayed anyway. She's that kind of woman. Tough-minded. Still want to talk to her?'

'I'll give it a bash,' Jack said.

He left it until one o'clock before he called Alison. He had no problem making the international connection, but the phone in the Banstead house rang for nearly a minute before she answered.

'Hello?' Slightly out of breath, a distracted tone to her voice.

'Alison? It's me.'

'Oh. Hello.' The voice dropping a note, another of her mannerisms lately.

'I'm calling from Kuwait. I'm in the apartment. The phones have just been reconnected and I thought I'd make contact as soon as possible.' She didn't respond, and he said: 'Are you all right? Have I woken you up or something?'

'At eleven in the morning? Hardly. I was out in the garden, trying to start the lawnmower. I've had to call Fred Reynolds out of his own garden to help,' she added reproachfully.

Fred Reynolds lived across the road and his garden was a model to the neighbourhood. 'You shouldn't have bothered him,' Jack said. 'I'll be home soon. Besides, you shouldn't use that mower. It's too heavy for you.'

'Somebody's got to cut the grass. You promised to do it before you went away. It can't be left at this time of year.'

'Then pay someone to do it, for God's sake!'

'We can't afford that sort of extravagance.'

'Ask bloody Fred Reynolds, then. He'll enjoy the chance to show me up.'

'Have you rung just to be rude to me, Jack?'

'Of course not.' It struck him that this argument, though no more ridiculous than many of their others, had an added absurdity for being conducted over a distance of three thousand miles. 'All right, I'm sorry you've got to mow the grass. And I'm sorry if that sounded rude. It wasn't meant to be. How are the girls?'

'They're fine. They're playing next door at the moment.'

There was another pause. She had not responded to his apology. So he'd forgotten to cut the grass. Diminished her in the eyes of the neighbours. Capital offence. He said rather acidly: 'I thought you might like to know that I was quite right to come back here. The flat is mostly intact. The Iraqis took some of our stuff but they didn't strip the place. I'm getting all the money out of the bank, as I'd hoped. And I've been offered some freelance work, but I don't know yet whether I'll take it.'

'When do you say you're coming back?'

'Within two or three days. I'll phone you again. But don't let me keep you away from the lawn. Give my love to the twins,' he said, and banged down the phone.

Jesus Christ, he thought, things were going from bad to worse. She could no longer bring herself to sound interested in anything to do with him. He couldn't get through to her, couldn't penetrate her moods or her deliberate, punishing silences. Punishing him for what? For the loss of his business? For taking her back to England only to humiliate her in the eyes of her friends? Or just for not living up to her own confused expectations of him? Worst of all, she had lost her sense of humour. More and more, it seemed to him, she was drawing on some deep well of bitterness that had always been there, successfully concealed only for as long as his money had held out.

After all the years in which he'd had to travel away on business of one sort or another, Jack realized that for the first time he wasn't looking forward to going home.

He recognized another thing. Somewhere in his subconscious mind a decision had made itself. He fished out the business card Dr Hamadi had given him, picked up the phone again and dialled the number. He gave his name to a switchboard operator and asked to speak to Hamadi; after a few moments a smooth male voice came on, speaking perfect English.

'Mr Rushton, I am Dr Hamadi's personal assistant. He's not available at present but he told me he was expecting you to call. Can I take a message?'

'Yes,' said Jack. 'Just tell him I agree to the proposal we've discussed. I'll get in touch with him about a further meeting.'

# 7

Al-Adeliya lay just south of the Third Ring, close to the university campus and roughly at the halfway stage along the methodical march of suburbia into the desert. Like the rest of Kuwait's satellite communities it was purpose-built, this time not for the rich but for the Arab white-collar class that had been emerging since the oil began to flow. No security gates here, but low-walled gardens in front of modest villas, and paved pathways giving access to small apartment buildings. A shopping centre reflecting Western and Arab consumer tastes side by side: a Sultan supermarket, a *halal* butcher, a Baskin Robbins ice-cream parlour. All the shops were closed and had their metal blinds down, but looked undamaged; evidently the Iraqi pillagers hadn't bothered coming this far out of town. On the streets, however, under the canopy of oil smoke, there was hardly a sign of life.

The address Jack had got from Vincent Hand was in an apartment block on Street Number Three, a low building with flaking cream paintwork, screened from the street by a row of hardy tamarisks. The smoke caught in his throat again as he left the car and approached the entrance. The building was on three floors with two apartments on each, facing each other across the stairwell. In the gloomy lobby was a rack of numbered mailboxes with cards slotted into them, the tenants' names written in Arabic but some also with their Romanized equivalents. He found the name Vincent had given him, Al-Fadni, in the slot for Apartment B.

It was one of the ground-floor flats. Just as he approached the door it opened in front of him. A plump

Arab woman stood in the opening, wearing a dark *abaya* and a veil. She'd been about to go out but she paused in surprise, or even shock, when she saw Jack. As he made an involuntary, questioning move towards her, she turned and fled back into the apartment.

The door remained open. After a few moments a black-haired boy of about twelve emerged, wearing a denim jacket and jeans. He studied Jack gravely and said, 'May I help you?'

'Perhaps. I'm looking for a Miss Dale Griggs.'

'She doesn't live here.'

'I believe not. But I was told I might find her through someone at this address.'

'You are a friend of hers?' the boy asked suspiciously. His manner was prematurely serious. Although Jack sensed that the woman, presumably his mother, still lurked in the background, the youth seemed to consider himself the spokesman for the family in the absence of a grown man.

'No, she doesn't know me. But my name is Jack Rushton and—'

'Miss Dale only came here for short visits. She has her own place to stay now but she asked us not to reveal her address. May I know why you want to see her?'

'I'm not at liberty to disclose that,' said Jack, falling in with the pedantic spirit of things, 'but I have an introduction from a mutual friend.'

The boy thought about that and reached a decision. 'I can't tell you where she lives,' he said, 'but I may know where to find her. At this time of day she is usually running.'

'Running?'

'In the stadium, just near by. If I go with you she may not mind meeting you.'

'All right,' said Jack bemusedly.

The boy called through the door to the woman. Perhaps he was asking permission to go out, but he phrased the request like a casual statement of fact. As they set off across the lobby he suddenly dropped his earnestness and became chatty.

'My mother is nervous,' he said. 'She became a nervous person during the occupation. My father was never at home. He was a resistance fighter, facing many dangers.' Proudly. 'During Desert Storm he went out and killed many Iraqis but was wounded himself. He's in the hospital now. We hope he will be home soon.'

'I hope so too,' Jack said.

'Miss Dale was like one of us. She went where others were afraid to go. She speaks perfect Arabic. She dressed as a Kuwaiti woman and carried guns under her *abaya*.'

The Qasma stadium was just down the road and the boy refused Jack's suggestion that they drive there. He introduced himself as Tewfiq Al-Fadni and said he was a pupil at the Al-Adeniya Secondary School. He explained that Miss Griggs had been a colleague of his father at the university, and had become friendly with the family after moving into an apartment down the road the previous June.

'That was after her husband gave her *talaq*,' he said matter-of-factly. 'You understand?'

'Divorce.'

'Yes. She gave him no sons.'

'Was that really the reason?'

Tewfiq looked at him in puzzlement. 'It is the usual reason,' he said. 'It is the custom. But perhaps there were other things. She said he was not a kind person.'

'She talked to you, then?'

'Quite a lot. She knows interesting things.'

Jack recognized in Tewfiq the type of confusion felt by young Arabs eager to absorb Western culture but having trouble reconciling it with their own traditions. To an intelligent man the experience of really getting to know a Western woman, of learning to respect and even admire her, could be an unsettling one. It opened up possibilities of conversation and stimulation that could make him wonder whether he wanted a submissive and housebound woman for a wife. It could even make him question the value of a social life spent entirely with other men.

Jack, however, had his own misgivings about dealing with Dale Griggs. The tough, unisex name seemed intimidating in itself.

The stadium loomed out of the smoke. The main entrance that gave access to the indoor sports centre was locked, but they found one of the gates to the spectator stands open. They climbed a wide flight of stairs that led out on to a middle tier of grandstand seats. The field below was a bleak oval of uncut grass, dead and dying, with the faint whitewashed markings of a soccer pitch still visible here and there. A running track with a damaged Sportflex surface encircled the pitch, and on its far side a solitary figure moved through the gloom at a steady, middle-distance canter.

'Miss Dale,' Tewfiq announced.

They went down an aisle to the low barrier at the edge of the track. Approaching them as she came out of the nearest curve into the straight, the woman must have seen them but did not acknowledge their presence. She wore black running shorts and a green T-shirt, white spiked shoes and a headband from which a long tail of blond hair bounced in time with her steps. She passed by the two spectators and began another lap, moving in the easy but concentrated way of a natural runner, harnessing energy, long legs with strong, stringy muscles going in rhythmical strides, her arms pumping close to her sides. Her head was thrust forward, showing straining tendons in her neck. Her profile was lean and angular, her face reflecting a bare minimum of stress.

She ran two more laps at the same pace and took the final hundred metres at a sprint, checking her watch at the moment she crossed an imaginary finish line. She wound down her stride over a dozen more paces, then lowered her head, coughing and resting her hands on her knees for a minute before straightening up. She walked to where a sports bag stood beside the barrier, took out a towel and buried her face in it.

'Come,' said Tewfiq.

He led the way along the railings and stopped a few feet from Dale Griggs. She still seemed in no hurry to acknowledge them, dabbing the sweat from her face and her neck. Jack had had an impulse to clap her performance and was glad he had resisted it. Finally she said, 'Hello, Tewfiq.'

'Miss Dale, I have brought a man to see you.'

Dale Griggs looked coolly at Jack and said nothing, waiting for an explanation. Seen close up she was tall and square-shouldered, her figure spare, small-breasted and supple. Her features were sharply chiselled, the cheekbones high, the nose and chin both prominent. Her eyes were light green and her skin had a natural tan. At a guess, she was in her early thirties.

'Hello, Miss Griggs,' Jack said. He leaned over the barrier and offered his hand, which she shook after a moment's hesitation. 'My name is Jack Rushton. Vincent Hand suggested where I might find you, and Tewfiq kindly took over from there.'

'What can I do for you?'

'It's a bit complicated to cover in a few words. I used to live here until last July and I've just got back from London. I'm a business consultant, but what I want to ask is more a personal favour . . .' He sensed that he was babbling a bit. 'Am I interrupting your training?' he asked.

She had taken off her spikes and was slipping the two halves of a grey, brushed-cotton track suit over her running gear.

'Business consultant?' Repeating the words, she seemed to be testing them for some hidden meaning. She pulled on a worn pair of Reeboks, then suddenly turned away and coughed again at some length. 'Goddam smoke,' she said when she'd recovered. 'No, there's nothing to train for. I was just timing myself at the end of my usual workout.'

'How was your time?'

'Bad. Around four minutes thirty.'

'For fifteen hundred metres? That sounds bloody good to me.'

'It's lousy,' she said dismissively. 'I used to run the mile in less than that. And my best over fifteen hundred was just under four-oh-four.'

'All the same, on this track, in these conditions . . .'

He gestured around at the smoke-laden air, but his attempts to praise her seemed only to irritate her. 'No credit where it's not due, please. My times these days wouldn't get me a place on my old college squad, not even in the best conditions. I peaked around ten years ago. It doesn't bother me. I do it now because it's a therapy, or maybe a compulsion.'

'What was your college?'

'Louisiana State, Baton Rouge.'

The way she pronounced it, he could now catch the hint of a Southern accent in her voice. 'What I wanted to talk about,' he said, 'was something that happened here during the occupation. Something you might be able to shed some light on.'

'Uh-huh? Is this the business part, or the personal?'

'A bit of both, really. Vincent said you could help me if anyone could. He told me you were involved with the resistance.'

'That's a delicate subject right now, Mr . . . Rushton?' She looked at him speculatively, clutching the towel to the side of her face. 'What's your interest in it?'

Jack glanced at Tewfiq, who hadn't joined in the conversation but appeared to be following it closely. 'I feel we ought to talk in private. No offence,' he said to the boy, 'but I'd like to have a few minutes alone with Miss Dale. If that's all right with you?' he asked her.

She thought about it for a moment. Tewfiq looked crestfallen, but then she spoke to him in Arabic and he brightened up. 'See you later,' he said in English, and scampered away up the steps.

Dale Griggs slung the sports bag over her shoulder and vaulted the barrier. She pulled off the headband and shook loose her hair, which fell, rather to Jack's surprise, in thick blond tresses all the way to her shoulders. Now that she stood beside him her face was almost on a level with his; its outlines, softened by the hair although devoid of make-up, no longer seemed so sharp. What he had seen as a rather scrawny toughness was really a healthy absence of spare flesh.

'Thank you,' he said. 'I was a bit worried about offending Tewfiq's male pride.'

'Oh, he's not too bad. I've been educating him. Actually, he's jealous of my company. I told him I'd go with him to visit his father in the hospital this evening.'

'He tells me his father was wounded in some shoot-out after killing a lot of Iraqis.'

'A forgivable overstatement. He did go out with a rifle when the allies invaded, but before he could do any damage he was hit by some shrapnel from what my countrymen are pleased to call "friendly fire". He's a brave man, though. They all were. After the first few weeks of the occupation they had to give up any idea of serious armed resistance. Too big a threat of reprisals.'

With the change in her looks had come a slight relaxation of her manner. She was friendlier, but the green eyes remained guarded. 'I'm heading for what passes at present for my home,' she said. 'We can talk on the way if you like, but I don't promise to be of any help.'

'My car is at Tewfiq's place. Can I give you a lift?'

'No. I'm just down the road, but in the other direction.'

They climbed the steps together and at the top Dale Griggs halted and looked around the stadium. She said: 'Do you find this place creepy?'

'No. A bit depressing, perhaps.'

'Then I guess you don't know what the Iraqis used it for. Torture. Executions. They brought the overflow here from the Nayef Palace. The wrong people, mostly: innocent civilians, women, young boys. They were kept in the changing-rooms downstairs, and when they were killed they were thrown in the swimming-pool. I'm the only one who uses the place now. I thought it might help exorcize my ghosts.'

'And has it?'

'I'm not sure yet.'

Her reference to the Nayef Palace had given him an opening. He said, 'Actually, it's one of those victims I'd like to talk to you about. I asked Vincent for an introduction to someone who had worked with the resistance. He gave me your name and then mentioned that you'd been a friend of Noura Hamadi's.'

She gave him a wary look. 'Noura? You knew her too?'

'No, but I met her father yesterday and he told me what had happened to her. And Vincent said he thought you were one of the last people to see her before she was arrested.'

'Maybe I was.' She shrugged. 'So?'

'I'm trying to find out more about it, Miss Griggs. I've taken on a kind of business commission from Dr Hamadi, and what happened to Noura has some bearing on it.'

'Ah. Money and Dr Hamadi. I'm not surprised you mention them in the same breath. By the way, I've always been charmed by British formality, but I'd feel more comfortable at this point with Dale and Jack.' She turned and began tripping down the steps towards the exit, leaving him to follow. She called over her shoulder, 'Did the doctor have anything to say about me?'

'No.'

'That doesn't surprise me either. I guess my name is *haram* in that family now. Forbidden, I mean. The old man blamed me for talking Noura out of her wedding plans. The fact is he didn't like to believe the girl had a mind of her own, however liberally he thinks he raised her. Easier to point the finger at infidel feminist trash putting wrong ideas in her head.'

'Did you?' Jack caught up with her halfway down the steps.

'Not intentionally. She came to me for advice and I gave it as objectively as I could. But I'd seen, months earlier, that marrying someone like Ahmed Khalid would be a disaster for her. They were both students of mine. That's to say, they were both spoilt, rich kids who'd been to school in England and were sent to while away some time at college until they were ready for their pre-ordained roles in life. In Ahmed's case, that meant attending a few classes in between partying and jetting around Europe, preparing himself for the family profession of international playboy. And Noura . . . well, I guess her father thought there was nothing wrong in letting her spend a few years studying something harmless like sociology, just as long as she was ready in the end to become a good Arab wife. But she'd begun to see herself differently. She was bright, eager to learn. She'd got some benefit from her education, and that made her confused. She was caught between the conflicting demands of her independence and duty to her family.

'She told me she wanted the perspective of another woman, a Western woman, on the problem, but I think what she was really looking for was confirmation of her own feelings. She was . . . like a little sister, looking to an older one for reassurance. And I'm ready to admit to a prejudice: I didn't want Noura to repeat my mistake. I was married to my own Arab playboy. And I left him. Which in Daddy's eyes made me unqualified to give any advice to his daughter, and probably a brazen slut as well.'

Dale gave an unexpected, self-deprecating grin. Jack had begun to like her directness. He remembered what Hamadi had said about Noura falling under the spell of people without respect for her own traditions.

They emerged from the stadium into the smoky half-light and walked across the street. 'Anyway,' she said, 'I guess that stuff isn't what you came to hear. What can I tell you that the doctor hasn't already?'

'When was the last time you saw Noura?'

'That's easy. Monday, September third. The night they arrested her.'

'You mean you were there when it happened?'

'Not exactly. But I'm not sure I should go into the details.'

'Can they matter now?'

'Now that the poor kid is dead? Maybe they don't matter to you, but in my case there are other considerations. I was told some things that I wasn't supposed to know. Daddy is a powerful man, and he doesn't like me. He and the other sheikhs who endured the occupation at a distance, like from Bahrain and Palm Beach and Monte Carlo, have reacted against people like me who were in here at the sharp end. Plus, my professional position here is uncertain. Until the university reopens later this week I don't know whether I still have a job. And they still owe me money. In a nutshell, I could easily lose my livelihood and my residence permit, especially if the good doctor should decide to put a word in the right ears. You must know how things work around here.'

'Perhaps I could help straighten that out. I seem to have *wasta* with the doctor.'

'Thank you, but that might just make further complications. Noura took me into her confidence about some arrangements her father had made.'

'I think I know about those arrangements. You wouldn't be breaking any confidences by talking to me about them. And none of it has to get back to him.'

'Then why don't we level with each other, Jack? Where do you come into this?'

They had gone a short way down a sidewalk, deserted apart from a group of small children who halted a desultory

101

game to stare at them as they passed. Jack thought for a moment and said, 'We seem to be discussing more or less the same thing. Fill me in on what you know and I'll tell you as much as I can afford to about what Hamadi wants.'

'That sounds like a pretty one-sided bargain.' But she laughed and said, 'Well, what the hell? There's another thing the doctor wouldn't like. The reason I was with Noura that night is because I was staying in her house. In the annexe that was being prepared for her and Ahmed, in fact. The servants knew, of course, but Noura swore them to secrecy. I was on the lam. After the invasion the Iraqis stopped all Westerners from leaving, and then they started rounding them up. I decided to go into hiding rather than risk what might happen to me if I turned myself in.

'Noura was a sweet girl. As I said, she'd started treating me like a big sister. I asked if I could stay out of sight with her over in Salamiya for a while, just until I could make other arrangements, and she didn't hesitate. It turned out I couldn't have had more seclusion, because Daddy had been fixing things behind the scenes. He'd bribed an Iraqi officer to have his soldiers protect the place . . .'

'Colonel Jalloul,' Jack said. 'The man who was supposed to help Noura leave the country.'

'You know the bastard's name? Then you probably know at least as much as I do. For what he called security reasons he never told Noura who he was, and he was using a false name that night, anyhow. He'd been in touch with her for two or three weeks. He'd send messages and sometimes he'd visit the house.'

'What kind of messages?'

'Just reassuring her that his plans were going ahead, I guess. He didn't give her many details, and I didn't ask for any. I did warn her to be careful about trusting him, but I have to say I saw no particular reason why she shouldn't. Obviously I was wrong.'

'Did you ever actually see him?'

'No, I kept out of the way when he was around. Except on the last night, when he arrived to collect her and I snuck out to see them leave. Even then, he was just a shadow in the courtyard.'

'Then how do you know about the name he was using?'

'Because I overheard him saying it. He was briefing her about their travel plans. They would be going together, on false papers showing them as man and wife. He would be called Ghani and she would be Fatma Al-Falaki. You know that Arab women keep their own names when they marry, even if they get to keep nothing else? He also gave her a wedding ring to wear.'

Jack nodded thoughtfully. 'What else did you hear?'

'He said he had a plane waiting at the airport, as he'd already promised. And then they left. I assumed she had got away, and then a few days later I heard she was being held at the Nayef Palace. By then I'd left the house and moved down here to the Al-Fadnis'. That's about it.'

Dale had stopped walking. They were at the entrance to another building similar to Tewfiq's. 'This is home,' she said. 'In fact, the apartment belongs to an American friend who turned himself in, and I just sort of took it over. I won't invite you in. It's not exactly equipped for receiving visitors.'

'Mine is much the same.'

They strolled into the open-fronted lobby. She took a key from the pocket of her track suit and paused by one of the doors. 'Aren't you forgetting your side of the deal, Jack? What is it about all of this that interests you?'

'As you guessed, it's to do with money. Indirectly, anyway. Hamadi wants me to tie up some embarrassing loose ends that were left over when Jalloul reneged on the deal with him. That is, assuming he did renege.'

'What do you mean, assuming?'

'Doesn't it strike you as odd that he should go to so much trouble over Noura if all he intended to do was betray her? I mean the visits to the house, the travel

103

arrangements, the details – right down to the wedding ring?'

'I guess I've never thought about it that way. I've never thought of him as anything but a double-crossing bastard. Are you trying to tell me different?'

'I don't know. I'm just thinking aloud.'

'Well, you can spare me the facts of Daddy's anguish, whatever they are. And if that's all, I'll say goodbye now.' She opened the door and he caught a glimpse of a hallway leading into an almost bare living room; behind another half-open door a mattress lay on the floor with bedclothes and a patchwork quilt neatly spread over it. She thrust out her hand and shook Jack's, more firmly this time. 'I'm sure I haven't been much help, but good luck anyway.'

'No, you've been terrific.' He hesitated. 'Do you have a phone here? In case I think of anything more to ask you?'

'It's not working. And I promise I've told you everything I know. It's been nice meeting you, Jack.'

'Goodbye, Dale. And thank you.'

She closed the door and he left the building. He walked to his car with an odd feeling of anticlimax, sorry that their talk had ended so abruptly, with such apparent finality. He'd begun to enjoy Dale's company. The sight of that mattress on the floor had been strangely moving, suggesting a precarious quality to her life that she was trying to disguise, that he sensed might even be something like his own.

It was half-past three before he got back to the Muthanna. Turning the corner beside the building, he noticed a police Land Rover standing by the front entrance but thought no more about it until he had left the Granada in the basement and was trudging up the stairs. As he entered the foyer, heading for the next flight up, he saw two men in khaki uniforms and black berets leaning against the porter's desk. They straightened up when they saw him and one of them called: 'Mr Rushton!'

He stopped, puzzled and a little apprehensive. The man who knew his name came towards him and Jack recognized one of the cops who had been in the outer office at the Nayef Palace the night before.

'Mr Rushton, you were not in your apartment so we waited for you here. We are sent by Major Al-Shaheb. He asks you to come with us, please.'

'Where to?' Jack asked blankly.

'Just to come. Not for long. Something he wishes to talk to you about.'

Jack wanted to ask more questions but sensed that the men either couldn't or wouldn't answer. Although logic suggested there was nothing sinister about the summons, he was uneasily reminded that this was one of the group who had taken part in the beating of the Palestinian suspect last night.

'All right,' he said, and followed the men from the building.

# 8

The policeman who had done the talking drove the Land Rover. His companion sat beside him and Jack crouched on the rear seat as they entered the junction beside the Muthanna and turned towards the Al-Jahra Gate. At least, he noted with relief, they weren't taking him back to the Nayef Palace. They joined the main westbound road and soon were speeding past Al-Shuwaikh Port and the suburbs that straggled beyond it along the shore of the Gulf.

Neither of the cops seemed disposed to talk, so Jack sat in silence and gazed at the passing view. More American military convoys, going in both directions. The shells of more abandoned Iraqi trucks, many of them stripped by scavenging bedouin of their wheels, doors and even engines. The high-rise apartment blocks of migrant Asian workers, outwardly untouched but looking neglected after the mass departures that had followed the invasion.

The suburbs thinned out and gave way to desert on one side, salty marshlands fringing the sea on the other. The air was much cleaner here than it had been in the city, although blotches of smoke lay on the northern horizon where the Raudhatain oil wells had been set alight. The bay became narrower, giving a hazy view of the Jal az-Zawr escarpment on its far side that was almost the only high ground in the country. The road they were on now was the main route to the Iraqi border and it was over there, at the Mutla Ridge, where Operation Desert Storm had reached its gruesome climax, where the Allied planes had trapped the main body of Saddam Hussein's fleeing forces and visited a terrible ordeal of destruction upon them.

Well short of there, the Land Rover turned on to a secondary road heading inland. Jack became uneasy again until he saw up ahead the concrete pillars of a gateway with a sandbagged guard post beside it, and the Kuwaiti flag hanging limp from a pole, and recognized the entrance to the Al-Jahra military base. Barbed-wire fencing stretched away into the desert on either side of the gate. Behind it were clusters of low, yellow-brown buildings and, in the distance, the control tower of an airfield.

The driver halted at a striped boom blocking the road just inside the entrance. The vehicle was apparently expected, for the sentries raised the barrier almost at once and they drove through, past neat rows of barrack huts, parade grounds made of compacted sand and vehicle parks crammed with American trucks painted in desert camouflage.

The place simmered with activity under the late-afternoon sun. Mechanics, stripped to the waist, crawled over tanks and self-propelled guns. Officers bustled in and out of an important-looking building that seemed to be the base headquarters, but the Land Rover passed this by and went down a side road that led to a group of huts separated from the main camp. They were identical to the others but were cordoned off by a high wall made of breezeblocks and topped with a double row of barbed wire. The painted wooden board outside it was inscribed in Arabic, but Jack needed no translation to identify it as a military prison.

The Land Rover stopped beside a gate of wire mesh guarded by military police in white helmets. The cops got out, telling Jack to follow, and after they'd exchanged a few words with the MPs the gate was unlocked and they were led inside.

There were three iron-roofed barrack huts grouped around a small parade ground, no doubt used for punishment drill. Two of the buildings had steel doors and rows of small windows screened with mesh; the third was apparently divided into offices, with wooden stable doors that opened on to a veranda. In contrast to the rest of the camp the place seemed strangely deserted. The tens of thousands of Iraqi POWs captured last month were being held elsewhere, in camps hastily prepared for them, and presumably not many Kuwaiti soldiers had done anything to merit a spell in detention in the short time since the liberation.

Major Al-Shaheb came to the door of one of the offices as Jack was steered towards it. Today he was casually dressed in a khaki safari suit and sandals. He looked tired, with a greyness beneath his dark skin, but his eyes were bright and he gave Jack a grin and a hearty handshake.

'I'm glad you could make it,' he said.

'At first I wasn't sure I was being given a choice.'

'I think you'll find your time isn't wasted,' the major said, either unaware of the sarcasm or choosing to ignore it. 'There's a man here I've arranged for you to meet. He may tell you more about your Colonel Jalloul.'

'Who is he?'

Al-Shaheb barked an order at Jack's two escorts, who turned and marched hastily away. He faced his visitor again and spoke with quiet satisfaction.

'He is one of the *Mukhabarat*, the secret police. We picked up three of them in Hawalli, the Palestinian quarter, in the early hours this morning. The interrogation of our little friend last night was quite productive, you see.' Pointedly. 'He gave us the names and addresses of some more of his compatriots who had been sheltering these snakes.'

The memory returned to Jack of the naked man, handcuffed and bleeding, and he wondered queasily how much more it had taken to prise this information out of him.

Al-Shaheb continued: 'These three were among those who did not succeed in escaping at the time of Desert Storm. They've been in hiding for nearly a month. We keep them out here, away from any possible contact with their sympathizers, until they are ready to tell us of the whereabouts of others. And while we prepare charges of war crimes against them.' He paused. 'The one who will interest you is a Lieutenant Daoud Fadel. He worked in the office of Jalloul at the time of his disappearance.'

'And knows something about it?'

'He told me a little. It's not a matter of direct concern to me – you understand? – so I have not questioned him closely about it. I leave that to you,' the major said magnanimously.

Jack felt as though he'd been offered an unwanted gift that he had no idea how to refuse. The notion of his interrogating an Iraqi secret policeman was weird, to say the least, and it brought him a sudden step closer to recognizing the bizarre nature of his undertaking. He didn't know whether he was up to it. Al-Shaheb was hinting loftily, however, that he was not going to make Dr Hamadi's business his own.

'Is this Lieutenant . . . Fadel? . . . willing to talk to me?'

'I will see to it that he does. He is perhaps the least co-operative of the three, but one can use subtle threats against such a man. I've told him it will be to his own benefit to meet you. Also, he speaks English. I've had him moved to a cell block on his own, where nothing will be overheard by his comrades or the guards. Shall we go?'

The policeman stepped down from the veranda. He set off briskly towards the farther of the two other buildings, and with Jack hurrying to stay beside him he continued talking.

'Fadel was appointed to Jalloul's staff soon after the occupation began. Military Intelligence is, of course, a part of the army structure, but the secret police insist on having a hand in everything. Officially a man like Fadel would have some sort of liaison function; in practice he was probably put there to keep an eye on Jalloul. He claims to have been just a clerk of some sort, but I have no doubt that he took part in the usual dirty business of the *Mukhabarat*: arrests, tortures, random killings. He acts tough, but in time we'll get a confession out of him.'

'And then?' said Jack.

They had reached the steel door at the gable end of the barrack hut. Al-Shaheb lifted a small flap that was set in the door at head height and bawled through the opening. When he turned to Jack his features had the same hard, professional look they had taken on the night before, once the bland pleasantries of Dr Hamadi's *diwania* were out of the way.

'Then he will hang, Mr Rushton. All three of them will hang, and they know it. They'll be given a fair trial but already there is no doubt of their guilt.'

'Then what can Fadel gain out of talking to me?'

'Hope, Mr Rushton. Even the most fatalistic of condemned men retains a little hope. He also has nothing to lose. What you want to know has no bearing on his own crimes, and if he co-operates perhaps he will earn a little goodwill.'

The heavy door swung open, pushed from within by one of a pair of MPs who stepped aside for them to enter and saluted the major. In the small vestibule were two folding chairs and a table at which the guards had been playing *sheshbesh*. From there a corridor ran down the centre of the building, flanked by five doors on either side. Heat had built up during the day beneath the iron roof, intensifying the smell of carbolic that filled the place. One of the guards led them to the last door on the left, slid back the bolt and opened it.

The cell was about three metres square and was furnished with an iron-framed army bed, a chair, a table and a prayer mat. Surprisingly, it had a flush lavatory in one corner with a washbasin beside it. There was even a towel rail with a khaki hand towel folded over it. The light from the unglazed window was reduced by the protective mesh to a near-twilight gloom, but the place looked clean and was not unduly cramped. Kuwaiti oil wealth had trickled down even to this level.

Lieutenant Daoud Fadel sat cross-legged on the camouflage-patterned sleeping-bag that covered the bed. He'd been given a pair of Kuwaiti army overalls that he wore with red plastic flip-flops, the overalls unbuttoned to the waist and showing beads of sweat among a few strands of black chest hair. He was a slender man of about twenty-five with a narrow face, curly black hair and a standard-issue Arab moustache. His eyes were his only remarkable feature; they were sapphire blue, as hard and bright as jewels against his sallow complexion.

His hands rested on his knees. He looked up at his visitors but otherwise did nothing to acknowledge their arrival. His gaze travelled from Al-Shaheb to Jack and back again, showing no curiosity. The policeman spoke a few gruff sentences in Arabic and Fadel settled his stare, with a hint of disdain, on Jack.

'Talk to him,' Al-Shaheb said carelessly. 'Ask him whatever you want. The answers won't interest me, just as long as he gives them.'

Jack felt more than ever inadequate to the task, but he pulled the chair over to the centre of the room and sat on it, facing the Iraqi. Al-Shaheb leaned against the door, saying no more, presumably ready to guarantee the promised co-operation.

'I understand that you speak English,' Jack began self-consciously. He waited for a reply, and when none came he went on. 'Lieutenant Fadel, my name is Jack Rushton. I'm a British civilian. I have no official position here, and no interest in whatever crimes you may be accused of in Kuwait. The major is doing me a favour by letting me talk to you about a matter that's quite unrelated to his own business with you.'

Again, no response. The prisoner's silence was contemptuous, but from his steady, concentrated look Jack knew the man was absorbing what was said. He plunged on with his explanation.

111

'I'm making enquiries about a Colonel Ibrahim Jalloul of the Iraqi Military Intelligence, who disappeared from Kuwait last September. I believe you worked with him during the occupation, in his office. I want to find out what became of him, where he might be now. Nothing more.'

This time Fadel did react. He uncrossed his legs and swung them over the side of the bed. The luminous blue eyes narrowed with hostility as he spoke for the first time, addressing Al-Shaheb in Arabic, in a thin but steady voice. The policeman responded and suddenly they were arguing incomprehensibly over Jack's head. He felt even more out of things, a foreigner and a bewildered interloper.

Finally the argument stopped and Al-Shaheb addressed Jack.

'He says he will not co-operate with the enemies of Iraq. He says he is a True Believer, and if God wills that he must die then he will do so honourably. I told him there are worse fates than hanging.' The major flashed an angry, gold-edged smile at Jack. 'I told him that if he doesn't help you I will turn him over to the families of those he tortured. That they will cut him to pieces slowly and leave his parts in the desert to be eaten by the jackals.'

If this was the policeman's idea of a subtle threat, Jack wondered how he would phrase a straightforward one. Fadel appeared unmoved by it anyway, withdrawing back into himself. Al-Shaheb spoke to him again and got a few words in reply. He made a show of disbelief.

'He still defies us. He says you have not done him the courtesy of explaining the purpose of your enquiries. Courtesy! To him! I've told the pig it's none of his business.'

'I can't go too far into the reasons . . .'

'Exactly. If I don't want to know them, why should he?'

'. . . but I'd like him to understand that I'm not an enemy of his country. That I'm not looking for Jalloul to make him answer for anything, only trying to help someone else.'

'You're wasting your time, Mr Rushton.' The prisoner's unexpected stubbornness was costing Al-Shaheb face, getting him flustered. He pushed himself off the wall and cracked his knuckles. 'Give me half an hour with him and I promise he will tell you everything.'

'No!'

Jack said the word more in nervousness than defiance, but it came out with unintended vehemence. The major paused and frowned. As Jack gathered his thoughts, trying to find a way out of this impasse, Fadel suddenly said: 'Let me speak alone to you.'

Jack turned in surprise. The request, in English, had been addressed to him. The prisoner's face had revealed only anger and defiance since the other two had entered the cell, but now there was anxiety in his expression. It occurred to Jack that for most of the time he had been talking about Fadel and not to him, almost avoiding the reality of his presence.

'I will speak to you,' the Iraqi repeated. 'Not with him here.'

'*Te'ban!*' muttered Al-Shaheb. 'Now the snake wants to make his own rules.' He moved threateningly forward but Jack held up a hand.

'Perhaps it would be best if we did talk alone.'

'He will lie to you, Mr Rushton,' the policeman protested. 'I will know when he's lying. You won't.'

'Let me try, please. You say you're not concerned with his answers, anyway.'

'As you wish.'

His back stiff with disapproval, Al-Shaheb went to the door and bellowed for the guards. He was let out of the cell and Jack waited until their footsteps had retreated to the end of the corridor before he turned back to Fadel.

The prisoner looked relieved. His sapphire eyes were vivid in the murky light, and Jack wondered again at their colouring. There were Turks and Kurds with blue eyes; perhaps Fadel's family had had an infusion of non-Arab

113

blood. He wondered as well whether the cell might be bugged, but thought it unlikely.

'What do you want to tell me?' Jack asked.

'You say you want Jalloul. You do not say why.'

'I'll tell you as much as I can without betraying any confidences. Before he disappeared, Jalloul made a certain arrangement with a man from Kuwait. A wealthy man with plenty of influence. *Wasta* – you understand? The arrangement involved a lot of money but it went wrong. There's no question of any criminal action against Jalloul, I just want to find him and straighten things out.' Jack hesitated, not quite sure how much English Fadel actually had. 'I'm acting on behalf of this Kuwaiti, as a sort of financial consultant. Do you know what that is? Do you follow me, Lieutenant?'

Fadel considered his reply. He said: 'Mr . . . Rushton? I studied English at school and at the University of Basra. I am by profession a translator. I understand you well.'

'I'm sorry,' Jack murmured. The rebuke had been as gentle as it was surprising.

'All right,' the prisoner said equably. He glanced towards the door. 'What I know is not for Al-Shaheb to hear. What does he promise for me if I talk to you?'

'He said you might want to earn some goodwill. I suppose he means favourable treatment, privileges. He didn't explain exactly.'

'He is a lying dog,' Fadel said with casual contempt. 'He will give me nothing. I suppose he told you also that I am a torturer. He will make up evidence against me so that he can hang me. It is useless to talk to Al-Shaheb. Perhaps you will listen.'

'Listen to what?'

'I am forbidden visitors; I have been given no lawyer. I am an innocent man but I will have no chance to show it. That is why I wanted to see you alone. I ask you to help me, Mr Rushton.'

Jack could not conceal his surprise. 'Me? I don't think I can do anything. I have no influence with the police.'

'But you have your rich friend. The one with good *wasta*. *Wasta* is everything here. Let him plead for me.'

Jack had the feeling that Fadel had taken control of the conversation and was steering it where it suited him. He was an intelligent man, and for someone who had been all but condemned to death he seemed remarkably self-possessed.

'Why don't we talk about Jalloul first?'

'It is him I am talking about.' The lieutenant leaned forward on the bed, speaking with a sudden earnestness. 'I want you to understand what I am. I am a True Believer. I am bound to speak the truth. I am an army reservist and I was transferred into the *Mukhabarat* only to work with documents and translations. It was not my job to interrogate or torture. But to Al-Shaheb we are all criminals, all to be hanged to give the Kuwaitis their revenge.

'When I joined the staff of Colonel Jalloul I had orders to report on him to my own chief, General Malik. Jalloul knew this and despised me for it. In spite of this, I grew to love him. I saw that he was a good man and a patriot. He had *baraka* – do you understand this word? It means the grace of God. I saw that he was disloyal in a way to Saddam Hussein, as I had been warned, but that others were greater criminals. I prayed to God for guidance and he showed me that the work of the *Mukhabarat* was that of liars and thieves. I saw that it had been against God for us to invade Kuwait. When I discovered evidence against Jalloul I did not denounce him.'

'What evidence was that?'

'Something that was worth more than his life.' Fadel paused to give effect to his words. 'Something I have kept to myself. I will not give it for nothing to Al-Shaheb.'

Jack was perplexed. It was hard to get the measure of the Iraqi through the florid, emotional language, harder still to believe in his overnight conversion. What he had to say might be quite intriguing, but they seemed to have moved a long way from what Jack had been hoping to discuss. 'Do you think Al-Shaheb would be interested in what you know?' he said.

'Of course. It's a matter of money, much money, and that is all these Kuwaitis care about. Do you think you can make your rich friend interested?'

'In exchange for some kind of clemency for you? I'm sure that would depend entirely on what this information was.'

'It's good,' Fadel said with conviction. 'Good for Kuwait and the greedy sheikhs who rule it.' He threw another glance at the door of the cell and lowered his voice even further. 'Are you a Nazarene, Mr Rushton?'

'A Chri:tian? Yes. More or less.'

'If I tell you more, do you swear by Jesus Christ to say nothing to Al-Shaheb or his police?'

Fadel was deadly serious. 'If that's what you want,' Jack said with misgiving.

'Swear it.'

'I swear by Jesus Christ,' he mumbled.

'Then understand that my life now also depends on this.' The strange blue eyes shone with intensity. 'It concerns gold. You know about the gold that was taken from the bank?'

'The Kuwait Central Bank?' Both Vincent and Al-Shaheb had mentioned the theft of bullion that had taken place soon after the invasion. 'The gold that was sent to Iraq?'

'Not all was sent. Some of it, a lot of it, was stolen. Colonel Jalloul knows what happened to it.'

# 9

The cell had grown hotter while they talked. There was perspiration on Fadel's brow as he hunched forward on the bed, getting his face close to his visitor's. Jack felt the sweat in his own armpits and pulled off his jacket. He leaned back in the chair, instinctively withdrawing from the intimacy of the prisoner's closeness, his rapid breathing and his fervent stare.

Jack began to think he should have paid more attention when Al-Shaheb had warned him that the Iraqi would tell him lies.

'You're saying that after the gold was taken from the Central Bank, some of it disappeared? What happened to it?'

'It was stolen,' Fadel said simply.

'By whom?'

A shrug, perhaps a little too nonchalant. 'I don't know. But Jalloul knows. He had evidence.'

'And where is this evidence now?'

'Gone. With him, I think. After he left, the *Mukhabarat* came and searched his headquarters. I was with them. They found nothing, but knew it had been there.'

'And you think this had something to do with his disappearance?'

'Of course.'

Jack sighed. Again he thought Fadel was trying to manipulate the conversation, offering bogus information in exchange for the chance of salvation that Jack seemed to represent. Last night Al-Shaheb had spoken casually about part of the gold consignment going missing, so perhaps the Iraqi's story was not based entirely on fantasy. Quite

117

likely it was an amalgam of rumour and speculation that he was trying to pass off as the truth. On the other hand, if it offered any clues as to what had become of Jalloul it had to be listened to.

'Let's try and start at the beginning,' he said. 'When did all this happen?'

'In the last week of August. I learned of it on the thirty-first. I know because that was a Friday. I was on duty in the headquarters and could not go to the *khutbah*, the weekly sermon, so instead I recited some *shurahs* in the office. I was there on my own. It was a good chance to make a search.'

'For what?'

'For something to give to General Malik. He was an impatient man. He wanted evidence of Jalloul's disloyalty. I had discovered nothing, and by then I had already resolved that I would not report on the colonel. But I needed something, some small piece of information that would do him no harm but would prove to General Malik that I was doing my job.

'The colonel kept a folder of private papers in his office, separate from the official files. I saw him one day, when he thought no-one was looking, replacing this folder in a special cabinet and then hiding the key. He taped the key beneath a drawer of his desk. That Friday I removed it and opened the cabinet. When I looked at the papers I found things that I knew at once were too dangerous to reveal.'

'Such as?'

'Passports. Also papers about the removal of the gold to Iraq. These were—'

'Wait a minute. Tell me about the passports.'

Fadel looked uncomfortable. 'The colonel had a passport that was in another name. A passport issued in Baghdad, with his photograph. Genuine in every way, with an exit visa allowing him to leave Iraq, but with a different name and details. Such a thing is not unusual for an intelligence officer who must travel . . . do you say, incommunicado?'

'Incognito. Then what made you think it was dangerous?'

'Well, I wasn't sure whether General Malik knew about it. Such a document can be issued only with the approval of the *Mukhabarat*, and if the colonel was under suspicion there might have been no approval. He might have got it some other way, and if the general learned of it the matter would be very serious. But this is not the important thing . . .'

'It may be important to me. What name was on this passport?'

'Mr Rushton, I told you that I loved Colonel Jalloul and would do nothing to help his enemies. I should not have mentioned this.'

'I'm not an enemy, Lieutenant. And it seems to me that the colonel is well out of harm's way by now. If you really want my help you'll have to tell me everything. What was the name on the passport?'

Fadel shrugged and said reluctantly: 'Ghani. Given name, Mohamed. It stated his profession as merchant.'

The same name Dale Griggs had overheard Jalloul using. 'You said *passports*. Plural. What others were there?'

'Only one other. Issued to a woman, and with an exit visa also. Her name I do not remember.'

Jack felt a flush of excitement. 'Fatma Al-Falaki,' he said. 'Does that ring a bell?'

'That could be it.'

'Does this look like her?' He took from his pocket the photograph Hamadi had given him and held it out. Fadel studied it and said, 'Pretty. Maybe that is her. But in the other picture she wore an *abaya*.'

'What else do you remember about the passports? When were they issued?'

'I was not looking for such details,' the Iraqi said helplessly. 'They both seemed to be new. The colonel's one had visas for some countries, but not used visas. Also entry stamps from Jordan, two with dates from earlier that month. These I noticed because I recognized the dates. The colonel had been absent from his headquarters at those times. He had said he was visiting Baghdad for staff meetings.'

Jack's interest had quickened even further. 'Do you remember those dates?'

'The fifteenth of August, and the twenty-eighth.'

Coinciding with Jalloul's meetings in Amman with Dr Hamadi. 'What other countries did he have visas for?'

'Turkey. France. And Switzerland, I think.'

'But no stamps showing that he'd actually visited those places?'

'No.'

'All right,' Jack said with satisfaction. 'Now tell me what else you found.'

'The really dangerous things. The papers about the gold.' Relieved to change the focus of the discussion, Fadel leaned back on the bed. 'First you must understand what was happening at that time. Orders came from Baghdad, as soon as the occupation began, to take the gold from the vaults of the bank. This was done on the first weekend we were here, but it took time to organize its removal to Iraq.

'To safeguard it, they sent these ten special trucks from Baghdad. Armoured trucks, the kind they use to carry money to banks, but painted to look like army vehicles. They returned the following weekend – the eleventh and twelfth of August, I think. The *Mukhabarat* were in charge of the convoy, but they had to ask Military Intelligence to arrange an armed escort, and the request was passed to Colonel Jalloul. The army gave them two armoured personnel carriers and a platoon of the Republican Guard.

'In Jalloul's secret file there were copies of all these orders. There was a – do you call it an inventory? – prepared by the army officer who supervised the removal of the gold from the bank. There was a manifest given to the man in charge of the convoy, stating what was in his cargo, and a receipt given by the Central Bank of Iraq when it was delivered to them.' Fadel gave Jack a significant, almost a sly, look. 'Between the first figure and the other two there was a difference. Just over forty tonnes of gold were taken from the bank here, but only thirty-six and a half tonnes was sent to Baghdad. In between, more than three and a half tonnes went missing.'

Jack did some rapid mental calculations. Three and a half metric tons of gold bullion – three thousand five hundred kilograms, a figure large enough in itself to stagger the imagination – broke down to roughly a hundred and twelve thousand troy ounces. At the free market rate of around four hundred dollars an ounce, that amounted to . . . nearly forty-five million dollars' worth.

He did not utter the figure aloud. Possibly Fadel had no idea of the values he was talking about. And possibly Fadel was lying through his teeth. What he had had to say about the passports seemed authentic; Jack had independent confirmation of the names Jalloul and Noura were supposed to have used on that September night, as well as the dates on which the colonel had travelled to Amman to see Dr Hamadi. But the story about the gold sounded simply absurd. It couldn't just have gone missing, not in a quantity like that, at least not without raising a panic.

'You're saying the stuff disappeared here in Kuwait, during those few days? And you think Jalloul knows where it went?'

'He must know. The papers prove it was missing, and he had the papers.'

'But that's not quite the same thing. You didn't see any indication that he was aware of what had actually happened to it?'

'It would be too dangerous to write down something like that,' the Iraqi said dismissively.

'Also, he can't have been the only one who knew. The gold must have been under guard, by soldiers or the secret police. Do you know where it was kept after it was taken from the bank?'

'No,' the Iraqi admitted. 'But where are those other people now? Dead on the Mutla Ridge? Fighting the Kurds? Executed for disloyalty? Colonel Jalloul is the one man you can be sure knows the truth. Tell this to your friend. Tell the Kuwaitis if they want their gold back they should find Jalloul.'

Jack considered. Unexpected as all this was, and even if Fadel wasn't lying or exaggerating, the question of the gold seemed hardly relevant to his own purpose. Indeed, it threatened to be a distraction. At least he had now confirmed the alias that Jalloul had been using. And it seemed clear that the colonel had had a line of retreat carefully prepared for himself: his insurance policy against action by his political enemies had apparently proved just as useful in helping him skip with Dr Hamadi's million dollars.

'When was the last time you saw Jalloul?' Jack asked.

'The Monday after that. The third of September. He worked in his office as usual and then returned to his quarters on the base. The next morning he was gone. The first we knew of it was when General Malik's men came. They searched everywhere. They found the key to the cabinet, but the folder of papers – the passports, the documents about the gold – all were gone.'

'Was any of Jalloul's work concerned with Kuwaiti civilians?'

'Not much. His job was military intelligence. Internal security was work for the *Mukhabarat*. Dirty work.'

'Do you know if he ever ordered the arrest of a civilian? Could he have?'

The Iraqi gave the hint of a cynical smile. 'Any officer could do that. But if he had, the *Mukhabarat* would want to know why. They would want the prisoner to themselves. The only Kuwaitis I know passed through his hands were soldiers captured during the invasion. They were interrogated and then sent to Iraq, the POW camps. And all properly treated.'

Jack was finding this blind loyalty a little irritating. He wondered how to phrase his next question without coming too close to betraying the confidence of Hamadi. He showed Fadel the photograph again.

'What would you say if I told you Jalloul arranged for this woman to be arrested? On a false charge of helping the resistance? And that, as a result, she was raped, tortured and murdered by your friends in the secret police?'

'I would say you must be wrong.'

'You think he had too much *baraka*? It happened at just about the time he disappeared, and shortly after he had been paid a large bribe to see that she left the country safely.'

'Jalloul would not do that,' Fadel said with conviction.

'Wouldn't harm the girl, or wouldn't take the money?'

'I can't say about the money. But if he made a bargain he would keep his part of it. Say that as well to your friend. And tell him that Lieutenant Fadel, who unjustly faces his death, is the man who helped you.'

Major Al-Shaheb gave Jack a lift back to the city. He seemed to have got over his huffiness at Jack's insistence on conducting the interview in private, and the only question he asked was: 'Did he co-operate?'

'As fully as he could, I think. He claims not to be a regular member of the secret police, just an army reservist.'

'I told you he would lie,' said the major with satisfaction.

'I have a feeling he may be telling the truth. About that, at least.'

'We will see when I question him myself,' Al-Shaheb said ominously.

He drove his Range Rover at homicidal speeds, stamping alternately on brake and accelerator, scowling and cursing the military traffic that cluttered the roads. This didn't encourage further conversation, allowing Jack to lapse into his own thoughts.

The vision of Fadel stayed with him, the blue eyes glittering with misplaced hope in the deepening gloom of the cell. He felt dissatisfied but also burdened by what the lieutenant had told him. If it was true, it seemed to confirm that Jalloul had skipped the country at exactly the time Noura Hamadi had been arrested. It suggested that he was using a false passport and that his travel plans included a visit to Switzerland, which made sense. But what about the other visas he had acquired, for France and Turkey? Why Turkey, of all places? And where, if anywhere, did the story about the missing gold come into it?

All that the Iraqi could offer in support of his claim was a glimpse at a few sets of papers, all of them now missing. There could be any number of explanations for the discrepancy he said he had found between the quantity of gold removed from the Central Bank and the amount taken out of Kuwait. There might have been a simple error in the original tally, for instance. And even if the figures were accurate, some part of the shipment could have been diverted elsewhere quite officially – if that word could apply to what had been an outright theft in the first place. Fadel hadn't been in any position to know.

There was something else about his story, though, something that didn't quite square up with another version of the events he had described. The discrepancy eluded Jack. All this had happened more than seven months ago in any case. If the gold had really gone missing the Central Bank of Iraq must certainly have been aware of it and have taken steps to recover it. It was too fantastic, too puerile even, to suppose that such a quantity of treasure could simply disappear.

On the other hand, this was the Gulf, the Middle East. Its history and its politics, some would say its thinking as well, were steeped in the kind of fantasy that few *nasranis* like himself were equipped to understand. And when it came to disappearances, there were people, families, whole households, who had vanished without trace from here during the Iraqi occupation. Not to mention the countless millions in currency, the entire contents of museums, warehouses full of goods, fleets of planes and vehicles, many of which would probably never be seen again. Why not forty-odd million dollars' worth of gold for good measure?

The man at the centre of it all, Colonel Jalloul, remained a bundle of contradictory impressions. Dale Griggs had seen no reason to distrust him and even Hamadi had once thought of him as a man of his word. Yet clearly their faith had been misplaced. The fact that Jalloul had been willing to accept a bribe was not, in this part of the world, a sure sign of an unscrupulous nature. What mattered was that in return he had made a promise that he hadn't kept; he had left Noura Hamadi to face a gruesome death. If that had been his intention all along, though, why had he gone to all the trouble of getting her a passport and arranging the finer details of her departure?

Unless the gold was indeed a factor. It kept intruding into the story of Noura's arrest and Jalloul's disappearance. It was possible that Jalloul himself had been involved in its theft. In fact it was quite easy to imagine that he might simply have abandoned his agreement with Dr Hamadi when he'd discovered he had bigger fish to fry. What was two million dollars, after all, compared with forty-five million?

Jack sensed that he was becoming unwillingly fascinated by the idea of Jalloul. Remembering the notes in English in Al-Shaheb's file, he was reminded of the time the Iraqi had spent on a staff officer's course at Camberley. Was there a chance of finding out anything back in England that might shed further light on the man?

As if this wasn't enough to think about, Jack seemed to have got himself involved in the fate of Fadel. He had promised to report the story about the gold to Dr Hamadi in the hope that it might win the young man some form of clemency. The more he thought about it, the flimsier it seemed as a bargaining counter. What was a fairy tale told by a member of the hated *Mukhabarat* going to count for? And who would care what happened to him? Not Al-Shaheb. Probably not Hamadi. And his own people least of all.

Dusk had been approaching when they had left Al-Jahra, and it was almost fully dark by the time the major jarred the Range Rover to a stop outside the Muthanna building.

'You are satisfied that you did not waste your time?' he asked. 'If there is anything else you want to know, you have only to say.'

'Thank you. As a matter of fact,' Jack said carefully, 'I was wondering if you had any information about someone whose name you mentioned last night. General Malik. The head of the secret police here during the occupation.'

'Omar Hassan Malik, God blacken his face. What about him?'

'Do you know what became of him?'

'Certainly. His little servant Fadel didn't tell you? He was sent to roast in hell,' Al-Shaheb said with relish, 'but not before he was roasted alive on the Mutla Ridge. He was in a truck full of *Mukhabarat* that was hit by a phosphorus bomb as they fled like rabbits from Desert Storm. A dozen of them, cooked to cinders. But papers were found in the cab showing that Malik was among them.'

Jack tramped up to his flat. Outside the door he found a plastic bag full of provisions that Vincent Hand had left for him: a loaf of sliced bread, some more processed cheese, a couple of US Army C-Ration cans of stewed beef and even a Sterno stove to heat them on.

He lit the gas lamp and fumbled with it about the apartment. He felt tired suddenly, the result more of emotional than physical exertion. Hungry, but lacking the energy to cook, he ate yet another cheese sandwich and then slumped into a chair.

Letting his thoughts drift back past Fadel and Al-Shaheb, he found himself recalling his encounter with Dale Griggs. It wasn't their conversation that came to his mind but the sight of her running alone around the track. In retrospect, he knew that in that unlikely setting he had found something erotic in the controlled, easy rhythm of her limbs and the bouncing of her blond hair. He could imagine hard, muscular buttocks moving beneath the shorts, and small breasts bobbing in unison with her strides. He visualized her stripping off after a run, her wiry body still damp with sweat. He took the idea further and saw himself with her, in her apartment. Perspiration had trickled from between her breasts, down over a hard, flat stomach. She smiled at him, took his hand and led him to that mattress on the floor . . .

He recollected himself with a guilty start. This was pure adolescent fantasy, a hard-porn daydream flickering across his half-asleep brain. Probably sexual frustration had a lot to do with it; it was months since he and Alison had made love, and he had begun to think they probably never would again. In the slow process of their estrangement they had passed some invisible point at which the idea of physical intimacy had become merely embarrassing.

Jack stood up and dragged himself off to bed, deciding he had better put Dale Griggs firmly out of his mind.

# 10

Jack met Hamadi at eleven o'clock the next morning, not at the Gulf Bank of Commerce this time but in the offices of the Hamadi Finance Corporation. These occupied two upper floors of a building in the Joint Banking Complex, which rose above the worst of the smoke still shrouding the city's lower levels. Jack was whisked up in a generator-powered lift. Stepping out into a lobby to one side of an open-plan work area, he was dazzled by the sunshine that streamed in through the windows. The offices overlooked the central commercial area towards the Dhow Harbour, but the view was like that of a blanket of dark cloud, pierced only by other tall buildings and the pale minarets of mosques.

The work area contained about twenty desks set among a profusion of houseplants, and a similar number of young men and women, in pale shirts or white blouses, who gazed at computer screens or talked on telephones or pecked at word processors; it was the smooth male secretary, however, wearing an Armani suit and a professional smile, who was waiting to greet Jack.

He was led straight to Dr Hamadi's own office, where a suspicion he'd begun to form was confirmed: the place had clearly been quite untouched by the occupation. The mahogany-panelled walls of the sanctum enclosed perhaps a thousand square feet of floor space, covered by a woollen shag carpet so immaculately white that it looked as though it had never been trodden on. The furnishings were few, simple and elegant: bookshelves decoratively hand-carved and filled with volumes bound in calfskin; a cluster of leather-covered couches around a coffee-table topped with mosaic; more flowering plants in marble pots;

a huge desk, also of mahogany, its top bare apart from a telephone console and a blotter pad of tooled leather.

Hamadi rose from the desk to greet him. He seemed in better spirits than on either of Saturday's occasions, warmly shaking Jack's hand and leading him to one of the couches. Unlike his employees he stuck to traditional dress, today a pale grey *dishdasha* and a head-dress held in place by an *agal* trimmed with ornaments of carved ivory. Catching Jack's wondering look, he confirmed that his offices had escaped being ransacked by the Iraqis. They had been taken over after the invasion, he explained, by a manager sent from the Ministry of Finance in Baghdad. Overwhelmed by the luxury of his surroundings, the man had ordered everything left as it was and for seven months had enjoyed the illusion that he was running a business empire.

'There was no work for him,' the doctor said. 'Our foreign assets had been frozen. Nothing was being imported or exported. There was no banking activity to speak of. All he could do was sit here and feel important. For an Iraqi bureaucrat, that would not present any great difficulty.' There was a note of that same irresistible contempt in his voice that Jack had heard among the guests at the *diwania*; but Hamadi quickly became businesslike.

'I'm pleased that you have agreed to take on my commission, Jack. I'm sure it's the right choice for us both.'

'I have to say that I still have reservations,' Jack said. 'I'm not sure I'm really the person for the job. You may be throwing away fifty thousand dollars.'

'I doubt it,' Hamadi said with a smile. 'In fact your modest assessment of yourself gives me an even greater confidence. It means you are realistic. Has Major Al-Shaheb been helpful?'

'He told me everything he could about Jalloul's background. He also let me speak to an Iraqi prisoner who worked in Jalloul's office at the time of his disappearance.

Interesting stuff, but it doesn't take things much further. We still don't know what became of the man.'

'Let me explain the background to my agreement with him. I began my search for someone who could rescue Noura by making confidential enquiries through a few of my trusted contacts among the exiled leadership of our country. It was Al-Shaheb who came up with the name of Jalloul. Since none of the usual lines of communication with Iraq were open, I had then to ask some of my business associates abroad to find a channel through which I could deal privately with the man. I gave no details of any of these people, beyond saying that my purpose was humanitarian but also had a commercial dimension. I knew that if Jalloul was the man I thought he was, he would take the hint.

'A few days later I was advised to contact a lawyer in Zurich named Dr Karl Zunckel. I had him checked out and found that he had represented certain Middle Eastern interests in Switzerland over a number of years. He is what they call there a *finanzamwalt*, a specialist in monetary and banking matters, and he has a small international clientele. When I approached him he confirmed that he was available to act as an intermediary.

'From this point on there were only three of us involved – Dr Zunckel, Jalloul and myself. Even now, Zunckel has no idea of the true background to the transaction. He met Jalloul only once, when he flew to Amman for the signing of the documents he had drawn up. We had them notarized at the Swiss Embassy there, and when he returned to Zurich he opened the bank account which he would operate as our nominee.

'Zunckel was professionally obliged to act in the equal interests of both parties. He has told me, as recently as this morning, that he has had no contact with Jalloul since that day in Amman. He fails to see what further help he can be. Nevertheless, I continue to pay him a large retainer to represent my interests, and he will have to be one of your starting points; the other will be the Handelsbank Bauer, through which the funds were transferred. After that you will be depending on your powers of persuasion and your investigative skills. Always remembering that my interest in the matter must be kept as far in the background as possible.'

Coffee had been sent for and was now brought in by Hamadi's secretary, in a solid silver pot on a tray that held only one cup. Once again Jack went through the Ramadan ritual of helping himself while the doctor abstained.

'Why did you choose the Handelsbank Bauer?' he asked. It was a name that was only vaguely familiar to him.

'It was Zunckel's suggestion. It's one of the smaller Swiss banks, old-fashioned and quite choosy about its customers. It doesn't do a lot of commercial business and so is not much in the public eye. Under the terms of the agreement, I deposited two million dollars in the account, half of which was immediately transferred to Jalloul. It was paid into a separate account under his own name which Zunckel arranged for him to open at the same bank. The second million was to be transferred in the same way at an unspecified date – once Noura was safely out of Kuwait, in fact – and the nominee account would then be closed. Each of us retained copies of the documents.

'This was not an ideal arrangement, but it gave me the best possible protection in the circumstances. Jalloul was an officer in the Iraqi army. He knew I could see to it that evidence of our dealings was sent to the right quarters in Baghdad, where they would provide a fine excuse to send him before a firing squad. In other words, he seemed to have far more to lose than I did. But he chose to run that risk and take just half what he could have had. And at the same time rid himself of Noura. Once he had used her as the pawn in his scheme, she no doubt became a liability.'

Jack sipped some coffee. 'Are you absolutely sure that's what happened?' he said.

'You imagine there is some other explanation?'

'Not necessarily. It's just that I've been struck by certain . . . inconsistencies. For someone who intended to betray you, Jalloul seems to have gone to a lot of trouble to carry out your wishes.'

'Please explain.'

'This Iraqi prisoner told me Jalloul had arranged a false passport for your daughter. And that confirmed an impression I gathered elsewhere that he was actually taking care of the details of her departure. Right up to the last minute.' Jack paused. 'He even provided a wedding ring so that she could travel as his wife.'

'Indeed? And where did you hear that?'

Mistake, Jack thought. The doctor was watching him intently; the warmth had gone from his eyes.

'I . . . was talking to a friend of Noura's.'

'What friend?' said Hamadi sharply.

'I'm afraid I can't tell you. I gave a promise of confidentiality.'

'Does that count for more than the promise you have given me?'

'They are two different things. To work for you effectively I have to win people's trust.'

Hamadi considered that. 'Very well, I will not press you further,' he said. 'But be careful in future about who you trust in return. Noura had friends whose influence on her was not good. There was one in particular who undermined her loyalty to her family and her traditions – the kind of person, in fact, who is not welcome in this country and may soon be asked to leave. If this is the person you have talked to then I advise you strongly not to do so again. I will not tolerate having my private affairs discussed with her.'

'You have to rely on my discretion,' Jack protested. 'If there were people you didn't want me to speak to you should have said—'

'Enough Jack, please.' Having shown his claws, Hamadi seemed anxious not to widen the argument. He patted Jack's shoulder and stood up. 'Let's continue with our business. The question of Jalloul's motives is not really relevant to your task, after all.'

He went to the desk and took an unsealed A4 envelope from one of the drawers. He opened it and handed a sheet of paper to Jack.

'Please read this,' he said.

The paper was expensive, cream-coloured bond bearing the letterhead, in English and Arabic, of the Hamadi Finance Corporation. The letter typed beneath it carried that day's date, 1 April 1991, and was addressed to Dr Karl Zunckel, Frohlichstrasse 106, 8051 Zurich. On a separate slip of paper, Zunckel's business and home phone numbers had been typed.

The letter read:

Dear Dr Zunckel,

This serves to introduce Mr Jack Rushton, who, as I mentioned on the telephone this morning, is authorized to act on my personal behalf in matters arising from the transaction I made through your office last August.

Please afford him every co-operation, including access to the relevant financial records and documents.

With thanks.

Yours sincerely,

Mustapha Sultan Hamadi

Sweet simplicity. The letter said nothing to anyone who was not familiar with the details, but it would allow Jack to get a handle on them. Maybe. There were still things he wasn't clear about.

'How did Zunckel get in touch with Jalloul in the first place?' he asked.

'Through connections of his own in Iraq. Since the war, he says, he can no longer make contact with them. So that, apparently, is a dead end.'

'And why did Jalloul open the second account in his own name, instead of going for some anonymous arrangement?'

'He said at the time that he needed direct access to the money. Later, of course, the reason became obvious: he could clear out the account without Zunckel or anyone else knowing about it. Which is what he has no doubt done.'

'The whole difficulty seems to hinge on a single legal point. Zunckel can't close the nominee account because he can't get Jalloul to sign a document authorizing him to do so. Couldn't he be persuaded to bend the rules?'

Hamadi gave a wan smile. 'Don't imagine that I haven't suggested it. I have hinted at spectacular rewards in return. But Zunckel is a Swiss,' he said hopelessly. 'Like their banks, he is correct, formal and too rich to be corruptible. Also he has a professional reputation to protect, and in his own way he stands to lose as much as I do. Anyway, such a tactic would solve only part of the problem. Jalloul, wherever he is, still possesses those incriminating documents. Assuming he can be traced, the only practical solution will be to get him to co-operate. It might, after all, be easiest if you could deal with him in person.'

Jack stared at him. 'That isn't what you were talking about the other night.'

'I know, but I've been thinking it over. You've been in business yourself; you understand the value of face-to-face contact. Jalloul may be shrewd, but he is, after all, a soldier, not experienced in financial matters. He may need to have the advantages of my proposal explained to him in simple terms.'

Like selling an insurance policy, Jack thought. Presentation, persuasion, closure. Maybe that was how he ought to start thinking about it. 'Let me ask you about my commission,' he said. 'When and how do I collect it?'

'If you care to stop off at the Gulf Bank of Commerce, you'll find that Latif has a cheque for fifty thousand dollars waiting for you. It's drawn on the American account of a foreign subsidiary of one of my companies, so there is no difficulty over the exchange control. Payment of the second fifty depends on how well you succeed with your enquiries. You understand that it's not possible to put this arrangement on a formal basis; we will simply have to trust each other.

'Please report to me by telephone, here at this number, at regular intervals. Shall we say every second day? Even if you have nothing new to tell me, it would be as well for us to stay in touch. In an emergency you can call me at home. In any event, do not discuss any aspect of our business with anyone but me.'

Hamadi stood up again, indicating that he considered the interview over. Jack said, 'There is one other thing. In exchange for the information I got from the prisoner yesterday, I had to promise to draw your attention to something.'

Jack recounted the substance of his conversation with Lieutenant Fadel about the missing gold and the documents he claimed to have seen. Though he kept it as brief as possible, he sensed Hamadi fidgeting with impatience. When he had finished the doctor said indignantly, 'In return for this . . . jumble of gossip, this fellow expects me to intercede for him?'

'I never mentioned your name,' Jack said pointedly, 'but he understands that you're a man with influence. He claims to be innocent of any crime against Kuwait, and he's offering what he knows in the hope of clemency. He thought your treasury might like to get its gold back.'

'It will come back anyway, Jack. The Iraqis have already been forced to agree to return everything that was stolen. If I remember the figure correctly, three thousand two hundred and sixteen gold bars were taken from the Central Bank. And so the same number will have to be handed back.'

'Is there any possibility that your daughter was somehow involved in an attempt to smuggle some of that out?'

'Of course not! I heard the same rumour, that some of the gold had gone missing. So what? As far as we are concerned, it is for those clowns in Baghdad to replace it.'

Jack hadn't expected to hear any different. He said: 'So there's no hope for Fadel?'

'That's not for me to judge. His case will be dealt with by our state security courts as impartially as all the others. And certainly I do not intend to get involved.'

As Jack stood up, Hamadi suddenly gave his familiar melancholy smile and clasped both of his visitor's hands in his own.

'*As salaam alaikum,*' he said. 'May God's peace go with you, my dear Jack.'

# 11

He got to the bank half an hour before it was due to close for the afternoon, but there was a long queue outside again and he wondered whether he would make it to the door in time. While he was dithering he felt a hand plucking at his sleeve and found Mr Latif beside him. It seemed the assistant manager had been alerted by a phone call to expect him, and under the baleful gaze of the waiting merchants he was ushered into the bank. *Wasta* to the rescue again.

Latif took him to the far end of the main counter and produced a paper-clipped set of documents. There was a second sterling bank draft for eight thousand, eight hundred and twenty-four pounds, representing the balance being released from his two accounts together with the interest that had accrued to them. There was a cheque for fifty thousand US dollars drawn in his favour on the account of a company called Hamadi Overseas Realty, Inc., at a Fifth Avenue branch of the Chemical Bank of New York. Receipts for both of these had been prepared for Jack's signature, together with a debit note for the amount withdrawn from his accounts and a form authorizing their closure.

He was about to sign this last document when a woman's voice interrupted him.

'Might have known you'd be in the VIP channel.'

Dale Griggs had approached from the direction of the tellers' windows. She stood watching him with a slightly sardonic smile.

'Dale! What brings you here?'

'Money, what else? Or rather the lack of it. I'm owed half a year's salary and all I get are promises.'

She was wearing black leggings, flat shoes and a loose-fitting yellow sweater, and she had a bulky leather handbag slung on a strap from her shoulder. Her hair looked newly washed, fluffed out to provide a wider frame to her features. She said: 'How's your work for the good doctor progressing?'

'Slowly.'

'It seems to give you status, anyhow. I saw you getting priority treatment while I was standing in line with the plebs.'

'Not my idea,' he said apologetically. He paused and made a decision. 'Listen, I'm glad I've bumped into you. If you're not in a hurry, there's something I'd like to talk to you about.'

Conscious that Latif was silently waiting, he scribbled his signature on the form. The Palestinian gathered up the documents, leaving only the two cheques on the counter. Picking them up, Jack was aware of Dale's glance sliding casually over them.

He said goodbye to Latif and strolled beside her to the door. 'I'd offer to buy you coffee,' he said, 'if anywhere was open.'

'As it happens, I know a place that is.'

She led him down a side street next to the Gold Market. She stopped by a door between two shuttered jewellers' shops and opened it to reveal a tiny, dim, nameless coffee house he had never known existed. Their arrival brought a dead halt to the conversations of the dozen or so male customers, but the owner came from behind his counter to give Dale an enthusiastic greeting in Arabic. He showed them to a table, wiping it vigorously before bustling off to fetch coffee.

'A friend from the resistance,' Dale explained. 'He managed to keep this place open right through the occupation. We used it as a message centre.'

'I heard you were pretty actively involved.'

'Guns under my skirt? You've been listening to little

Tewfiq,' she said dismissively. 'It wasn't that exciting. It could be scary; at times it could even be boring. There was a lot of waiting around. What I did mostly was courier work, keeping the various cells in touch with each other. Keeping out of sight of the *Mukhabarat*. And finding ways of sending out reports on Iraqi troop dispositions to the spooks waiting across the border in Saudi. I've begun to wonder what it was all for, frankly. To put the same old fat cats back at their feeding bowls, as far as I can see.'

'It's one of those that I wanted to talk to you about. I think I owe you an apology. I'm afraid I may accidentally have dropped you in it with Hamadi this morning.'

'How so?'

He explained how he had casually let slip to the doctor one of the details of Noura's departure from the house at Salamiya on the night of her arrest, and how Hamadi had instantly guessed at the source of the information.

'I didn't mention your name and neither did he, but we both knew who we were talking about. He certainly seems to have a hang-up about you. He got going about what a bad influence you'd been on Noura, and he hinted that he didn't expect you to be allowed to stay here much longer. I imagine he's quite capable of making his own wishes come true.'

'Oh, he sure is,' Dale said; but she seemed to be taking the news calmly. 'Well, I never thought I had much chance of staying, anyway.'

'All the same, I shouldn't have drawn his attention to you. He, quote, advised me, unquote, to have nothing more to do with you. But I was going to come out to your place and warn you.'

This was only half true. Jack hadn't actually decided whether he wanted to risk looking like a bloody fool in Dale's eyes. He was also afflicted by an absurd self-consciousness over the erotic daydream he had had, almost as though she might somehow have been reading his mind. It wasn't as though he had knowingly made her into an object of his lust; her sexual attraction arose from the more subtle appeal of the lively, intelligent woman he saw behind her athletic body and her American candour.

'Thanks, but don't worry about it,' she said. 'Truth to tell, I'm not too sure I want to go on living here. Especially on sufferance. I have a feeling the delay in giving me my back pay is their cute little way of telling me I'm no longer wanted. No job plus no Kuwaiti husband equals no residence permit.'

'What will you do then?'

Two small finger-cups of strong, sweet coffee had been placed on the table. Dale sipped at hers and shrugged. 'I've been planning to take a vacation in Europe anyway. I need to get away from this place. I did a sabbatical year at the Sorbonne and I have friends I want to look up in Paris. After that, go back home and look for another job, I guess. Not that any good college has a crying need for one more sociologist. Especially one in her thirties who's still researching for her Ph.D.'

'I'm afraid I've never had more than a vague idea what sociology actually is,' Jack confessed.

'I suspect that neither do a lot of my students. The theory is hard to grasp and the literature is full of jargon. What it comes down to is how people interact with each other. Psychology is about the behaviour of people as individuals, right? But people are social animals, and sociology is about how they behave as groups, and as members of groups. Starting with the family – that's my own field – and moving right on up to whole populations. In a complex society like ours, most people belong to a lot of separate or overlapping groups. By the ring you're wearing I guess that you're married. That means you're part of a mechanical solidarity group: one based on a sentimental attraction of similarities.' She gave him a mischievous grin. 'Does that make you any the wiser?'

'Not really,' he said. 'And that doesn't sound much like my marriage these days.'

'Oh. Have I goofed? Well, if it's any consolation, none of the research I'd done into marriage did anything to save my own from being a disaster. My husband was the sort of Jekyll and Hyde character that some Arab men can be when they have one foot in their own world and another in the West. When I met him in the States he was all charm and urbanity. When I came back here with him he turned into a thirty-year-old patriarch. I made the most obvious mistake of all: I thought I could change him. I guess he must have thought the same about me. You know the four things a Muslim traditionally looks for in a wife? Piety, status, wealth and beauty. And my score was zero in all four departments.'

'I'm afraid I can't agree,' Jack said. 'Not on the last point, anyway.'

Dale gave an unaffected laugh. 'I wasn't fishing for praise. When I look in the mirror I see a pretty haggard stand-in for the Southern belle my mother wanted me to be. But thank you, Jack, you're good for my ego.' The green eyes held his gaze for slightly longer than they needed to; there was interest as well as amusement in them. 'The way you say you're *afraid* before you express an opinion . . . is that British politeness again, or your own reticence?'

'A bit of both, perhaps. It's a habit I should get out of.'

'No. It's part of your charm.'

'I'm sure it's nothing of the sort.'

His turn to deflect a compliment. A moment of silence followed in which they both seemed to consider the personal turn that the conversation had taken. Jack was a little surprised at his own boldness. He was out of practice at flirting. The next move, if there was going to be one, was hers.

'How much longer are you staying here?' she asked.

'I think I'll have to leave tomorrow.'

'Daddy's work won't wait, huh?' There was a definite hint of regret in her voice, but now she chose to end the

141

banter. 'Well, I guess I have to go now. I have a date with myself at the stadium.'

'I can give you a lift. I've got time on my hands today.'

'Thanks, but I'm driving a jalopy that came with my squat.'

She spoke easily but with finality. She was telling him that in spite of the attraction that had flickered between them she wasn't interested in a one-night stand.

They rose to go. Jack signalled to the proprietor and tried to pay for the coffee, but the offer was refused with elaborate gestures and a short farewell speech to Dale.

They walked together back towards the bank. Reduced to small talk again, he asked Dale to tell him about her running career.

'You don't follow track, do you?' she said.

He didn't know what she meant for a moment. 'Athletics? Only from an armchair.'

'I guessed those times I mentioned yesterday didn't mean much to you. No false modesty: I used to be one of the six fastest women milers in the world. Yes, it's true,' she smiled, detecting his surprise. 'I was due to run the fifteen hundred metres at the Moscow Olympics in nineteen eighty, and then our squad pulled out under political pressure. Goddam Jimmy Carter playing macho man with the Soviets. Running is the main reason I never got round to earning my Ph.D. Louisiana State had a great track team; by the time I got my Master's I was spending more time training than studying. But I don't regret it. I broke collegiate and state records; I went on improving my times, and I began to think I could get right to the top. Trouble was, the competition was exceptional. Maybe you *have* heard of Mary Decker?'

'Of course.'

'Mary was the best woman runner of my generation, and it was my ambition to beat her. But she started earlier than I did. She'd broken her first world record at sixteen, and she always stayed ahead. I did run her a close second four times in national meets, but she just had that edge, that extra level of determination that I couldn't rise to. When you're looking at margins measured in hundredths of a second, it's what's going on in your head that makes the difference. Mary needed to win more than I did.

'Anyway, I think I lost heart after the Moscow business. I told myself I had more cerebral interests – not that my academic credentials are all that wonderful. A doctorate is almost a *sine qua non* in the States, even for a humble assistant professorship.'

Jack had been thinking while she talked. As they reached her borrowed car, a Toyota several years old, he said: 'Since you seem to believe I'm so polite, I'm going to surprise you by asking something that's probably none of my business. Will you be all right for money?'

She looked at him blankly. 'Sure. As long as my back pay comes through.'

'Because I can let you have some if you're in a spot. I think you saw the size of that cheque I was given. I feel a bit guilty about it, frankly. It's Hamadi's money, and I reckon he owes you something.'

A little flustered, she said: 'You're right. You have surprised me. It's very kind of you, Jack, but no. I'll be OK. Even if I wasn't, I wouldn't feel right about taking money from you. We hardly know each other.'

'Now who's being reticent?' he said with a grin. 'Perhaps we have only just met, but I'd like to consider you a friend. If you change your mind, get hold of me through Vincent.'

'OK,' she said, still looking a bit bewildered. Then she thrust her face forward and kissed him on the cheek. 'Thanks, Jack. You're a nice man. Good luck.'

# 12

At eight o'clock the next morning Jack was ready to leave. In what was now an established ritual he joined Vincent for breakfast and they listened for the last time together to the World Service news.

The plight of the Kurds in northern Iraq was growing desperate. Their guerrilla forces had been routed by Saddam Hussein's army and hundreds of thousands of people were now said to have fled into the mountains along the Turkish border. The radio carried a clip from an interview in London with one of the main Kurdish rebel leaders, Abdel Karim, pleading for the West to intervene and save his people from torture and genocide. Karim, it seemed, was also one of the informants who had helped in the investigation of the thefts of money from the Iraqi treasury by Saddam Hussein and his associates, and he was questioned briefly about it.

Jack listened rather absently. He had been preoccupied since last night with domestic details, sorting through the things in his flat and making ruthless decisions about what was worth keeping. It had been an unexpectedly depressing business, the breaking up of a former home seeming to foreshadow what might happen to his present one. In the end he had given up the idea of saving any of the furniture or other bulky items; he had given a few things to Vincent, and in return the Irishman had undertaken to sell everything else and send on the proceeds. Jack was taking with him only what would go into his luggage.

He locked the apartment and unscrewed the door handle, the absence of which still provided its only protection. He gave the keys to Vincent, and then they carried his suitcases down to the basement and loaded them in the Granada. They said goodbye and promised to keep in touch. Then Jack set off.

Along the road to the border things looked just as chaotic as when he'd arrived. The oil-well fires were still burning. The ubiquitous military traffic slowed his progress for several kilometres, and smoke impeded it further, but when he had passed the Burgan field the fug suddenly lifted to show the desert flooded by brilliant spring sunshine. He took this as a good omen, picking up speed and letting his thoughts drift along positive lines.

He was going home fifty thousand dollars richer. That much was certain. There was another fifty thousand in prospect if he could pull off the deal for Hamadi, and possibly a whole lot more if he could negotiate a share for himself of the one million dollars still blocked in the account in Zurich. These were pretty heady figures; what he couldn't quite understand was why he was not more excited by them. The money had an unreal quality, something just as intangible as the services required of him in return. The more he thought about these, the less inclined he was to accept Hamadi's bland assurances about how simple it was all going to be. Something was missing – no, probably several things were missing – from the complicated patchwork of fact, speculation and prejudice that formed the background he had to work against.

Perhaps he shouldn't let this bother him. He had a job to do; what had gone before it was none of his concern. But despite himself he kept seeing a human dimension to it. He imagined the cruel death of Noura Hamadi in the Nayef Palace, and he heard a doomed Iraqi babbling in his dark cell about stolen gold. He also remembered the tug of desire he had felt for Dale Griggs, and regretted that he was unlikely to see her again. He had come to Kuwait in search of answers about himself; he was leaving, it seemed, with his mind full of questions about other people.

Near the Saudi border he was held up in a line of traffic. An American supply truck had skidded off the road into the sand and a huge towing vehicle was dragging it out. Edging past the scene of the accident, Jack felt his memory jolted. A connection fell into place that was so simple he wondered why on earth it hadn't occurred to him before.

He crossed the frontier with little delay this time and reached Dhahran early in the afternoon. Half a dozen dogs yapped at him when he rang the doorbell of the Patley penthouse and he got his usual warm welcome from Sylvia, who pressed a late lunch of cold chicken and salad on him. Immediately he had eaten he phoned the local office of British Airways. They told him the direct flight to London the next day was full, but he got a reservation on one leaving for Jeddah in the morning, with an onward connection arriving at five-thirty in the evening.

After asking Sylvia's permission, he made a call to Alison.

It was midday in England, a time when she had usually finished her morning's housework and would be relaxing with a cup of coffee and the newspaper. She managed to make it sound inconvenient to talk all the same.

'I can't collect you at the airport,' she said when he told her his plans.

'I wasn't expecting you to. I'll take the train. How are the girls?'

'They're both starting colds. I think I'm getting one too.'

These days Alison would never admit to being completely well. He had thought he might cheer her up by telling her about the cheque for fifty thousand dollars he was bringing home, but something stopped him. Why should that have to make any difference to the way she felt? He told her he would be home around seven o'clock the next evening, and after they'd exchanged a few more remarks he hung up.

Sylvia had been out on the terrace, watering her plants and endeavouring not to eavesdrop, but she could hardly have missed the chilly tone of the conversation. When she came in he said: 'Alison and I aren't getting on too well these days, I'm afraid.'

'I guessed as much.'

'That was clever of you. I didn't think I'd given anything away the other night.'

'It was all in what you didn't say, dear.' Beneath her blue rinse and her easy Canadian drawl, Sylvia was a woman of considerable insight. She sat down on a couch, shooed off a couple of shih-tzus and beckoned to him to join her. 'Eric and I have been worried about you. Not to mention those sweet little girls. And I don't mean just recently. Things had begun to go wrong before you left Kuwait, hadn't they?'

'I think I can date it fairly precisely, in fact, to the time when my business started to look shaky.'

'And you expected your wife to be supportive at a time like that? But instead she was just the opposite?'

'Exactly. For better for worse, for richer for poorer. She became obsessive about money. She got discontented, started to withdraw into herself, pick arguments over nothing. Decided she didn't like Kuwait any more. Now she's home in England and she's still no happier. I've almost given up trying to please her, frankly.'

'If you'll pardon my bluntness, Jack, I don't think you ever will. Some couples are so similar in temperament that they were born to be together: the types who tell you they've never had a cross word in their lives. Others, like Eric and me, have differences that complement each other and make the relationship stronger. But you two are just way off each other's wavelength. The money you used to make was just papering over your problems.'

'You could see all that?'

'I'm not going to take sides,' Sylvia said, 'because I like you both for different reasons, but I used to feel that Alison never knew who she really was. She was like a child who hadn't found an identity for herself and had to go on making up roles. She found a role as your wife and the mother of your children, but she's grown tired of playing it.

'She also never had a father she could admire, so she looked up to you instead. It isn't the thing nowadays for a woman to admit to being dependent on a man, but that's what she is. And I guess the moment you began to seem less than perfect she felt threatened. Her daddy gambled his money away and she thought you would create a secure, happy new world for her. Whereas what you needed was a grown-up woman who could share your problems as well as your successes. It wasn't a healthy basis for a lifelong relationship.'

Jack looked at Sylvia with a new respect. She seemed to have hit on something that he had been too close to see for himself. 'So I should feel sorry for her instead of angry? That's easier said than done.'

'I know. But maybe you should try talking to her about it.'

'We don't talk about anything, Sylvia, least of all our feelings. And even if we did, she would never accept that analysis of herself. I did suggest marriage counselling, but she said if we couldn't sort out our own problems no-one else would be able to.'

'So you think it's all over?'

'I'm beginning to think so.'

'Then the agony aunt's advice is not to let it drag on. Finish it before the bitterness gets too strong, for the sake of all four of you. Recognize that if she's ever going to be happy then it won't be with you. And go out and find that grown woman you need.'

Soon afterwards Sylvia sent for her driver and went out shopping, leaving Jack to have his first shower in three days and change into fresh clothes. The ones he had worn in Kuwait still carried an odour of oil smoke. When Eric came home from work at four-thirty the two of them went out on the terrace. Displacing more dogs from the cane chairs, they sat and drank iced tea and looked out towards the Gulf, over the deceptive acres of grass and shrubbery that had been planted to make a home from home for Americans.

Eric was a shrewd Nova Scotian whose eyes shone with good humour behind gold-rimmed bifocals. He wanted to hear at first hand about the state of things in Kuwait, and Jack told him circumspectly that he'd been given a commission to chase up some money that had gone missing during the occupation. Eric repeated a story he had heard about a Kuwaiti merchant fleeing across the border on the morning of the invasion, carrying his life savings in the form of a bag full of gem diamonds. This gave Jack an opportunity to raise a subject on which he wanted the benefit of the older man's knowledge.

'I remember you telling me you made quite a lot of money playing the gold market at one time,' he said. 'How did that come about?'

'Oh, I was just a small-time speculator and it wasn't a killing, exactly,' Eric said; he seemed pleased to retell the story all the same. 'It was back in the early seventies, not long after the two-tier pricing system had come into operation. It allowed gold to find its own value on the free market, alongside the official rate that was still fixed at thirty-five dollars an ounce. The odd thing was, the markets didn't seem to know what to make of it at first, and for a couple of years the new price hovered at not much above the old one.

'Now this seemed crazy to me. I didn't know much about gold at the time, so I went out and learned everything I could. The official rate had been pegged at thirty-five dollars since nineteen thirty-four. It was obviously artificial. The real value of gold had certainly gone up since then – and I found out that unofficial buyers were prepared to

149

pay a lot more for it. Well, I backed a hunch and it paid off. A run on gold began a few months after I'd bought in. It went on going up and up, and at the time of the first big oil crisis in 'seventy-three it shot through the ceiling. I'd got in at forty dollars an ounce, and I sold at a little under two hundred. A profit of . . . what? Nearly five hundred per cent in three and a half years.'

'I'd call that a killing,' Jack said.

'Not when you consider that it rose a few years later to over eight hundred. But nobody could have foreseen that.'

'It's not an area I'm familiar with. If I wanted to invest in gold, how would I go about it?'

'Simple as buying ice-cream. You'd go to an authorized dealer, or maybe a bank, and you'd write them a cheque. They'd give you gold bars and a certificate proving your ownership, or if you wanted they'd hold them in safe keeping for you.'

'Let's say I took the bars and later wanted to sell them somewhere else. In another country, for instance.'

'No problem, as long as you could prove they were yours. But what I'm saying applies only to the richer countries, really, which have done away with most of the old restrictions on private ownership of gold. In countries with unstable currencies or weak trading positions, they're still in place. They're needed to prevent hoarding and protect foreign reserves. The only way to buy or sell gold in a place like India or Russia is on the black market.'

'So presumably there's still something to be gained out of smuggling it.'

'You bet there is,' Eric said. 'And nowhere more so than right here in the Middle East. The big markets are India and Pakistan; people there still count their wealth in gold, and there's probably billions of dollars' worth held illegally in private hands. I believe a steady supply still travels down the Gulf in dhows, gets offloaded on the coast between Karachi and Bombay. Then there are the overland routes from Turkey.'

'Turkey?'

'You sound surprised. As every second-rate guidebook will tell you, Turkey straddles the East and the West. It has borders with half a dozen countries. It was on the main trade route between Asia and the Mediterranean as far back as the time of Alexander the Great. Smuggling is at least its second oldest profession.

'As a matter of fact I did some business once with a man I know in Istanbul who used to have the whole unofficial gold trade sewn up.' Eric took on a look of sly, wistful amusement when he remembered shady episodes from his past. 'Quite a fascinating character called Manolis Zakarios. Retired now, I believe. A phanariot Greek, one of those people whose families have been there since the Byzantine era. In fact, they still call the place Constantinople. By profession he was a wholesale jeweller. By vocation he was a smuggler.

'It was all quite respectable. He had agents all over the Middle East who'd buy gold from anyone who wanted to sell, no questions asked. He'd bring the stuff into Turkey, melt it down and recast it into little ten-ounce bars, then ship it out to the hottest markets. He had a wink-and-nod arrangement with the authorities: as long as he used Turkey purely as an entrepôt and he wasn't costing their treasury anything, they let him get away with it. It brought a lot of foreign exchange into the country. They've turned all law-abiding since then and tightened up their rules. But we've come a long way from your original question.'

Not necessarily, Jack thought. He poured more iced tea and said: 'I'm not thinking of buying gold, actually. Between you and me, I'm trying to work out how somebody who had stolen some might go about offloading it.'

Eric shot him a look. 'You haven't got desperate and found your way into some racket, have you?'

'No. It's a question that arises from this job I've taken on. A purely hypothetical question, at the moment.'

'OK. Hypothetically, how much gold are we talking about?'

'I don't have an exact figure, but I worked it out to be between forty-five and fifty million dollars' worth.'

Instead of looking surprised, Eric made a sceptical face. 'Somebody's been shitting you, Jack. Nobody ever had that much hot gold on his hands. Not all at one time, anyway.'

'I'm not saying I believe it. But I realized just today that the figures at least make a curious kind of sense.' Jack had decided there was no harm in entrusting all his thoughts to Eric. He took out a sheet of paper on which he'd done some arithmetic. 'The gold is supposed to be part of the booty that the Iraqis took from the Central Bank of Kuwait. What is definite is that three thousand, two hundred and sixteen bars of it were removed from the vaults. Working on the values I was given, I'm assuming those were the standard international mint bars, four hundred troy ounces each. A total of one million, two hundred and eighty-six thousand, four hundred ounces, or just over forty metric tons.

'At the current price of around four hundred dollars an ounce, that adds up to nearly five hundred and thirteen million dollars' worth. Now, what I was told was that a little under ten per cent of that went missing. Call it three hundred bars, conservatively, or a hundred and twenty thousand ounces. Roughly forty-eight million dollars' worth. Ten per cent, Eric: there's a significance to that figure.'

Jack recounted parts of the conversations he had had with Major Al-Shaheb and the Iraqi prisoner, Fadel. Both had told him about the ten armoured vehicles that had been sent from Baghdad to collect the gold. It was only this morning, when he'd seen the American truck being pulled out of the desert sand, that he'd remembered Al-Shaheb's casual reference to one of the vehicles breaking down. Only nine of them had returned to Iraq.

'Ten per cent is roughly one truckload of gold, Eric. I'd been wondering how it had been possible for part of the consignment to go missing without a whole lot of people knowing about it. Well, that could be the answer: one of the trucks was made to disappear. I didn't see any importance in it at the time; if I had, I'd have asked more questions before I left Kuwait.'

'So,' Eric mused, 'let's assume the bad guys have got this truck full of gold, and let's ask ourselves what they might have done with it. First of all, consider how much of it there is: I'm talking volume and weight, not just value. Give me a minute.'

He went indoors and returned shortly with a calculator and a book which he showed to Jack: it was an old copy of the *Minerals Yearbook* published by the United States Department of Mines. 'I remember this had some useful statistics in it. Here we are. One international mint standard bar of gold measures seven inches by three and five-eighths by one and five-eighths. Let's find its volume and multiply by three hundred.' He got to work on the calculator. 'A little over seven cubic feet. Say three feet by two by a foot and a bit. Now in theory you could almost hide a stack that size under your bed, but the problem would be the weight: the stuff is so heavy it would fall right through your floor. You could even fit it into a couple of big suitcases, but you'd need a crane to lift them. Gold has one of the highest specific gravities of all metals – nearly twice as high as lead. A hundred and twenty thousand troy ounces comes to . . . let's see, three thousand, seven hundred-odd kilograms, or about eight thousand, two hundred pounds. That's over three and a half tons, whichever way you look at it. So, you see, it's easy to hide but difficult to transport.

'The first thing I'd want to do is stash it somewhere safe so it wouldn't have to be moved around any more than necessary. The second thing: find a buyer or a middleman who doesn't deal on the official market. There's a given amount of gold in bank vaults around the world, about a billion ounces of it at the last count, and the people who operate on the international markets know pretty exactly where it all is at any one time. In practical terms, what they're mostly dealing in is pieces of paper, credit and debit notes representing sales and purchases. A bar of gold could notionally change ownership a hundred times, a thousand times, without ever leaving Fort Knox or the Bank of England.

'When an actual physical transfer of bullion takes place, it's usually by way of some international trade-off. A government that doesn't have strong foreign reserves or a good line of credit, for instance, might have to pay directly in gold for some of its imports. And when that happens, every unit of bullion can be separately accounted for. Each bar has a set of assay marks and serial numbers stamped on it. An expert can tell at a glance where the bar was minted and when. And naturally there's an international register of any that have been stolen.

'In other words, you couldn't take the gold you're talking about to a reputable dealer. You'd have to go to someone willing to take the risk of disguising its origin, probably by breaking it down into smaller units before it was resold.'

'Someone like your friend in Istanbul?' Jack said.

'Zakarios? In the old days, maybe. Like I said, the Turks have cleaned up their act. They're trying to join the European Community and they have to look respectable. Which is not to say there aren't still some freebooters around who don't have to depend on official connivance. But with a quantity like that, I don't know. I can see a syndicate getting involved, perhaps, to spread the risk. It'd be a huge capital investment with no quick return. Selling it would have to be a long-term operation, a few thousand ounces at a time. Even a market like

India could get flooded by that much coming in all at once.'

'What was the business you did with this Zakarios?'

Eric smiled and playfully rubbed the side of his nose. 'Still between you and me? After I'd bought my gold I got a little panicky. The price didn't move at first and I began to think I'd overextended myself. I decided to hedge my bets a little by offloading some of it on the black market. Drove into Turkey with half a dozen bars hidden in the door panels of my car. Zakarios gave me seventy-five dollars an ounce against the forty I'd paid: chicken feed, as it turned out. The sly old bastard acted like he was doing me a favour. I should have trusted my instincts.'

They talked on until Sylvia returned and joined them on the balcony. As dusk crept in over the Gulf the amplified wail of muezzins began to drift across the city in the call to evening prayer. Later, when the mosques had emptied and the restaurants had opened, the three of them went out and gorged themselves, like the Arabs breaking their fast around them, on red caviare and grilled shrimps, stuffed lamb, smoked aubergines and sticky-sweet baklava.

The abundance of rich food after his three days of spartan living in Kuwait no doubt contributed to the lushness of Jack's dreams in the Patleys' air-conditioned guest room later that night. Shining bars of gold, stamped with dollar signs and seven-figure sums, were spread out at his feet. Photographs flickered before him in which the same two subjects, Colonel Jalloul and Noura Hamadi, struck poses for the camera. Dale Griggs, naked and sweaty on her mattress, clasped muscular thighs around his hips and drew him inside her with a little gasp of delight.

He woke up briefly, feeling a warm, guilty but pleasurable wetness in his pyjama trousers, drowsily wallowing in the fantasy that had bubbled up again, this time in the crudest physical way. Some part of his mind was obviously determined to hold on to it.

*Part Two*

# 13

The flight to Jeddah the next morning added two hours to what would have been a six-hour journey home. When Jack arrived at Heathrow he couldn't face the further hassle of a succession of commuter trains at the evening rush hour, so he splurged on a taxi all the way to Banstead. He wanted to be in time to see the twins before they went to bed. And, after all, he reminded himself, he was carrying a cheque for fifty thousand dollars in his wallet, together with drafts for nearly sixteen thousand pounds. It was almost as much money as he'd ever had in his own hands at any one time, but it still seemed faintly illusory.

It seemed even more so once the taxi had turned off the M25 into an area where the outer suburbs of London poked a finger into rural Surrey. Banstead was a placid dormitory town and Prescott Gardens, where Jack lived, had always struck him as the archetypal English middle-class street. After the harsh desert environment of the Gulf its pocket-sized front gardens, flawlessly manicured for the spring, looked impossibly green and well-watered; daffodils were blooming and maple and beech trees were in leaf. In the fading light, lamps glowed invitingly behind the curtains of neat detached houses, most of them of the inter-war Georgian or Tudor type. Across the road from his own house, Fred Reynolds' lawn was as smooth as a bowling green.

It was undoubtedly a pleasant place to live, a suburban environment that everything in his background and temperament suited him to inhabit. Why, then, did he find no contentment in coming back to it? He had lived here happily enough before they had moved to Kuwait, but on his return he had found something oppressively uniform about the place. His neighbours' families were all much alike in age, size and income bracket. Their conversations were polite, their opinions commonplace. Their houses were furnished and decorated in the same cautious, inoffensive way, and even their cars were of similar makes and price range. They were nice people; they simply weren't interesting. You wouldn't come across anyone like Eric Patley or Vincent Hand at one of their Sunday-morning drinks parties; and you certainly wouldn't meet a Dale Griggs.

He had changed and Alison hadn't. She had rediscovered a liking for Prescott Gardens. She shared school runs with her neighbours and enjoyed their weekend get-togethers. She went shopping on Saturdays as the other women did, while their husbands mowed their lawns or took their cars to the car wash. She liked the predictability and the sense of continuity it seemed to represent. She fitted in where he no longer did, and this in turn had some bearing on the failings in their marriage.

She came to the front door as he was fumbling for his keys. She greeted him with a constrained smile and a kiss on the cheek, the coolness of the gesture immediately overwhelmed by the shrieking welcome of the twins, running from the kitchen in their pyjamas and red dressing-gowns. He swept them off their feet and held them aloft, squeezing them and submitting to milky kisses and sticky-fingered hugs.

'We missed you, Daddy,' said Camilla.

'You were gone for ages,' said Claudia.

'It was only five days, sweetheart!'

'Well, it seemed like ages.'

'Was it scary in Kuwait?'

'It was a bit weird.'

'Did you bring us presents?'

'Wait and see.'

The girls' dinner had been interrupted so all four of them went to the kitchen and sat around the pine table. While the twins continued their meal of scrambled eggs, toast and milk, Jack opened his bags and took out treasures salvaged from the flat: two teddy bears and other favourite soft toys, Claudia's moth-eaten Garfield and Camilla's one-eared donkey. He also produced the things he had bought in the duty-free gift shop at Dhahran, two Swatch watches for the girls and a bottle of Fidji scent for Alison.

'A bit impersonal,' he said apologetically, 'but I didn't have time for any real shopping. There's nothing to buy in Kuwait.'

'You shouldn't have bothered,' Alison said. She poured Scotch and water for them both and Jack savoured his like nectar.

'Ah. I'd forgotten how good that can taste.'

The twins strapped on their watches but were more delighted about the return of their old toys. They competed for their father's attention with a barrage of questions, more to do with the immediate details of his trip than the state of their former home. Seven months is a long time in the life of a pair of six year olds, and the apartment in the Muthanna complex was already a hazy memory to them. In turn he listened patiently to news from their own small world.

'Rachel at school has got chicken pox,' Camilla announced.

'We're going to get it too,' Claudia said confidently. 'You stay off school for a week.'

'I thought you liked your school.'

'We don't like Miss Jackson. She's our new teacher. Mrs Fox has gone to have a baby.'

'A baby fox!'

Fits of giggles, splutters of milk. They did have slight colds, but there was no sign that Alison had caught one. Gathered round the table with the twins prattling on, they might have been an average loving family involved in each other's doings. Jack had known for a long time that the

161

reality was different. Alison, quietly watching the girls with an indulgent smile, knew it too. He noticed that she had dressed up a bit for his return, in a narrow black skirt and a tan silk blouse she had bought in Kuwait, and had caught up her light brown hair with a gold clip, but he suspected this was part of the keeping up of appearances as well.

Soon it was the twins' bedtime, and their protests were overcome only by Jack's offering to read them an extra-long story. He did so sitting on a chair between their beds, where they could both see the illustrations, and by the time he was near the end they were nodding off. He kissed them good night, turned out their lights and quietly left the room.

Though she was careful not to point it out, Alison had clearly gone to some trouble in her arrangements for their own dinner. They never used the dining room unless they had guests, but she had set the table in their big kitchen with the best dinner service and the silver cutlery they had got as wedding presents. She'd cooked a feather-light crab soufflé, a roast joint of pork that she served with new potatoes and French beans, and an apple crumble. She had also opened a good bottle of St Emilion.

He told her about his trip. He was grateful to have something to talk about, and she listened with at least an outward show of interest to the account of his dealings with the bank and the meetings with Dr Hamadi. He spoke only in vague terms about the commission he had taken on, skating over the details without seeming evasive. He made two deliberate omissions, though. He still did not mention the fifty thousand dollars he had been paid, not because he wanted the money to himself but because he was certain now that it would colour her attitude to him. And, without quite knowing why, he said nothing about Dale Griggs.

He went on to describe the state in which he had found their apartment and their possessions.

'It's impossible to ship stuff back at the moment. And I didn't think there was anything worth going to that much trouble over, frankly. Vincent will keep an eye on the flat and sell the furniture when he thinks he can get a decent price. If that's all right with you?'

'Of course.'

They were drinking coffee now and their conversation had taken on the over-polite tone that meant it was running out of steam, threatening to come to a halt. Emboldened by the few glasses of wine he had drunk, he suddenly said: 'Have you been thinking things over while I've been away? About us, I mean?'

She looked at him without expression. 'Why do you ask?'

'Don't think I'm ungrateful for the effort you've put in tonight, but it makes me wonder.' He gestured around at the remains of their dinner. 'You didn't want me to go, but you've welcomed me back. Are you trying to tell me something?'

Alison rested her elbows on the table, laced her fingers beneath her chin and said, 'I have made one decision. I'm going to sleep in the spare bedroom from now on.'

The announcement came as such an anticlimax that it made him laugh. 'For Christ's sake, what do you suppose that's going to achieve?'

'Nothing, probably. I just want more space to myself.'

'Well, it won't make much difference to our sex life,' he said grimly. 'But perhaps it is a good idea. It may bring things to a head. I've been thinking even if you haven't, and the conclusion I've reached is that our marriage is dying, if it's not dead already. Do you agree?'

'I suppose so.'

'You suppose so. Is that as close as you're going to get to having an honest discussion about it? What's gone wrong between us, Alison?'

'You tell me.'

'All right, I'll try.' Though the makings were there for another pointless quarrel, he attempted to speak calmly. 'The accepted wisdom in these things is that there are always faults on both sides, but it's my admittedly biased point of view that most of our problems arise from your attitude to me. It changed as soon as my business began to fail. It made me think that the only worth you'd ever seen in me was the material kind. In fact, you've never gone short of anything, not even in the last eight months. And at the risk of sounding immodest I'm going to say I don't believe I've ever been anything but a good husband and father. I've also gone out of my way to find out what's been bugging you, how I can help you. You just don't respond. You don't seem interested in making this marriage work any longer, and I'm on the verge of giving up trying myself.'

'Are you asking me for a divorce, Jack?'

'I'm saying that unless you can change your attitude, that's the way we're heading.'

Alison spoke with a sudden decisiveness. 'Then let's get a few things clear. If you want a divorce I want full custody of the children. I want the house signed over to me and I want an equal division of all our other assets – as they stand now, that is, before you fritter any more of our savings away.' Her voice had taken on a new, hard edge; there was a marble-cold look in her eyes that he seemed never to have seen before. 'It's not up to me to change, Jack; it's for you to decide whether you'll meet my terms for getting rid of me. I've already seen a solicitor.'

'Just a minute, just a minute . . .' He was shocked by the transformation of her mood, taken completely off guard. 'It's not just a question of what I or you want. I started out trying to discuss things with you. I didn't expect to be given a list of demands.'

'No discussions, Jack. The divorce court will give me the house and custody of the children anyway. If I pushed for it, I'd probably get a good chunk of any future earnings you might happen to make as well. I'd prefer a settlement that will allow me to salvage what I can from this marriage now – and yes, I do mean in material terms. I told you I'd made one small decision; I didn't say I hadn't been thinking about bigger ones.'

He was aware of having been drawn into a trap of some kind, but unsure of its dimensions. 'You've just gone ahead and worked this all out behind my back? Have you thought about anything apart from the money? Have you considered how it would affect the girls? They'd be heartbroken.'

'Of course they would. But you're the one who brought the thing up. Are you starting to have second thoughts?'

'I'm trying to take in some of the implications, that's all. Somebody had to raise the question. We couldn't go on living the way we have been.'

'We certainly couldn't. I'm not buying your self-righteous waffle about being a good father and husband. What matters to me is that you've let me down, lost nearly everything we had. For eight months you've hung around here like Mr Micawber, hoping that something will turn up, too good to go out the way Reg did and earn yourself a living. Do you know you're something of a laughing-stock among our neighbours?'

'You mean the likes of Fred Reynolds?' he retorted. 'The world's champion lawn-mower? It really hurts to hear what he thinks of me.'

'You go gallivanting off to Kuwait, spending more of our money, coming back with some Mickey Mouse scheme that will lead nowhere. Well, at least you've got our savings out of the bank, and I intend to see that I get my fair share of them. You'll never succeed as an independent businessman, Jack; that's why I'd prefer to take what I can get now. Think about it: a divorce on my conditions now, or a messy wrangle in the courts later.'

Jack was speechless for a few moments. Remembering how he had become aware a few months ago that Alison was a stranger to him, he realized that the experience should have been a warning. There had been far more bitterness and resentment simmering beneath her apathetic surface than he could possibly have guessed.

With an effort he restrained his temper. He said, 'So that's it, as far as you're concerned?'

'That's it.' She stood up from the table. 'I'm going to wash the dishes now, and then I'm going to bed.'

He stalked out of the kitchen. In the sitting room he poured himself a whisky and slumped into an armchair, feeling his senses reel under the impact of belated shock. He was even shaking slightly. It wasn't just the discovery of a side to Alison he had never known was there; he was stunned also at the thought that she actually despised him. And this was the woman Sylvia Patley thought he should feel sorry for? In a funny way, though, Sylvia had been right. Alison's view of the world wasn't that of an independent woman. Denied what she wanted, she could think only of hitting back at the source of her frustration. Screwing him for everything she could get out of him was just another, debased form of dependence. Reflecting further, he found that he was more surprised than hurt by her expressions of contempt for him. He knew his own worth, he considered, and nothing she said could undermine it.

On a practical level, there was one thing he could be positively glad about: if she could be selfish, he need have no scruples about being the same. He hadn't mentioned the money he'd got from Dr Hamadi, and now he had no intention of doing so. It looked as if he might need it to survive on.

The television had been left on with the volume turned down. He stared at it in a daze, feeling suddenly exhausted after the day of travelling and an evening of emotional strain. One of the late-night news magazine programmes was on, dominated, naturally, by events in the Gulf. Few pictures were coming out of the separate conflicts in Iraq, so a succession of talking heads mouthed silently at intervals between snatches of library footage.

Jack got up to pour himself another drink. As he did so, his attention was caught by a caption that flickered on to the screen. It appeared beneath the face of a voluble middle-aged man, being interviewed in an anonymous indoor setting.

The caption identified the speaker as *Abdel Karim, Iraqi opposition leader*.

Jack found the remote control and turned up the volume. Abdel Karim was a distinguished-looking man with silver hair and gold-rimmed glasses. 'Unless the West sends help to the Kurds immediately,' he was saying in impeccable English, 'these events will end in tragedy. We have indications that Saddam Hussein is regrouping his forces . . .'

Karim was the same Kurdish political leader who had been interviewed on the World Service yesterday morning. Jack had read descriptions of him as a man who'd spent years of exile in England, who was under sentence of death in Iraq for his activities aimed at overthrowing Saddam's regime. He was also one of the people who had helped in preparing the report on the theft of money from the Iraqi treasury.

As he talked on, Jack was struck by an odd notion. Karim was just the kind of man who would be in a position to know, or at least to make a well-informed guess, about what might have become of someone like Colonel Jalloul. These exile groups all seemed to have their own sources of information inside Iraq, and they could hardly have failed to be aware of the disappearance of a senior military intelligence officer. But how to go about approaching such a man? Jack had no credentials he was free to reveal, no official position to buttress him. On the other hand, if he had guessed right about Hellig Associates being involved in compiling that report, at least he did have a contact there.

He turned off the television, went to the phone and dialled Reg Kilmartin's number.

His former partner had a little mews house off Ennismore Gardens in Kensington. When he answered the phone Jack apologized for the lateness of the hour and said: 'Reg, I was wondering if you could do me a favour. Well, a couple of favours, possibly.'

'Anything I can, Jack.' Reg had taken more blame on himself than necessary for the failure of the business and would be anxious to make any amends he could. 'What is it?'

'Would I be right in thinking that Hellig's had some hand in producing that report that's just been published on the money stolen from Iraq?'

'Sure thing. Kroll's of New York did most of the work on it but they commissioned us to carry out some of the enquiries at this end. I had nothing to do with it myself, though.'

'Could you get hold of a copy of the report for me?'

'Well, I don't know,' said Reg uneasily. 'Only selected parts of it have been made public. The rest is confidential. A tricky business from the legal point of view, naming banks and companies that might have had funny money invested in them, knowingly or otherwise. Can you tell me why you want it?'

'I'm involved in a confidential job myself, Reg. A bit along the lines of the work you and I used to do, but with added complications. I need to do some research without making it too obvious what I'm looking for. What I also want from you is an introduction to someone. Riding on your professional coat-tails, so to speak, I'd like to get in touch with Abdel Karim, the exiled Iraqi politician.'

'My God, Jack! That's like asking to meet Salman Rushdie. The man lives in hiding, in fear for his life.'

'But the media have access to him. He seems to have them eating out of his hand at the moment. And since I gather he helped Hellig's in compiling that report, someone there must be in contact with him. If you could just get a message through asking for a brief private meeting, to exchange information that might be to our mutual benefit . . . You know you can trust me. Nothing I see or hear is going to go any further.'

'I'll ask about it,' Reg said. 'And I'll see what I can do about the report. Let me call you in the morning.'

'There's one other thing I'd like you to think about in the meantime. When was it that you left the Army?'

'Longer ago than I care to remember. Nineteen seventy-six.'

'Do you know anyone who could give me an introduction to somebody at the Staff College in Camberley? Somebody who would have records or at least recollections about a foreign army officer who was there around nineteen eighty?'

'Now that really is out of my league,' Reg said. 'I was just on a short-service commission, before I decided that God didn't intend me for that kind of life. Camberley is where career soldiers get tested to destruction; I never got within an ass's roar of the place.'

'Give it some thought, will you?'

'All right,' Reg said with a sigh. 'I'm beginning to think Salman Rushdie would be easier after all. How's Alison, by the way?'

'Oh, you know. Difficult.'

Leaving Reg to ponder on that, Jack finished his whisky and tramped up to his newly single bedroom.

# 14

The next morning Jack awoke in a strangely optimistic mood. He couldn't pin down the reason, but he thought his conversation with Alison had something to do with it. It had cleared the air if nothing else, ending what he could now see had been months, perhaps even years, of uncertainty between them.

Within a few minutes, a heaviness returned to his thoughts as he considered a future of separation from the twins. Would he end up like other divorced men he knew, pathetically collecting his children for their weekly period of 'access'? Maybe he should fight for custody, or contest the divorce: was that even possible nowadays? And if so, could he afford it?

He found it hard to contemplate the horror of such a business, and he didn't feel like facing Alison this morning. She was moving about downstairs, getting the twins ready for school, and a few minutes later he heard the three of them trooping out to her car. As soon as she had driven off he went down to the phone, taking advantage of her absence to call the number of the lawyer who had represented Dr Hamadi in Zurich.

He stated his name to the answering telephonist and within a few moments he was speaking to Dr Karl Zunckel. A man with a gravelly voice and precise English diction, he seemed keen at once to take charge of the conversation.

'Good morning, Mr Rushton. Our mutual client has already informed me that you would be in touch with me. No names, if you please – it is advisable not to be too specific on the telephone, I think. I should make it clear at once that I don't believe I can be of any more help to

170

you than I have been to him. He knows everything there is to know about this matter. To be quite frank, I am not at all sure what purpose would be served by your coming to see me.'

'I have to start somewhere, Dr Zunckel, and I think a discussion with you could be very useful. I'm thinking of—'

'I understand what your principal's intentions are,' Zunckel interrupted. 'Unfortunately, it has been difficult to convince him that I have no way of taking the matter any further. It is in a state of impasse. A legally binding covenant is involved, as well as strict banking regulations which cannot be circumvented.'

'I'm sure you know a lot more about them than I do,' Jack said firmly. 'Which is why I'd appreciate the benefit of your advice. I hope to fly to Zurich tomorrow morning and I'd be grateful if you'd fit in a meeting with me early in the afternoon.'

'At so little notice, I am not sure that will be possible.'

'Since your client is paying both of us, Dr Zunckel, I think we ought to treat his problem with some urgency. In the meantime I'd like you to set up an appointment for me for later tomorrow with someone from the Handelsbank Bauer.'

'Mr Rushton . . .' The lawyer's tone became patronizing. 'Perhaps you're not familiar with the confidential nature of Swiss banking. Nobody there is going to talk to you.'

'Not even if I want to invest some money with them? That's all I have in mind for the moment.'

'I see,' said Zunckel, nonplussed. 'Very well, I'll see what I can do. To be perfectly candid, I think you and our client are looking for a miracle.'

'I'll phone again and tell you when I'm arriving.'

Pompous ass, Jack thought, putting down the receiver. Dr Zunckel sounded like the kind of lawyer who was fonder of talking than of listening. And behind his expressions of candour he seemed extraordinarily determined to discourage Jack's efforts. Well, Hamadi had suggested that the man would be difficult to deal with, and Jack hoped he would not have to depend on him too much. Meanwhile, he had other business to attend to.

He went back upstairs and showered, shaved and dressed. He was ready to leave the house just before ten o'clock when the phone rang. It was Reg, mumbling furtively from his desk at Hellig's.

'I've got what you were looking for,' he said.

'The report? That's terrific. Can I come and collect it?'

'Not here, please,' Reg said hastily. 'Let's meet for a quick bite of lunch at Walpole's. I may have made some progress on that other thing by then.'

'Abdel Karim? That's even better. Dare I ask if you got anything on Camberley?'

'Not much luck there, as I warned you. I've lost touch with the people who stayed on in the Army after I'd left. But I do have an old pal who remembered that one of our company commanders moved to the college as an instructor around the time you were talking about. Man named Thorpe. Major David Thorpe. Retired now, but still lives somewhere around Camberley. What he might remember about any one officer who did a course there is anybody's guess. That's the best I can do for you.'

'I'll try and find him,' Jack said.

'Remind him about our regiment: the Royal Green Jackets. That'll be your entrée. See you later. One o'clock all right?'

'Fine.'

'Oh, and bring some serious ID with your photograph on it, just in case. Preferably your passport.'

Jack called directory enquiries and asked for the number of a Major David Thorpe in the Camberley area. After some delay, the nearest they could get to it was a Colonel A.D. Thorpe with an address in Green Lane, Sandhurst.

172

Jack tried the number but got no reply. It occurred to him that the place was less than half an hour's drive away; he might just have time to get over there, if only to establish whether the major and the colonel were one and the same person. But the only car he and Alison had between them these days was her Honda Civic, and he did not want to have to ask her for the use of it.

He heard her coming in by the back door just then, and he went through to the kitchen to find her unpacking some shopping. They greeted each other with studied politeness, neither of them mentioning the discussion of the night before. He told her he would be out until at least mid-afternoon, and sensed that she shared his own relief that they would escape each other's company.

It was a blustery spring day, sunshine alternating with fast-moving rain clouds. He walked the short distance to his bank in Banstead High Street, where he paid the two sterling drafts from Kuwait into his deposit account. He also bought five thousand Swiss francs' worth of travellers' cheques before crossing the road to a travel agency. He paid for a return ticket to Zurich and got a reservation on a flight leaving at ten o'clock the next morning, together with a booking for one night at a hotel where he had stayed before. Finally he walked to the station and caught a train to Waterloo.

'I don't know if you realize quite how cagey they have to be,' said Reg Kilmartin. 'These Kurdish exile people, I mean. They don't take any chances. They've got an office over at Bethnal Green, but naturally you can't just walk in there and ask for Abdel Karim. There's a drill to be followed, the same one they use for arranging clandestine press and television interviews. They trust me because I'm from Hellig's. I take you there and introduce you, vouch for you, and after that you're on your own. I gather that if they accept your bona fides they'll arrange a further rendezvous and take you to meet the man somewhere else.'

'Thanks, Reg. You've been terrific.'

'I'm not going to say it was nothing, because actually it was quite something. Smuggling that thing out wasn't exactly easy, either.' Reg pointed at the report, in a large manila envelope, which lay between them on the bar counter at Walpole's. 'Not to be shown to anybody else, and none of the information in it to be attributed to Hellig's or to me. For God's sake, don't leave it in the taxi.'

'Don't worry, I know the score.'

They sat with plates of beef salad and a glass of wine each at one end of the bar. Jack wasn't sure whether his former partner appreciated the irony of choosing Walpole's as their meeting place. It was off Moorgate in the heart of the City, just around the corner from the offices of Hellig Associates, and it was where the two of them had often furtively retreated to plot their escape from Hellig's all those years ago. A staid Dickensian chop-house in those days, it had since succumbed to fashion and become a wine bar, serving quiches and salads and vegetarian lasagne to health-conscious yuppies from the financial service companies.

As well as producing the report by Kroll Associates of New York, Reg had greeted him with the news that he had managed to arrange an appointment for that afternoon with Abdel Karim. It was in Reg's nature to complain of the impossibility of doing things and then to do them all the same. As he had reminded Jack last night, he hadn't been cut out for the Army, but neither did he seem very much at home in the City. A big, soft-featured man who favoured blazers and slacks over the ubiquitous double-breasted suits, he had something of the look of a golf-club secretary slightly gone to seed.

'Better eat up,' he said, glancing at his watch. 'We've got to leave in five minutes.'

Jack took the report out of the envelope and glanced through it. It was a hefty document of a hundred pages or so, with a glossy cover bearing the Kroll Associates logo and the word *Confidential*. There was a general introduction, followed by a series of chapters detailing the movement of funds out of Iraq over the past several years and the equities that had been purchased with them. These were broken down in turn into legitimate government investments and private, apparently irregular ones made by individuals or through companies set up in foreign countries. Lot of figures, lots of names: the report would no doubt repay detailed study, but its scope was far too wide to understand at a glance. There were two or three appendices at the back, giving more detailed lists of equities and of Iraqi nationals who owned them.

A name sprang out of one page, making Jack pause midway through raising a forkful of salad. Mohamed Ghani. The name on Colonel Jalloul's false passport, the one he had used on the night he had collected Noura Hamadi from her house.

*Ghani, Mohamed*, the entry read. *Baghdad businessman. Holdings: 200,000 Unilever 5½%, 1988–93; 150,000 First Chicago Overseas Finance 4½%, 1986–96; 175,000 Hamersley Iron Finance* . . .

'Time to go,' Reg interrupted.

The list went on. Mohamed Ghani was named as the owner of around a dozen European and American securities. The figures quoted were their par values in a number of different currencies: dollars, Swiss francs, Dutch guilders, German marks. In anybody's money, the supposedly fictitious Mr Ghani was clearly a millionaire.

This added a puzzling new dimension to the business. But Reg was fidgeting and there was no time to read further. Jack paid for their lunch and they left.

The taxi that they hailed in Moorgate ploughed through heavy traffic, past the Bank of England, the Stock Exchange and the towers of steel and glass that had sprung up around them in the years since Jack and Reg had first worked in the City. Soon they were out of it, however, passing through

Whitechapel into shabbier regions of the East End that he hardly knew. Turning up Cambridge Heath Road, the taxi stopped after half a mile or so just past Bethnal Green tube station. Reg told the driver to wait, and led Jack past a strip of lawn to a cul-de-sac where a row of three-storeyed Victorian houses stood in odd isolation, facing the busy road and backing on to a railway cutting. A few of them were in residential use to judge by the fresh paint on their doorframes and window boxes full of spring flowers; the others had the down-at-heel appearance of low-rent office accommodation and conformed to the generally depressed look of their surroundings. A street sign identified the place as Paradise Row.

One of the buildings had strong iron bars over the windows of its two lower floors. Removing any doubt that this was their destination, there was also a police car parked conspicuously outside, its two occupants eyeing Jack and Reg as they halted at the door. The brass plate beside it said: Kurdish People's Democratic Party.

In spite of its run-down appearance the building had impressive security, a stout oak door with two deadlocks, a peephole and a videophone entry system. A speaker beside the door crackled into life when Reg pressed the buzzer.

'Mr Kilmartin from Hellig Associates,' he announced himself.

'What's your business, Mr Kilmartin?' said a disembodied male voice.

'I've brought Mr Rushton for the appointment made through my office. I have a letter of introduction here.'

'Put it through the letterbox, please.'

Reg did as he was told. A minute went by before the voice said: 'Does Mr Rushton have some identification?'

Reg raised an eyebrow at Jack, who fished out his passport and held it up for inspection through the video scanner.

'Anything else?' said the voice.

'A business card. A driver's licence.'

'Put them all through the letterbox, please. They'll be returned to you in due course.'

The documents vanished through the flap. Jack and Reg waited awkwardly on the doorstep for another two or three minutes, conscious of the camera's scrutiny, before the speaker came to life again. Instead of inviting them in, the man behind the door said: 'Mr Rushton, please follow these instructions carefully. Walk back the way you came. Cross Bethnal Green Road and turn right. Go as far as the post office and wait in front of it. Thank you.'

They looked at each other and shrugged. Apparently this was all that the Kurdish People's Democratic Party intended to reveal of itself. They went back to the roadside, where Jack thanked Reg and watched him leave in the taxi before following the directions he'd been given.

Among the run-down, almost featureless East End streets, he found the post office after a five-minute walk. He stopped outside it and stood looking about, not knowing what he was waiting for. The roadway was choked with traffic. A motorbike pulled in a few yards away and he thought for a moment it had come to meet him; but its rider, a courier in a black-visored helmet, ignored him and trotted into a newsagent's shop.

Ten minutes went by and Jack began to feel faintly absurd. He supposed the Kurdish exiles had good reason to be nervous but he failed to see the point of such crude subterfuge. He also began to wonder whether he'd been wise to surrender his passport and driver's licence to someone he hadn't even seen.

A few spots of rain fell and he took shelter in the doorway of the post office. As he turned to face the road again a battered Bedford van drew up sharply at the kerb. The sliding door on its near side was drawn back and a dark-skinned man was beckoning from the opening.

'Mr Rushton! Here!'

He went over to the van. 'Get in, get in,' the man said,

smiling in spite of the urgency of his tone, making room for Jack to clamber through the door. It was rammed shut immediately, and almost before he could take stock of his surroundings the vehicle was nudging out into the traffic.

He sat down on one of two long benches behind the driver's seat. Apart from the driver there were two men in the dim, windowless rear of the van: the one who had called to him and another who sat beside him, facing Jack. They both wore leather jackets and jeans and they had the muscular, seam-splitting build of Middle Eastern wrestlers. They looked friendly, however, and the one with the smile said: 'We are Abdel Karim's bodyguards, Mr Rushton. This is how we must deal with everyone who meets him. Please let me search you.'

Jack submitted to the probing of powerful hands that patted his body up and down in search of weapons or hidden microphones. The Kurd peered into the envelope containing the Kroll report and passed it back. From a pocket of his jacket he took Jack's passport and driving licence. He studied the passport photograph briefly, comparing it with the face in front of him, before handing the documents over. He seemed anxious to be reassuring, and a moment later Jack understood why.

'We're going to blindfold you, Mr Rushton,' he said.

'*What?*'

'It's a necessary precaution.' Still smiling, the bodyguard produced a broad strip of heavy black cloth. 'It's better that you don't know where we are going.'

'Who do you suppose I'm going to tell, for God's sake?'

'I have to insist that you co-operate. It's safer for Abdel Karim, and safer for you.'

Jack sat back with a sigh and allowed the Kurd to fit the blindfold over his eyes, knotting it behind his head. Just now they didn't seem to be going anywhere much, for the van had barely travelled a few yards before getting caught in a snarl of traffic. From behind, he thought he heard the growl of a motorbike starting up; perhaps that was another of the necessary precautions.

They drove, slowly at first and then at increasing speed, for what seemed about forty minutes. The Kurds conversed quietly in their own language, leaving Jack feeling even more isolated behind his blindfold. Out of idle curiosity he tried to work out the direction they were taking, but soon he became disorientated. To judge by the diminished sound of traffic, they had reached somewhere in the outer suburbs when the van came to a decisive stop. The driver did a slow reverse turn and cut the engine.

'We're here, Mr Rushton.'

He heard the door slide open. The Kurd whom he thought of as Smiler took his arm and helped him out. They went a few steps before passing through a doorway into an atmosphere of spicy cooking smells: a kitchen. From there he was led along a carpeted floor, turned to the left and guided to a seat. He felt fingers fiddling with the knot of his blindfold and suddenly it was whipped away.

The light around him wasn't strong but it made him flinch and close his eyes for some seconds. They watered as soon as he opened them and he had to wipe them with his fingertips, gradually bringing his surroundings into focus. He was in a room of modest size that was apparently doing double duty as a drawing room and office. The high ceiling and the bay window suggested it was part of an older type of house. The curtains were drawn and the only light came from a lamp standing on a desk; untidy heaps of papers and bulging file covers overflowed from the desk and covered every other level surface: the tops of two filing cabinets, a coffee-table, even an area of the floor. Otherwise the furnishings were comfortable in a shabby, nondescript way, among them the sofa on which he found himself sitting and a swivel chair behind the desk, from which Abdel Karim had risen to greet him.

'Good afternoon, Mr Rushton,' he said. He had Reg Kilmartin's letter and Jack's business card in his hand. 'I apologize for the inconvenience you've been put to. There is no alternative, I'm afraid. Over the years the *Mukhabarat* have made three attempts to kill or kidnap me, and I feel it's particularly important at present not to offer them a fourth opportunity.'

Karim looked like a tired man, but he had retained a good-humoured briskness. He held out his hand and Jack stood up and shook it. Smiler was still in the room and Jack was aware now that other people were moving about the house. Somewhere in the background a telephone was ringing. Karim said: 'You'll understand, I hope, if we keep this rather brief. So many awful things are happening to my people in Iraq and Turkey that I am overwhelmed with work. But if you and I have a common enemy in Saddam Hussein, then let's listen to each other.'

'That isn't quite what . . .' Jack began, but Karim had turned to Smiler and was addressing him in Kurdish. The bodyguard left the room, closing the door behind him, and Karim gave his attention to his visitor again.

'Where do we begin?' he said.

Fifty yards away, at the corner of Cricklewood Lane, Ali Shakir waited five minutes before heaving his motorbike off its stand, starting the engine and cruising down the road.

A gentle downhill slope, a long line of redbrick Victorian semis on either side: a typical street of the north London suburbs. Each house had its own scrap of front garden, and some had just enough space to have had garages squeezed in beside them. The house that had been the destination of the Bedford van was one of these.

The road was called Plumtree Road, though no trees of any kind grew on it, just as there seemed not to be any woods in Cricklewood. Such vagaries of the language had puzzled Ali Shakir and his younger brother when they had first come to serve in England eighteen months ago; now they could look back and laugh at the naïve, literal-minded village boys they had been. Ali took pleasure in knowing how easily he had adapted to life here, how readily he had understood its codes, how quickly he had grasped the geography of London and submerged himself in its multiracial diversity. Not even his new superior, the man he called the Mudeer, knew this great city as well as Ali did.

He did not succumb to the sin of pride, though. He knew that God had given him a mission. Like the Mudeer, like Saddam Hussein himself, Ali had been chosen to serve a cause.

The occupants of the van hadn't spotted him as he followed it. He was sure of that; otherwise they would certainly not have led him straight here. Now, as he travelled slowly down Plumtree Road, looking right and left as if searching for an address, he was confident that he drew no attention to himself. Motorcycle couriers were everywhere in London, more numerous than taxis and even more anonymous in their standard uniform of crash helmet and black leathers. Those from the smaller firms did not even wear a sign indicating who they worked for.

Passing by the house he had identified, he was careful to show it no more interest than he did any of the others. The van, which he had seen being reversed through the gateway, was no longer visible; it must have been shut away at once behind the doors of the garage attached to the house. Presumably there was an internal door between them. Bay windows upstairs and down were the building's only distinctive feature, and heavy curtains were drawn across the lower one. There was no sign of a burglar alarm, and no evidence that the police were guarding the place; that would have defeated its purpose anyway.

A panel of coloured glass was set into the upper half of the front door, and above this the street number of the house was picked out in brass lettering. It was 48.

Ali Shakir rode on, turning the next corner and doubling back towards Cricklewood Lane before he halted again, well out of sight of the house. He pulled off his gauntlets, noticing how excitement had suddenly made his palms sweat.

He had waited nearly a week for this moment. In a wider sense, it was the culmination of everything he had trained and prepared for over the past eighteen months. God had rewarded his patience. Watching the offices on Paradise Row from different vantage points, avoiding the scrutiny of the police who protected it, observing how the Kurdish renegades dealt with the reporters and other visitors who arrived there, he had followed a dozen false trails before finally understanding how their system worked.

'There is no god but God,' he murmured to calm himself. He unzipped the leather jacket, took out his mobile phone and called a number in central London. It was answered by his brother, who passed him on at once to the gruff, suspicious voice of the Mudeer, their director.

'Here is young Ali, *ya-ustaz*,' he said respectfully. 'I think I have found the traitor. I have followed a Nazarene to his house.'

# 15

'So,' said Abdel Karim, 'there is not much that happens in Iraq that escapes our attention. We know many of their horrible little secrets. The Ba'ath Party has had absolute power now for well over twenty years, and of course power corrupts, nowhere more so than in the Middle East. During the first period of United Nations sanctions – in the middle of what was supposed to be an economic crisis – there were people making fortunes importing Mercedes Benzes and Scotch whisky and designer clothes. And, of course, exporting the profits. And who were these people? Officials of the Ba'ath. And army and secret police officers. The Iraqis liked to think of themselves as the Prussians of the Middle East, efficient and honest and straightforward, a cut above other Arabs, but now they're the worst of the lot . . .'

Like all people devoted to a cause, Karim was a fluent and obsessive talker. He chain-smoked and paced the over-furnished room, and stabbed a finger at the air to emphasize the points he was making. His conversation was wide-ranging and vastly knowledgeable, and sometimes a bit hard to get to grips with.

'Could I just bring you back to some details in this report?' Jack said. He had the Kroll Associates' dossier open on his lap. 'I'm especially interested in the man named here as Mohamed Ghani. You say you think it's a false name?'

'If there were really a wealthy businessman in Baghdad of that name, then we would know about him,' Karim said. 'Almost certainly he has been invented to cover the true identity of someone in the army or the security

183

services. Perhaps even more than one. They have dozens of these false sets of credentials, possibly hundreds of them, ready-made for people to step into: passports, citizenship papers, driving licences. Ostensibly they exist to allow Iraqi spies and agents to travel and live undercover abroad, but they are just as convenient for hiding the real identities of people moving money around.

'These privileged cronies of Saddam Hussein have been allowed for years to tap into the foreign revenue accounts. A lot of the dollars that Iraq earns from its oil sales have been re-exported almost as soon as they arrive, into banks in the West. And then laundered through investments in shares, bonds, real estate . . .'

Jack said: 'Mohamed Ghani, or whatever his real name is, seems to have put most of his money into the international bond market. Have you any record of where the bonds were issued?'

'Usually for a big issue there is a consortium of banks involved. But wait, I may have an index here.' Karim went to his desk and began hunting through the chaotic heap of files. He opened and closed several before finding what seemed to be the right one. 'Remind me of the names.'

Jack stood up and joined him, with the report open at the page of the appendix where Ghani's holdings were listed. Karim flicked impatiently through sheets of typed records as Jack recited the titles of respected multinationals and state-backed enterprises that had sought to raise working capital on the bond market: Unilever, Thyssen, Krupps, and public utility companies in half a dozen countries. In turn, Karim read out the names of the banks that had had a share in floating each issue.

There was one thing that all Ghani's securities had in common. The Handelsbank Bauer in Zurich was the only bank that had sold bonds in every one of the companies.

Coincidence? It was possible.

Karim slapped the file shut. 'Does that tell you anything?'

'I'm not sure. It's quite usual for someone who has money to invest but no expertise in the markets to put himself in the hands of a bank, which then recommends various purchases and manages the portfolio for him. Naturally the bank is inclined to favour its own issues, because it often picks up a special commission on them. That's what could have happened with Ghani. But it's also usual in Switzerland for a foreigner to be recommended to a particular bank by someone on the spot. Do you have the names of any brokers or middlemen who might have been involved?'

'I'm afraid not. You know how secretive the Swiss can be. Besides, Kroll's were interested only in establishing a direct connection between the Iraqis and their holdings, not in the people in between.'

'That index of yours wasn't incorporated into the report, then? Could you let me have a copy of it?'

'Certainly. We have a photocopier upstairs.'

Karim detached four or five pages from the file, went to the door and called to someone. A young woman appeared and listened to his instructions. Perhaps the index would be more revealing once he'd had a chance to study it, Jack thought. For the moment it seemed to raise more questions than it answered. Colonel Jalloul had signed the agreement with Hamadi and opened his account at the bank under his real name, so he could hardly have switched to the alias of Mohamed Ghani for the purpose of buying bonds. Besides, the million dollars Hamadi had paid him would have covered only a fraction of the investments credited to Ghani. Unless he'd already been holding assets under that name and had not revealed the fact. This, however, seemed to contradict another impression of the man that Abdel Karim had referred to.

Jalloul's name hadn't rung any bells for Karim at first, but then he had looked up his files and found confirmation from a source in Baghdad that Jalloul was indeed missing. He had been posted to Kuwait at the start of the occupation, and he never came back. There was no indication that he had been recalled to Iraq, or arrested or executed. He had simply disappeared.

Karim closed the door and Jack heard the woman's footsteps retreating up the stairs. He said: 'There's no evidence that Jalloul was one of the people with their fingers in the till?'

'None that I have seen. That was a privilege reserved for the sort of party lackeys I told you about, and he was apparently not one of those.'

'Politically out of favour?'

'Politically,' said Karim, 'he was not an enthusiast, and that's all it takes to be distrusted. You mentioned that Jalloul was under suspicion by General Malik of the *Mukhabarat* – now there was a typical product of the regime. A bully, a thug, a yes-man and a crook.'

'Was Malik one of the favoured few?' Jack indicated the Kroll report.

'Certainly. But his name isn't there because we never found any evidence connecting him with funds being milked out of the treasury. And since he's dead now, we probably never will. But perhaps there is your answer to the question of what became of Jalloul. Malik could have had him quietly eliminated while they were both in Kuwait.' Karim paused and glanced at his watch. 'Unless you have further questions, Mr Rushton, I believe I've told you everything I can. What was the information that you thought might interest me?'

'It isn't hard information, exactly. In fact, I can't call it anything much stronger than gossip.'

He began to tell the story about the missing gold. Halfway through, he was interrupted by a knock at the door and the woman assistant entered. She handed the photocopies to Karim and left. Before Jack could carry on, the Kurd halted him with a gesture.

'Let me save us both some time. Yes, I know of these rumours about the gold. In fact, I asked my people to check some of them out, but nothing can be pinned down. By all accounts there *was* a shortfall in the amount that was delivered to Baghdad, but there are conflicting stories about how much was missing. One version I heard was that part of the consignment was flown out of Kuwait to northern Iraq – to Kurdistan, in fact, my part of the country – and taken on to somewhere else by road. But that is just as impossible to verify as any of the other yarns.'

'Assuming it is missing,' Jack said, 'the Iraqis haven't been in a position to try to recover it over the past few months. And the Kuwaitis don't seem to care as long as they get compensated for it. So if there really is a pile of gold stashed somewhere in the Middle East, nobody is looking too hard for it. It isn't quite as hot as it might be in other circumstances. It would make a nice little windfall for someone.'

'No doubt,' said Karim with a smile. 'But there is also gold at the end of a rainbow, isn't there? There's nothing like a story of missing treasure to get people's imagination going.'

Or to attract the interest of hard-up revolutionaries, Jack thought. Karim's dismissive attitude didn't quite square with the trouble he had taken to chase up the rumours. But he was looking at his watch again and Jack guessed he was close to outstaying his welcome.

It was approaching four o'clock when he was escorted from the house. He submitted more resignedly this time to the blindfold that was tied in place before he was guided out to the van. Karim's friendly bodyguards said they were heading for central London and could drop him wherever he wanted. He said any tube station would be fine, and twenty minutes later he was blinking into the dull afternoon light beneath an Underground sign at Baker Street.

He caught a train back to Waterloo. In the concourse of the main-line station he went to one of a row of open telephone cubicles, intending to try the number he had been given for Colonel Thorpe in Sandhurst and then realizing he had left it at home. He rang directory enquiries again, forced almost to shout out the name and address over the background din of the station. He dialled the number they gave him and again got no reply.

In a dither he wandered across the concourse. Perhaps he should do what he'd been contemplating earlier and go straight to Thorpe's home. It should be easy enough to get there from here. He still didn't know whether this Thorpe was the same one Reg had referred to, let alone whether he could be of any help; all the same, this evening offered the last chance Jack would have to make contact with him before leaving for Zurich tomorrow.

He stood studying the complicated timetable boards. Like most Londoners he knew where his own trains went, and roughly when, but was unfamiliar with the other loops of the outer-suburban network. To get to Sandhurst he would have to change at Guildford, or was it Aldershot? He was still trying to work this out when he was distracted by a crackling announcement that the 4:44 Inter-City to Southampton would soon be leaving from Platform Ten, stopping at Woking and Basingstoke and . . .

Woking was near enough to his destination and the express train would get him there sooner. With three minutes in hand, he hurried to the ticket office. The crowds were just beginning to swell towards their rush-hour flood but he reached a vacant window quickly and bought a one-way ticket. As he turned away he bumped shoulders with a man close behind him who must have had the same idea, a slight, foreign-looking young man in dark clothes who'd been standing next to him at the information boards.

Muttering an apology, Jack ran to the barrier of Platform Ten. He made the train with half a minute to spare and found a window seat just as the train jarred into motion. The seat faced back down the platform and he could see that he had been the last to board. The other

188

man either hadn't got his ticket in time or had changed his mind.

A few minutes later, as the train was rushing between the grey back walls of the south-west London suburbs, Jack's thoughts were thrown inexplicably back to the young man. Something about him must have imprinted itself on Jack's subconscious, but he couldn't identify it. The familiar cast of features, perhaps, of a Gulf Arab – but, no, there were plenty of those to be seen in London. Maybe it was the way the man had stood so near to him, both at the timetable boards and at the ticket window, almost as though he wanted to speak to him but had lost the courage. Come to think of it, someone had been standing close behind him when he'd made that phone call as well.

Then Jack remembered the way the man had been dressed. The resolution of one doubt has a way of banishing others. He forgot his earlier speculations as he recognized that what he had found odd, or at least out of place, about the man, were the black leather trousers and jacket, and the black, dark-visored helmet that he carried. Why would a man dressed for riding a motorbike be thinking of catching a train?

The answer, no doubt, would be even more banal than the question. Jack dismissed it from his mind.

# 16

He reached Woking at a quarter past five and took a taxi from the station. It would be a ten-mile journey, the driver said, warning him obliquely about the likely size of the fare. Jack asked him about getting back and he said public transport would be a problem after six o'clock; if Jack didn't expect to be too long it would be advisable to have the cab wait for him.

The driver was talkative. He had opinions on many topics, though his favourite one appeared to be the incompetent or antisocial behaviour of other motorists. Only half-listening, Jack leaned back and watched the passing scenery. Though usually regarded as part of the London stockbroker belt, this corner of south-east England, where Surrey, Berkshire and Hampshire met up, was also the heartland of the British military establishment. Pleasant old towns like Aldershot, Guildford and Camberley were home to thousands of army families, and the landscape between them was dotted with camps, depots and training centres. Of these institutions the two most famous were the Army Staff College and the Royal Military College; although conventionally known as Camberley and Sandhurst, the driver took the opportunity to explain, they actually shared the same extensive grounds. He pointed them out as the taxi crossed a bridge over the River Blackwater, a broad sweep of parkland with a lake in the middle and beyond it just a glimpse of buildings, looking like rambling extensions to a great country house.

Sandhurst itself was a village of prosperous Home Counties proportions and Green Lane was exactly what you would expect of it, narrow and leafy and lined with

190

cosy period houses. Among them, the address of Colonel A.D. Thorpe was a bit of an oddity, a small detached bungalow of pale yellow brick, only a few years old, standing in a garden not yet mature enough to have any character. Walking up the flagstoned path, however, Jack could see that considerable work had gone into edging the lawn, weeding the borders and shaping the low griselinia hedge, suggesting that the owner was not lacking in energy.

There was a notice tacked to the front door, crudely hand-printed on a square of cardboard. It said, mystifyingly, VEGETABLES, and had an arrow pointing to the right.

Jack rang the bell and heard it echo through the house. He waited a minute and rang it again, but by now he was sure no-one was going to answer. He stepped away and was about to follow the direction of the mysterious sign when a man appeared around the corner of the bungalow, a rather wild-looking man with a lined, weather-beaten face and unkempt grey hair. He wore an Aran sweater with holes in the elbows, and a pair of frayed corduroy trousers tucked into wellington boots. The boots, the trousers and his hands were caked in mud. He carried a garden fork which he brandished at Jack in a vaguely threatening way.

'You were supposed to be here this morning,' he called.

'I'm sorry . . .?' Jack began nervously.

'So I should think. Why can't you people stick to your arrangements? I take it you have at least brought my Rotovator?'

The tone of sternness was a little diminished by the man's lilting West Country accent. Jack said: 'I think there's some confusion here. I'm looking for a Major, or possibly a Colonel, David Thorpe.'

'Lieutenant-Colonel. No confusion. I rose one rank on retirement.'

'What I meant was that you must be mixing me up with someone else. I'm Jack Rushton, and your name was given to me by a former fellow-officer of yours. I apologize for turning up without notice. I've tried to phone you twice today.'

The unlikely figure of Colonel Thorpe had moved closer. He was studying Jack suspiciously in the evening light, and now he glanced towards the front gate and saw the waiting taxi. He relaxed and gave a chuckle.

'My mistake.' He stepped forward, offered his hand and then remembered the mud and withdrew it. He laughed again, this time with a mischievous awareness of his visitor's own embarrassment. He knew that Jack had taken him, in those clothes and with that strong accent, for a gardener or a casual workman.

'I've been expecting a Rotovator to be delivered. A tilling machine, that is. Nobody ever turns up when they say they will these days. And you wouldn't have got me on the phone because I'm mostly out of doors at this time of year. I went into the organic vegetable business when I retired,' he explained, pointing to the cardboard notice, 'only the local council won't let me put up a proper sign. Who do you say sent you?'

'A chap called Reg Kilmartin. Used to be with you in the Royal Green Jackets.' Colonel Thorpe frowned as he tried to recall the name, and Jack hurried on. 'He was my business partner until recently. He thought you might be able to tell me something about a man who was once a student at the Staff College.'

'The Green Jackets, eh? That *was* a long time ago.' Thorpe was still struggling to remember Reg Kilmartin. He glanced up at the fading light. 'I'm planting out some lettuce seedlings and I've got to finish before dark. Come round the back.'

Jack followed him down a path at the side of the house. Its modest front garden had been deceptive; a narrow strip of ground to the rear opened out on a much wider one running about eighty yards to the wooden boundary fence. Almost all of it was under intensive cultivation. Two long greenhouses occupied one side of the land; the rest was either planted or being made ready for planting. Rich crops of spinach, broccoli, cabbages, leeks and cauliflowers stood in military-straight rows; likewise newly dug potato and onion drills, and lengths of wire mesh set up to support peas and beans. There wasn't a weed in sight.

'You look after all this yourself?' Jack asked.

'My wife used to help me but she died last year.' Thorpe waved a hand as though to ward off any offer of sympathy. 'It's an acre and a half; anyone should be able to make a living from that. We built this house when I retired, and bought what used to be a paddock over there. Once we were established we started getting customers from miles around. Got shops and restaurants buying regularly from me now.

'Not many overheads to this if you plan it properly. Nothing wasted, everything recycled. No weedkillers or chemical fertilizers, just good vegetable compost and manure from cows that haven't been fed on animal protein. The soil will repay you if you respect it. No, I'm not one of those New Age types,' Thorpe said with a grin, 'burying quartz crystals by the full moon and all that, but I'm afraid I may have become a bit of a sage. This was something I'd always wanted to do. I'm a son of the soil, from Dorset farming stock.'

He led Jack to a newly dug and raked bed beside the greenhouses. Jamming the fork in the ground, he knelt beside a tray of seedlings and began scooping holes for them with a trowel, setting each one in place and packing the rich tilth around its roots. He seemed to have absorbed himself so instantly in the task that Jack hesitated to speak again.

Eventually, he said: 'You'll have to pardon my ignorance. What exactly do people go to do at Camberley?'

'They don't just go there,' Thorpe said sternly. 'It's a privilege offered to a few outstanding officers who are considered to have top-brass potential. They go through an intellectually rigorous course in a variety of disciplines.

Strategy, planning, logistics and other subjects. Not everyone gets through the course. Those who do get three magic letters after their names: PSC, Passed Staff College. Known in the trade as Practically Second to Christ.'

He looked up and chuckled once more, not wanting to be taken too seriously. 'The subject I taught was guerrilla warfare, theory and practice. Saw it at firsthand in Malaya, Kenya, Cyprus, Aden. As for the theory, nobody's ever stated it better than Sun Tzu. He was a Chinese general in the fifth century BC. Another sage. The man who said every battle was won before it was fought. Who first said: Know your enemy. Where he's weak, attack him. Where he's strong, avoid him. The basis of all good strategy, really. Who's this fellow you want to talk about?' Thorpe asked abruptly.

'He's an Iraqi. He was at Camberley in nineteen eighty, and apparently he passed out with honours. He was a captain at the time, called Ibrahim Jalloul.'

Jack couldn't be sure, but he thought he saw a momentary wariness in the colonel's eyes. He said: 'I've got a photograph of him, taken while he was here, if that's any help.'

He took out the group picture that Major Al-Shaheb had given him. He showed it to Thorpe, pointing to the ringed head in the second row. The colonel studied it briefly, his expression revealing nothing now, before turning back to his lettuces.

'Where did you get that?' he said.

'I was given it in Kuwait, together with some details about his background. I'm looking for more.'

'Nineteen eighty, eh? That was the year the first Gulf War broke out. We had quite a few chaps from the Middle East in the college at the time,' Thorpe said vaguely, 'under various military assistance agreements. Iraqis, Turks. Even some Iranians, but they stopped coming because our government had put their money on Saddam Hussein against the Ayatollah. Never thought that was a good idea myself, but that's bound to seem the wisdom of hindsight.' He turned and gave Jack a meaningful look. 'If I happen to remember Ibrahim Jalloul, I would need to know exactly why you were interested in him.'

He had repeated the name with a casual fluency that made Jack feel almost certain it was familiar to him. Perhaps he had been talking to give himself time to think.

'Jalloul is a colonel now, in Iraqi Military Intelligence. At least he was, until last August. He disappeared in Kuwait, leaving a rather complicated financial tangle behind him. I've been asked to try to find him.'

'Disappeared? How?'

'Just vanished.' Jack wasn't going to tell the whole story without an offer of something in return.

'And what are you, Rushton? Some sort of private detective?'

'Not exactly. I'm a business consultant. I'm working on behalf of a man who did a deal with Jalloul. There's no question of any legal action being taken against him; in fact, it would probably be to his advantage to settle this mess.'

'And you came to me just on the off-chance that I might have known him?' Thorpe said dubiously.

'Yes. If you do remember him, I'd be grateful for anything you can tell me that might suggest where he's gone. In confidence, of course.'

Thorpe had finished pricking out the seedlings. He got to his feet, picked up a water hose and began gently spraying the plants. Glancing at Jack again, he seemed to be weighing him up, considering whether he was to be trusted. Finally, he said: 'How much do you actually know about Jalloul? As a person, I mean.'

'Hardly anything, really.'

'And do you realize that I'm still subject to the Official Secrets Act?'

'No, I didn't. Does it matter?'

'It's binding for life. Nonsensical, perhaps, but there it is.' He paused. 'I can't see that it'll make any difference now. I'll tell you what I can, provided I have your word that my name is kept strictly out of it. Whether it'll be of any use to you is another matter. There's an aspect to this that may still be sensitive, which is why I mentioned the Official Secrets Act.'

'I can promise you absolute confidentiality,' Jack said.

'Good. I did recognize that photograph, and I have a particular reason for remembering Ibrahim Jalloul. He got himself into a bit of a mess here as well, you see. But satisfy my curiosity on one point first. You say he's disappeared. Do you know what's become of his wife?'

'Wife?' Jack said blankly.

'Didn't you know he was married?'

'No. Oh, yes, as a matter of fact . . .'

'As I recall from my time in Aden, Arabs are almost always married by their mid-twenties. In fact, anyone who isn't is considered a bit peculiar.'

That was true, Jack reflected. He remembered a passing reference that Al-Shaheb had made to a wife whose position might have helped Jalloul's career. In a patriarchal society it was not something that any man would want to emphasize.

'In his case,' Thorpe said, 'it was rather more complicated. When I refer to his wife, I don't necessarily know who I'm talking about. There were two women in his life at the time, you see: one Iraqi, one French. I know they don't practise polygamy in Iraq, at least among Jalloul's class, so if he is married now it would have to be to one or the other.' Seeing the bewildered look on Jack's face, he grinned: then he glanced up at the gathering darkness. 'I'm going to have to start at the beginning, I see. I'm finished out here anyway. Time to offer you a drink, I think.'

# 17

The yellow-brick bungalow, unprepossessing from the outside, revealed an interior that was surprisingly warm and welcoming, with a strong accent on wood. The shining teak floors, mahogany wall panels and bookshelves made it like a scaled-down version of a much grander house. Jack had asked the taxi driver to wait a bit longer, and while Colonel Thorpe went to change from his workclothes he sat in a drawing room cluttered with what he supposed were the scavengings of the soldier's travels. A silk-cushioned sofa and chairs made of Indian cane were grouped around the fireplace, overlooked by a display of African tribal masks. A big ebony chest supported a tray of beaten Arab brass holding bottles and decanters. On the floor in one corner a small stuffed crocodile peered from behind a Chinese lacquered screen.

When Thorpe rejoined him he was wearing a green cashmere pullover, cavalry twill trousers and brogues. He had washed off the mud and slicked down his wild grey hair, and looked presentable almost to the point of elegance. He lit the fire that was prepared in the grate, poured whisky for them both and sat facing Jack across the hearth.

'I have no idea where you might find Jalloul,' he said, 'but I'll tell you what I know of the period he spent at the Staff College. I want to emphasize that my role was purely peripheral, that I was just called in to give my advice about him. Or, rather, about the mess that I mentioned.

'He arrived in June of nineteen eighty on a six-month course. It was pretty intensive, and there was hardly any leave apart from weekends. The officers from foreign armies – those from poorer or more distant countries, at least – rarely got a chance to pay a visit home. They could feel a bit lost, thrown back on each other's company; Jalloul, I remember, struck up quite a close friendship with a fellow from the Turkish army.

'We did have arrangements for trying to give them a bit of social life. We'd organize parties and sightseeing trips to London, and those of us with families living near by would ask them home for an evening or to spend a weekend.

'It was on one of those weekends, quite early in his stay, that Jalloul met this French girl, Nadine – I forget the surname. She was an au pair, living with the family of a major called Ralph Purchase over at Farnborough, and Jalloul and his Turkish friend were invited to stay there. Well, Jalloul and the girl fell for each other. Instantly and heavily. The attraction was understandable. They were both rather fish out of water in this country, probably both a bit lonely. She was a pretty girl, perhaps the first European woman he'd ever got to know. As for him, he had that sort of innocent charm that Arabs can have. He also wasn't strongly religious, and he was actually quite westernized in his thinking.

'This was more than infatuation, or at least it quickly became more. They weren't children. He was twenty-nine or thirty, she was about twenty-three. They fell seriously in love and they wanted to spend the rest of their lives together. There was just one small obstacle: Jalloul had a wife in Baghdad. He'd been married for three years.'

'Did Nadine know about the wife?' Jack asked.

'Oh, yes. He was completely honest with her. Technically there was nothing to stop him getting a divorce and remarrying: that's easily done in Arab countries, as you know. The difficulty was that he came from a poor family and his wife, apparently, was from a rich and quite powerful one. I believe they were well in with the people around Saddam Hussein. If he'd gone back and announced that he was ditching her for some Western slut . . . well, it would have been disastrous. It would have meant the end of his army career. He would also have dishonoured his wife's family, and that might be positively dangerous. They hadn't fully accepted him anyway, since he was a Shi'a Muslim and they were Sunnis. It wasn't impossible that he'd be arrested, accused of some political crime, perhaps executed. They have a word out there for that sort of patronage.'

'*Wasta*,' said Jack.

'That's it. Jalloul was willing to face his responsibilities, but he couldn't take Nadine back to Iraq and neither could he stay here. Then things got even more complicated.'

Night had fully fallen and Thorpe stood up to close the curtains. Before sitting down again he replenished their drinks.

'Nadine went home to visit her family that September. They were country people from somewhere in the Franche-Comté region, I believe. While she was there she went to see the family doctor, who confirmed what she'd begun to suspect. She was pregnant. She thought about the implications, and when she came back here she told Jalloul what she'd decided. She was going to keep the baby, regardless of what happened to them. She wasn't putting pressure on him; she was just one of those women who love children and find the idea of abortion abhorrent.

'This left him with the choice of going back to Iraq, resuming his career and giving up Nadine and the child, or finding some way of staying with her in Europe. But neither of them had any money to speak of. He had no way of earning a living and no right of residence. He could acquire French citizenship by marrying her, perhaps, but he'd need to get a divorce first, and to do that he'd have to return to Iraq anyway. He even confided in his friend from Turkey – don't remember his name either – and asked what the chances were of settling there.

'He was running out of time anyway. Iraq had just gone to war with Iran, and he thought he might be recalled to regular service. At that point he threw himself on the mercy of the British Army.

'He asked for a meeting with our commandant, told him the whole story and made an odd request. He wanted to know if he'd be allowed to stay here as a political refugee, on the grounds that he'd face persecution if he returned home. Well, the CO was a bit taken aback, but he promised to make an informal enquiry to the Home Office. He was told that any such request would be turned down flat: Jalloul's problem was personal, not political, they said, and he couldn't possibly qualify for refugee status.

'When he heard this he came up with another idea: even more bizarre on the face of it. If he couldn't have Nadine now he was prepared to wait, bide his time, make some plan to provide for their future. Now we're at the sensitive bit I mentioned. His idea was this: he would go back to Iraq, he'd rejoin his unit . . . and become a spy.'

Thorpe leaned back in his chair, smiling at Jack's astonishment. 'Yes, he was willing to provide our intelligence services with secret military information from Iraq in exchange for money paid into a foreign bank account. He had it all worked out. He'd do it for a fixed period, say three or four years, and then he'd find some way of getting a divorce and slip out of the country. He'd talked it over with Nadine and she was willing to go back to France, have her baby and wait for him.'

'And what happened?'

'Well, the CO didn't want the college involved. He had its reputation to consider. It was bad enough that a student had got involved in an extra-marital affair, but it would be a lot worse if Camberley came to be seen as a place where foreign officers were recruited to spy on their own countries. He called in a couple of us – the instructors who knew Jalloul best – to help him make a decision.

'The view that prevailed was that we ought to put Military Intelligence discreetly into the picture and let them take it from there. Personally I thought they would be mad not to try and do a deal with Jalloul. His idea wasn't at all far-fetched. Iraq wasn't just some tin-pot dictatorship; it was a major oil producer engaged in a war with another one. Everything that happens in the Gulf affects the strategic interests of the West. Firsthand intelligence from out there would have been invaluable.

'What happened did nobody any good in the end. It became a hot potato that no-one wanted to handle. MI passed it on to the spooks in London, the Secret Intelligence Service, who in turn felt obliged to put it up to their political masters. We never heard officially what the outcome was, but the CO was quietly tipped off that the answer was no. SIS said they thought Jalloul's motives were suspect. Behind that, I imagine, was the fact that our government saw the Iranians and their Islamic revolution as the real threat at the time. Even if we were technically neutral we were secretly hoping for Iraq to win that war. It might not look very nice if one of their officers should happen to be exposed as a British agent.

'In the catalogue of lost opportunities, that must rank with the man who said nobody would buy sliced bread. Can you imagine what it might have meant to have someone supplying intelligence from Iraq right through the early eighties? If we'd had a proper assessment of their intentions and capabilities, we might have been forewarned about the invasion of Kuwait, perhaps even have prevented it. But that's the wisdom of hindsight again.'

'So what did become of Jalloul?' Jack asked.

'The story ends in an anticlimax, I'm afraid.' Thorpe shrugged and sipped his whisky. 'He wasn't summoned back early, he finished his course in December and had no option but to go home. Nadine went back to France and duly had her baby, I gather. Ralph Purchase's wife stayed in touch with her for a while. Perhaps she and Jalloul had some agreement to join up again one day, but from what you tell me it can't have happened. Perhaps the passion fizzled out.'

'Have you any idea where I could find Nadine now? Would Mrs Purchase know?'

'Well, I wonder,' Thorpe said dubiously. 'You could be raking up some painful memories. And the business about the spying is still sensitive.'

'That needn't be mentioned. And I'd be as discreet as possible about everything else.'

'All right, I'll ring her. Pour yourself another drink.'

Thorpe left the room and a minute later could be heard murmuring into the phone in the hall. Jack stood up but did not refill his glass, conscious of some need to keep all his wits about him. Instead he wandered around the room, examining the colonel's exotic artefacts until he returned, flourishing a slip of paper torn from a notepad.

'I don't know if this will help,' he said. 'The Purchases and the girl did write to each other occasionally – well, woman, she'd be thirty-three or four now – for about three years after she went home. Then they lost touch. She'd had a baby boy in April, eighty-one, and at the time of her last letter she and the child were still living with her family. This is the address. It's a village not far from Belfort, I gather. But, of course, she could be anywhere by now.'

Jack took the note and read what Thorpe had written: Nadine Schuster, Vaux-sur-Autruche 90203, Territoire de Belfort.

'There's no phone number. Or if there is, she never gave it. She also never mentioned Jalloul in her letters. You could be on a wild-goose chase.

'I feel as if I've been on one for several days,' Jack said with a grin. 'But thank you, Colonel, this could be very helpful. I'm grateful for your time, and I won't waste any more of it.'

'Just leave my name right out of any other discussions you have,' Thorpe said, 'and that will be thanks enough.'

'By the way, I got a glimpse of some files on Jalloul while I was in Kuwait,' Jack said. 'Intelligence files. And there were some notes typed in English among them. Do you suppose the SIS might have passed their old report on to the Kuwaitis?'

'It wouldn't surprise me. They're supposed to be our latest allies, after all. If we couldn't make use of him, perhaps they could. Goodbye, then. And good luck with your investigation.'

'Good luck with your vegetables.'

They shook hands and Jack left the house. The taxi driver had dozed off in his seat and he started when Jack opened the rear door.

'Sorry,' he said. 'I've had a long day.'

'I don't suppose you feel like driving me to Banstead, then?'

'Banstead? Halfway across London, isn't it?'

'It isn't that far. But God knows how long it would take me on the trains.'

'It's your money,' the driver said, pulling away from the kerb and glancing at the meter, which already showed a healthy tally. A short way down the narrow lane he winced at a dazzle in his mirror as a car started up behind them and its lights came on at high beam.

'Country drivers,' he muttered. 'Never dip their bloody lights. Never yield properly at junctions. Drive slowly in the fast lane and don't keep their distance.'

Confounding two of these generalizations, the car behind immediately dimmed its beams and then maintained a respectable gap between itself and the cab as they threaded their way out of Sandhurst. Undeterred, the driver kept up his litany of complaints about rural motorists, but this time Jack wasn't even half-listening. He had learned a great deal in the past few hours and he was trying to put it all into some kind of order.

Alison wasn't in when he got home just after eight o'clock. It turned out that she'd gone across the road for a drink with the Reynolds, and their teenaged daughter and her boyfriend had come over to babysit. They had hired a couple of videos and asked if he minded their staying to watch them. He told them to take their time. He checked on the twins, found them fast asleep and went back downstairs to the kitchen. There was no sign that Alison had included him in her catering arrangements for the evening, no cartoon-style dinner-in-the-oven note: he guessed the two of them were long past the stage where he could expect that sort of thing. Last night's meal had been in the nature of a farewell feast.

He heated soup from a can and took it through to the dining room. When he had eaten he opened the Kroll report and read it, for the first time, from cover to cover. Then he spread the pages of Abdel Karim's index on the table and turned back to the section of the report that listed the names of those Iraqis favoured with the ownership of substantial foreign assets. Making notes on a pad, he began the same laborious process of cross-checking that he and Karim had employed in the case of Mohamed Ghani.

It took him over an hour to go through them all. When he had finished he had a list of five names to go with that of Ghani. The single factor they had in common was that all their holdings were in bond issues that had been floated by the Handelsbank Bauer. The total value of the bonds was in the region of twenty-six million dollars.

Jack stood up and paced about the room, trying to assess the significance of what he had learned, feeling himself on the brink of a discovery that was both tantalizing and scary. It had occurred to him, riding back in the taxi, that he might be going off at a tangent with this business of the bonds, letting himself get distracted from his main purpose of tracing Jalloul. Now, he sensed, he had got an entirely new slant on the whole thing.

There was another small piece of research to be done. He went through to the drawing room, to a section of the bookshelves where he kept maps and guidebooks retained from holiday and business travels. Among them he found a Michelin road map of France, which he spread out on the coffee-table. The Franche-Comté region wasn't marked as such on the map, but by scanning the eastern half of the country he quickly located the town called Belfort. It was the prefecture of a tiny department of the same name, tucked down in the south-eastern corner. The village of Vaux-sur-Autruche, which had been the home of Nadine Schuster, was not shown, suggesting it was not a place of much significance. One thing that did strike him about Belfort was its proximity to the Swiss border, which at its nearest point was only about twenty kilometres away. From Zurich it couldn't be much more than a hundred and fifty. He could drive there and back in half a day.

Which reminded him that he'd better book a taxi to take him to the airport. On the hall table beside the telephone he saw for the first time a message that Alison had written on the memo pad.

It said: Dale Griggs. And gave a phone number.

Jack blinked disbelievingly at the name. The number began with 071, the prefix for central London. Couldn't be. It must be part of an international code. But the code for Kuwait was 965, and phone numbers there had no prefix.

There was no indication of what time Dale had phoned. Through the hall window Jack glanced across at the Reynolds' house, wondering if he should go over there and ask Alison to explain this bald message. But that might be awkward. No doubt she was busy consolidating her neighbours' sympathy with horror stories about her marriage. Besides, he had never mentioned Dale's existence to Alison and had no idea what they might have said to each other on the phone. What it came down to was that the sight of her name was enough to bring back an irrational sense of guilt: that bloody dream again.

He dialled the number. A man's voice answered, without enthusiasm: 'Henderson Hotel.'

'Miss Dale Griggs, please.'

'Hold on.'

Taped country-and-western music filled the earpiece for a time. When a woman's voice came on he still wasn't sure it was her.

'Dale?'

'Yes.'

'It's Jack Rushton.'

'Jack!' She sounded delighted. 'I'd about given you up.'

'What are you doing here?'

'I told you I was coming to Europe on vacation. Turned out to be sooner than I expected. I was expelled from Kuwait yesterday, and the first flight I could get out of Saudi was to London.'

'Expelled?'

'Yep. They refused to renew my residence permit, told me to leave right away. No more than I expected, but kind of sudden all the same. So here I am in the good old Henderson Hotel in Bloomsbury. Listen, is it embarrassing for you to talk?'

'No. Why?'

'Your wife didn't sound exactly overjoyed to get my call,' Dale said. 'Surprised, then kind of peeved.'

'Yes, I suppose she would be.'

'Things still like that, huh? Well, I don't want to be the cause of any extra grief. If you want to just forget that I called—'

'No, of course not. What's on your mind?'

'This is going to be embarrassing, so bear with me. You remember me saying I was having problems getting my back pay out of the Ministry of Education? Well, they still haven't forked out, and now that I'm not in the country to needle them, God knows how long it will take. I do have some money back in the States, but it's tied up in stocks and it'll take a couple of weeks to get over here. My credit cards are up to their limits and . . .'

'And you're short of cash. Before you ask, yes, I do remember offering to let you have some. The offer still stands.'

'I hate having to ask, Jack, and I wouldn't if there was any alternative. Right now I don't even have the price of the air fare home. It would be a very short-term loan, I promise.'

'How much do you need?'

'Is five hundred pounds too much?'

'No. The only problem is getting it to you. I'm flying to Zurich tomorrow morning.'

'Could I come see you tonight, then? No, I guess that wouldn't be a good idea. Is there someplace near your home that we could meet?'

'I'm out in the suburbs. It would take you ages to get here.' He glanced at his watch. 'Listen, I'll bring it to you now. Where is your hotel, exactly?'

'Russell Square. But really, Jack, I can't expect—'

'I'll be there in an hour or less.'

He cut short her protests and put down the phone. The two teenagers were still in the sitting room and he asked them if they would mind staying on a bit longer. Whenever they wanted to go home, he suggested, they should ask Alison to come back.

He felt a tremor of illicit excitement as he closed the front door behind him and went to the garage. Starting Alison's car and easing it down the drive, he saw a curtain twitch at a downstairs window of the Reynolds' house. He guessed with malicious satisfaction that this would give them all something new to talk about.

# 18

It was an easy run into London but he had to circle Russell Square twice before he spotted the Henderson Hotel, sandwiched between a number of similar small establishments.

He parked the car and went inside. The lobby was furnished with nondescript easy chairs in which two or three guests sat watching a late programme on television. A night clerk, presumably the owner of the dispirited voice on the phone, sat behind the desk and gave Dale a covertly lascivious look as she rose from a seat near by and walked past him to greet Jack.

Her blond hair was down and fluffed out around her face, with a stray ringlet falling against one cheek. She was wearing a chocolate-coloured woollen dress, dark brown tights and a leather belt that emphasized her narrow waist and bony hips. She was lightly made up and didn't look tired after her journey; if anything she seemed fresher and more cheerful than she had been in Kuwait.

She smiled and kissed his cheek, then gestured apologetically around her. 'It isn't Claridge's,' she said, 'but at least I knew it wasn't going to break the bank. I've stayed here before. Refuge of penniless American assistant professors putting in research time at London U and the British Museum. It's so good of you to do this, Jack. I can't tell you how much I appreciate it.'

'It's no more than I promised in Kuwait.' He glanced round and lowered his voice. 'It's all in cash. I don't think I should give it to you here.'

'Come up to my room,' she said. 'I can offer you a drink, which is the least I should do.'

She led him, past the longing gaze of the clerk, to a tiny lift that churned its way up to the third floor. The Henderson had suffered the fate of other old London houses converted into hotels, of having its room space severely curtailed by the introduction of a lift shaft and bathrooms, so it was all odd corners and awkward turnings. Dale's room was down a corridor to the rear of the building, a narrow cell into which a single bed, a combination fitted wardrobe and chest of drawers, a miniature desk and a chair had been ingeniously crammed. There were also a hand-basin and a shower cubicle. Velvet curtains concealed what Jack suspected was a view of an air shaft.

Dale hauled a shoulder bag from the wardrobe and took out a bottle of Remy Martin. 'Thank God for duty-free,' she said. 'None of this stuff in Riyadh.' She found two toothglasses, and while she opened the bottle and poured the brandy Jack took out his wallet. He removed the wad of twenty-pound notes that he had plundered, through a cash dispenser in Banstead, from his bank and credit card accounts, and placed it on the desk.

It caught her eye as she handed him his drink. She looked at him suspiciously. 'How much is that?'

'A thousand. I thought what you asked for was too modest.'

'Jack, I can't accept that!'

'I think you ought to. Perhaps it'll save you selling your stocks. Not a good idea with the markets as they are.'

'But if I don't get the money the Kuwaitis owe me I'll have trouble repaying you.'

'It isn't a loan, Dale. And it's not really a gift from me, if that makes you feel any better. I told you, it's Hamadi's money, and I think he owes it to you. Especially now, since he probably helped get you kicked out.'

'If I'd known you were going to do this I would never have asked.' She had flushed slightly, both embarrassed and pleased. Exaggerating her Southern accent, she said,

'My Mama always told me to accept compliments and gifts with good grace, so I won't go on quibbling about it. But I do intend to repay you.'

Jack shrugged. 'I don't want to argue either. Let's just see how it works out. In the meantime I suggest you put that money in the hotel safe as soon as possible.'

'Well, isn't it time we sat down?' she said rather feebly.

He took the chair while she perched on the edge of the bed, crossing her legs. The room had so little floor space that their knees were almost touching. It struck him that this was the first time she had been able to anticipate meeting him, and he wondered if she had made a positive effort to look her best.

'Cheers.' She raised her glass and took an appreciative swallow. 'I really do hope I didn't embarrass you by leaving that message.'

'Don't worry about it.'

'I probably shouldn't have called, remembering what you'd said about your marriage. I told your wife I was someone you'd met in Kuwait. Maybe she thinks I'm some tramp that you picked up there. I mean, you and I both know that she has no cause to be jealous, but when people are unhappy for other reasons jealousy often finds its way into the picture. I've been there myself, so I know. I don't want to add to your problems.'

'You couldn't make them any worse, believe me. She finally made it clear last night that she wants a divorce. As for what she thinks about anything else, I just don't know. We don't talk. So whatever she imagines you are can't make any difference.'

'Good. But the rest of it is tough.' She glanced at the cash that still lay on the desk. 'I guess you didn't tell her about that, huh?'

'God, no! One thing she does have definite opinions about is money. Mainly she reckons I don't earn enough of it to keep her in the style she would like to become

210

accustomed to. She's right, I suppose. I'm afraid I haven't done too well for the past couple of years.'

Dale said with amusement: 'There you go being afraid again, Jack.'

'Maybe justifiably, this time. What do the middle classes fear more than poverty? The trouble is, I can't get worked up about money the way other people do. I've seen some of its nasty side effects. In fact, I've helped bring some of them about.'

'How?'

'Didn't I tell you I used to be a financial investigator?'

The brandy was warming and powerful; he could feel it making him expansive. And she was easy to talk to, giving him her full attention, watching him with steady green eyes over the rim of her glass as he told her about his time at Hellig's.

'As an example of what I mean,' he said, 'there was an old family baking and milling firm here in London, down the river a bit, near a place called Silvertown. They made very good bread and a special kind of ginger cake. During the seventies they'd gone public so that they could expand to supply a couple of supermarket chains. They also owned a few of their own retail outlets, but the heart of their business was still an old mill with a hundred yards of river frontage, where barges delivered corn and they ground their own flour. They had a staff of about a hundred. They made consistent, modest profits and they kept their shareholders happy.

'We spotted this company for one of our clients. He wasn't a believer in modest profits, and he wouldn't have known a good ginger cake from a bar of soap. He was an asset-stripper. All that interested him was that hundred yards of river bank.

'He bought up shares in the bakery, through a number of shell companies, until he'd acquired a controlling interest. It cost him about nine million pounds. Within three months he had broken the firm up and sold it off in separate lots.

The brand name went to a processed-food corporation. The shops were bought by a discount chain. The workers lost their jobs. The mill was sold to a property development company in which our man also had a major interest. The site is now a yuppie condominium with a marina attached. A hundred apartments at a quarter of a million each: not a bad return. And . . . this is the final irony – do you know what they call the place? Baker's Wharf. It was that kind of thing that drove me out of that business.'

Dale nodded approvingly. 'Good for you. I hope you made a stirring farewell speech.'

'Of course not. Nothing I did was going to make any difference to the system. But it made me feel better not to be part of it.' Seeing her reach for the brandy bottle, he said, 'No more for me. I've got to drive. Besides, I'm talking too much. It's time I left.'

'There's no rush as far as I'm concerned.' Dale poured herself a small drink and then spluttered with unexpected laughter. 'Do you know what I just thought? You've been with me up here, what, twenty minutes? You walk out, and right afterward I take a thousand pounds down to that creepy night clerk and ask him to put it in the safe . . . He's going to think I'm one hell of a high-priced hooker!'

Jack laughed as well, but rather more uncertainly. There had been nothing contrived in the casual way she had invited him to her room, and there seemed to be no innuendo in this joking reference to sex. It might even be a way of keeping the subject at arm's length. Yet her physical nearness to him was a reminder of the powerful attraction he had felt for her back in the coffee house in Kuwait. Unless he had been fooling himself, she had felt it as well. On the other hand, in her case it might have been a mere passing inclination. The way she was looking at him now, with bright eyes and a relaxed smile, made him wonder again whether she was aware of those guilty private desires of his, and whether she found them exciting or just amusing. The signals were confusing.

'How long are you staying in London?' he asked. Taking refuge in the ultimate cocktail-party question.

'Three or four days, I guess. Then I'll head for Paris, catch up on those Sorbonne friends and spend some time oiling my rusty French. And you're going to Zurich? It seems the boot is on the other foot this time.'

'What do you mean?'

'The last time it was me asking you how much longer you'd be in Kuwait. It seems we're destined to meet only fleetingly at the world's crossroads, Jack.'

'It looks that way. But I hope we'll stay in touch.'

'Of course we will.'

He stood up, pushing back the chair to make room to get out. He felt a little deflated, the way he had the first time they had met, that she took their parting so much for granted. She stood as well, smoothing down her dress as she followed him to the door. He opened it and turned, expecting to peck her on the cheek again, but she had stopped just out of range. She stood with her arms folded across her breasts, her look now faintly sardonic.

'I told you the other day you were a nice man, Jack. One of the nicest things about you is that you don't even know you're desirable. Why would any woman want to give you up?'

He stood in the doorway, staring at her.

'Why would any man give you up?' he said.

He reached out and touched her face, just where the loose ringlet brushed her cheek. Her skin was warm against his palm. She didn't flinch, didn't move except to twist her head slightly, rubbing the cheek under his hand like a cat asking to be stroked. He stepped closer, feeling a surge of disbelieving excitement. He put his arms around her waist, drew her close and kissed her on the lips. Her body pressed into his. She explored his mouth briefly with her tongue and then pulled gently back, holding him by the shoulders, looking him full in the face.

'Do you want to break the mould, Jack? Would you like us to stop just meeting and missing each other?'

'Yes.'

'So would I. There's nothing I'd like more than to hop in the sack with you right now, but in twenty minutes' time you'd be looking at your watch, worrying about getting home, thinking about your trip. I want it to be good when it happens. I want to take it slowly. We've both been through shitty marriages, Jack, and we deserve a better start than that. Besides, it's . . . such an obvious thing to do, isn't it? I hate doing the obvious.'

'How do you want to handle it?'

'Why don't you call me when you get back? We can take it from there.'

'I've got a better idea. Come with me tomorrow.'

She began to laugh but he said: 'I'm serious. You were planning a holiday, weren't you? Why not start in Zurich? Go on to Paris afterwards if you like. If we want to get to know each other it's the best chance we'll have. What's there to stop you?'

She was smiling, shaking her head. 'I don't know. It just doesn't seem like you to be so . . . impulsive. Maybe you'll have changed your mind by the morning.'

'No.' Strangely, he was not at all surprised by his own impetuosity. He was in a state of euphoria that made anything seem possible. 'Listen, if it's the money you're worried about I'll pay your fare and your hotel bill. But I don't want you to feel under any obligations. We'll have separate hotel rooms. And if it'll make you feel better you can actually help me. There's someone I need to trace in France, right across the border, and you'd make a better job of it than I would. Even if your French is rusty it's bound to be better than mine. You can be my research assistant.'

Dale was still hesitant, but he could see that she was taken with the extravagance of the idea. 'Just like that, huh? But you're leaving in a few hours' time.'

'I'll call the airport now, make sure I can get an extra seat. Come on, let's just do it!'

Six miles north-west of Russell Square, the Range Rover turned off Cricklewood Lane at a junction indicated by Ali Shakir. It travelled for a hundred yards or so before he told the driver to stop.

They were in a street called Orange Grove Avenue, another name of the sort that had once puzzled Ali. It ran behind Plumtree Road, and the house opposite which they were now parked, number 26 on the avenue, was the one that backed on to number 48 on the road. They were identical in most respects, one difference being that number 26 had no garage. Instead, the concrete-paved drive that led down the side of the house was blocked off at the rear by a head-high brick wall with a small gate set in it.

All this Ali had established in daylight. Now it was well after midnight, the street was deserted and most of its houses, including number 26, were in darkness.

There were four of them in the Range Rover. Ali had guided them here but the man who drove was in overall command, the Mudeer who had taken charge four months ago of their work in London. He was a taciturn man, like a wise and stern father to them, who commanded their total respect. From a canvas bag he took out and distributed equipment to Ali and his two younger comrades, his brother Issa and a newly trained man named Osman. Each was given a pistol already loaded, a balaclava mask and a pair of black cotton gloves. The pistols were 7.62-millimetre Makarovs with silencers screwed on to their barrels. They checked and cocked the weapons and tucked them awkwardly into their waistbands, then put on the hoods and gloves before slipping out of the vehicle. Ali carried the bag containing the other things they would need.

For a few moments they stood in the shadow of a high privet hedge while the Range Rover moved off. Then Ali led them across the road and went quietly down the drive of the house.

They easily scaled the wall at the end, waiting in silence to be sure their intrusion had not been heard before crossing an overgrown back garden to another wall, the one that divided this property from 48 Plumtree Road.

Ali hoisted himself up, clinging to the rough brickwork. With only his head exposed, he peered through a margin of shrubbery to survey the rear of the Kurds' house. There was a light on outside the back door and another glowed dimly from somewhere on the ground floor, but there was no sign of movement. The bedroom windows upstairs were dark. There was no floodlighting and, as he had observed earlier, no alarm and no evidence of guard dogs; the house was protected only by its suburban anonymity, and yet this did not lessen its dangers. There had not been time to subject it to a full surveillance. They knew nothing about its layout or the routines of its inhabitants, or how many henchmen the renegade kept here to protect him. All they were certain of was that they must take the traitor while they knew where he was. For the rest, in the English phrase Ali liked to use, they must play it by ear.

He swung a leg over the wall and straddled it, signalling to the others to follow. As soon as they had dropped into the shrubbery he began to work his way through the shadows at the edge of the garden to the back door. Like most houses of its age and type, this one had had a modern kitchen extension built on at the rear. The door had glass panels in its upper half, and by the light above it he saw that it was secured by a deadlock and an internal bolt. There was a full-length window beside it, however, divided into two sections. The lower part of the frame contained a pane of glass about two feet high by three across.

Kneeling by the window, Ali took a roll of wide parcel tape and a knife from the bag. Cutting strips of the tape swiftly from the roll, he stuck them vertically and horizontally around the edges of the pane, making

216

sure their ends clung to the frame, and then placed two lengths diagonally across it. He wrapped a square of muslin around the butt of his pistol, and with four muffled taps he broke the pane neatly and almost silently at its outer edges. Peeling the ends of the tape back, he lifted the broken slabs of glass in one shaky rectangle out of the frame.

'God is great,' Ali muttered in gratitude. Again he waited, watching and listening for a minute, before beckoning to the others.

They crawled through the opening one by one. In the dark kitchen they drew their pistols and stood close together, hearing only the sound of each other's breathing. Still carrying his bag of equipment, Ali moved to the inner door and eased it open.

A wide, unlit hallway running to the front entrance. A staircase with a door on either side of it, the one on the left closed, the other one open with a light on in the room behind it. Western pop music playing softly, a smell of cigarette smoke. Somebody in there for certain, probably whichever of the bodyguards was on duty for the night.

They paused and then went in single file down the carpeted hall. Ali got to a couple of feet from the open door and signalled to the others to wait where they were. He pressed his back against the wall and edged along it, the pistol held close to his side.

Suddenly the other door opened. A door to a room he had assumed was unoccupied. A shaft of light fell from it and a man emerged, about to cross the hall, starting to say something to whoever was in the opposite room, then halting in disbelief as he saw the armed and hooded figure in front of him.

The man wore thin-framed glasses that glinted faintly in the dim light. He carried some sheets of paper. He uttered a guttural word of surprise.

Several things happened at once. Ali was just as astonished as the other man, and stood facing him for a moment with the pistol still hanging in his hand. He sensed rather than saw Osman, just behind him, raising his gun, and he swung round to slap down his arm. Their orders were to take the renegade alive. At almost the same moment another shape sprang from the open doorway on the right, the figure of a stocky man in a leather jacket. A bodyguard, taken by surprise but still moving swiftly and lithely, wielding a revolver which he aimed two-handed at Osman.

There wasn't the slightest chance of stopping him. There was a mighty explosion and a muzzle flash, and Osman grunted and reeled across the hall. The Kurd swung his gun in search of other targets but Ali had his own pistol levelled by now, and with the sound of the shot ringing in his ears he fired at the bodyguard's head, hearing the soft plop of the silenced pistol followed by the sharper sound of the bullet smacking through bone. Blood sprayed in dark blotches against the wall. The Kurd dropped to his knees, then fell on his side across the doorway.

The air was filled with smoke, reeking of cordite. Abdel Karim still stood by the door of his office, slack-mouthed and numb with shock. Ali stepped towards him, past the collapsed form of Osman, and became aware of a movement at the top of the stairs. He turned in time to see another Kurd, in pale pyjamas, dazedly raising a gun, but Issa had already spotted him and fired twice across the banister. The man gave a groan of pain, fell back on the landing and slid halfway down the stairs.

Ali jammed the muzzle of his pistol into Abdel Karim's ribs.

'Down!' he said. 'On the floor!'

As Karim dropped to his knees, Issa raced up the stairs. Ali forced the Kurd down on his face and heard from the upper floor a man's shout and a woman's scream, interspersed by four or five snaps from Issa's silenced pistol. He felt himself shaking as he knelt beside Karim and reached into the bag for more of the parcel tape. Still half-deafened by the revolver shot, he knew that the plan they had made for a swift, quiet operation was in disarray. There would be no time now to search for the documents which were their other objective.

Karim had not spoken a word since his first grunt of surprise, and he did not try to resist or protest as Ali fastened bands of tape over his mouth and his eyes. He plucked a length of cord from the bag and tied Karim's wrists behind his back. As Issa came clattering down the stairs he went into the office, pulled back an edge of curtain and looked out. The Mudeer had parked the Range Rover where they had arranged, just a few yards down the road. Lights had come on in one or two of the houses opposite, and although no-one had ventured out on the street it seemed certain that the revolver shot had been heard and the police summoned.

Ali pulled Karim to his feet and then crouched beside Osman. He jerked the hood off his comrade's head and saw a lifeless stare in his eyes. The Kurd's bullet had gone through his chest and the carpet beneath him was soaked with blood. There was no pulse; he did not seem to be breathing. Ali signalled to Issa, then seized Karim by the back of his jacket and unbolted the front door.

'We can't leave him here,' Issa said, staring down at Osman.

Ali hugged his brother and said: 'You did well. Osman will find peace with God. But we can't let him impede us.'

He opened the door, pushing Karim ahead of him, and they all lurched clumsily out into the cold spring night.

The Range Rover's engine was running and the door to the rear cargo deck was open. They bundled Karim inside and threw over him the sheet of black plastic they had ready. From the driving seat the Mudeer stared at them, an unspoken question in his eyes at the absence of Osman. But there was no time to explain. They dived into the back seat as the car swung away from the kerb.

*        *        *

219

It was after two o'clock when Jack got back to Prescott Gardens.

Its houses were completely in darkness now, and this time no curtain moved in the Reynolds' window as he backed the Honda into the garage. A car that hadn't been there earlier was parked outside their house, though, another and more anonymous Japanese model; glancing back at it as he unlocked the front door, he was almost sure he caught a movement in the back seat. The Reynolds' daughter and her boyfriend? Probably there was some heavy petting going on, although it seemed a bit late, and why they should choose to do it under the parents' bedroom window was a mystery.

Jack felt indulgent towards them. He was in love himself. There was no other way of describing the strange, almost adolescent sense of joy that had taken hold of him. The fact that it was still physically unfulfilled gave it an even headier quality. In spite of the punishing day he'd had he felt pumped up with excitement, as if he'd been taking stimulants, and was not in the least tired.

He averted his gaze from the car and let himself quietly into the house.

# 19

There was no avoiding an encounter with Alison the next morning. He was up well before she was, though, and had ordered a minicab and dressed and packed for his journey by the time she and the twins came down for breakfast. For a while they were saved the necessity of conversation through the chatter of the girls.

'Are you going away *again*, Daddy?'

'I did tell you. It'll just be for a couple of days this time.'

'To Switzerland? Where's that?' said Camilla.

'It's in the Alps,' Claudia said. 'Stupid.'

'Oh, yes. Heidi lived there. Miss Jackson read us the story.'

'It's about this girl who had to go and live in the mountains with her Grandad because her parents got divorced,' Claudia informed them.

'They didn't get divorced,' Camilla said. 'They died.'

'Divorced!'

'Died!'

'They got divorced, didn't they, Mummy?'

'I'm afraid I've forgotten most of the story, darling.'

Eventually Alison shooed them upstairs to get ready for school. Jack watched for any sign that she'd been affected by this innocent exchange, but saw none. She leaned back against the kitchen counter and said: 'The next time you want to borrow my car I'd appreciate it if you asked.'

Seizing on the only tangible objection she could find to his absence last night, he said: 'I didn't think you'd be needing it. And I didn't want to interrupt your fun across the road. I had to drive up to town in a hurry.'

'To see that woman?' she said stonily.

'Dale Griggs? Yes.' He held her look, keeping his tone casual. 'She's helping me on this project. As a matter of fact she's coming to Zurich with me.'

'She told me she'd only just met you.'

'That's true. And she was worried that you'd think she was some bit of fluff that I'd picked up in Kuwait. Well, she isn't. She happens to have a skill I can use.' He wasn't lying, but he wondered whether he was explaining too much. 'It's a bit late to start feeling jealous, isn't it?'

'What makes you think I am? It's just that if you've found yourself another woman I'd prefer you not to rub my nose in it.'

'Alison . . .'

But she gave him no chance to reply, stalking off upstairs and leaving him to wonder which of them was being more hypocritical.

Thanks to the time difference he was able to phone Dr Zunckel's office in Zurich just after eight o'clock. The lawyer wasn't in yet, but his secretary was familiar with Jack's name and sounded friendly enough. He told her his flight was due in at one o'clock; she said she'd already pencilled him in for an appointment at two.

'What about my request for a meeting at the Handelsbank Bauer?' he asked.

'Yes, that has been arranged for three-thirty, sir.'

After the researches he had carried out last night, Jack was now ready to back a hunch. 'Do you think we could change that around?' he said. 'The bank first, and then Dr Zunckel?'

Her tone became a little less amiable. 'It is very short notice, sir. If you really think it's necessary . . .'

'I do, rather.'

'I'll see what I can do. I will ring you back shortly.'

He used the interval to make a final check on the contents of his wallet: plane ticket, passport, driving licence, cash, travellers' cheques. The phone rang almost immediately but it wasn't Zurich, it was Reg Kilmartin. He sounded wary and tentative. There was a radio or television blaring in the background; presumably he hadn't left home for the office yet.

'Jack, have you heard the news?'

'What news?'

'Obviously you haven't. Our friend – the one I arranged for you to meet yesterday – has been kidnapped.'

'*What?*'

'There was some shoot-out last night at a house in north London, presumably the one they took you to. Two or three of his bodyguards killed. They're talking about it on the television news now. Look—'

'Hold on,' Jack said. He dropped the receiver and ran into the sitting room. He found the television remote control, turned it on and flicked through the channels until he got what he guessed was the right picture: a slow pan along a suburban street, lengths of blue-and-white police tape drawn across it and fluttering in the breeze, then the camera settling on a redbrick house that looked no different from any of its neighbours except that the front door was open and people were moving in and out of it. The usual cutaways: knots of bystanders, police cars with flashing blue lamps. To judge by the light, the filming had been done first thing in the morning. A reporter was reciting a voice-over.

> '. . . *Neighbours on this quiet street in Cricklewood heard a commotion at about one o'clock this morning. Police, who arrived within a few minutes, found a scene of carnage. Three men and a woman lay dead in different parts of the house. One of those killed is believed to have been among the gunmen who carried out the attack, himself shot dead by a bodyguard. And Abdel Karim, one of the most vocal opponents of the Iraqi regime, is missing. He's presumed to have been abducted and there are fears for his life.*'

The reporter appeared on camera, an earnest young man in a pale trenchcoat talking against the background of the street.

> '*The police have arranged a news conference for later this morning. In the meantime they're refusing to speculate publicly about who may have been responsible for this attack. Inevitably, though, the finger of suspicion must point towards agents of Saddam Hussein's regime. Even now, they may be interrogating Abdel Karim about the clandestine activities of his party inside Iraq. This was supposedly a secret address, one of a number used by the Kurdish leader as a safeguard against precisely such an event . . .*'

Jack went back to the phone, feeling shaky and disbelieving. Reg said: 'Well? Was it the house?'

'I don't know. I never saw it from the outside. But I suppose it must have been.'

'Grisly coincidence, eh? Listen, the main reason I'm phoning is this. I'm sure the police will be talking to you—'

'Why me?'

'They're bound to want to interview anyone who's visited Karim recently. Just, as they say, to eliminate you from their enquiries. They may want to see me as well, to confirm that I set up the meeting. I don't intend telling them about the Kroll report and I'm asking you not to mention it either. It can't make any difference to them, but it could certainly land me in the shit with Hellig's if they found out I'd leaked it to you.'

'Of course.' Jack was about to tell Reg that he was flying to Switzerland and wouldn't be available to be interviewed, but he stopped himself. 'Unless they actually ask, I don't see why I should say anything about it.'

He put down the receiver and stood in a daze. The homely interior of that house, with its worn furniture and its cooking smells, came back to him vividly; it was grotesque to imagine it being so violently invaded, the affable bodyguards and the young woman assistant now dead, Abdel Karim dragged off to some other, perhaps more ghastly, fate. Through his immediate shock, however, Jack was aware of a deeper unease. He felt involved in what had happened. The enemies of the Kurds must have been planning their attack even while he was visiting the house only, what, nine or ten hours earlier? No doubt that was merely what Reg had called it, a coincidence, and yet with hindsight he seemed to recall, around some of the events of yesterday, an indefinable sense of disquiet, a feeling that now lay like a shadow across his mind.

More practical thoughts interposed themselves. Reg was right; the police would be trying to find out how the killers had traced Karim to that address, and would almost certainly want to talk to him. But that might raise difficulties of its own. Though he could probably avoid mentioning the report that Reg was worried about, he would have to explain his reasons for visiting Karim. How much detail could he give them without betraying Dr Hamadi's confidence? And how much could he avoid telling without making them suspect he had something to hide? Either way, he had a feeling they weren't going to like what he was up to. They might subject him to lengthy and even hostile questioning. Altogether, it seemed quite a good idea to be leaving the country for a couple of days.

The doorbell and the telephone rang at the same time. His taxi had arrived, and he signalled through the window to the driver to wait a few moments while he answered the phone. It was Zunckel's secretary, telling him she had managed to rearrange his appointments. He would now see Dr Paul Buchmann, the investment director of the Handelsbank Bauer, at two-thirty, and Dr Zunckel would make himself available at four o'clock. Another doctor: together with Hamadi, that made three of them.

He ran upstairs, kissed the twins goodbye and told Alison he would be in touch, a promise she received without enthusiasm. He picked up his bag and left the house.

In passing he observed that the strange car that had been parked across the street early this morning was gone. He had no reason to notice another car, a Ford Sierra, pulling out from the kerb further along Prescott Gardens as the taxi drew away from the house. The shadows of yesterday, the half-formed suspicions, were submerged in any case by the thought of his meeting Dale.

At Heathrow she was waiting where they'd arranged to meet, beside the Swissair reservations desk in Terminal Two. She was dressed as though for a business trip in a pale grey suit of brushed cotton, a black silk shirt and black knee-length boots. Their heels raised her height by a couple of inches, and her face was exactly level with his when she kissed him.

'Good-morning.'

'Good-morning,' he said. 'I had a horrible notion that I might find a message here saying you'd changed your mind.'

'I wouldn't go back on my word.' She returned his smile but caught a seriousness in his manner. 'Is something wrong?'

'I'll tell you when we're sorted out here.'

He used a credit card to pay for the ticket he had reserved last night and they checked in. With a few minutes to spare before their flight was called, they sat over coffee in the departure lounge. Jack had no doubts about taking Dale completely into his confidence, but the whole story would have to wait until they were on the plane. For now he merely repeated what he had learned that morning. She had heard the news as well, on the radio in her hotel room, but had had no reason to connect Abdel Karim to Jack. When he had finished she said with concern: 'Does all this have anything to do with your project?'

'Not as far as I can see. It's just by chance that I went to see him yesterday.'

'But if they've kidnapped Karim they'll interrogate him, won't they? What if he mentions your visit?'

'All we talked about were some things he had on his files. They wanted him for more important reasons, because he's an enemy of Saddam. I can't think that they'd be interested in me.'

'I think you should have gone to the police, Jack.'

'I don't see how I could have helped them. It would only have caused complications and probably a delay.' He studied her over his coffee cup. 'It would also have kept me away from you.'

Once Issa Shakir had seen the couple go through the passport barrier, there was no point in lingering at the airport. He was grateful to leave, anyway. It had been a long night's work, starting with Cricklewood and then taking over the surveillance of the Nazarene, and he was tired. In the terminal car park he sat in the Ford Sierra and used his mobile phone to report to the Mudeer. Then he set off to return to the safe house.

It was in Finsbury Park, a long drive off the M4 along the North Circular Road and then a southward turn through Wood Green. The house was in another of those long, monotonous Victorian terraces, each with two storeys over a basement, but it faced out on the park and backed on to a row of shops, and thus had the advantage of not being overlooked. It was also in an area almost totally occupied by people of Asian and Middle Eastern origin, in which the presence of Issa and his comrades went unnoticed.

He parked the car, went to the front door and gave a coded rap on the knocker. The door was opened by Ali, who signalled to him to go straight downstairs.

The basement had once been a separate flat. It had two rooms, front and back, and the rear one with its adjoining bathroom had been long prepared for its role as an interrogation room. Its flimsy door had been replaced by one of heavy oak, and its one narrow window was blocked off by a frame fitted with soundproofing material. No scream of pain or cry of help would ever be heard beyond its walls. It was furnished only with a bed and a spindle-backed wooden chair, and lighted by a single overhead lamp.

In the middle of the room Abdel Karim sat on the chair, bound to it by his wrists and ankles. He had been there for eight or nine hours and his head hung forward as though he were asleep, but Issa saw that he was staring at the floor. Sitting on the bed and facing him, absently cradling a silenced pistol, was the Mudeer.

He was a man who liked to dress expensively and stylishly, but now his suit was rumpled and his shirt was grubby and sweat-stained. To judge by his drained and exhausted expression, the questioning had not been going well. He nodded at Issa and then returned his attention to the prisoner.

Karim looked in a worse mess than when Issa had last seen him. He still wore the clothes in which he had been captured, and his jacket and shirt front were stained with the blood that had run from his nose and his split lips. His glasses had been removed; through swollen and blackened eyes he gave a myopic, indifferent glance at the newcomer before looking down at the floor again.

'Our friend is still not being very co-operative,' the Mudeer informed Issa. 'That's why I asked you in here, to help convince him that we needn't be so disagreeable with each other.'

Karim raised his head for a moment. 'You know I have nothing to say to any of you,' he said hoarsely.

'On the contrary, in time I expect our conversation will be rich and rewarding. One of our young comrades sacrificed his life to help bring you here. That should indicate how important we think it is that you speak to us.'

'What help do you expect? I know you are going to kill me anyway.'

'I do have a choice in the matter, Abdel Karim, and so do you. I prefer if possible not to use forceful means. I thought you might want to make it easier for yourself. And if not that, then easier at least for your friends.'

'If you think I will believe any promise of yours, then you're wasting your time. And if you imagine I will betray my comrades in Iraq—'

'I don't mean only those snivelling renegades,' the Mudeer interrupted, 'although we will discuss them in due course.' He stood up and began circling the chair, toying with the pistol and looking down reflectively at his prisoner. 'You have friends here, in this country, whose activities are of interest to us. Like the Nazarene who visited you yesterday.'

Karim looked up in surprise. 'He's not a friend. It was the first time we'd met.' Seeing the Iraqi's disbelieving look, he went on: 'He is nothing to our cause, he's just an English businessman.'

'What business is he doing with you?'

'None. Many people come to see me for different reasons. Journalists, politicians, wellwishers. This man was introduced by a financial concern that I've had dealings with, but all he wanted was to check some information.'

'What information?'

'About matters on my records. Things that are long past, that have nothing to do with your politics or mine.'

'Then what harm is there in telling us about them?'

'It was understood that we spoke in confidence.'

'Tell him,' said the Mudeer to Issa, 'what this man has been doing since his visit to the renegades yesterday.'

'We followed him to Waterloo Station. There, he was heard enquiring about the address of a man who was until recently a colonel in the British army. He caught a train to Woking and went to visit this man. We picked up his trail from there and followed him to his home, where we resumed surveillance early this morning. We learned that his name is Rushton. He left for the airport and met a woman, and they caught a plane together to Zurich. The woman apparently is not his wife,' Issa concluded primly.

'What has all this to do with me?' Karim protested. 'I can't account for the man's movements. I know almost nothing about him.'

'Because you don't want to know?' the Mudeer said. 'We will make further enquiries about this man. If he has been in collusion with you it seems very likely to me that he is an enemy of our people.'

'Don't be a fool. He has no interest in what goes on in Iraq, and he can do you no harm. I swear that to you by the Prophet. Let the matter rest. Your business is with me. Why not get on with it?'

Issa, in spite of himself, could admire the dignity and conviction with which Karim spoke. The Mudeer, however, still circling the chair, showed no sign of being impressed even by the serious oath the Kurd had sworn. After the wasted hours of questioning he had got his teeth into something and was holding on to it.

'If you are so sure of this man's innocence,' he said, 'then convince me of it as well. Otherwise, anything that happens to him will be your responsibility.'

'Your promises can mean nothing to me,' Karim said wearily. 'But I suppose that if you intend to kill him you will do so anyway. Very well. You are right: his name is Jack Rushton. For his sake, not for mine, I will repeat to you exactly what he told me.'

The Mudeer looked up and nodded again at Issa, this time in a silent signal for him to leave the room.

# 20

The Swissair plane landed at Zurich shortly after one o'clock on a cool, sparkling spring day. There was an unexpected queue at the taxi rank, so it was almost an hour before Jack and Dale reached the Meilenhof Hotel off the Limmat-quai.

Jack dropped Dale with their luggage at the entrance, leaving her to check them into their rooms, do some shopping and enquire about hiring a car. Then he carried on across the Munsterbrucke to the left bank of the river. Here, in the financial heart of the city that was the only part of it he was familiar with, he found the Handelsbank Bauer at the far end of Talstrasse, across from the Botanical Gardens.

Its appearance was that of a large old town house, and its style of doing business belonged to the days when banks disguised themselves as gentlemen's clubs. Through the glazed and brass-plated double doors, a marble-floored entry hall led into an elegant reception area. This was a place far removed from the nuts and bolts of commercial banking; indeed, the only sign that it dealt in money at all was a single teller's position tucked away in one corner, where a male cashier was counting out large-denomination Swiss notes.

A woman with an efficient manner was in charge of the reception desk; Jack gave her his name and told her he had an appointment with Dr Buchmann to discuss a personal portfolio. He made a point of mentioning that the arrangement had been made through Dr Zunckel's office; she seemed familiar with the name. Now was the time to test that plausibility of his that he had boasted to Dr Hamadi about.

After checking a desk diary the woman said: 'You're a few minutes early, Mr Rushton. Would you mind taking a seat?'

'Actually, while I'm here, I have another small piece of business to do. Dr Zunckel and I are working together on behalf of an associate in the Middle East, and I have to deposit some money into the accounts of several of our clients. I can tell you the names but I'm afraid I wasn't given the account numbers.'

'That's no problem. I'll look them up and you can pay the teller.'

She produced a small stack of deposit forms, printed in German, French, Italian and English. He left blank spaces against the amounts to be credited and wrote as the names of the account holders Ibrahim Jalloul, Mohamed Ghani, and the five others he had singled out from the Kroll report. The woman took the forms, went to a computer terminal to the rear of her desk and keyed in the names. She scribbled some details on a slip of paper and returned, frowning slightly.

'I have verified Mr Jalloul's account, but we seem to have no customers by any of these other names.'

'That's odd. I do know that they all bank with you.' Jack feigned incomprehension for a few moments, then brightened. 'I've just thought . . . the accounts may not be held in their own names, but by Dr Zunckel as their nominee. Would you mind trying under that name?'

The woman looked dubious but checked her computer files again. When she came back she said, 'Yes, Dr Zunckel has a number of nominee accounts here. But they are Form-B accounts, which means they were opened under confidential covenants between him and his clients. We have no record of the beneficial owners of the deposits.'

'I see. I'm not familiar with your procedures, but this does seem to be just a technicality, and to save me the inconvenience of coming back . . . Would it be possible for you to phone Dr Zunckel's office and establish which are the correct accounts? I don't need to know which they are, just as long as you do; that would protect their privacy, wouldn't it?'

'I can try,' the woman said, 'but I doubt that they will release such information even to the bank.'

She went away again, this time to a telephone at the back of the room, out of his hearing. Jack lingered apprehensively by the counter, watching her make the call. For all their habits of discretion, banks tended to be quite trusting towards people who were putting money into them rather than taking it out. He had used similar strategems before; whether this one would work depended on how the woman worded her request and how quick on the uptake Zunckel and his staff were.

The receptionist was on the phone for a couple of minutes. When she returned for a third time she was shaking her head. 'I'm sorry, but they refuse to identify any of the accounts. There is nothing more I can do.'

'But they did confirm that there are such accounts? Held on behalf of all these people?'

'Well, they didn't sound unfamiliar with them,' she said, slightly puzzled. 'They went away to check and came back saying the matter was confidential.'

'I see. Well, thank you for your trouble. Obviously I'll have to take this up with Zunckel himself.'

She had told him all he needed to know. More, in fact: the one big surprise was to learn that Colonel Jalloul's account, presumably the original one, was still open. He went through the motions of completing the only usable deposit slip, copying out the eight-digit account number on the form and the attached receipt, then handing them to the cashier with a payment of one hundred Swiss francs.

He got back the stamped receipt and sat down to wait. At a cost of about forty pounds, paid into Colonel Jalloul's account, he had established several important facts that would otherwise have been virtually impossible to ascertain.

At half-past two he was shown into the office of the invest-ment director. The room was a continuation of the prevailing old-money theme of the bank's public areas, and Dr Paul Buchmann was a pale, serious man of about Jack's own age, whose English was as smooth as his manners. Once they were seated at his desk he asked to see Jack's passport and took a note of the number, then offered him tea or coffee. Jack refused both. He produced his cheque for fifty thousand dollars and they got down to business.

It didn't take long to agree on the essentials. Jack would open a deposit account in which a reserve of five thousand dollars would be kept. The balance would go into a separate securities account and be used to make a spread of conservative investments: international bonds, the same sort of assets into which the funds of Mohamed Ghani and the others had been channelled. Interest and dividend payments, Buchmann explained, would automatically be reinvested unless Jack chose otherwise. Should he wish to realize any of his capital, he need only notify the bank; some of the bonds could be sold within a few days and the proceeds forwarded to him.

'In other words,' Jack said, 'I need never set foot in the bank again.'

'Not if you don't wish to.'

'Very convenient. Even more so for those who've never had to come here in the first place.'

Buchmann looked at him blankly. Jack went on. 'I mean the customers whose names you don't know, the ones who shelter behind intermediaries. What will happen to them when these new laws come in later this year? The ones that require you to give the Swiss government a list of the actual holders of accounts?'

He had kept his tone light, at the level of idle curiosity. Buchmann shrugged and said: 'They will have to identify themselves. Or, if they prefer to retain their anonymity, they will have to seek it in some other jurisdiction. Actually, some have already been encouraged to do so. Swiss banks no longer want to be seen, rightly or wrongly, as havens for the funds of criminals and tax evaders. But none of this is relevant to your situation. The account holders' register will be available only to the Federal Banking Commission. In exceptional circumstances, such as when fraud is suspected, selected access may be allowed to the police or the courts. For all practical purposes, your relationship with the bank will remain as confidential as ever.'

Jack leaned back in his chair. 'I wasn't thinking of myself, actually. I was wondering how you'll ascertain the identities of these other people. Are the nominees who protect them going to lead them in here to show their faces? And if so, how will you know that they really are who they claim to be? In my case, for instance, you've glanced at my passport but you know nothing about me except that I was introduced by one of those nominees.'

The banker was not put out by what was now, obviously, a deliberate digression from their business. He sat very still and maintained his professional composure.

'What exactly are you getting at, Mr Rushton?'

'Are you sincere in saying that you don't want any tainted money in your coffers?'

'Perfectly sincere.'

'I ask because some Swiss banks have been known to turn a blind eye to such things in the past.'

'That has never been the case with us,' Buchmann said crisply. 'On the other hand, we can't treat every investor as a potential criminal. But you are . . . a business consultant? May I know the purpose of your questions?'

'Bear with me, Doctor, and I may be able to do you a favour. But I'd want one in return.'

'Is this the true reason you are here?'

'No, I want you to manage my money for me as well.'

'Go on.'

'With your laws being tightened up, I imagine you'd like to be able to identify some of this dubious money,

235

with a view to . . . as you put it, encouraging it to go away. I believe your bank may have been deliberately used for the laundering of such funds, Doctor. Many millions of dollars, in fact, stolen from the Iraqi treasury. Have you seen the report that's just been produced by Kroll Associates?'

'Ah, come now.' Buchmann lost a little of his detachment. 'That report is already old news. The investments it names are in shares and bonds bought on the open market, through a great many banks and brokers. It does not single out any one institution.'

'That's true. But it needs to be read in conjunction with other information. Kroll has identified individuals through their assets but has skipped over the routes by which they were acquired. I've examined the range of bonds purchased on behalf of some of these people, *and* I've compared them with the names of the third parties who issued the bonds. I've come up with six portfolios that were almost certainly put together through your bank. Six people, at least one of them using a false identity, have got twenty-six million dollars in stolen Iraqi money on your books. I have all their names, or at least their aliases: Mohamed Ghani, Sharif Hayawi, Mohamed Rashid, and three others. And I have a good idea that Dr Karl Zunckel is the nominee who controls all their accounts.'

Buchmann was watching him steadily. 'Only an idea, Mr Rushton? Dr Zunckel is a respected lawyer and these are serious allegations. I hope you can support them with more than conjecture.'

'Take a careful look at his records and they should tell you most of the story. But there's more.' Jack took out and showed the receipt for the hundred francs he had paid into Jalloul's account. 'This man is an Iraqi army officer suspected of a war crime, the torture and murder of a woman in Kuwait. The purpose of his opening of an account here was to hide the proceeds of a crooked ransom deal. He, at least, used his own name. The others may well all be going under false ones. I don't think it will look very good for you, when the time comes to draw up that register, to have people like these on your books.'

Buchmann remained outwardly calm, but the rapid movements of his eyes suggested an inner conflict. Maybe he was wondering if he was about to face a blackmail demand. 'Evidently you have done some considerable research,' he said. 'Perhaps now you'll tell me what its purpose is.'

'I have nothing to gain from it financially. I'm representing a client who has more money than he will ever need. He happens to be in a personal difficulty because of the actions of at least one of these people I've mentioned.'

'Let me rephrase my question. What do you, or this client of yours, hope to get out of raising these matters with me?'

'To confirm what I've told you, and to prove other things for myself, I need to look at those accounts, Doctor. Zunckel's nominee accounts, and this man Jalloul's. A look, that's all.'

'That's *all* . . .?'

'And I want a promise that you won't tell Zunckel I've seen them until I've spoken to him myself.'

'Mr Rushton, you are asking me to break the most fundamental rule of my profession. It's out of the question.'

'I have to follow similar rules in my own job, Doctor. For instance, I learned purely by accident about the way your bank has been used. How you deal with it is your own business. Since it isn't relevant to my purposes, I don't intend to tell anyone about it, not even my client. But I also know that rules sometimes have to be bent. You can help me, and help yourself, by letting me see those accounts. I'm on the side of the good guys, if that makes you feel any better.'

Buchmann thought for a few moments. 'Let's make sure there are no misunderstandings between us. If the next thing I say is no, what is the next thing you say?'

'I didn't come here to make any threats. Why not just say that as matters now stand, I see no reason why anything said in this office should ever be repeated outside it? Except to Zunckel, and if I'm right he won't be complaining.'

The banker gave a thin, humourless smile. 'I thought you introduced yourself as an associate of his.'

'I am, after a fashion.'

'He could be an innocent party to these transactions.'

'It's possible.'

'Then let us say we are both acting in his interests.'

Without another word, Buchmann swivelled his chair to face the computer terminal beside his desk. He tapped some commands into it, and while he waited for a response Jack moved his own chair around to where he could see the screen.

Vertical columns sprang into view, a display of file titles in German. Buchmann selected one, then made a further choice from a second list that was presented. *Zunckel, Dr Karl Wolfgang*, appeared in the top left corner of the screen, followed by a dozen or more groups of numbers.

'Where do you want to start?' Buchmann said.

'Take your pick.'

The banker pecked at more keys. A balance sheet appeared, the credit column showing a six-figure sum carried forward, the debits eked out in five-figure amounts. The space left for the client's name was blank. The document was headed *Depositenkonto*.

'Deposit account?' Jack said.

Buchmann nodded. 'The figures are in Swiss francs. The debits represent drawings transferred into investments.'

'It doesn't say much. Can we concentrate on the securities?'

Another set of keystrokes, a different image on the screen. This one was called a *Depotauszug*. Again there was no name attached to it, but a list of bond titles occupied one column, with those beside it detailing quantity, par value, current price and market value. Jack took out the notes he had drawn up last night and within a few moments he had found a page that corresponded almost exactly to the listing on the screen. He was looking at a current statement of the bond holdings of the man named Sharif Hayawi. Their market values were given in various currencies but they added up roughly to the equivalent of about two and three-quarter million dollars.

Jack took a deep breath and exhaled slowly. 'Let's have some more,' he said.

Within ten minutes they had gone through all Zunckel's nominee accounts. They had found six sets of figures that corresponded to the holdings of the six Iraqi names Jack had singled out from the Kroll report, starting with Hayawi and ending with Mohamed Ghani. He was the richest of them all, with assets totalling nearly seven million dollars. There was also a balance sheet for what was clearly the original joint account set up for Jalloul and Hamadi, with the Swiss franc equivalent of two million dollars credited to it and a million immediately withdrawn. The overall picture was very close to the way Jack had imagined it.

Buchmann had got quite absorbed in the enterprise and by now was almost friendly. When his telephone rang he dismissed the caller quickly and turned to Jack with a grin. 'Your . . . associate, Dr Zunckel, trying to reach me. Apparently he's in a panic over some enquiry that our receptionist made to his office.'

'My doing,' Jack confessed.

'Bending the rules for the good guys again? Well, we have one more bad one to deal with.'

He keyed the number of Colonel Jalloul's account into the computer and another balance sheet appeared on the screen. It was a deposit account statement and it bore Jalloul's name without an address. The details it recorded were simple to the point of starkness. In the credit column was an opening balance of one million, two hundred and eighty-seven thousand and some hundreds of Swiss francs, the equivalent of one million dollars transferred from the joint account. The entry was dated 29 August last year, and some interest had been added at the end of December. Before and after that, nothing. The debit column was blank.

Jack stared at the screen in amazement.

Jalloul's account had not been touched since the day it had been opened.

# 21

From his voice on the telephone Jack had imagined
Dr Zunckel to be a heavy, slow-moving man with
a self-satisfied manner. He wasn't far wrong in this
assumption; what he had not been expecting in addition
was a dandy.

Zunckel was in his mid-sixties. His face was smooth
and round as a football, with vivid but but rather watery
blue eyes, a tuft of white hair and a Colonel Sanders goatee
grown to disguise a receding chin. He was perhaps forty
pounds overweight, and his ruddy complexion suggested
chronic high blood pressure. In place of the expected
lawyer's pinstripes he wore a biscuit-coloured suit, a dark
brown shirt fastened at the cuffs with heavy gold links,
a silk, floral-patterned tie and beige Gucci loafers with
gold buckles. A red carnation was in his buttonhole and
a brown silk handkerchief spilled from his breast pocket.

Jack and he sat in armchairs facing each other across
a hearth. The room they were in was far too hot, with a
fire of pine logs burning in the grate in addition to baking
radiators, and from time to time Zunckel pulled out the
handkerchief and dabbed at the moisture on his face. The
temperature alone did not account for his discomfort. He
had begun by being angry and indignant, but had run
out of steam; trying to sound reasonable, he spoke with
a mixture of bluster and self-pity.

'Nothing I have done is illegal, Mr Rushton. I have
spent more than thirty years building up this practice,
and my reputation rests on the correctness of my dealings
with the authorities here as well as on mutual trust and
understanding between me and my clients.'

'I don't doubt that, Dr Zunckel. I'm just asking you to confirm a few guesses I've made.'

'It's my understanding that you were commissioned to find, if possible, this Iraqi, Jalloul, and reach an agreement with him allowing the closure of his joint account with Dr Hamadi. Had you succeeded in this, the matter could have been settled in five minutes. Instead you have meddled in an unscrupulous and unethical way in the business of other clients of mine. Listen . . .' he said over a threatened interruption. 'I do not feel obliged to account to you for what you have learned. Nevertheless, I will explain the background. Perhaps then you will not judge me so harshly.

'Much of the success of my practice has come from connections I have built up in the Middle East, especially in Iraq. My involvement there began in the nineteen sixties. The Iraq Petroleum Company, which belonged to Western interests, was to be nationalized, and I helped to negotiate terms of compensation for the European partners in the consortium. The job took up a good deal of my time for almost ten years. That was also a period of political instability, a succession of military *coups* and dictatorships. In the course of my visits to Baghdad, some highly placed Iraqis began asking me to handle private business for them. Banks and major industries were also being taken over by the State, and large personal fortunes would be lost unless ways could be found of investing them abroad.

'This was not work that I welcomed but I found it difficult to refuse. You know the Middle East; you understand the importance of doing favours for the right people, and how impatient and demanding they can be. My reputation apparently spread; I became known as what you call in English a "fixer". Naturally, the whole thing was a political minefield. I tried to be careful who I dealt with but, frankly, it wasn't always possible to be certain of their standing.'

Zunckel flicked the handkerchief like a duster over his features. 'I will not go into details. Enough to say that I was able to settle most of these people's affairs satisfactorily. The nationalization of the oil industry was completed in the early seventies, and after that I had less occasion to go to Baghdad and fewer requests for help. The political situation had also settled down. More people had access to foreign currency, and those with the right connections had channels through which to invest it.

'Then began the Iran–Iraq war. There was a point, around the mid-eighties, when Iraq looked in danger of losing it. I was approached once again by people who wanted favours. This time it was not only industrialists and bankers, but others who feared for the future—'

'People like these?' Jack held out the list of six names culled from the Kroll report.

'Those among others,' Zunckel admitted grudgingly.

'Who are they? I mean, who are they really, behind their pseudonyms?'

'Mr Rushton, as far as I am concerned they are who they say they are. I had only limited contact with them, and since the Gulf War I have had none at all. Now I've been as candid as possible with you—'

'But not candid enough, I think,' Jack said harshly. 'It's taken me about twenty-four hours to establish that one of these names, Mohamed Ghani, is an alias. Are you saying you haven't worked that out for yourself over four or five years? It's a false identity almost certainly used by a member of the Iraqi secret police. It was also used for a time by Colonel Jalloul.'

'I cannot explain that,' Zunckel said, mustering his dignity. 'All I can say is that I have met Ghani and Jalloul, and they are two separate people.'

'Dr Zunckel, you've invested twenty-six million dollars on behalf of these six men without caring much who they are or where their money came from. But soon your banking authorities here are going to start caring. Actually none of that concerns me, but I have to remind you that Dr Hamadi is paying both of us to represent him. I want to be sure there's no conflict between his interests and those of these others.'

'How could there be? They are quite separate interests.'

'But connected through you. Hamadi had been given the name of Jalloul, and because of your reputation as a fixer he came to you asking to be put in touch with him. How do you explain Jalloul's using the alias of your other client, Ghani? And how is it that the bank account you opened for Jalloul hasn't been touched?'

'That, I assure you, is news to me. It's also his business, not mine.'

'You say you met Jalloul only once, in Jordan when the documents were signed. Who had found him for you? Was it Ghani?'

Zunckel was busy with his handkerchief again, and his face was redder than before. He sighed heavily and said: 'Ghani was merely returning a small favour to me, acting as yet another intermediary. If he had some private connection with Jalloul, I know nothing about it.'

Jack hunched forward in his chair. 'I think you'd better tell me more about Ghani, Doctor. It strikes me that whoever he really is, he may hold the key to the whereabouts of the colonel.'

'There is almost nothing to tell,' Zunckel protested. 'I have heard nothing from him or any of the others for six or seven months.'

'Dr Zunckel, I want you to give me access to all your records on Ghani and Jalloul and these other five Iraqis. The alternative is for me to report what I know to Dr Hamadi and tell him that you're refusing to co-operate. I have no idea what he'll choose to do about that, but I do know that I wouldn't like to have an enemy with his resources. He told me you were too rich to be corruptible, but I rather imagine he could buy and sell you and all your other clients with the change in his pocket. On the other hand, if I can tell him you are co-operating, I needn't go into any details. The choice is yours.'

The lawyer shifted uncomfortably in his chair. He gave Jack a resentful look and then glanced again at the list of names. 'Do you understand that these people could be dangerous?'

'I certainly do.'

'Wait here a moment.'

Zunckel stood up and waddled out of the room. Jack rose as well, to get away from the fire, and strolled to the window. It overlooked a garden ablaze with cherry blossom. The offices of the *finanzamwalt* had turned out to be some distance from the financial centre, occupying a substantial grey-brick villa just off Bellerivestrasse on the east shore of the lake. The woman who had met him at the door had seemed rather apprehensive; he took her to be Zunckel's secretary and guessed that it was she who had committed the indiscretion of replying too incautiously to the query from the bank.

The room into which she had shown him was one set aside for receiving visitors, another variation on the theme of the club lounge, with a floor of black-and-white marble squares, a leather sofa and armchairs, and a table on which newspapers in half a dozen languages were spread out. Jack turned away from the window and scanned the news pages of the *Financial Times*. It was an early edition and probably it wouldn't have bothered much anyway with the shooting and kidnapping in Cricklewood, but there was plenty about the plight of the Kurds in their homeland. The Turkish army had taken measures to halt the flood of refugees trying to cross into the country; up to two million of them were now said to have fled into the mountains. In Iraq, more of the atrocities carried out by the secret police were being uncovered. In other circumstances the implications of these events might have seemed a million miles from this cosy room; Jack had a sense now that they had drawn uncomfortably close.

When Zunckel returned he was followed by his secretary carrying a heap of box files. She set them down nervously before hurrying out of the room. Zunckel loosened some papers from their bindings in one of the boxes and handed them grudgingly to Jack.

'Here are details that Ghani provided when he first became my client. A copy of his passport is attached.'

The top sheet was a printed form in German, headed *Verwaltung von Wertschriften*. It was a standard authorization, apparently, allowing Zunckel to manage funds on behalf of a client. The details, such as they were, had been completed in a European hand: the surname Ghani, the given name Mohamed, and a post office box address in Baghdad. A signature was scrawled at the bottom and the form was dated 9 May 1986.

The second sheet was more revealing. It was a photocopy of two pages of an Iraqi passport, the headings printed in English and French as well as Arabic. The name, Mohamed Ghani, was given in its romanized form, his date of birth was recorded as 6 February 1941, and his height as one metre eighty. His occupation and place of birth were written in Arabic.

On the opposite page was a photograph. A man of chunky build wearing a jacket and tie. A wide, jowly face scowling at the camera. Dark hair and moustache, unsmiling eyes with heavy bags beneath them, making their owner look older than his stated age of forty-five. He had the aggrieved look of an insomniac, and he certainly wasn't Jalloul.

'How did you meet Ghani?' Jack asked.

'Through other clients in Baghdad. Friends of friends: as usual, I was under an obligation to help. He was introduced to me as a businessman with funds he wanted to invest abroad.'

'What business was he supposed to be in? And where did his money come from?'

Zunckel gave a helpless shrug. 'Some things, in places like Iraq, it is better not to know. And Ghani did not encourage me to ask. He told me never to contact him directly, and the only address I had for him was that box number.'

'What else have you got on him?'

'Only details of his investments.'

The lawyer surrendered the file to Jack, who skimmed quickly through it. There were receipts and advice notes, securities and deposit statements, all more or less confirming the picture he had built up at the Handelsbank Bauer. For just over four years a steady trickle of funds had been reaching Zunckel for investment in Ghani's proxy accounts. Nice round figures, a hundred thousand dollars here, fifty thousand dollars there. And always in dollars, the currency used in the sale of Iraq's only export worth mentioning, oil. The payments had stopped at the end of last July, just before the invasion of Kuwait.

The other files contained similar sets of records for Zunckel's five other Iraqi clients. Their authorization forms were all dated later than Ghani's, and Zunckel explained that they had been introduced and vouched for by Ghani himself. More favours being repaid, no doubt, more flies gathering at the honey pot. For Colonel Jalloul there was virtually no paperwork at all, not even a copy of his passport, since he had elected to manage his account at the bank himself.

'I'm going to want copies of those passport pages,' Jack said. 'And blow-ups of the photographs, if you can manage it.'

'Mr Rushton—' Zunckel began to object again, but Jack cut him short.

'Just for my own reference. Nothing you've told me or shown me needs to jeopardize your relationship with your clients. Just think how happy Dr Hamadi is going to be when I tell him what a help you've been.'

Resignedly Dr Zunckel sent for his secretary and gave her the papers to copy. Looking weary, he went back to his chair by the fire. Jack sat down opposite.

'So you have no idea what's happened to any of these people since the Gulf War, and you're sitting on twenty-six million dollars' worth of their assets. Isn't it strange that not even one or two of them should have turned up? Just to see how their investments were doing?' Zunckel shrugged again and Jack said: 'All right, you can't tell me what you don't know. There are just a few small details I need to be clear on. If this Ghani is so elusive, how did you reach him to get in touch with Jalloul?'

'We had an arrangement in case of anything urgent. He had given me a phone number in Baghdad at which I could leave messages, day or night. I phoned and he called back within a couple of hours. I explained what was required, and two days later Jalloul himself phoned me.'

'Is that number in Baghdad still working?'

'I have no idea.'

'You mean you haven't tried it? Then it's not strictly true to say you've lost all contact with Ghani, is it? Why didn't you try to reach him when Hamadi told you about his difficulty?'

'Because I was sure that Ghani wouldn't be willing to help.'

'Why?'

Zunckel hesitated. 'Another circumstance had intervened. It really is of no relevance.'

'Perhaps you'd better tell me all the same, Doctor.'

'Look, it was nothing. It was a foolish notion . . .' Zunckel was trying to work up his indignation again but the fight had gone out of him. He dropped his hands into his lap. 'That phone call in the middle of August wasn't the last conversation I had with Ghani. He called me again, later that month, I think, looking for some assistance that I refused to give. He became annoyed. The discussion ended on a somewhat unfriendly note.'

Jack waited. Zunckel went on: 'He wanted my advice on the sale of some gold bullion. Quite a lot of it, I gather.

I told him I had no expertise in such matters, and I wasn't willing to recommend him to anyone else who might help. I didn't even want to hear the details, but he insisted on giving an explanation of sorts.' With an odd lack of irony the lawyer added: 'It didn't sound like the kind of thing that anyone reputable would want to touch.'

# 22

Entering his room at the Meilenhof Hotel, the first thing
Jack saw was a note on the hotel stationery that had been
left at the foot of the bed. Written in the rounded, legible
hand that was characteristic of Americans, it said:

> Gone to drool at the windows of the shops on the
> Bahnhofstrasse. I've found some maps that may lead us
> to Ms Schuster, and I've rented a car that we can pick
> up whenever we want.
> See you soon.
> Love,
> Dale.

His bag was standing on a luggage bench and he went to
unpack it. He was still preoccupied by his conversation
with Zunckel, and it was only when he opened the wardrobe
that he realized there was something oddly lived-in about
the room.

Dale's clothes were hung in the wardrobe and stacked
on the shelves beside it. Her small suitcase was tucked in
beneath them. When he looked around he saw the boots
she had travelled in discarded at the foot of the wide bed.
She had arranged for them to have a double room.

This commitment touched him with a mixture of longing
and guilt. There was more involved here than those sexual
fantasies of his, there was a suggestion of a faith in him that
he didn't think he'd earned. Although more eager than ever
to see her again, he was conscious of an immediate need to
be alone and gather his thoughts. It was five-thirty Swiss

time, making it seven-thirty in Kuwait, so he called Dr Hamadi at home. The tycoon himself answered, his tone light but peremptory: 'Hamadi.'

Jack wasted no time on pleasantries. He sketched in as briefly as possible the progress he had made so far, leaving out names and details, and then said: 'There's something that I need to have checked urgently at your end, Doctor. Have you got a fax machine at home?'

'The Iraqis stole it. It hasn't been replaced yet.'

'In your office, then? I'd like you to ask Major Al-Shaheb to take a look at some photographs and documents and see if he can make some quick IDs.'

'Yes, the one in the office seems to be working. Send them there and I'll have them collected at once and call you back.' Hamadi paused. 'It sounds as if you're on to something positive. Are you any nearer to tracing our friend?'

'I might be,' Jack said noncommittally. He told Hamadi the number of the hotel and wrote down the fax number the doctor gave him. Then he left the room and went down to the lobby. He had not been strictly truthful in telling Zunckel he wanted the Iraqis' IDs purely for his own purposes. But then, he reflected, neither had the lawyer been particularly honest with him.

The Meilenhof Hotel catered mainly to a business clientele. There was an office across from the reception desk that provided secretarial and travel services, and he handed over the papers to be faxed. With the copying machines in Zunckel's office his assistant had managed to blow up the passport photographs to postcard size, and although they were rather fuzzy they should serve their purpose provided they were reproduced with reasonable clarity at the other end.

The hotel fax machine signalled that the number in Kuwait was receiving. The transmission lasted five minutes, and when it was over he took the documents back and returned to his room. There was nothing to do now but wait.

Dale came back at six o'clock. When he made a silent gesture around the room she said: 'I thought it might save you some money. I hope you don't think I was presumptuous.'

There was still an awkwardness about their new intimacy. 'Of course you were,' he said lightly. 'But you presumed correctly.'

Among the glittering shops on the Bahnhofstrasse she had made only one purchase, a tiny gift-wrapped package that she handed to him with a smile. It contained a pair of silver cufflinks that she'd had engraved with his initials.

He kissed her. 'Thank you. But why?'

'Just to celebrate our arrival. I hope you like them. I realize I don't know anything about your tastes.'

'Enough to know that these are perfect. And extravagant. And unnecessary. But appreciated.'

Jack got down to practicalities. He explained that he couldn't leave the hotel until Hamadi had called him back, so they went down to the bar for a drink and reserved a table in the restaurant for dinner. Against a background of cocktail Muzak and the conversations of foreign businessmen he told her everything he had learned that afternoon from the doctors Buchmann and Zunckel. He ended by repeating what the lawyer had said about the last phone call he'd received from the client who called himself Mohamed Ghani.

'Ghani spoke in vague terms about being a member of a syndicate that owned a quantity of gold bullion. He claimed they'd been planning to ship it out of Iraq to be sold, but had been prevented when the United Nations sanctions were imposed. Trying to make it sound as legitimate as possible, Zunckel said.

'Ghani wanted advice on how this little difficulty could be circumvented. What red tape would be involved in moving the gold between countries, proving ownership and so on. What he seemed to be hinting at was that Zunckel might come up with some way of laundering the stuff, just as he'd laundered Ghani's money: in effect, putting it on the official market by disguising its origins. Well, Zunckel's been involved in a few dodgy transactions in his time, but he knew better than to touch this one. He fobbed Ghani off with excuses and apparently made him angry, but he did ask the question that anyone in his position would: how much gold was involved? Millions of dollars' worth, Ghani said.'

Dale had been watching him over the rim of her glass. 'And this was just before the time Noura was arrested and Jalloul disappeared? More than a coincidence? But it doesn't sound as if Ghani and friends were any too sure about what they were doing.'

'Exactly. It's one thing to get your hands on a heap of bullion, but quite another to turn it into cash. To do it officially, you have to prove that you're the legitimate owner. But there is a thriving unofficial market on the side. At a guess, I'd say that's where these people would have turned once they realized they weren't going to get any help from Zunckel.'

'Melt it down and ship it to India, the way your friend in Saudi suggested?'

'Something like that. But they'd still need help from a middleman.'

The head waiter came to tell them that their table in the restaurant was ready. There was fresh asparagus on the menu, and they ordered that and stuffed breast of veal with a bottle of Swiss Dôle du Mont recommended by the *sommelier*. They continued to speculate for a while on the subject of the gold, but nothing they came up with seemed to shed any more light on the real purpose of their enquiries.

Dale had more solid information to report. She had bought a French guidebook and some detailed road maps, on one of which she had found the village called Vaux-sur-Autruche, the last known home of Nadine Schuster. It was a tiny spot just to the east of Belfort, which, in turn, was a hundred and fifty-odd kilometres from Zurich, an easy two-hour drive. The proximity of the two places was another thing that had come to seem more than a coincidence.

'So we go there tomorrow?'

'It's a long shot, but we can't afford not to try.'

Along the M1 motorway, the traffic charging north out of London seemed unabated well after the rush hour was over. Juggernauts and long-distance coaches crammed the two inside lanes, trapping cars between them in an endless stampede of light and noise. Faster vehicles cruised by to the right, but Issa Shakir stuck to the inside lane, keeping the Ford Sierra a careful distance behind the nearest truck.

Ten miles out he took the turning at Junction Six, the first practicable place to double back along the motorway without looping off on to a secondary road. Halfway back to London, he followed the signs that pointed to the Scratchwood service area, filtering left and crossing a road bridge that gave access to the brightly lit petrol station, parking area and restaurants. He didn't stop, but kept to the left lane and swung across a second bridge, going down the ramp that led back on to the southbound carriageway. Thin traffic just here, nothing immediately in front or behind, and the darkness around the Sierra was emphasized by the stream of light from other vehicles rushing by on the main carriageway. Issa kept the speed steady at thirty miles an hour until he was halfway into the filter. Then he said to his brother in the back seat: 'Now!'

Ali had kept his left hand clasped to the back of Abdel Karim's jacket all through the journey, and the silenced pistol in his right hand jammed into the renegade's neck. Not that he thought the Kurd, bound and gagged and blindfolded, had any hope or intention of escaping, but just to keep him frightened.

Ali leaned across Karim and released the door catch. Then he shot him in the head.

The force of the bullet threw him out of the car, and he hit the hard shoulder of the road and rolled along it and off it like a bundle of rags, disappearing almost at once into the dark. The door slammed itself shut as Issa accelerated, getting up to fifty miles an hour before he joined the main stream of traffic towards London.

An hour later, in the safe house in Finsbury Park, the Mudeer received the two brothers' report in silence. They had found him in the drawing room, dressed immaculately once again and watching the news on television. He wasn't one for giving praise too freely, and tonight he seemed especially preoccupied, but at last he grunted and said: 'That was well done. In spite of the loss of our comrade Osman, our tracks remain well covered. The Kurd will soon be found, but no-one will know where he has been. More importantly, no-one will know what we have learned from him.'

The Mudeer looked at Ali and Issa significantly. He had not allowed them to be present during much of his interrogation of Karim, but in the brief periods Ali had spent in the room he'd had the impression that the Kurd wasn't saying very much.

'Our country has many enemies,' their chief went on, 'as you have been trained to appreciate. We have rid ourselves of an important one, but there are others more than willing to continue his work. Not all of them are as obvious as the Kurd. Among the most subtle and dangerous are economic enemies: people who attack the wealth and stability of our state for their own greedy purposes. These must be rooted out and crushed.'

The Mudeer paused. 'It is clear from my questioning of the Kurd that the Nazarene, Rushton, is one of these.

He has business interests in Kuwait. He is an accomplice of the opportunist sheikhs there in a new conspiracy to undermine and weaken us.'

The potent words sent a thrill of apprehension through Ali. 'Does Rushton's journey to Zurich have to do with that?' he asked.

'Very probably. I can tell you in confidence that over the years our leadership has wisely moved sums of money in secret to Switzerland, to keep them from the grasp of the very criminals and thieves who now plunder our country under the protection of United Nations sanctions. The arrangements are in the hands of a few selected men, and the details need not concern you. It is enough for you to understand that Rushton and the Kuwaitis have hopes of seizing this money, and that they must be stopped. There is more to be learned first.' He gestured at the television. 'The police here are now extremely vigilant. For the present we must risk no more forceful actions. But I have plans for both of you over the next few days.'

Jack woke up and for an instant didn't know where he was. Then he was aware of the warmth of Dale's body pressed against his in the unfamiliar bed.

They had left the light on, and when he raised his head from the pillow he saw a tender, knowing smile on her face. 'I'm sorry,' he said. 'How long have I been asleep?'

'Just a few minutes.'

His left arm lay across her firm, flat stomach. Lifting it to look at his watch, he saw it was just after eleven. Not that he had to bother about the time. Neither that nor anything else could diminish his extraordinary feeling of elation. For the first time in eight years he was in bed with a woman other than Alison; not just any woman either, but one who had more than fulfilled all the desires he had had for her. The feeling went beyond the satisfaction of male conquest, though, beyond guilty physical pleasure; in fact, he had no sense of guilt at all. In making love to

Dale he seemed to have rediscovered something he had lost long ago, a true sense of shared wanting and delight.

It was she who had made the decisive move. When they'd finished dinner and Dr Hamadi still hadn't returned Jack's call, they had gone back to the bar for coffee and brandy. After they'd been talking for half an hour she had stood up and said simply: 'We can't wait down here all night.'

In their room, it had happened just as he'd imagined it. She had slipped unselfconsciously out of her clothes, taken him by the hand and led him to the bed.

When she lay on her back as now, her small breasts all but disappeared, emphasizing the hard, boyish strength of her body. There was a yielding softness to her lips, though, and when he kissed her she drew his tongue into her mouth. They lay for a couple of minutes with their mouths working greedily at each other in a miniature simulation of coupling, until with a sudden mutual urgency they locked their bodies together and he slid into the wetness between her thighs. This time their ardour was even stronger than before, and it was amazing how close to the reality his fantasies had been: Dale's muscular legs clasped around his back, drawing him in so deep that he had the sensation of almost disappearing inside her; and then a simultaneous climax, Jack hearing her whimpers of pleasure and feeling the successive, shivering spasms of her orgasm as his own lust was released.

They separated and lay side by side for a while, looking at each other in a kind of wonder at the strength of their passion. Eventually it was Dale who spoke, striking the light note that seemed necessary.

'I think we're pretty good at this, huh?'

'I think we're brilliant. And I'm glad you made me wait.'

The call from Kuwait came ten minutes later. When he answered the ring on the bedside phone, Jack was greeted not by Hamadi's voice but by the rougher tones of Major Al-Shaheb.

'Mr Rushton? I'm sorry to call so late, but finally I think I have the information you wanted. What use it will be to you is another matter.'

'Why's that?'

'These six photographs you sent me . . . May I ask how recently they were taken?'

'Between three and five years ago, more or less.'

'Then that makes sense. I thought at first there had been some mistake. You see, I have been able to identify all six of these men from our records, but . . .'

Al-Shaheb hesitated like someone unwillingly breaking bad news. 'Go on,' Jack prompted.

'Well, all of them are dead.'

'Dead?'

'All wiped out together,' the major said with more enthusiasm. 'All burned alive on the Mutla Ridge, in February. I think I have already mentioned the incident to you.'

Jack recalled the conversation they'd had after his visit to the prisoner Fadel. 'You mean the truck full of Iraqis that was hit by a bomb? The one that killed General Malik?'

'Precisely. And ten or eleven others. These pictures of yours correspond to those of half a dozen men that I have on my files. Under their real names, of course. The ones on their passports – Ghani, Hayawi and the rest – are false.'

'Then who were they really?'

'That's what I'm trying to tell you. They were identified by the charred scraps of paper that were found with their bodies. A crowd of *Mukhabarat* swine fleeing from their crimes, and among them the biggest pig of all.'

'Malik himself? You mean he was one of these six?'

'There's no doubt of it. The man whose name you have as Mohamed Ghani was, in fact, Omar Hassan Malik, chief of the *Mukhabarat* in Kuwait. The five others were all his lackeys, all now burning in hell with him. I don't know what lead you've been following, Mr Rushton, but it looks as if it has run out on you.'

Jack put down the phone in a daze. A vision of that scowling face came back to him. The character of Ghani as the ringleader of a gang of crooks had already taken shape in his mind. To recognize that Ghani had been one and the same person as Jalloul's chief enemy required a leap of logic that was beyond him.

# 23

The N1 autobahn out of Zurich cut through the snow-patched hills of Aargau and descended into the Swiss Rhineland, following the course of the river for a time and giving occasional glimpses of it. Wide loops of blue water twinkling in the sunshine, steep, thickly wooded slopes on the far bank hinting at the forbidding terrain of the Black Forest behind them. Downstream from Rheinfelden the river widened and became like a second motorway, traversed by a steady traffic of barges and passenger boats.

It was Saturday morning, another cold but cloudless day. Dale had gone for a run first thing, and after snatching a light breakfast they had set off at ten o'clock in their hired Volkswagen Golf. Cocooned in a warm afterglow of intimacy from the night before, they didn't talk much but found no need to search for words. Their separate selves seemed to belong to a distant past; their situation had the dangerous illusions of a honeymoon about it, Jack knew, but he wanted it to go on for ever.

He had pushed what he had learned from Al-Shaheb last night to the back of his mind. There was no sense in trying to understand the inexplicable.

They reached Basle or, rather, passed it by, in less than an hour: a collection of church spires huddling around the Rhine before the river twisted away to the north. There was a sense of being at the heart of Europe here, with Germany and France both on the doorstep; indeed, they were still in the suburbs of the city when they came to a border post and were waved casually through.

They were in the French department of Haut-Rhin, in the region of Alsace. The main route to Belfort was the motorway via Mulhouse, but they chose a secondary road heading due west that looked likely to take them more directly to the village called Vaux-sur-Autruche. The nature of the countryside had changed, from the grand to the picturesque. Sleek cattle grazed on gently sloping pastures and rooks swarmed behind ploughs, searching the newly turned earth for worms and grubs. The villages and small towns they passed had German names – Ranspach, Tagsdorf, Altkirch – but their look was French: the avenues of pollarded plane trees, the squares with their *monuments aux morts* from two world wars. After fifty kilometres they crossed the Rhine-Rhône Canal, and a few minutes later a roadside sign welcomed them to the Territoire de Belfort.

It was an odd but significant little corner of France. On the map it appeared as a tiny wedge driven into a gap between Alsace and Franche-Comté. And a gap was precisely what it was, as Dale instructed Jack from the guidebook she had bought: an opening between the Vosges mountains and the Jura, a strategic passageway through which invading armies had marched from the earliest times. In 1916 it had been touch-and-go whether the German General Staff would choose Belfort or Verdun as the site of the battle intended to bleed France to death.

A sign to the left pointed them down departmental route number 29, the road they were looking for, but gave no indication that it led to Vaux. It was a narrow road flanked by high hedges, and after winding through two or three small villages that were named on the map it became little more than a country lane. Past a small schoolhouse and then a hump-backed bridge over two converging streams, it made a sudden left turn and then looped back around a cobbled square overlooked by a dozen houses.

Jack halted the car and looked at Dale in puzzlement. 'Is this it?'

'It must be. But we'd better ask.'

The place had an abandoned, vaguely down-at-heel appearance, and seemed hardly to add up to a village. There

261

was no church or other public building in the square, just a fountain that looked as if it hadn't worked for years, a small shop with a sign saying *Epicerie*, and a nameless café adjoining it. A couple of tractors were parked outside the café, and agriculture made other trespasses on the human habitat: a metal barn occupied one side of the square, and there were patches of cow dung on the cobbles.

As they stepped out of the car, Jack sensed Dale sharing his own sudden misgivings. They had come equipped only with the name of Nadine Schuster, with no real clue to her connection with this tiny hamlet. It was a literal dead end, a strange point of origin for a woman who had once had an Arab lover; and one, moreover, who had once volunteered to become a spy in order to stay with her.

Dale glanced at her watch and then around at the deserted square. 'Just after twelve. The sacred hour of the *déjeuner*, bad time to go knocking on doors. I guess we should try the café. No, here's someone we can ask.'

A small boy had walked into the village from the same direction by which they had entered it. He looked dressed for school, in corduroy trousers, a white shirt and dark pullover, and was presumably on his way home for lunch. He seemed rather nervous as they approached him across the square, but when Dale addressed him he gave her a tentative smile.

'*Bonjour. Est-ce que tu habites ce village?*'

'*Ouai?*' A question within the answer.

'*Il s'appelle comment?*'

'*Ici, c'est le village de Vaux, madame,*' the boy replied politely. He was ten or eleven years old, with the shyly curious manner of a country child. In spite of that his features were strongly formed, giving him a prematurely adult look. The prominent nose, the narrow jaw and the liquid brown eyes harked at origins from another time or place. The Midi, perhaps, or even one of the former French possessions in North Africa.

'*Bien*,' Dale said. '*Alors, peut-être tu peux nous aider. Nous cherchons une dame qui a habité ici dans le temps. Elle s'appelle Nadine Schuster. Est-ce que tu la connais?*'

The boy's smile vanished. He didn't answer, but stared at her in confusion. It was hard to guess what had caused this sudden change in his manner, but on that well-defined but innocent face there was something very like fear.

'*Qu'y a-t-il?*' Dale asked. '*Tu a compris ce que j'ai dit?*'

He chewed on his lip and lowered his gaze to the ground, where he was twisting the toe of his shoe about on the cobbles. Then he looked up with a more definite apprehension at Jack, as though whatever threat he had sensed came from this silent male presence rather than from her. In a moment of intuition, Jack thought he had understood the boy's fear. He reached out a hand in what was meant to be a reassuring gesture, but that proved the breaking point. The child's lower lip was quivering. He flinched back with a whimper of fright and ran away across the square.

Dale said: 'You scared him! You should have left him to me.'

'Sorry. But I don't think it's really me he's frightened of.'

He watched the boy run to the *épicerie*, yank open the door and go inside. From the decisive way he had moved, there was nothing random about this choice of a refuge. Jack went after him at a trot, ignoring Dale's further protests. He was remembering another three-way encounter, between himself, Dale and the Kuwaiti youth called Tewfiq and he knew what it was he recognized in this boy: not Provence, not North Africa, but Arab. Not just a general look this time, but a particular one. He knew instinctively that the boy was the true reason for their coming here.

Dale caught up with him as he reached the glazed double doors of the village shop.

'Jack, do you want to get arrested for child molesting or something?'

'Just trust me. Please.'

An entry bell on the door rang as they stepped into a cool, dark cave smelling pungently of cheese and smoked meats. Fat Alsatian sausages hung above a glass counter displaying hams and tubs of liver pâté and *choucroute*, none of them looking very fresh. There was no-one behind the counter, but from an open doorway to the rear came a medley of sounds: the piping treble of the boy cut off by urgent adult voices, the residual clash of cutlery on plates betraying a French country family disturbed at their midday meal. A moment later an old man in a grubby grocer's apron emerged from the door, to be immediately brushed aside by a much younger and tougher one in a workman's *bleu de travail*. He glared at the newcomers and said: *'Qu'est-ce que vous voulez?'*

*'Pardon, monsieur'*, Dale began. *'Nous avons seulement demandé des directions à vôtre fils—'*

*'Etienne. Mon neveu, pas mon fils. Mais je sais ce que vous lui avez demandé. Qu'est-ce que vous voulez suggérer?'*

*'Nous lui avons pas voulu de mal.'*

The man's hostile stare continued. The old grocer lingered in the doorway and from behind him the boy, Etienne, peeped out. Nothing but fear could have evoked such a reaction in these people. They had been anticipating trouble.

Dale turned nervously to Jack. 'I knew we shouldn't have come in here. This is the boy's uncle. He seems to think we were trying to frighten the child.'

'Tell him we're sorry,' Jack said. 'Tell him it was just by coincidence that we spoke to Etienne. That we didn't realize it was his mother we were asking about.'

'His mother?'

Dale stared at him in bewilderment. He went on: 'Ask this man if his name is Schuster. Tell him it's his sister we're looking for: Nadine, Etienne's mother. And that we're not here to cause any problems.'

The man had caught something of Jack's drift and said: '*Vous connaissez mon nom. Comment?*'

'They're going to insist on an explanation,' Dale said.

'Tell them as much as you need to.'

She began to speak, interrupted now and then by remarks and questions from the two men. There were other people in the living room at the back of the shop, and in response to a whispered summons Etienne turned away to join them. Then the bell at the front door pinged and three hefty farmers in blue overalls came in. Someone must have gone through the back entrance and alerted the tractor drivers from the café next door. Hands on hips, they formed a solid, menacing semicircle behind the two strangers.

Dale paused in her conversation and said to Jack: 'I think I've convinced them that we don't mean any harm. They admit that Nadine does live somewhere near here. They are her brother and father. Apparently she isn't married, but Etienne is her little boy. He comes here for lunch from school every day. Beyond that, they're stonewalling. I've told them we want her to help us trace a man she used to know in England many years ago, but they say that's her own business. They won't have us meddling in it.'

'Is that a tacit admission that it's Etienne's father we're talking about?'

Once again the boy's uncle was quick on the uptake. '*Son père?*' he said gruffly. '*Il n'a pas de père.*'

'*Tout le monde a un père, monsieur,*' Dale retorted. '*C'est pour son propre bien que nous le cherchons.*'

'*Pourquoi est-ce qu'on devrait vous croire?*'

'*Vous pourriez être n'importe qui,*' the old man put in.

Dale talked back to them with spirit, getting into her stride with the language. She spoke without interruption for a couple of minutes, raising her voice and wagging an admonitory finger, and when she had finished the two men looked much less certain of themselves. They glanced at each other and the younger one made a decision. He gave a gesture of dismissal to the three farmers, and when they had trooped out he said grudgingly to Dale: '*Attendez. Je vais téléphoner.*'

Father and son returned to the room at the back, closing the door behind them, leaving Jack and Dale strangely alone in the shop. 'What did you say to them?' he asked admiringly.

She was full of suppressed excitement. 'I told them they were being foolish not to trust us. I said that since we'd managed to trace Nadine Schuster here, others with less kindly intentions might be able to do the same, and that they'd be better off sharing their knowledge with us than hiding it. That thought really bugged them. Remember what I told you about the mechanical solidarity group? This family is obviously scared of something, and I knew what it was as soon as you'd made the connection between Etienne and his mother. The way that kid reacted to us! He'd been warned to beware of strangers – not just the run-of-the-mill strangers that all parents warn their kids about, but people asking questions about his mother. Foreigners. But why? The two of them must have been living quite peaceably in this backwater for the past ten years or so. Maybe she kept the name of the boy's father a secret, maybe not, but either way she had nothing to be afraid of. Why the sudden anxiety?'

'Because she knows Jalloul is on the run? That people might come looking for him?'

'Exactly. And how could she know unless she'd been in contact with him?'

Jack turned to stare out through the glass doors, from the gloom of the shop into the sunlit square. He was struck again by the shabbiness of this village, and Dale's thoughts gave an extra dimension to the reasons he had imagined for Nadine's returning here and staying for so long. They also put a question into focus that Jack had never paid much attention to: who exactly did Jalloul have to be afraid of? Who might come looking for him? Vengeful Kuwaitis?

Western war crimes investigators? Or the *Mukhabarat*, still chafing at his disappearance seven months ago? The man who'd appeared to be the main enemy in his own camp, General Malik, had since been killed, as Jack had learned last night from Al-Shaheb; but that still left a number of other possibilities open. Maybe Nadine Schuster would have some answers.

Her brother emerged from the back room, his phone call presumably made. His expression gave nothing away; he nodded curtly and said, '*Venez*.'

Colonel Thorpe had used his newly delivered Rotovator to till a patch of ground at the top of the paddock, and this morning he was spreading compost to prepare the site for maincrop potatoes. He'd been interrupted once by a restaurant owner who called to pick up an order of broccoli and leeks, and again by a retired couple he knew who chatted to him for ten minutes before departing with a single cauliflower. There was a tranquillity about this place that made people feel in no need to hurry about their business. He didn't really mind, but his heart sank slightly when he saw yet another caller coming round the side of the bungalow.

This was a stranger and unusual looking for a customer, a young man in blue jeans and a loose-fitting windcheater who paused at the corner of the house before spotting Thorpe and picking his way past rows of vegetables towards him. His appearance was foreign, possibly Middle Eastern, the colonel thought, and he looked barely into his twenties. He stopped a few feet away and gave a friendly smile.

'Colonel . . . Thorpe?' Hesitating slightly over the name.

'That's me.' Thorpe stuck his spade into the ground. 'What can I do for you?'

'I beg your pardon. I have stopped you in your work. I will not delay you long.'

The young man's English was correct, rather formal, probably not much practised. He had bright brown eyes and curly black hair. The apology for the interruption was a point in his favour, though there was a certain cockiness to his manner that made Thorpe wonder how seriously it was meant.

'You may perhaps be able to help me. I am trying to find a friend of yours. A Mr Jack Rushton.'

'Rushton?' The colonel was taken aback. He hadn't exactly forgotten his visitor of two nights ago, just hadn't thought much about him since. 'He's not a friend, just someone I met the other day. Don't you know where he lives?'

'I do. But he is not at home. He has gone to Zurich. I wonder if you know where I could find him there?'

'Not a clue. He didn't even mention he was going.' Annoyed now, Thorpe said: 'The talk we had was meant to be confidential. Who on earth sent you here?'

The man didn't reply directly. 'There is some mistake, I am afraid. I have not met Mr Rushton, I was just given his name. I am trying to help him with some urgent business of his.'

'Well, you've come to the wrong place,' Thorpe said briskly. 'I hardly know him either. He turned up on my doorstep, just the way you have . . .' The memory struck a faint warning note. 'Can you explain what help you want to give him?'

'That too is a private matter. He may perhaps have told you that he is involved in some sensitive work.'

The colonel studied the young man more carefully. Sure of himself all right, and definitely from the Middle East. He had a gleam of sincerity in his eyes that almost hinted at fanaticism. Perhaps he had something important to tell Rushton about the missing Jalloul. On the other hand he might be fishing for information, but this seemed a peculiar way to go about it.

'What we talked about was entirely our own business, I'm afraid. I don't expect to hear from Rushton again, but if I do perhaps I could give him a message.'

'Thank you. You could tell him I have news for him about a friend he was looking for. A friend from Kuwait.'

Thorpe relented slightly. There might be some genuine mix-up here, not a deliberate breach of confidence. Sloppy of Rushton all the same. He didn't want to be unhelpful, or so he told himself. In fact, for once, curiosity got the better of his ingrained discretion.

'Could I tell him that it's good news?'

'Oh, yes. Very good news.'

'This . . . friend . . wouldn't happen to have vanished in Kuwait seven or eight months ago, would he?'

The young man smiled broadly. 'I think we both know what we are talking about, Colonel. But I cannot say more.'

'I understand. Well, if I do happen to hear from him . . . I don't think you mentioned your name.'

'Mr Rushton wouldn't know it. But it is Ali Shakir.'

Nadine's brother, driving a beaten-up 2CV, had led Jack and Dale a short distance back along the way they had come. Just past the schoolhouse he turned on to a bumpy, unpaved track that ran between dusty farm hedges, then met up with another departmental road. Almost immediately the car swung to a halt beside a row of three or four single-storeyed cottages. Jack drew up behind it.

The cottages were small and plain, with slate roofs and whitewashed walls, lacking in any self-conscious adornment. Not unattractive but not quaint enough, at a guess, to have excited the interest of second-home buyers among the French middle class, and so probably still serving as the houses of farmworkers. They also had the disadvantage of facing directly on to the road, which led across open country towards a town dominated by a castle. This was evidently a minor route to the old fortress town of Belfort; in the middle distance was a collection of flat-roofed buildings that looked like an industrial estate.

Schuster got out of his car. He gave no indication that Jack and Dale should remain where they were, so they followed him to a house at the centre of the row, through a gate and across a tiny garden to the front door. His knock was answered by a young woman, probably in her late teens, who disappeared at once towards the rear of the cottage and left them to find their own way in.

A dark, low-ceilinged hallway. Open doors on either side giving glimpses of a living room and two small bedrooms. Down a step at the end of the hall, a turning to the right showed a kitchen with a telephone on the wall among a row of pans and skillets. From beyond another closed door, straight ahead, came the only sound of life in the house, a cacophony of shrill little voices like the cries of different species of birds in an aviary.

Schuster opened the door. Behind it was a room that must have been added on to the back of the cottage. It was bigger than any of the others, with wide windows and yellow-painted walls plastered with brightly coloured posters and the crude paintings of children. Four or five toddlers were down on the carpeted floor, surrounded by building blocks, wheeled toys and plastic tricycles. In the middle of the room, a couple of older ones knelt on benches around a table covered in oilcloth, tongues curled out in concentration as they wrestled with plasticine figures or smeared finger-paints on sheets of paper.

A woman wearing a flowered pinafore over a polo-necked sweater and jeans presided at the table. She was in her early to mid-thirties and pretty in a slightly faded way, with blue eyes and lank brownish-blond hair that she brushed back from her forehead as she looked up, without expression, at her visitors. Nadine Schuster, the au pair from Farnborough, was still looking after other people's children.

'*Les voici,*' said her brother by way of introduction. With a note of warning he added: '*Tu sais tu dois pas trop dire.*'

'*Je sais, je sais,*' she said.

Schuster left the room without another word. Nadine watched him go and then stood up and suddenly smiled at her visitors. It was a cautious but natural smile, and it immediately broke the tension.

'*Mon frère*,' she said resignedly to Dale. '*C'est un têtu.* A . . . hard case, do you say? You are English?'

'I'm American. My friend here is English.'

They introduced themselves, shaking hands with what seemed an odd formality in the circumstances. Two of the toddlers, suspicious of the strangers, were clinging to Nadine's legs; another had started to cry. The young woman who had answered the front door came in to pacify him. Nadine spoke a few words to her and then said, 'They have their lunch now, and then they sleep. We'll go somewhere else to talk.'

She gently detached herself from the children's grasp. Leaving her assistant in charge of the crèche, she led Jack and Dale to the sitting room. It was small and stuffed with ageing furniture, and they had to pick their way past rickety low tables before they found room to sit down.

Nadine said: 'You will excuse me if my English is not too good, please. It's long since I spoke it.'

'It seems excellent to me,' Jack said.

She fished in the front pocket of her pinafore, removing a collection of crayon stubs and crumpled bits of paper and dumping them in a big ashtray, before she found a packet of Gitanes. She offered them around and was refused. When she lit one herself she drew on it lightly, without any sign of nervousness. Jack realized he had been preparing himself for someone different, a sad and lonely woman perhaps, or on the other hand a prickly and defensive one. Nadine appeared to be neither. Surrounded by children and the shabby comfort of the cottage, she seemed placid and not discontented, a young earth-mother, and certainly she didn't share her family's paranoia. Her figure was still good, though thickened slightly, and in the steady eyes, clear skin and wide mouth he could see

271

traces of the youthful freshness that had attracted Jalloul all those years ago.

'You have met my boy, Etienne?' she asked.

'We spoke to him by chance in the village. I'm afraid we gave him a bit of a fright.'

'*Po-po-po!*' She gave a dismissive wave but did not take up the subject. She seemed in no hurry to get to the point, explaining that she had opened the crèche once Etienne had started school. The children were mainly those of people who worked in the factories in Belfort; today being Saturday, she had only a few of them in her charge. Since she had no qualifications, the only alternative would have been a factory job for herself. This was more fun and it gave her a small but steady income, enough to keep her independent of her parents.

It was a strange monologue. She spoke as though nothing outside this village had ever been part of her life. But eventually, she said: 'So you are looking for Etienne's father. You did not hope to find him here, did you?'

Dale and Jack glanced at each other. Dale said: 'Can we just verify one thing? His father is Ibrahim Jalloul, an Iraqi army officer?'

'That's right,' she said uneasily.

'Are you still in touch with him?'

'For many years, yes, but no longer. I saw him for the last time in June last year. After that, in August, we spoke on the telephone.'

It was hard to penetrate her blandness. Jack said: 'Your family, and Etienne himself, seemed very scared about the fact that we were looking for you. Is that because you expect Colonel Jalloul to make contact with you again? Or because they think others will come searching for him?'

'*Po-po-po!*' Nadine repeated, stubbing out her cigarette. 'His grandparents and his uncle frighten him with talk about strangers. They get scared about things they don't understand. Nobody is looking for Ibrahim. And I do not expect to hear from him.'

They waited. She swept her hair back off her face again. 'I don't know what you want with Ibrahim,' she said, 'but I don't think I can help you. I think he is dead. In fact, I am sure of it.'

# 24

Jack had begun revising his opinion of Nadine Schuster as
soon as they had met, and now he was forced to reconsider
again. He had put that placid demeanour down to a certain
lack of imagination; now he knew there was something
stronger behind it. Her stoicism had served her well during
the ten years of her intermittent love affair with Jalloul,
and in recent months it had helped her to resign herself
to what she obviously regarded as a form of widowhood.

She was a woman who could create her own contentment.
In imagining her pining away for an unrequited love,
Jack had merely been yielding to a stereotype. Sitting in
that over-furnished little room listening to her talk about
the relationship, he began to understand that it had been
Jalloul who'd been the one more dissatisfied with their
predicament, who felt guilty about failing to keep his
promises to her, who insisted that she deserved better
than she had. The conventional roles of a married man
and his hopefully waiting mistress had been reversed.

'I had more than he did,' she said simply. 'I had
Etienne. I had my home and family here. Ibrahim had a
wife he hated but whom he could not leave. He lived
in a country where there was no trust, no certainty, and
money only for favoured people. He liked the army, but
he knew that if he rose too high in it his life would be in
danger. He wanted to get away but he never could. When
the chance came, he lost it.'

From the end of 1980, when Jalloul had returned to
Iraq from his course at Camberley and Nadine had come
back here to have her baby, they had stayed in touch.
They wrote to each other and spoke on the telephone.

They met only when he could find excuses to get out of the country; given the demands imposed on him during the eight years of the Iran-Iraq war, that was no more than two or three times a year. He would visit her here for a few days at a time, and on some occasions when he couldn't make it this far she had taken Etienne on trips to Turkey to meet him there. Too much risk would have been involved in bringing them to Baghdad.

In spite of these difficulties they seemed to have remained devoted to each other. They were a strange match, characters from an old-fashioned love story. Jalloul adored Nadine and his son. He continued to search for ways to get out of Iraq and join them, but without money he could give them no security. His wife's family were important enough to make or break his army career, but had no intention of allowing him access to the golden circle of graft and corruption that had made men like Dr Zunckel's clients wealthy. Jalloul lived on the salary of an army officer, paid in Iraqi dinars. If he fled the country he would need more than was required merely to provide for Nadine and Etienne; he would be branded as a deserter and a traitor, and he would need enough to ensure that they remained out of reach of the long arm of the *Mukhabarat*.

Such a windfall, the sort he had once imagined the British would pay him for becoming a spy, continued to elude him. Until last August.

'I was surprised when he telephoned me. That was about two weeks after the invasion of Kuwait, and I was sure he would have been sent there and was worrying about him. To telephone from Kuwait was impossible but he was speaking from Amman, in Jordan. He told me he had made an arrangement that would give him two million American dollars. It would be ready for him at a bank in Zurich in two or three weeks.

'He always travelled through Switzerland when he came to see us here, to conceal the real purpose of his journeys. This time, he said, Etienne and I should be ready to go away with him. It would not be safe for us to stay here; we would have to go into hiding for a time and later we would find a new home, perhaps in some other part of France.

'Two weeks later he called me again, also from Amman. Everything was arranged, he said. He would be in Zurich soon and would phone me when he got there. He could not yet say exactly when that would be, because there was a complication.'

Nadine tossed back her hair and lit another cigarette. '*I* did not want this money, you understand? It was what he said we needed. What this plan was to make him suddenly rich, I don't know. He told me nothing and I didn't ask. I know that much money is made by Iraqis – wrongly, slyly? – in French we say *en cachette* – but I know that Ibrahim would not do anything dishonourable.' She paused. 'He told me that to make this arrangement work he needed the help of certain people he was not sure he could trust. He would have to choose the time of his departure carefully, to be sure that his plan was not sabotaged. Those were the last words he spoke to me. I did not know then that he was in greater danger than he was telling me.'

'He just never arrived?' Jack said.

'He never arrived.'

'But have you no proof that he's dead?'

'Have you any proof that he's alive? If he was, he would find a way to let me know.'

She had spoken calmly, but now she drew on the cigarette as if she needed it. Jack said: 'Did you make any enquiries about him?'

'Enquiries to whom? The Iraqis? They had just attacked Kuwait, they were *les méchants* of the world, nobody there would tell me anything. And what would my questions be? "Where is Ibrahim Jalloul, who has been ten years my lover? Who has a wife of his own in Baghdad?"'

'Who were these people that he didn't trust?'

276

Nadine shrugged. 'The usual ones. The ones he used to say did not trust *him*. The political police.'

'Then how can you be sure they didn't put him in jail? Keep him from making contact with anyone?'

'Why don't you believe me?' she said, showing her first slight sign of exasperation. 'It's not just my instincts that are saying it to me, it's . . .'

She was about to say more, but stopped herself. Her conviction that Jalloul was dead was so strong that she hadn't bothered to enquire more than casually about the purpose of their questions. Feeling he owed her an explanation, Jack described the arrangement her lover had made to get Noura Hamadi out of Kuwait. He told her that the first million dollars of the payment had reached the bank in Zurich and remained there, unclaimed, and that ownership of the second million was now the subject of a legal difficulty.

'That's the reason I keep coming back to the question of whether he's still alive. If he is, I want to offer him the chance of settling the problem. Arranging to let him have some or all of that second instalment. It's money that he wanted you and Etienne to have.'

He did not really expect her to rise to this bait. She sighed and said: 'I thank you for your concern. But . . . I don't know how to say this, because I have promised not to speak about it. But I must try to convince you. I will speak with . . . *circonlocution*, you understand? If you also will treat it with discretion?'

'Of course.'

'Apart from this business of the two million dollars, there was something else. Something Ibrahim was involved in, or knew about. Something, again, that I am sure was not dishonourable. But I don't know what it was, so it is no use for you to ask me. That's what men do, isn't it, hide things from women to protect them from worry?'

They do with women like you, Jack thought. Nadine put out her cigarette and immediately lit another one.

'When Ibrahim was in Amman the second time, he made another telephone call. Not to me, to a friend in Turkey, in the army there. I did not know what it was they spoke about, but it concerned this involvement, the thing that was making complications about his leaving Kuwait. The friend has told me since that it is for my own good not to know, at least for the present. I accept that. There is nothing more I can tell you.'

They sat in silence for a few moments. Then Jack said: 'This . . . involvement, whatever it was, is the thing that's made you so certain Colonel Jalloul was killed?' She nodded. 'And you really haven't the slightest idea what it was about?'

This time she didn't bother to reply. Dale said: 'Was this what you brother meant when he told you not to say too much? *Tu sais tu dois pas trop dire,* he said.'

'My brother!' she echoed, making a face. 'He loves me, but he is another one who wants to protect me. That's why there was this fuss about Etienne. One month ago they all got a fright because someone came looking for me. Like you, a foreigner asking for me in the village. It was only my friend, visiting from Turkey.'

'Is that when he brought you this news?'

'No. He spoke to me first on the telephone in September, after Ibrahim disappeared. The call from Amman had made him concerned. He phoned several times after that, very anxious to know if I had heard anything. This time he was just on vacation in Switzerland and he drove here to see me. Still worrying. The three of us were very old friends.'

Jack sat forward tensely. 'Without betraying any confidences, Miss Schuster, do you think it would be possible to get this friend of yours to talk to us?'

She drew on her cigarette and looked at them both in turn. 'If he will say nothing to me, why should he speak to you?'

'Because I have an idea – only an idea – that I may know something about the business. It could be to his advantage if we exchanged information.'

'You don't understand. He is a senior man in the Turkish army. He will not speak to a stranger, a foreigner, about a confidential matter. I can't even tell you his name.'

'Couldn't you try to convince him? Have you got some way of reaching him?'

'I have a phone number in Istanbul, but . . .'

'Please call him for us, Miss Schuster.'

She was still dubious. 'I think you are wasting your time, but . . . Will you pay for the call?'

'Naturally.'

'Then wait here, please.'

She stood up and left the room, closing the door behind her. In spite of that, a minute later they heard her talking on the telephone in the kitchen, her voice reaching them faintly over the fretful sounds from the crèche. She seemed to be speaking in English, but they couldn't make out anything that she said.

She came back five minutes later, stuffing a slip of paper into her pocket.

'It's as I thought,' she said. 'It is out of the question for him to talk to you. I can do nothing more.'

'Did you make the point that we might be able to help him?' Jack asked.

'I told him. It made no difference.' She saw their disappointment and added: 'If all you are looking for is proof that Ibrahim is dead, then I don't think this man could help you much more than I can. I trust him completely. The three of us became friends when I lived in England, while Ibrahim was at the army college there. Later, when Ibrahim was back in Iraq, when we used to go to meet in Turkey, we used to stay with him and his wife in Istanbul. Not so risky as a hotel, and cheaper.' Nadine hunted in the front of her pinafore for her cigarettes again, discarding more debris into the overflowing ashtray. 'One day perhaps he will tell me more about what happened. Until then . . .'

'When he came to see you last month,' Jack said, 'did he say anything more about this . . . complication that had put Ibrahim in danger? Did he suggest that it had been sorted out?'

'He told me nothing new.'

'Do you remember when exactly he visited you?'

'It was . . . a Sunday afternoon. It must have been the first Sunday in March.'

The telephone bell pealed from the kitchen and Nadine left the room again. Jack stood up and looked out of the cottage window, at the drab view across the road. So near and yet so far, he thought; all the progress he had seemed to be making had come to a halt in this dead-end village. Nadine was probably right: he could do nothing to disprove her conviction that her lover was no longer alive. Other signs pointed that way as well. In spite of the hope he had pinned on talking to her Turkish friend, on reflection it seemed likely that he would only have heard the same point of view repeated. The things he had learned in London and Zurich had been relevant to his task just as long as they led him towards the possibility of finding Jalloul. Now they were only incidental. They were murky and venal and perhaps even dangerous, but the bank accounts of seven dead men and rumours about missing gold were not what Hamadi was paying him to look for.

Dale had been preoccupied behind him. When Nadine returned she didn't sit down but stood by the doorway in a tacit invitation to them to leave.

'That was the telephone service,' she said. 'The price of the call was fifty-five francs.'

As they drove out of Vaux, they both admitted to being famished. A few kilometres down the road they stopped the car and dived into the first restaurant they saw, in a village called Dannemarie. The *plat du jour* was roast rack of spring lamb, and they ordered that with a bottle of light red Alsatian wine.

'I hate cow-like women,' Dale declared.

'Is that how you see her? I thought she was pretty admirable, standing by her man all that time.'

'Let's play cynical for a minute. Let's say that in spite of Nadine's starry-eyed view of lover boy, what he really was was your average shit. That he never intended to tie himself to her once he got out of Iraq. That like a lot of other married men he went on telling his girlfriend that she was the one he really cared for, that one day he'd leave his wife for her. Waiting for the day he gets into some big money and can disappear to the Bahamas, and meanwhile using her whenever it suits him.'

'For the sake of a free screw a couple of times a year?'

'Some men will do strange things for a free screw, believe me. If he decided to ditch Nadine he might even have gotten his Turkish pal to hint to her that he was dead.'

It was an original point of view, but not one that Jack could accept. 'Nadine may have the patience of a cow,' he said, 'but she's not stupid. She'd have seen through him if he wasn't sincere. Besides, he really seems to have loved the boy. And if you want proof that he never made it out of Kuwait, that untouched bank account says it all.'

'So you buy her story in full?'

'I think she was telling the truth as far as she knows it, and it ties in with the facts that we do have. The two million dollars. The two phone calls from Amman, coinciding with the dates Jalloul was there to meet Hamadi. I think he did intend to get Noura out of Kuwait. He was keeping his part of the bargain, but something went wrong at the last minute. He was captured, probably by his old enemy General Malik, and either killed on the spot or executed in some Iraqi dungeon.'

'Maybe. But I still don't trust all that *circonlocution*. I think Nadine is relying on more than guesswork. Not even she would accept the sort of vague explanation she gave us about this other thing Jalloul was involved in, that may or may not have led to his death. And I don't believe she put a very convincing case to her friend in Turkey about talking to us.'

'As a matter of fact, I have an idea that I know who this Turk is. Jalloul formed a friendship with a Turkish officer when they were both students at Camberley; Colonel Thorpe told me about it. Another thing: did you notice me asking exactly when this friend paid her his visit? It was the first Sunday in March – the third of the month. That was just three days after the end of the Gulf War, in which Turkey was heavily involved. Half its army was stationed on the border with Iraq. Can you see one of its officers swanning around Switzerland and France on holiday?'

'So he came specially to see her?'

'Yes. Quite why, I can't work out. But none of that is any real help. My job was to trace Jalloul, and now I have to accept that he's probably dead. Malik is dead too, so we'll never know where he came into it. And Noura is dead. Who's left to say what really happened on that night you saw her off to the airport?'

'So what now?'

'I'll have to tell Hamadi the case is closed.'

'Why so negative all of a sudden, Jack? There is one thing you could do. You could talk to this Turk yourself.'

'What would that achieve? Perhaps Thorpe could dig up his name for me, but . . .'

'Even if he can't, I have his phone number '

With a mischievous look she opened her handbag. She took out a slip of paper that had been crumpled and then unfolded, and flattened it on the table. A long number was scribbled on it in red crayon, starting with the digits 19-90-1.

'Care to bet on that being the international code from here to Istanbul? Nadine copied down the number from somewhere and stuck it in the front of her apron after she'd made the call. Then she threw it out. I retrieved it from the ashtray.'

He grinned at her. 'Are you sure your talents are best suited to sociology? If not, I can recommend you for a job as an investigator. But, I have to repeat, what does it achieve? I get his name and I call him, and he slams the phone down.'

'Don't give him the chance. Don't call. Go find him.'

'I couldn't justify that. Even if he did agree to talk to me, I don't believe that what he said would change anything. Besides . . . we seem to be talking about what *I* should do. If I were to fly to Istanbul, where would that leave you?'

'I don't know. I guess I'd go on to Paris, the way I planned.'

In sudden alarm he said: 'I don't want that to happen, Dale. I want us to stay together, for as long as we can.'

'Well, just as it happens,' she said with a smile, 'so do I.'


They were back in Zurich by late afternoon but there was no point in trying to phone Colonel Thorpe until the evening. Neither of them needed to wonder how they should fill in the time. They hung the DO NOT DISTURB sign on door of their room and went to bed.

When Thorpe answered his phone at eight o'clock, British time, he seemed oddly unsurprised to hear from Jack. In fact, he sounded rather indignant.

'I'm not too impressed by your idea of security,' he said. 'Are you using me as a message centre or something?'

'What do you mean?'

The colonel told him about a visit he'd had that morning from a rather odd young man named Ali Shakir. The name meant nothing to Jack, but Thorpe's account of the conversation they had had sent a shiver of apprehension through him.

'He knows I'm looking for . . .?' Jack bit back the name of Jalloul. 'And that I'm in Zurich? But he can't know, unless . . .'

'Unless what? I must confess that I wasn't a model of prudence myself. It crossed my mind that he was on the prowl for information, but I ignored the advice of my master Sun Tzu: Pretend inferiority to your enemy.'

Jack assured Thorpe that he had told no-one about their meeting. Whoever Ali Shakir was, he must have learned of it some other way. By the time he had satisfied the colonel on this point he was so distracted he had almost forgotten why he was phoning.

He asked Thorpe if he could find out the name of the Turkish officer who had been at Camberley with Jalloul. After some grumbling about this being Saturday night, about nobody being able to remember that far back, he agreed to see what he could do.

Dale came out of the bathroom and saw the look on Jack's face.

'What's the matter?'

He repeated what Thorpe had told him. 'There's only one way they could know I've been trying to trace Jalloul,' he said bleakly. 'They must have got it out of Abdel Karim after they kidnapped him. You were right to be concerned about that . . .'

'They? Are we talking about the *Mukhabarat*?'

'Who else would be interested? But I never told Karim I was coming here. They've been following my movements. Why?' An even more startling thought struck him then. 'Jesus! My family.'

He dialled the number in Banstead at once. Camilla answered the phone, whooping at the sound of his voice.

'Daddy! Are you still in the Alps?'

She told him Alison was out with the Reynolds for the evening and they had a babysitter in. The news reassured him; she wouldn't have left the twins if she had any serious cause for worry. He spoke to Camilla and Claudia in turn, asking them what was happening at home and listening patiently to accounts of their doings. No untoward event, no visit from a stranger for instance, would have escaped comment by those two busybodies.

When he said goodbye, after telling them he wasn't yet sure when he would be home, he felt a little less alarmed. He considered phoning Reg Kilmartin and asking if there was any news about Karim, but thought better of it; Reg didn't know he was in Zurich, and now the fewer people who did know, the better.

'It doesn't sound as if they've been asking questions at my house,' he said to Dale, 'perhaps because they didn't need to. Somehow they know I'm here. Why are they interested in *me*?'

'Because they think you know something that affects them, presumably.'

'But I don't, damn it! All Karim can have told them is that I wanted to find Jalloul, and that I'd come across some financial details about a man called Ghani. But Ghani was General Malik, who is now dead. And if Jalloul is dead too . . . they must have known that my enquiries wouldn't lead anywhere.'

'You talked to Karim about something else,' Dale said. 'You talked about the stolen gold.'

He stared at her. 'That *can't* be the reason. Neither of us knew anything about it worth speaking of.'

'But now you know more. Jack, I've seen the *Mukhabarat* at work and I don't think you should waste time trying to analyse their motives. I think you should get out of here. Head straight home, call the police and get yourself some protection.'

He tried to collect his wits. It was a scary feeling, scarier than he would have imagined possible, to think of nameless people tracking his movements, people who wouldn't stop short of kidnapping and murder to achieve their ends. It had thrown his thoughts into disarray as well as stretching his nerves, which were suddenly jangled by the ringing of the phone.

It was the hotel switchboard, asking if he would pay for a reverse-charge call from England.

Colonel Thorpe said: 'You're in luck. Purchase's wife, the woman that French girl worked for, has come up trumps again. She remembered the name of the Turk. It's Yashar Delkin.' He spelt it out. 'He had the rank of acting major at the time. But they never heard from him after he left Camberley, so God knows where he is or what he's doing now.'

Jack thanked him and said: 'If you get any more queries about me, please don't tell anyone where I am.'

'All right. I'm not going to ask what you're up to, but it sounds a bit dicey. Remember something else from Sun Tzu: When capable, pretend to be incapable. When near, you should seem to be far away; when far away, seem near.'

On this bewildering note of advice he rang off. Jack sat on the bed, staring at Dale. She was right; it would be sensible to get out of Zurich. There was nothing more for him here, anyway. On the other hand, he shouldn't let himself be panicked into flight. This was a big city and surely he would not be easy to find. Besides, if he did go back to London and talk to the police, what could he say without revealing the background to his recent activities? He had promised to keep Hamadi's agreement with Jalloul a secret, a promise that had been easy enough to make at the time but that now seemed a burden.

Dale could be right about another thing. The gold. No matter how hard he tried to dismiss it as an irrelevance, it kept re-emerging, demanding his attention.

Perhaps he was only seeking excuses not to go home to Alison's frostiness and the bitter dregs of their marriage. But in spite of the conclusions he had come to after talking to Nadine Schuster, what he had just learned from Thorpe could justify his continuing what he had begun.

He could make one more attempt to find out what had happened to Jalloul.

He searched in his address book for Eric Patley's number in Dhahran. One more contact, one more link in a chain that now drew him towards the settling of unfinished business.

He dialled the number. While he waited for it to ring he said to Dale: 'Yes, I'll get out of Zurich. But London isn't the right place to go just yet. If you meant what you said about us staying together, how about coming with me to Istanbul?'

*Part Three*

# 25

The road from Yesilköy airport ran along the shore of the
Sea of Marmara, parallel to the railway line that carried
the more intrepid kind of traveller the last few miles of the
long journey from western Europe to its eastern edge.
The sunshine of early afternoon was strong and the water
was deep blue, the coastline littered with rickety wooden
jetties and beached fishing boats. Inland, huddled slums
alternated with high-rise blocks of flats. For a time the view
was blocked by the towering grey heights of the old city
walls, and then a turn in the road revealed a hilly skyline
surmounted by the breathtaking domes and minarets of
St Sophia and the Blue Mosque.

The taxi ground its way into Istanbul, a blur of
chaotic impressions after decorous, orderly Zurich. Ancient
American cars jostled and hooted for road space among
milling pedestrians. The Galata Bridge across the Golden
Horn seethed with street traders, food sellers and Sunday
strollers. Things were quieter up among the shabby
buildings of Beyoglu, part of the old European quarter,
where the taxi dropped them in front of the Second Empire
façade of the Pera Palace Hotel.

It had to be the Pera Palace or nothing, Dale had
insisted. The hotel had been built a century before to
accommodate travellers arriving on the Orient Express,
and, in consequence, was almost as famous as the train
itself. The interior seemed to live up to her expectations:
the lobby and the adjacent public rooms were all plush
seating, dark wood panelling and gilt-framed mirrors; the
lift was an ornate contraption of wrought iron – the oldest lift
in Turkey, the bellboy who took them up in it informed

them proudly. The room he showed them into had a small balcony overlooking a garden, and a huge bathroom with a marble floor and a bath big enough for three people.

Dale hummed contentedly as she unpacked her clothes and hung them in the wardrobe. Jack's mood was not so buoyant. He did not regret their decision to come here, but felt less easy than he had about the circumstances that had led to it. Consulting the travel office at the Meilenhof Hotel, he had learned that there was no chance of getting a flight to Istanbul until this morning; even then, it turned out that the quickest way had been to travel via Frankfurt. At the airport there he had picked up a couple of British Sunday newspapers just flown in, and read that Abdel Karim had been found dead, shot through the head and dumped at the side of the M1. He appeared to have been tortured first. If proof were needed of the ruthlessness of the people who had now shown their interest in Jack himself, there it was in black and white.

The murder of Karim, though, was only a side bar to the main stories. The consequences of the Gulf War were now focused here in Turkey and the papers were full of pictures of Kurdish refugees, huddled in their thousands on bare mountain slopes along the Iraqi border. Western planes were about to start dropping supplies to them, but the relief that this would provide seemed entirely inadequate to the problem. In Ankara, Turkey's president was discussing the crisis with the visiting American Secretary of State.

'Well, where do we start?' Dale said.

She had bought a map and a guidebook at the airport. They had the names of two people in Istanbul, Nadine's friend Yashar Delkin and Eric Patley's old acquaintance, the retired gold smuggler Manolis Zakarios, but they had addresses for neither. There was no telephone directory in the room so they went downstairs and asked a receptionist for help. He found several Yashar Delkins in the phone book; the one whose number corresponded with the one Dale had filched from Nadine lived at a place called

Yildiz Kalesi. Jack couldn't be sure, but he thought the man had lifted an eyebrow slightly at the mention of the name. As for Zakarios, all that Eric had been able to tell Jack was that the jewellery shop that had once been a front for his operation had been in the Phanar, the old Greek district of the city. But they were in luck again: three or four people called Zakarios were listed, one of them with the first name Manolis; his address was in a village named Sariyer, which the receptionist said was some way out along the Bosphorus shore. They could get there by bus or boat, he told them, but if they were in a hurry he suggested a taxi.

Dale had already located Yildiz Kalesi on her map. 'It's next to Yildiz Park, on the way to Sariyer,' she said. 'We can stop there first.'

Jack had his briefcase full of documents with him. Good manners would normally have suggested phoning both men before turning up, but they had decided to arrive unannounced, offering no chance of being avoided. The receptionist said they needed a taxi driver who spoke English, and sent the bellboy out to find one. He returned shortly, followed by a grave, middle-aged man who led them out to a vintage Pontiac, down on its springs but with its paintwork and chrome highly polished. Dale gave him the address they wanted and he merely nodded before setting off.

The taxi negotiated more noisy streets and busy squares, down to a waterfront crowded with mosques, cafés, small hotels, and an occasional crumbling Ottoman palace. Cargo ships lay at anchor in the straits and ferries ploughed across the mile-wide strip of water that separated Europe from Asia. In spite of the hotel receptionist's assurance, the traffic along the coastal road was dense, the taxi reduced to a stuttering crawl. Finally it turned to the left, up a road that ran beside terraced parkland with ornate pavilions set among cypresses and firs. Higher up the hill was a grassy embankment with stonework exposed on it, the remains of what looked like some old fortification. About halfway along it the driver swung into a narrow opening, on to a sandy road that ran dead straight between high walls, a curious kind of alleyway cut through the embankment. After a hundred metres or so it made a sharp right turn, and here the car halted at a pair of mesh gates topped with barbed wire.

From the doorway of a sentry's hut behind the barrier a soldier emerged, dressed in combat fatigues and with a machine carbine slung from his shoulder, and scowled at them suspiciously.

'This is it?' Jack asked with misgiving.

'Yildiz Kalesi,' the driver confirmed. Jack had begun to suspect that the man actually had no English, but now he said: 'Yildiz Fort. You have the permission to visit?'

'No, but—'

'No permission, no visit.' The driver pointed at a sign beside the gates that said: *Askeri bolge; arac giremez.* 'Military area. No entry,' he translated.

'Now he tells us,' Dale muttered.

'We'll have to try to talk our way in. Will you help us?' Jack asked the driver.

The soldier had been joined by another one, but they showed no inclination to approach the gates, let alone open them. In fact, as the three visitors stepped out of the car the sentries unslung their carbines and pointed them in their general direction. The roadway behind them led past a stand of eucalyptus. Beyond that half a dozen modern bungalows were grouped, and in the distance were other buildings with a functional military look. The whole area was surrounded by a high barbed-wire fence, with more guards patrolling inside it. What Jack and Dale had taken for a simple street address was evidently an army residential compound, and a well-protected one, at the edge of the park they had passed by.

'Can you tell these men we'd like to see Yashar Delkin?' Jack said. 'That we don't have a prior arrangement to visit him, but it's an important matter and if they would just ask . . . ?'

The driver called to the sentries and they exchanged a few sentences in Turkish.

'It's what I told you,' he said, turning back to Jack and Dale. He pointed up the hill. 'Over there, Istanbul army headquarters. That way, Instanbul War College. Here at Yildiz Fort is officers' houses. Nobody can go in without the written permission.' He crooked a little finger to indicate a gun being fired. 'Terrorists. They must be careful of terrorists.'

'I understand that they're only doing their duty,' Jack said, 'but we've come a long way to see Mr Delkin, and if one of them would just go and speak to him, or phone his house . . .' He pulled out his passport. 'Look, they can see that we're foreigners, not terrorists. They can tell him it's an urgent matter about a friend of his in France,' he improvised.

Another exchange ensued between the soldiers and the driver, who eventually shrugged and said, 'It's no good. Anyway, they say General Delkin is not here to ask. He went away this morning.'

'*General* Delkin?'

The Turk gave him a look that was almost as sceptical as the sentries'. 'You ask for a man you don't know? They say he is a . . . general of brigade? The *Jandarma*,' he added with a significant air.

'A brigadier-general?' Dale said. 'But what's the *Jandarma*?'

'Gendarmerie.' The driver held his wrists together to suggest handcuffs. 'Special military police. Fighting terrorists.'

'Can they tell us when he'll be back? Or where we can find him? Or even just let us talk to someone in his house?'

This time the driver's questions were met with sharper answers and impatient gestures. 'They will say nothing,' he reported nervously. 'They say to go now or they arrest us.'

Jack seethed with frustration as they got back in the car. So near and so far again. It had all seemed a bit too simple, he supposed. They should never have let themselves imagine they could just turn up in Istanbul and expect Yashar Delkin to be available at their convenience.

Reading his thoughts, Dale said: 'Sorry. It was my idea originally. Not such a good one, huh?'

'I took up the idea. It's not your fault. But we've lost the initiative. Knowing what he is now, it hardly seems likely that he's going to be accessible to two complete strangers. Particularly since he's already refused to talk to us once.'

And yet, Jack thought, the fact of what Delkin was, a brigadier-general in a branch of Turkish military security, made it that much less probable that his visit to Nadine last month had been merely casual. It made the idea of talking to him even more tantalizing. Delkin had obviously risen through the ranks even faster than his Iraqi friend and former fellow-student, Jalloul. More than ever, Jack was convinced that Delkin knew something definite about the circumstances of Jalloul's disappearance, and that the hunch he himself was following was right.

'Delkin was obviously at home yesterday when Nadine called him,' Dale said. 'Maybe he didn't go away this morning. Maybe those jokers were told to turn away any strangers who turned up.'

'Perhaps they were just lying to save themselves the bother of arguing,' Jack said. 'We've got to find another way of reaching Delkin.'

'Let's work on it. Meanwhile let's hope for better luck with Zakarios.'

Even in the richer days of large oil revenues, the *Mukhabarat* had never had a lot of money to spend on elaborate organization or sophisticated equipment. One result of this was that its young agents were taught to be self-reliant as well as thrifty. The new Mudeer was particularly insistent on these two points. Although with his expensive tastes he seemed to be quite wealthy in his own right, he was not fooled into believing that money was any substitute for hard work when it came to gathering intelligence. He taught his disciples that there was no point in paying for information that could be had for nothing, just as there was no sense in being devious when it was possible to appear straightforward.

This approach had produced results for Ali Shakir from the old soldier, Thorpe, and it might work again here in Zurich.

Ali and Issa had arrived on a midday flight from London, carrying Egyptian passports. The first thing they did was go to the tourist office on the Bahnhofplatz and pick up a comprehensive list of the city's hotels – not for themselves, for they intended to check into a modest pension on the Sihl-Quai, near the industrial quarter. At the newsagent's stand in the adjoining station they bought thirty francs' worth of phone cards and then occupied two adjacent telephone booths in the concourse. Dividing the list between them, they began calling every hotel and asking if a Mr Rushton was registered.

It was a simple procedure, one that the Mudeer would have described as eliminating the obvious. Rushton was a businessman, not a trained agent who automatically covered his tracks. Unless he and his woman had friends in Zurich to stay with, they had to be in a hotel.

Ali's fourteenth call yielded information, though not quite the sort he had hoped for. The switchboard operator at the Meilenhof Hotel told him Mr Rushton had checked out that morning.

'That is Mr Jack Rushton, from England?'

'That's correct.'

'Do you know where he has gone, please?'

The operator asked him to wait. After a minute she came back on the line. 'He left no forwarding address, sir, but our travel office says he bought tickets for flights to Istanbul.'

'Thank you.'

There was enough credit left on his card for a quick call to London. When he told the Mudeer what he had learned he was relieved that his chief did not sound disappointed. He seemed quite pleased, in fact.

'Very good,' he said. 'Get to Istanbul as quickly as possible. Phone me again once your arrangements are made, and I'll see to it that you are met.' There was a moment's silence on the line. 'We have good friends in Turkey. From our point of view, he couldn't be in a better place.

'I think his woman may still be with him,' Ali said.

'Then we must assume she shares his knowledge. In which case she must also share his fate.'

Where the city began thinning out to the north, the Bosphorus was overlooked on both sides by wooded hills dotted with houses and patched with the spring colours of lilac and wisteria. Two great road bridges crossed the straits but the taxi kept to the European shore. Along it, what had once been small fishing villages had, all too obviously, become weekend retreats for the better-off, invaded by ugly flat-roofed villas, bars, restaurants and places advertising themselves as *diskoteks*.

The road was still choked with traffic, and it was after five o'clock before they reached Sariyer. After stopping to ask directions, the driver guided the Pontiac a short way past the village, took a left turn and stopped at an impressive gateway.

The barrier here seemed just as formidable as the one at Yildiz Fort. Visibly at least there were no armed guards, but there were heavy barred gates eight feet high, set between thick stone pillars. There was a bellpush in one of the pillars, and an electric eye and an entryphone speaker: domestic security, California-style. Jack rolled down his window to ring the bell, conscious again that they had lost the advantage of surprise.

A male voice erupted from the speaker. A response that Jack recognized as Greek: *'Oreste?'*

'Mr Zakarios?'

*'Perimenete, parakalo.'*

There was a lengthy wait before another, throatier, voice came on: 'Yes?'

'Mr Manolis Zakarios?'

'Yes?' Cautiously, as though by admitting it he might be giving something away.

Jack gave his name, told Zakarios he was a friend of Eric Patley's and said Eric had suggested he look him up while he and a friend were visiting Istanbul. He apologized insincerely for not phoning beforehand, saying they'd just been out sightseeing when they realized how close they were to the house.

There was a brief silence before Zakarios said: 'Come in. You'll join us for a drink.' The speaker clicked off and a few moments later the gates groaned open.

A driveway twisted uphill for perhaps three hundred metres between lines of horse-chestnut trees. There were terraces on either side planted with citrus and olives, and the only attempt at a formal garden had been made on levelled ground at the top, where a small lawn was bordered by footpaths and rose bushes. Overlooking this stood a villa, not one of the seaside cubes but a strange confection of pale stone and decorative marble. Nineteenth-century Ottoman kitsch, three storeys high, with a pantiled roof and wrought-iron balconies; the marble, in alternating slabs of grey and green with touches of pink, had been inlaid around the windows and the front door, and in vertical columns from the ground to the roof.

Off to one side, a chauffeur was polishing a black Rolls-Royce. Half a dozen other cars were parked on the gravelled forecourt.

Not wanting to look too businesslike, Jack left his briefcase in the taxi. The front door, which had a security camera above it, was opened by a uniformed maid who led them silently through a large hall to a door from behind which came a buzz of conversation. She opened it to reveal a drawing room in which nearly two dozen people were gathered.

The windows gave a spectacular view of the Bosphorus. There was more coloured marble covering the floor and the lower half of the walls. Among those seated or standing about the room were several middle-aged men and women, a few younger ones, children ranging from ten or eleven to the late teens, and a very old couple on a *chaise-longue* in one corner. The men were in suits, the women in print dresses and hats. At the centre of an admiring circle was a woman with a baby in her arms, wrapped in an elaborate brocaded gown. Huge arrays of food were set out and the room was filled with flowers. A manservant in a white jacket was going round with champagne.

Dale and Jack exchanged embarrassed glances. Although the guests did not seem put out, nodding and smiling at the newcomers, it was clear that they had gatecrashed a party.

The old man rose to greet them, with the aid of a silver-headed cane. He was yellow-skinned and completely bald, and he wore natty, dark grey pinstripes and a black bow tie with white polka dots. He appeared to be well into his eighties and was small but robustly built, with hunched shoulders and a roguish expression that gave him the look of an elderly but still lively chimpanzee.

They introduced themselves. 'I am Manolis Zakarios,' the old man said, giving them an arthritic handshake. 'And this is my family. Wife, children, grandchildren, sons-in-law, daughters-in-law, and one great-grandson.' He waved his stick towards the baby. 'Today he has been christened. Come. Eat and drink.'

'I really am sorry to burst in on you like this,' Jack said. 'If we'd known . . .'

'Never mind, never mind. Friends of Eric Patley will always be welcome. How is Eric?'

Jack brought him up to date with Eric's news while the servant poured them champagne and Zakarios pressed them to select from bowls of caviare, boiled shrimps, stuffed vine leaves and cheese pastries. Then he took them round and introduced them to his wife and his offspring and their spouses. They were handsome, dark-eyed people, phanariot Greeks whose origins went back to pre-Ottoman days, Orthodox Christians whose forebears had somehow survived Constantinople's turbulent history.

'We were here before there was any such place as Turkey, you know,' Zakarios said with a chuckle. 'In fact, we were here two and a half thousand years ago, before Christianity or Islam were thought of.'

They chatted in a desultory way to the relatives. Zakarios's wife spoke only Greek and Turkish, but the younger people all had some English and the old man's was excellent. Eventually he grew tired of standing, and Jack found him a chair and sat beside him.

'I gather you were in the jewellery business,' he said.

'For nearly sixty years, until I realized there was more to life than work. So I retired and moved out of the city.'

'Who runs the business now?'

'Two of my sons. Of course it's not what it was when Eric knew it,' Zakarios added.

The remark seemed pointed, but at least it was opportune. Jack said: 'He told me you used to have quite an international operation.'

'I think he was exaggerating. What else did he say?'

'That you both had an interest in . . . well, the unofficial gold market?'

'Ah! Those gold bars that he brought here in the panels of his car?' Zakarios grinned. 'I think Eric imagined he was pulling a fast one on me. He thought the price was about to fall. I knew it would go up. But it's not so easy to predict things nowadays. The unofficial market is much more difficult than it was. And I am no longer involved in it.'

'But others have taken over?'

'Maybe.'

Jack waited. Zakarios continued: 'It isn't a question I would advise you to pursue, Mr Rushton. It's a dangerous business. For an amateur, and a foreigner . . .'

'I think you misunderstand,' Jack said. 'I'm not interested in buying or selling gold.'

'But you're interested in something.' Zakarios's eyes twinkled in the comical chimpanzee face, but his tone was serious. 'Why else would you be here? You don't think I believe that you just happened to be passing my door, do you?'

Jack hadn't expected the point of the discussion to be reached so quickly. He was tempted to prevaricate, but instead decided to come clean.

'All right, Mr Zakarios. I've come to ask you a favour. I want your advice, and the benefit of your experience.' He glanced around the room; nobody seemed to be paying them any attention. 'I've been given the job of tracing a missing Iraqi who may have stumbled on a plot by some of his countrymen to steal a consignment of gold bullion. The gold itself isn't my concern; it's only by getting closer to it that I stand any chance of finding out what happened to this man. I need to know how, and perhaps through whom, these people might have been planning to sell it. It's only a guess, but I think it's a reasonable one, that they might have chosen to do it here in Turkey.'

The old man sat reflectively sucking his yellow cheeks, watching Jack closely. 'What I told you still applies,' he said. 'The market can be a dangerous place even if you are not selling or buying. In my day there were rules – unofficial ones, but rules all the same. Contracts were made and kept. Now it's different. In this country it's gone underground, and so it attracts people who don't like to be seen in the daylight. If you poke into their burrows, the chances are you'll get bitten.'

'I know enough to be careful. And to keep anything you care to tell me to myself.'

'And the young lady? Is she aware of this . . . under-taking of yours?'

'Completely.'

'Then bring her through to my study,' Zakarios said, heaving himself to his feet. 'What I have to say will take only a few minutes, but I can save you the trouble of repeating it.'

# 26

The study was along a side passage of the villa, a room too large for its purpose and looking as though it wasn't much used in any case. It was furnished with a dainty writing desk, a sofa and a few chairs in the French Empire style, and an ornate bookcase that held only a scattering of books. Zakarios lowered himself into a chair and Jack and Dale sat on the sofa.

'First tell me more about this gold you believe has been stolen,' the old man said.

Jack related as much as he thought necessary about the disappearance of part of the bullion taken from the Kuwait Central Bank. He repeated the rumour Abdel Karim had heard about the gold being flown to northern Iraq, and also what Dr Zunckel had told him in Zurich about Ghani and his enquiry about the possibility of offloading it on the official market. Zakarios smiled at the innocence of this notion.

'So where do you think it is now?' he asked.

'The man who called himself Ghani is dead,' Jack said. 'And so are several of the people who were probably involved with him. But there must be others in the know. I don't see how they could have moved it out of Iraq as long as the country was in a state of siege. They knew that from the start, and they planned to leave it there until the crisis was over. My guess is that it's probably still there. But sooner or later they've got to get it out, and the logical way of doing so is through Turkey. Am I on the right track?'

Zakarios thought for a moment, then pointed with his stick at the bookcase. 'There is a map up there. Save my legs. Fetch it for me.'

There were several folded maps crammed on to one shelf. The one he wanted was a double-sided road map of Turkey, published in Germany. He got Jack to open it on the floor at his feet to show the eastern half of the country, then jabbed his stick at the lower right-hand corner.

'Here is the border between Turkey and Iraq, among the southern Taurus mountains of Kurdistan. There are only two roads across it. But it is desolate country and people who know the mountains well can find other ways to get across them. Often I used to buy small quantities of gold that were brought out this way, usually by Kurdish refugees carrying whatever valuables they could bring: jewellery, old coins, hoarded ingots. In normal times, using guides and pack mules and travelling by night, it would not be impossible to transport an amount even as big as the one you mention. But things are not normal. The Kurds are carrying on a guerrilla war against the Turks. The whole area has been under military control for several years, and now with the Iraqi Kurds coming across the mountains . . . well, it seems hardly the right time for such a venture. On the other hand, maybe your guess is wrong and the gold has already been moved. And even sold.'

'If it had been,' said Dale, 'would you have picked up some inkling of it?'

Zakarios gave his quizzical grin again. 'As I've told your friend, young lady, I have been out of that business for a long time. But one never completely escapes from it. I hear things through my sons. If that much gold had been released on the market, it would not have gone unnoticed.'

'If or when it is brought out, then, what's likely to happen to it?'

'Firstly you can't assume that it will all arrive at once. Dividing it into smaller quantities lessens the risk that it might all be seized. Then, obviously, a plan must be in place to move it on as quickly as possible. I doubt that your Iraqis would have the opportunity to melt it down and export it piecemeal, as I would have done.' The old man poked at the map again. 'See where those two roads lead, after they cross the frontier? One towards Iran, the other westwards to the seaports at Iskenderun and Mersin. That is part of the Silk Road, the ancient trade route between Europe and the Orient, and it is the more likely choice. To transport the gold safely, these Iraqis will need help from people here that they can trust, and if a few Turkish palms can be greased as well, so much the better. Above all they will need protection. The *Jandarma* are vigilant, and nowadays they would not turn a blind eye to smuggling on that scale. Not that they are all above being corrupted.'

'The gendarmerie would be responsible for a matter like this?'

'Yes. They are paramilitary police, a division of the army responsible for internal security and for law enforcement in rural areas.' Zakarios looked at them gravely. 'I will not go into details about the trade that I was in, but I can say that it used to be reputable. We had understandings with the authorities, and we had no violence. The system worked to the advantage of everyone, including the Turkish government. Now there are no controls, and what's left of the business is in the hands of criminals. Some of them ordinary crooks, but others claiming to act for political causes, which makes them unreasonable as well as vicious.

'You probably know that the Turks have many terrorist groups to contend with. There are the Kurds who fight them in the east; there are Islamic fundamentalists who have attacked synagogues, here in Constantinople; and there are Marxist revolutionaries who blow up soldiers and wage war against the rich. Why do you think my house is so well protected? But there is another organization that is less familiar to outsiders. Have you heard of *Emegin Birligi*? In English known as the Grey Wolves?'

They shook their heads. 'They were a right-wing party in the days of Ataturk,' Zakarios said, 'but later they began calling themselves Marxists and took up arms against the Turkish government. In the seventies they were involved in bombings and political assassinations but they degenerated, if one can use such a word, into gangsters. Still, they maintain links with Palestinian extremists and they have also done some dirty work on behalf of the Ba'athists in Iraq.' He paused. 'As I told you, I hear things. These people are opportunists. They're involved in protection rackets and smuggling. If you want to know who your Iraqis may have sought help from here, you need look no further than the Grey Wolves. But I suggest that you don't look too closely.'

Jack shrugged. 'We wouldn't know where to start, anyway. Do the police here know about this connection?'

'In a general way, I'm sure they do.'

'The reason I ask is that the only other contact we have is with an officer in the gendarmerie. He might be interested in what you've told us, but . . .'

'But you don't want to embarrass me? I think there is no fear of that. These are only my opinions, remember. I have no secrets, but also I know nothing definite. The Turks would be too proud to come for advice to a phanariot, but if they did I would tell them exactly what I have told you.'

'And what would you suggest that they do?'

'Watch out for a ship arriving at Mersin or Iskenderun without specific sailing orders. It's a route that I sometimes used myself.' Zakarios smiled again. 'That's all I can tell you. And now if you don't mind, I must go back to my family.'


The sun was setting by the time they left the villa. The water of the Bosphorus had turned from vivid blue to an oily, leaden grey, and the ships heading up and down the channel had their navigation lights on. Along the coastal road the Sunday traffic was even worse than it had been on the outward journey, and by the time they reached the outskirts of the city it was fully dark.

At first the taxi driver flatly refused to take them back to Yildiz Fort. They didn't know what Turkish soldiers were like, he said. If they arrested him they might also impound or confiscate his car, which would be a far more serious matter for him than spending the night in jail. Eventually, but still with reluctance, he agreed to park on the road outside and accompany them on foot.

They tramped along the sandy floor of the alley that led through the embankment. It was an odd feature, but even in the dark a second viewing made its original purpose clearer. The fort that had once stood here was just one more of the Byzantine ruins in which Istanbul was smothered, a spot that didn't rate a mention in Dale's rather inadequate guidebook; and this passageway had been a ditch between the inner and outer ramparts. It was about eight metres deep and six metres across, and no doubt it had been a formidable obstacle to attacking crusaders and Ottomans. The walls that flanked it, and the overgrown banks on either side, seemed to be all that was left of the building. Strong light came from up ahead, beyond the turning leading to the gates, and when they reached the bend they could see that the entrance and the approach to it were illuminated by powerful lamps.

Jack also saw, with foreboding, that the same pair of guards were on duty. The sight of three people walking towards them out of the night seemed to alarm them more than the arrival of the taxi had, and their carbines were levelled almost before the visitors were within shouting distance.

'*Dur! Dur!*' one of them called sharply. The driver stopped walking and indicated to Jack and Dale that they should do the same.

They stood still, exposed within a circle of remorseless light.

'Ask them if General Delkin is home yet,' Jack said. 'And tell them the message we have for him is even more urgent now.'

The announcement, bellowed from twenty metres away, was met with the same hostility as before. The driver exchanged several remarks with the soldiers and then said nervously, 'They say nothing. Only that we must go.'

'Please tell them—'

But the Turk had lost what little enthusiasm he had had for this enterprise. 'No more, no more!' he muttered, shaking his head, and turned away to head back for the road. Jack stood where he was for a moment, tempted to go nearer and try to reason with the guards himself, but Dale sensed his thoughts and said: 'Forget it. You stand too good a chance of getting shot. We'll find another way.'

Despondently they retreated from the compound for a second time. As they began to follow the taxi man a car swept around the bend ahead of them, catching them in its headlights. It slowed down as it approached the gates and stopped when it drew level with Jack and Dale.

The car was one of the smaller BMWs. The driver's window was wound down and a woman's face was framed in the opening, attractive Turkish features fringed by thick black hair. She looked about forty. She gave them a friendly smile and, surprisingly, spoke to them in perfect English.

'Are you lost?'

'Well, not exactly,' Jack said. 'We're visitors here, and . . .'

'I can see that. I thought I should warn you that you've wandered into a military area. The sentries can get a bit agitated if—'

She was interrupted by footfalls from the direction of the gates. One of those excitable soldiers had come out and was running up to the car, clumsily wielding his carbine but at least not pointing it at anyone. He addressed the woman respectfully but then began to jabber at her, making gestures at the two foreigners. She looked at them in some wonder and finally dismissed the guard with a few brusque words.

She said to them: 'You wanted to see my husband?'

They were reduced to silence for a moment. Dale, the first to recover, said: 'You're Mrs Delkin?'

'That's right. Is this something I can deal with?'

They both began talking at once and she silenced them with a wave. 'Before you go into details, I can tell you he's not here. He went back to Hakkari today, near the Iraqi border. I don't expect to hear from him for a while.'

'But do you have some way of contacting him?' Dale asked.

'He's on the border most of the time at the moment. There is a crisis down there and as you can imagine he's a busy man. In an emergency I can get a message to him through the army. But is this an emergency?'

'It's a professional matter, not a personal one, but we can't pretend it's a case of life or death,' Jack admitted uneasily. He hesitated about even trying to explain. Nadine Schuster had said she and Jalloul had stayed here with Delkin and his wife, so obviously that was no secret, but was Mrs Delkin aware of anything beyond that? Might she be frightened of helping them if she was told too much? 'Your husband already knows who we are,' he said, 'and if he's told that we're in Turkey he'll guess what we're doing here. I know it's an odd request, but all we need is a few minutes of his time, even if it's only on the phone. We may be able to give him information that's important to his work.'

'Won't somebody else do?'

'Not really. And we have come a long way to see him.'

Mrs Delkin considered for a few moments but seemed satisfied not to probe any further, accustomed no doubt to the confidential nature of her husband's job. 'I'll see if I can help,' she said. 'I can do nothing now, but I'll try and reach him in the morning.'

She wrote down their names in an address book she took from her handbag. When Jack remarked on how good her English was she gave him a look of amusement that was also a warning not to patronize her. 'It ought to be,' she said. 'My father was a diplomat in London for many years. I was at Benenden School with Princess

Anne. Phone me tomorrow,' she added crisply, 'let's say at twelve o'clock, and perhaps I'll have some news for you.'

Suitably chastened, they left the fort and found their driver sulking in his Pontiac down the road. He got them back to the hotel in time for dinner.

Issa and Ali Shakir reached Istanbul on one of the last planes to arrive that evening. It was the only one on which they'd been able to find seats at short notice, a charter flight from Frankfurt filled with Turkish *gastarbeiters* going home on holiday. The two Iraqis felt uncomfortably exposed among them, but the Turks were in a noisy, celebratory mood, drinking heavily and taking hardly any notice of them.

With their Egyptian passports they got through the immigration and customs controls quite easily and then, ignoring the solicitations of hotel touts and taxi drivers, they left the terminal building. Following the instructions relayed through the Mudeer, they crossed the road and entered a poorly lit car park. They turned to the right between the first and second rows of vehicles and had almost reached the end before they heard the sound of a car door opening just to their left.

They stopped walking. The car was a big American model. A man was standing beside the driver's door, dimly outlined against the distant lights. He called softly to them: '*Merhaba*.'

Ali and Issa remained silent. The man said in English: 'Can I help you?'

'We're looking for a friend,' Ali said.

'I am your friend,' the man replied. He stepped forward and studied them more closely. He was no older than Ali was, with a slight build and the shifty look of a fugitive. 'You are the brothers from London and I am your guide.'

'What can you show us?'

'Everything.'

With these coded preliminaries out of the way they relaxed a little. The Turk gave them a brief hug of greeting

311

and led them to the car. Another man was sitting in the front passenger seat, and he merely nodded to them as they climbed into the back. The first man started the car and headed it carefully out of the parking area. They were well clear of the airport before he spoke again.

'We will not introduce ourselves,' he said. 'It's safer if we do not know each other's names. Trust us. We are your friends here. You will choose the time and place for your operation, but we will guide you and supply you. Everything you want will be ready first thing tomorrow.'

'Weapons? Ali asked.

'A choice from many. Also transport, intelligence and a safe house afterwards, until we can arrange for you to leave the country.'

'You've been told why we are here?' Ali asked with slight misgiving.

'Trust us,' the man repeated. 'We had to know; otherwise how could we help you? Already we have saved you the trouble of locating your targets. They are staying at a hotel called the Pera Palace.'

# 27

It was warm enough the next morning for Dale and Jack
to sit out on the balcony of their room for the breakfast of
brown bread, figs, white cheese and strong, milkless tea
that was brought up to them. After that, they had nothing
much to do before phoning Delkin's wife at midday.
Dale went for a run along the Golden Horn, returning
at ten-thirty. She was planning to spend the rest of the
morning washing her hair and arranging for the hotel to
do some laundry, so Jack went out for a while on his own.

He strolled up Istiklâl Cadessi to the huge open square
at Taksim, the hub of the modern city, and called in at
a travel agency. It had occurred to him that if General
Delkin proved willing to talk to them in person they had
better have some plans in hand for getting to Hakkari.
He remembered it vaguely as a place on the map that
Zakarios had shown them the night before, but it turned
out to be much more remote than he had imagined, in
the far south-east of Turkey and high in the Taurus
mountains. The woman in the agency was amused when
he asked about flying there; the nearest airport was at
Van, nearly two hundred kilometres to the north, a four-
hour drive away. There were five flights a week to Van;
all of this week's were fully booked, the woman said, and
there were long standby lists of foreign journalists trying
to reach the Iraqi border and report on the exodus of the
Kurds.

Somewhat deflated by this news, he returned to the
hotel. Dale had changed into narrow black trousers,
low-heeled boots, a white shirt and a black blazer, with
a coloured scarf loosely knotted round her neck. He sat

on the bed and watched her inspecting herself, in the wardrobe mirror, fluffing out the newly-washed hair that curled softly around her face. It struck him that with everything they'd done over the past three days, with the travelling and the endless analytical discussions, they had hardly talked about themselves. Although they had made love many times since that first night in Zurich, passion hadn't led to introspection. What they felt about each other seemed to go without saying, as though a sense of deep contentment had grown up between them without either of them realizing it.

Suddenly he said: 'I think you're the grown woman I need.'

'What?' She turned to him in puzzlement.

'Sylvia Patley, Eric's wife, told me I ought to cut my losses with Alison. Said she was . . . still partly a child, too emotionally dependent on me, and that what I needed was a grown-up woman who could really share things with me. I suppose what I'm saying is that I'm in love with you, Dale.'

It was the first time either of them had mentioned the word love. She'd been watching him seriously and now she gave a little shrug, almost of embarrassment. 'Are you sure about that, after three or four days?'

'Actually it's eight days since we first met. Some people court and get married in less than that time.'

'Well, for what it's worth, Jack, I feel the same about you. Only I'm more cautious about expressing it, because one thing I don't want to do is catch you on the rebound. You're emotionally vulnerable right now. I know you mean what you say, but I don't think you should go too fast. I don't want you making any declarations that you may regret later.'

'There won't be any regrets. I know that it's all over with Alison. As soon as I get back home I'm going to have to move out. On the other hand, I'm not going to push you into any decisions. I just want you to think about staying with me. Since you're out of a job, maybe it would be easier to find one in England anyway.'

'What about your kids?'

'That's going to hurt. It'll be tough on them. But it would be tougher in the long run if we stayed together just for their sakes and they had to spend the next ten years watching us maul each other to shreds.'

'I'll repeat my first observation about you: you're a nice man, Jack. All right, I'll think about it.' She bent over and kissed him on the cheek, then glanced at her watch. 'And hadn't you better think about making that call? It's just after noon.'

Mrs Delkin answered on the second ring. She was brief and businesslike. She had sent a message to her husband through the headquarters of the *Jandarma*, and he had sent one back: he would call her at two o'clock and would speak to the two foreigners on her phone. She would be at the compound gates just before then to see that they were allowed in.

'Let's celebrate,' Jack said when he'd put down the phone. 'We'll have an early lunch here and then leave. A bottle of champagne to kick off with, I think.'

'Fine by me. But do we have anything to celebrate yet?'

'Our future.'

'Don't go too fast,' she repeated, but with a smile this time. 'Do you know something? You've stopped being polite with me. You don't say *I'm afraid* any longer.'

Ali and Issa had watched the woman leave the hotel and come back. They had watched Rushton go out later and also return. They could easily have taken either of them anywhere in the crowded streets of Beyoglu, but they needed to take them together.

The brothers went on waiting.

They had been there since eight o'clock that morning, half an hour after setting off from the dingy apartment in the Kumkapi district where the Turks had put them up for the night. The man who had greeted them first at the airport drove them in a black Oldsmobile, and his companion followed in a Mercedes, a back-up car to be used afterwards. They could not tell where Rushton and the woman would go when they did leave the hotel, and so a prearranged plan was out of the question. They would follow, and they would seize the best opportunity to strike.

The Turks had driven across the Galata Bridge, up the hill and through the main entrance of the Pera Palace, then into the car park on its north side. From where the Oldsmobile was positioned, in the shade of a row of fan palms, Ali and Issa could observe the front door of the hotel without attracting any attention to themselves.

Ali glanced down at the floor of the car, where their weapons were hidden beneath a blanket. From the selection they'd been shown they had chosen two Hungarian AMD sub-machineguns, a type they had trained with, powerful cut-down versions of the Russian AKM assault rifle. They had also brought half a dozen hand grenades, in case they were needed, already primed and stuffed into a plastic carrier bag. The Turks had an abundant arsenal, though the quality of their personnel did not seem so impressive. They were willing and obliging, but not dedicated in the way of true militants. The man who had driven them was restless and jumpy, forever retuning the car radio in search of fresh *türkü* music, occasionally even getting out to stretch his legs or talk to his comrade in the Mercedes parked behind them. Ali also suspected that he didn't know his way around Istanbul quite as well as he pretended; although he'd tried to disguise the fact, he had taken a couple of wrong turnings on the way to the hotel.

Towards half-past twelve cars began turning up with increasing frequency, taxis and limousines disgorging parties of businessmen arriving for lunch. If Rushton and the woman didn't come out within the next few minutes, Ali estimated, they were probably eating in the hotel restaurant and wouldn't emerge until two o'clock or after. He did not relay this thought to the Turk in the front seat, who was fidgety enough as it was.

They had got into the restaurant just in time to avoid the rush, and they had finished lunch by one o'clock. On yesterday's reckoning it would take forty minutes to drive to Mrs Delkin's house, so Jack sent for a taxi and they finished their champagne while they waited for it. By what seemed unlikely to be a coincidence, they were greeted in the lobby by the same man who had driven them yesterday; after the exorbitant fee he had charged, Jack suspected he had been hanging around the front of the hotel in the hope that his English-speaking fares were planning another long journey. At the mention of Yildiz Fort he made a face, but he took them out to the Pontiac and set off into the frenzied city traffic.

It was Issa who spotted them leaving. He nudged Ali urgently and pointed, and now his brother saw them too, Rushton in the same light-brown suit he had worn earlier, but carrying a briefcase this time, the woman changed into black trousers and a jacket. They were following a grey-haired man from the door of the hotel across the forecourt.

'Drive!' Ali said to the Turk.

The man had fallen into a stupor and it took him a couple of seconds to gather his wits and start the Oldsmobile's sluggish old motor. By the time he was heading it out of the car park their quarry had disappeared through the front gates.

They caught up with the couple in the street outside, just as the rear door of a taxi closed on them. The car moved off and the Oldsmobile lurched after it, closely followed by the Mercedes.

Ali groped under the blanket for his gun, cocking it and then resting it across his lap, keeping it below the level of the windows. Issa did likewise and they both stared tensely forward, keeping the taxi in sight. It took a left turn a short way from the hotel, and then a right, staying in narrow streets until it reached the main post office and swung on to Istiklâl Cadessi. The traffic was heavy and slow. Half a dozen times the taxi halted, offering the brothers the opportunity of an ambush but no hope of getting clear from it. Entering Taksim Square the car gained some speed but then suddenly turned again, downhill through a cluster of little streets and on to the Bosphorus waterfront.

Ali relaxed slightly. Though he didn't know this city it was obvious that the taxi was moving away from the centre, to where the traffic would be lighter and their getaway simpler. He glanced around to be sure the Mercedes was still following, then said: 'Drop one car behind them. And don't lose them.'

The Turk did as he was told. He was still jittery but seemed in control of himself. This road was as congested as any other they had been on but it was leading them towards a distant prospect of hills and open coastline. One stop in the right place, or even at the couple's destination, was all it would take.

For twenty minutes the three cars moved in fits and starts along the waterfront. Sometimes there was a break in the traffic that allowed them to pick up speed, the Oldsmobile's ancient speedometer needle shuddering up to forty miles an hour, but soon they would be down to a crawl again. Ali had got used to the idea that they were heading out into the hinterland, so he was alarmed when the Turk said suddenly: 'They're turning!'

The Pontiac was at a green traffic light, signalling left and waiting for oncoming vehicles to pass. With the Oldsmobile stuck two cars behind it, the taxi driver spotted a gap and took the turning just as the light changed to amber.

'Go after him!' Ali said to the Turk.

'But . . .'

'Do as I say!'

The light was red now. The Turk spun the wheel and accelerated, crossing to the wrong carriageway and swerving wildly across the path of cars emerging from the junction. With horns blaring angrily around them he swung into the turning and straightened up.

Ali spotted the taxi a hundred metres ahead, moving uphill on a road almost free of traffic. Glancing behind him again, he saw that the Mercedes had somehow made it across the junction as well.

'Where does this road lead?' he demanded.

'Yildiz Park, I think.'

'You *think*? Can we get out of there in a hurry?'

'Yes.'

Ali was not sure he could believe the Turk. But their only choice now was to keep following the taxi, which continued up the winding road for a minute or two. The park was there, on the right, and then the road travelled for a distance beside a high mound of stone and grass. Here, suddenly, the taxi stopped.

It pulled in beside the mound, which formed a steep embankment to the road. On Ali's instruction the Turk halted fifty metres behind it, and they sat staring forward in puzzlement. They had Rushton and his woman where they had wanted them, out in the open. It couldn't matter what had brought them here, but some instinct made Ali wonder why they had stopped in this odd spot, whether everything was really as easy as it looked.

Both rear doors of the taxi opened and the couple got out. Although the Oldsmobile was clearly in their view now and might even look suspicious, they didn't give it a glance. Obviously they had no idea that they'd been followed. They stepped across the sidewalk towards what Ali suddenly realized was an opening in the embankment, a narrow roadway lined with stone, and disappeared through it.

'What's in there?' he asked.

The Turk didn't even try to pretend this time, just gave a helpless shrug. Ali made his decision.

'Let's take them now.'

The Mercedes had pulled in behind them and he signalled to the other Turk to keep it there. The Oldsmobile driver moved out on the road, passed by the waiting taxi and turned into the opening.

The cab driver had refused to approach the compound even on foot this time, but today it wasn't going to matter. Mrs Delkin would see them in through the gates and they would have no need of an interpreter. Jack looked at his watch as they made their way along the ditch: five to two, perfect timing.

The sound of a car's engine reached them when they were about halfway to the gates, and they both glanced around. A big black car, another of those rickety old American jobs that were everywhere in Istanbul, had come into the entry and was bouncing towards them on worn springs. Jack instinctively took Dale's arm to guide her to one side and let the car pass.

Ali quickly sized up the situation. This roadway was long and narrow, Rushton and the woman were trapped in it. It *was* easy. They could be taken without even the noise and risk of shooting.

'Run them down,' he said calmly to the Turk.

Jack saw that Dale was still looking back. Holding her arm, he felt the sudden tension in her body and knew something was wrong.

The car was picking up speed, the pitch of its motor rising. It was travelling abnormally fast over this short distance, its wheels churning up sand, and instead of keeping to the centre of the ditch it was veering towards them.

320

For a moment it crossed his mind that the car was out of control, its driver perhaps slumped over the wheel with his foot jammed on the accelerator. Then through the windscreen he caught a blurred impression of three faces looking intently towards them, and had a horrible certainty of what was about to happen.

Dale said: 'Run!'

Jack dropped his briefcase. They began racing towards the compound entrance, keeping close to the wall. The turning that led to the gates was fifty metres away and almost at once Jack knew they wouldn't make it. The car was gaining on them rapidly, the roar of its engine amplified by the stone walls. Dale, the runner, had got a start on him and was widening the gap. He threw a despairing glance over his shoulder and saw the car only a metre or two behind, edging in to crush him against the wall.

Turning his head threw him off balance. As the car drew level it slowed and lurched sharply towards him, narrowing the gap. He stumbled then, cannoning off the side of the car and into the wall and sprawling on the ground. He felt a wheel go over his left arm and then the vehicle hit the stonework right in front of him, the front wing slamming into it first and then the whole of its side scraping against the wall with a shriek of crumpling metal.

Jack lay on the ground, staring through a haze of shock at the bulging rear end of the car. The impact had jarred it almost to a halt but now it was moving again, accelerating, in fact, as its driver swung out from the wall. Jack realized the fall had saved his life. The car had struck the side of the ditch just where he would have been if he'd stayed upright. They must have thought they had run him over. And now they were going after Dale.

He saw with horror that she had stopped. She stood about twenty metres away, staring back past the car at where he was lying. He scrambled giddily to his feet, feeling for the first time a heavy numbness in his arm as he signalled to her to run.

She turned and dashed for the end of the ditch. The car picked up momentum, but although Dale was hampered by her boots she was well into her fluent sprinting stride within a second or two. The car closed the gap as she neared the bend, to ten metres and then to five. For a moment it blocked Jack's view of her and with a sick feeling he waited to see her knocked aside or flung into the air. Instead, the next glimpse he got of her was as she cut across to the right, blond hair streaming out behind her, and dodged around the corner.

The car swung heavily after her. Jack followed at a blundering run.

They were within a metre of the woman when she reached the sharp bend, but she gained some more distance as the Oldsmobile was forced into a wide turn around it. The ditch had opened out on to a bare stretch of sandy ground, and when the car began catching up on her again she was several metres to their right. Forget running her down: she was agile and now she had space to manoeuvre in, but the gap between them also gave Ali a field of fire for a broadside from his sub-machinegun.

He had it out of the window, the muzzle resting on the sill and aimed at the woman as they drew level with her.

'Look!' the Turk suddenly said.

Ali didn't know what he was talking about and for a moment didn't care. He and Issa were both watching the woman. She glanced towards them and Ali saw the terror on her face as he got her in his sights and squeezed the trigger.

At that moment the panicky Turk slewed the car violently to the left. The gun jerked and the burst of shots blew chunks out of the wall a metre behind its target. The woman dived to the ground.

'A trap, a trap!' the Turk was shouting. He had crashed down into second gear and stamped on the accelerator and was skidding into a tight circle on the sand, steering them back towards the ditch. Only then did Ali and Issa see the gates, the barbed wire and the soldiers, no more than four or five metres away. The sentries had their carbines raised and now they opened fire.

Jack heard the shooting begin a second before he reached the corner. Four or five rapid bangs from a heavy automatic weapon punctuated the howling of the car's engine, then there was a series of overlapping bursts from lighter guns. Rounding the bend, he saw the car with its battered right side swerving away from the compound, two men leaning out of the back windows and firing gangster-style towards the gates. The car was slithering about as its driver tried to gain speed in too low a gear, and the gunmen didn't seem to have much chance of hitting anything. The soldiers must have been alerted by the sound of the collision; three or four of them were crouched behind the gates, taking careful aim as they fired back through the mesh. An emergency siren had started up somewhere, adding to the deafening noise. There was no sign of Mrs Delkin. For a horrible moment when he saw Dale lying on the ground he thought she'd been shot, but then she began squirming away in search of cover. Jack thought he ought to do the same, but he couldn't take his eyes off the scene.

Bullets were hitting the car with sharp tinny sounds. It seemed almost out of control for some moments but then it straightened up and came charging towards the only escape route. Even as it gathered speed one of its rear doors flew open, the lock perhaps burst by a bullet, and one of the gunmen tumbled out and rolled across the ground.

Jack ducked around the corner, pressing his back to the wall as the car approached. Entering the ditch, it swerved again and clipped the wall opposite him, losing what speed it had gained, and he saw that both its back tyres were flat. It passed him by without its occupants noticing him, intent only on escape now, and began weaving a slow, unsteady course towards the exit.

A few moments later the first of the sentries reached the corner at a run, ramming a fresh ammunition clip into his carbine. The car had got perhaps thirty metres into the ditch and was trapped in it as surely as Jack and Dale had been. The soldier raised his gun, took deliberate aim and fired four bursts of shots.

The rear window splintered and caved in. Riddled with holes, the car faltered, wobbled about for a few metres more and then came to a stop. The soldier waited for a time, watching for any movement. Half a dozen others ran up to join him and they spread out across the roadway and began to move cautiously forward.

It was over, Ali knew. Until a few moments ago he had believed he had a chance, just a chance, of reaching the other car and getting away; but as soon as that final volley had hit the Oldsmobile and he'd felt it shuddering to a halt he was certain the Turk had been shot.

Ali lay on the floor of the car, where he had fallen when he was wounded in the same blast of firing that had blown Issa out of the door. The bullet had hit him in the face, passing through both cheeks and smashing some of his teeth; the pain was immense and he bled profusely, but he knew he was not close to death.

He raised himself slightly, just enough to see the head of the Turk lolling against the door frame, the windscreen in front of him shattered and holed by the bullets that had gone through him.

Ali felt calm, analytical even, and more despondent than afraid. The Turk was wrong about their having walked into a trap; it was the stupidity of these people, and his own willingness to condone it, that had ruined everything. It was the kind of failure the Mudeer would use one day as an example to other over-eager young men. The knowledge that he had let the Mudeer down was almost as humiliating as the failure itself.

Apart from a distant siren there was a strange silence outside the car, but he knew the soldiers would be creeping up on it. If he moved or showed himself they would instantly shoot. He still clutched his sub-machinegun and could fight until they killed him, but there was no guarantee of such an outcome. He might be badly wounded, captured and interrogated by the Turks before they hanged him as a terrorist. Probably that would be poor Issa's fate; he sought a tidier one for himself.

With another part of his mind he had begun praying. He let go of the gun and groped under the blanket on the floor for the bag of hand grenades. He was quite without fear now, and he was weeping for Issa. He got hold of a grenade, pulled out its pin, eased it back into the bag and let go his grip on it, releasing the safety lever. The four-second fuse began to smoke and sputter and he hugged the bag to his body. He was praying all the while, and thinking of Issa as he recited the passage on martyrdom from the *shurah* of the Imrans: 'Never think that those who are slain in the cause of God are dead. They are alive, and well provided for by their Lord, rejoicing that those they left behind have nothing to fear or regret . . .'

The soldiers were still twenty metres from the car when it blew up. There was an orange flash and a sheet of flame, a gigantic roar and a pressure wave that knocked some of the men off their feet. Shrapnel clanged against the walls and a grey-brown cloud of smoke and dust instantly filled the ditch.

Standing further back, Jack felt the pressure wave as a hot wind pushing him against the wall. Bits of glass and metal rained down around him, and as the smoke began to clear the car became visible again, a scorched shell with its roof torn off and windows blown out. A few flames licked around its petrol tank. Of its occupants there was no sign at all, as though they'd simply been vaporized or fused to the metal.

He had no intention of taking a closer look. His ears were ringing and his left arm, swollen inside his jacket, was aching badly. He turned away and went to find Dale.

Rounding the corner, he saw that three vans painted in army green had come out of the gate. Soldiers and military police in white helmets were swarming all over the place. Some of the MPs were helping Dale briskly to her feet; others were hustling the gunman who had fallen out of the car towards one of the vans. He was handcuffed and his shirt front was smothered in blood.

Jack started towards Dale and then stopped. Incredulously, he realized that she was handcuffed as well. And she wasn't being helped; she, too, was being roughly propelled to the vehicles.

He began running towards them, opening his mouth to call her name, but almost at once he heard a warning shout from his right. Three of four more MPs were trotting towards him, led by a man with the two stars of a lieutenant on his helmet and a large pistol in his hand. Jack stopped again and tried to say something, but the officer pointed the gun at his face and gestured impatiently for him to put his hands on his head.

It dawned on him then that until the confusion was sorted out, he and Dale were going to be treated as suspects. And this wasn't the time to argue. He raised his arms and the MPs closed in, seizing him and pushing him against the side of a van. Hands patted up and down his body and delved into his pockets, extracting everything that was in them. His arms were jerked down and he felt handcuffs being snapped around his wrists.

# 28

He got no chance to talk to Dale. They barely had a moment to exchange a helpless glance before they were bundled into separate vehicles and driven off.

Jack was made to sit on the floor of the van, against the bulkhead, while half a dozen military police occupied the two benches down the sides. With his wrists fastened behind him he was jolted around and the ache in his injured arm was growing. He found he was also trembling, no doubt a symptom of delayed shock. The van had no windows; the only light that entered it came from narrow slits below the roof, and he could just make out the features of his guards under their white helmets as they watched him with passive curiosity. It would be useless to try to explain the situation to them; he could only hope he would soon be passed on to someone in authority with the sense to listen to him.

The journey lasted about twenty minutes. When the van stopped and the doors were opened he saw it was parked in an enclosed yard at the rear of a building, a place of fairly recent design but anonymous function. There was no sign of the vehicle that Dale had been put into. To judge by the noise of traffic from beyond the walls, he was back in the city centre.

He was led through a bare little vestibule and down a whitewashed corridor; at the end of it was a barred gate with a counter beside it where another military policeman was waiting, together with the lieutenant who had arrested him. Without a word the officer reached out and began to undo Jack's tie.

'Do you speak English?' Jack asked.

The lieutenant gave no sign that he even understood the question.

'Please listen to me.' Jack tried to sound reasonable. Even if they couldn't follow his words, perhaps he could make his meaning clear. 'You're making a mistake by arresting me. Those people were trying to kill me. You know General Yashar Delkin? I was on my way to his house. His wife will verify that. Do you understand?'

The officer seemed unimpressed by this name-dropping. Still saying nothing, he removed the tie and unfastened Jack's belt and handed them both over the counter. Then he took him by the shoulder, opened the barred gate and pushed him through it, down a short passageway to a heavy steel door.

The cell behind it was tiny and almost bare, and smelt of urine. Once they were inside it the policeman stepped behind Jack and began removing his handcuffs.

'If you insist on arresting me then I demand that you notify the British Consulate. *Ingiltere Konsoloslugu,*' Jack said, dredging up a phrase he had seen in Dale's guidebook. 'I also want to know where Miss Griggs is. My friend, the American woman? And I want to see a doctor,' he added, pointing to his aching arm as the cuffs were released. 'Doctor. *Medecin. Arzt.*'

It was hopeless. The lieutenant stared at him briefly and then spoke to him for the first time, producing what might or might not have been his only words of English. They had an ominous ring.

'You wait,' he said. Then he left, slamming and bolting the door behind him.

Jack stood looking around the cell. It contained a metal bunk with a thin, plastic-covered mattress, a squat pan in one corner and a bucket of water, apparently to flush it with. That was all. It was without a window; the light came from an overhead lamp encased in steel mesh. Compared to this the Iraqi lieutenant, Fadel, was living in the Kuwait Hilton.

He subsided on to the bunk, feeling more disorientated than ever. It was an absurd irony that he should be arrested after an attempt on his life, but it was getting less funny by the minute. He didn't even know where he was. He had never been arrested before, let alone for doing nothing wrong. He supposed it would be bad enough if it happened in England, but there at least he could have communicated with his captors. Here, it didn't seem impossible that one misunderstanding would lead to another, that he might be detained for days or even weeks.

Even more frustrating was the knowledge that the attempt to kill him had proved that his quest for information had been leading him on the right path. Somebody thought that what he knew, or guessed, was important enough to make him worth eliminating – and Dale too, because the gunmen had certainly been after them both. It was now vital that he speak to General Delkin.

He worried about what had become of Dale. This presumably was an all-male place of detention, so they must have taken her somewhere else. He wasn't going to blame himself for bringing her to Istanbul, since it had been a joint decision; nevertheless, it was his business that had led them here, and for that he couldn't help feeling responsible.

He examined his pockets. The military police had taken his passport, traveller's cheques, wallet and credit cards. He took off his jacket and delicately rolled up the left sleeve of his shirt. The car wheel had gone over his forearm and there was livid bruising and a swelling all the way from the elbow to the wrist. He supposed he should be thankful that the damage wasn't worse; the sandy ground had probably cushioned the impact. Obviously there were no broken bones but there might be crushing of the muscles or some other internal injury. His watch was still working and he was amazed to see that it was only two-thirty, barely half an hour since their arrival at Yildiz Fort.

There was nothing left to do but wait. Feeling suddenly exhausted, he stretched out on the bunk and fell into an uncomfortable doze.

He was aroused by the sound of the bolt on the door being slammed back. The lieutenant and another MP entered the cell, the officer snapping his fingers and gesturing for Jack to accompany them. A glance at his watch told him it was a quarter past three.

He didn't bother trying to ask where he was being taken. The two men marched briskly beside him, back down the corridor and up a flight of concrete stairs. They stopped at the first of a row of unmarked doors and the lieutenant rapped on it. A voice invited him to enter.

The room into which Jack was led smelt of dust and looked as though it wasn't regularly used as anything but a storeroom. Boxes full of papers were stacked on wooden shelves that rose to the ceiling against two walls. The window had no curtains or blinds and overlooked a vehicle park. The only furnishings were a plain deal table and two metal-framed chairs.

The man who sat behind the table was young and slim, with silky black hair, a carefully trimmed moustache and watchful brown eyes. He wore a khaki uniform with a red armband, and there were three stars on his shoulderboards. A captain, one step up from the lieutenant, which Jack supposed was an improvement.

He spoke briefly to Jack's escort. The lieutenant clicked his heels and left the room. The other MP took up a position by the door. Without expression, the captain gestured to Jack to take the chair facing him.

The briefcase he had dropped in the ditch at Yildiz Fort stood beside the table. The documents removed from it lay in front of the officer, with the photocopies made in Zunckel's office at the top. Next to them the passport and the other possessions that had been taken from Jack were arranged. There was also a thin green file cover, a portable tape recorder, a notepad, a metal ashtray, a Zippo lighter and an open packet of Maltepe cigarettes. These the captain pushed across the table towards Jack.

'Smoke if you wish.'

'No.' The offer sounded more like a concession than an invitation. 'Let's get down to business. I want to know where I am, and where my friend Miss Griggs is. I want to know why we've been arrested, and who you are.'

'This is the Kisla barracks. I am *Jandarma* Captain Yekta. Your American friend is at the Selimiye barracks, across the straits. You have both been detained for questioning about a serious terrorist incident.' The captain rattled this off with an easy assurance, lighting a cigarette for himself. Then he opened the passport, glanced at the photograph and compared it with Jack's face. 'And your name is Rushton?'

'That's what it says, doesn't it?' Jack replied testily. 'I assume you've been given the job of questioning me because you speak English, Captain, so please understand this: I realize I have some explaining to do, but I object to being treated like a criminal. I was a witness to that incident, not a perpetrator.'

'Only a witness?' Yekta raised an eyebrow. 'You told the lieutenant somebody had tried to kill you. If that is so, perhaps they will try again. You should be glad to have our protection.'

So the military policeman had understood him after all. 'Protection isn't what it feels like. You have no right to lock me up against my will.'

'Under the Turkish penal code we have every right.'

'Did the lieutenant also tell you that I want to see a doctor? And someone from the British Consulate?'

'A doctor will attend to you shortly. The request for consular assistance has been passed to the appropriate authorities,' Yekta said blandly, 'but of course these things take time to arrange. I was hoping we might clear this up before any outside intervention becomes necessary. For the moment I would like us to have an informal discussion. Why not start by telling me your view of what happened this afternoon?'

'It's not *my* view. It's what did happen. Those men in the car tried to run me over. They did the same to Miss Griggs. After that the shooting started.'

'What's your connection with those men?'

'I have no connection with them. I don't believe I've ever seen them before.'

'Then why do you think they were trying to kill you?'

'I don't think it, I know it.'

'Who are the people in these photographs?' The captain pointed to the papers taken from the briefcase.

'I believe they were officers of the *Mukhabarat*, the Iraqi secret police. I've been told they're all now dead.'

'Dead?' said Yekta incredulously. 'Do you usually carry pictures of dead men around with you?'

'You'll have to let me start at the beginning. I—'

'Are you familiar with a terrorist organization called *Emegin Birligi*?' Yekta interrupted. 'The Grey Wolves?'

'I've heard of them,' Jack said uneasily.

'How have you heard? They are not much known outside Turkey.'

In the way the Turk framed his questions and jumped from one subject to another, Jack recognized a deliberate attempt to throw him off balance. What was more, it was succeeding.

'I didn't know they existed until I arrived here. Look, Captain, I'm not trying to be difficult, but there's a short cut through all this. Miss Griggs and I went to Yildiz Fort this afternoon to see Mrs Delkin, the wife of General Delkin. We met her last night, and then this morning she arranged for us to talk to her husband on the phone. She was meant to meet us at the gates. Ask her. She'll confirm it all.'

'We have already asked her. She does confirm those details. She was walking to the gates when the shooting began.'

'Then what's the problem?'

'The fact that you met her doesn't prove anything. You were two strangers asking to talk to her husband but refusing to say why. She has no way of confirming your identity. And at present neither do I.'

'You've got my passport,' Jack protested. 'You've got my credit cards and—'

'Passports can be forged, cards can be stolen. In a matter like this we have to be quite certain who we are dealing with. We are checking the authenticity of your papers with the British authorities, but that, too, will take time. Meanwhile, you can make things easier for both of us by co-operating.'

'I'm trying to do that,' Jack said. 'But General Delkin knows the background. I'd find it easier to explain to him.'

'The general is not available.'

'He was available at two o'clock, and he was going to talk to me on the phone. That should say something about my bona fides.'

'I have spoken to the general too,' the Turk said with studied casualness. 'He knows no more about you than his wife does, except that he has already refused to talk to you once. This time he agreed to do so at her request, but only out of courtesy. He intended to advise you not to go on wasting your time as well as his. He has plenty of work to do on the border. He has asked for a report on this matter, but has left me to handle it.'

Jack gave a despondent shrug. Yekta opened the green file, extracted two photographs from it and slid them across the table. 'I will begin by asking if you recognize either of these men.'

They were composite mug shots, full-face and profile, two youngish men of Middle Eastern appearance looking startled by the camera flash.

'I've never seen them,' Jack said.

'Members of *Emegin Birligi*.' Yekta stubbed out his cigarette and lit another. 'Both with previous records, both wanted until today for various terrorist and criminal offences. One was arrested in a car outside Yildiz Fort shortly after the shootings and the explosion. The other, his friend and regular fellow-criminal, was killed in the car that was blown up. Of the two that were with them, one was also killed and the other captured. The Turk who survived has already identified them as two Iraqis who entered this country last night on false Egyptian papers. Now tell me why they wanted to kill you, Mr Rushton.'

'Why not ask them? The ones who survived.'

'We are doing so even now. But I want to hear your version.'

'It's a long story,' Jack said with a sigh.

Yekta pressed a button on the tape recorder. 'Tell it to me anyway. I have plenty of time.'

It took nearly half an hour to tell. Jack could see no way to avoid recounting any of the information he had been given, and the only detail he insisted on keeping to himself was the identity of Hamadi. Captain Yekta didn't press him on this point. He listened mostly in silence, making notes on his pad and lighting more cigarettes, filling the room with smoke. The soldier who stood by the door was finding it hard to suppress a cough.

When Jack had finished Yekta switched off the recorder, sat back and was silent for a minute. Then he said: 'So. You are asking me to believe that you travelled all this way in the hope of meeting someone who had already refused to talk to you, and that all you wanted to discuss with him was something that is only a theory in your own head.'

'When you put it like that—'

'And that for the sake of this theory the Iraqi secret police were prepared to kill you?'

'The fact that they tried seems to prove that I'm right.'

'Other things puzzle me,' Yekta said. 'After the kidnapping of this Kurd, Karim, you knew the police would want to question you, but you went ahead and left England. Why?'

'I didn't want to be delayed.' Jack knew this wasn't going to sound good. 'Also, if I'd talked to the police they'd have wanted to know the whole background, and I was obliged not to reveal it. I didn't think I could help them much anyway.'

'Was that for you to judge?'

'Perhaps not.'

'You certainly had things to hide. When you accepted the commission from this man in Kuwait, didn't it worry you to know that murder and blackmail had given rise to it?'

'Yes, it did. But nothing could change what had happened. I was helping him out of an immediate difficulty.'

'And also helping yourself out of financial trouble,' Yekta said. 'Another thing: I find it hard to take seriously this idea about the smuggling of gold into Turkey, but if you believed it yourself why did you not take steps to inform our authorities?'

'What could I have told them? I don't know anything for certain. I was hoping General Delkin might tell *me* something.'

'You knew enough to go and discuss it with the phanariot, Zakarios. I have to say that I do not find your story satisfactory, Mr Rushton. What is it that you are not telling me? Were you hoping to get your hands on this gold yourself?'

'For Christ's sake!' Jack exploded. He had had enough of the Turk's self-righteousness, enough of everything. 'I may have stuck my neck out a bit, Captain, but I'm not that stupid. I've told you everything I know, and I don't bloody care whether you believe it or not. I'm not answering any more questions until someone from the consulate comes to spring me out of here. And when that happens, I'm mentioning your name as part of a formal complaint about the way I've been treated.'

The MP at the door had been jolted into alertness by this outburst, but Yekta sat unmoved. 'Very well,' he said. 'I cannot force you to co-operate. But please be under no illusion that any representations from your consul will secure your release. For the present there is no question of your leaving these barracks.'

'For the present?' Jack said numbly. 'How long does that mean?'

'For as long as necessary. This is what I will tell your consul: I have a suspected Arab terrorist in my custody who may have tried to kill your citizen Mr Rushton. I am detaining Rushton firstly for his own protection, and secondly because he refuses to co-operate fully in my investigation. If I release him and return his passport, he may flee the country and be unavailable for further questioning. Alternatively, there may be another attempt on his life. It's an argument that will be well received, I assure you.' Yekta rapped out an order to the guard on the door, who stepped forward and put a hand on Jack's shoulder. 'I advise you to think matters over carefully, Mr Rushton. Perhaps we will talk again later.'

Back in his cell, Jack was visited after an hour by an army doctor who examined his arm, bandaged it up, fashioned a sling for it and gave him aspirins for the pain. He spoke only halting English but confirmed that no bones were broken. Apparently unaware of Jack's circumstances, he advised him to get the arm X-rayed for possible muscle damage when he got home.

Nothing else happened for the rest of the afternoon. At half-past six a military policeman brought him a tray with a meal of lamb stew and rice that was surprisingly edible, though he didn't have much appetite. Before the guard left, and again when he returned to collect the tray, Jack tried to ask him if there was news of anyone's arriving from the British consulate. The man was not unfriendly but he shrugged uncomprehendingly.

Jack lay down on the bunk again with a creeping sense of despair. Matters were far worse than they had looked when he'd first been arrested. He saw now that coming to Istanbul on the off-chance of meeting Delkin had been a mistake. Innocent though it was, it was bound to seem unconvincing to a man like Yekta, and with Delkin refusing to intercede on Jack's part it would appear even more so. Now that Yekta had got it into his head that he was hiding something, how was he to be persuaded otherwise? What could Jack say that he hadn't said already? He found himself wishing he did have more information up his sleeve, and began to understand why prisoners under interrogation tried to satisfy their captors by confessing to crimes they hadn't committed.

He fell asleep again. Just before half-past eight the cell door banged open. It was the lieutenant, accompanied by another MP. Although the officer still didn't speak, his manner seemed a little less curt; knowing now that he did have some English, Jack said: 'Is it someone from the consulate?'

The lieutenant made no reply. Jack felt his spirits lifting slightly as they marched him along a corridor and up the stairs again. It was possible that Yekta had been bluffing about the consul's inability to get him out of here. At the very least the Turks couldn't deny the consulate access to a prisoner, and once he got a chance to tell his story to a British official wheels would surely begin to turn on his behalf.

They halted at the same door as before. The lieutenant knocked and Captain Yekta answered.

It was pitch dark outside the uncurtained window and the room was lit only by a single dim bulb. Jack's heart sank when he saw that Yekta was on his own, this time standing by the table. There was a change in his demeanour as well, though; he seemed wary rather than hostile as he looked the prisoner over.

'You've had your arm attended to, I see.'

'Yes.'

'Have you any complaints about the conditions in which you are being detained?'

'Only about the fact that I'm here at all. Does your sudden concern for my welfare mean that you've heard from my consulate?'

'I will come to that in a moment. First I have other news for you. We have now extracted a certain amount of information from the Iraqi who was captured after the shooting today. It appears his name is Issa Shakir. He was—'

'Shakir!' Jack interrupted. 'That was the name of—'

'Yes, Ali Shakir, the man you told me had visited your British army acquaintance in England, was Issa's brother. Ali was blown up in the car today.' For the first time Yekta gave him a smile, a self-satisfied baring of even white teeth. 'Issa has been too distraught with grief to put up much resistance to our interrogators. It seems the two of them had orders to kill you, although they were never told exactly why. They followed you to Zurich and then here to Istanbul, where they had the assistance of the Grey Wolves. The instructions came from their superior in London, a man who apparently is the resident head of the *Mukhabarat* there. It was he, too, who ordered the kidnapping and murder of the Kurd, Karim.'

Jack felt a strange blend of relief and excitement. 'So you believe me now?' he said triumphantly. 'You admit I was right? My story checks out all the way, doesn't it?'

A hundred other questions crowded his mind, but he paused. Yekta's smile had given way to a look that warned him not to get carried away. 'What is it, Captain? Have I missed something?'

'You asked about the British consulate. Yes, they have been in touch with us. They have been informed that they may visit you on Wednesday if you have not been released by then.'

'In two days' time? But what's to stop you letting me go now? This clears everything up, doesn't it?'

'Unfortunately it also creates further complications. The consulate has been told that you will not be available. You are being moved out of Istanbul.'

Now Jack saw something that he had missed while his eyes adjusted to the gloom. Beside the table stood not only his briefcase but also a travel bag, his own bag, brought here from the Pera Palace.

'Moved to where?' he said disbelievingly.

'You are being taken to Hakkari,' Yekta said. 'You will leave at once and your American friend will join you *en route*. I cannot explain further, except to say that General Delkin wishes to question you both in person.'

# 29

He was as much a prisoner as ever but he was being treated with some deference now, almost apologetically. He was given his bag and allowed a few minutes in an adjacent washroom to clean up and change into fresh clothes. Then the lieutenant and three other military policemen hurried him back to the vehicle park at the rear of the barracks, where another van was waiting. There were no handcuffs this time, and the guards allowed him to share a bench with them, offering him unwanted cigarettes and miming their concern over the state of his bandaged arm.

He had got over his initial dismay. In fact, despite the questions that remained unanswered, he had begun to feel there was an element of bluff involved in this after all. They no longer had a pretext for holding him; and it was General Delkin who wanted to see him now, not the other way round. He suspected that if he'd complained loudly enough and again demanded to see his consul they would have given in and released him. However, he had put up only a token protest. This was almost certainly the only chance he would get of meeting Delkin, and it was worth paying the price of remaining formally in custody.

The lieutenant was still pretending to speak no English and wouldn't tell him where they were going. This time the journey in the stifling, windowless van seemed interminable. Once it was clear of the city traffic it travelled smoothly and fast, but another two hours went by before it turned off and halted twice at what Jack supposed were checkpoints. When it made a final stop and the doors were flung open he found he was far out in the country, on a breezy plain beneath a moonlit sky, with the lights of a town twinkling in the distance. Closer to hand were the control tower and buildings of what could only be a substantial military air base.

It was twenty minutes to midnight but the place was buzzing with activity. A dozen or more troop carriers were lined up at the front of the main building; when Jack was led inside he saw that it was filled with soldiers in camouflage fatigues, wearing the red armbands that he now knew identified the *Jandarma*, squatting and sitting among their piles of gear. Through the windows facing out on the apron three big transport planes were visible, their holds being loaded with cargo.

The military police escorted Jack down a side passage and the lieutenant knocked on a door at the end. It opened to reveal a plain little waiting-room, furnished only with a bench that ran along three of its walls. Facing the door, between two guards of her own, sat Dale.

She leaped to her feet with a look of delight that turned to alarm at the sight of his arm.

'Jack! They didn't tell me you were injured!'

'You should have seen the other fellow,' he said with a grin. 'Well, you did see. This isn't serious. Really.'

She ran forward, hugging him and kissing him greedily on the mouth. Then she held him by the shoulders and studied his face. She looked tired but not distressed, her green eyes bright in spite of the shadows around them. She had got her luggage back too, and had changed into a wide skirt of dark brown tweed and a knitted cream top.

'What the hell is going on, Jack? They kept me locked up for six hours, grilled me as if I was Patty Hearst and then rushed me out here as though they couldn't wait to get rid of me.'

'Likewise. I know about half the story. I'm hoping General Delkin will tell us the rest.'

'Well, it's wonderful to see you, anyway. I thought you were dead when that car went for you.'

'I thought you'd been shot.'

'Then there you were, getting up and walking like Lazarus while I stood there like a dummy . . .'

'I saw them pushing you into the van and wondered if I'd ever see you again . . .'

They stood exchanging reminiscences for a minute and then sat down together, with two MPs for company. The ones who had escorted Jack had left.

'I guess this place counts as the VIP lounge around here,' Dale said. 'How come we're suddenly in favour with these people?'

He repeated what Captain Yekta had told him about the admissions made by Issa Shakir. Her own captors in the barracks across the Bosporus hadn't explained any of this, but had at least been more forthcoming than Yekta about what was in store for them now. They were at the Eskisehir air base, she said, two hundred-odd kilometres east of Istanbul. They would be travelling to Van in the south-east on a transport plane carrying reinforcements to the border region; then they would be taken on to Delkin's headquarters at Hakkari.

'Of course I objected at first,' she said. 'Like you, I was screaming about my rights and demanding to see my consul. But when they told me you were going anyway I agreed to come along. Still, I don't quite see what Delkin wants us there for. The information we've given must have been relayed to him, plus everything they've screwed out of this Issa. What more can we tell him?'

Jack had thought a good deal about this on the way out from Istanbul. 'I'm not sure,' he said. 'The man who questioned me talked about further complications, so maybe something else has changed. On the other hand, it could be a convenient way of keeping us out of circulation for a day or two. They can tell our consulates, hand on heart, that we're not being treated as suspects and are co-operating with their enquiries. But, since we've had to be moved out of Istanbul, we're not available to be seen. Hence, less pressure on them

341

to release us. I don't think they can afford to let us go.'

'In case we blab to the newspapers or something?'

'Well, the whole thing is pretty sensitive. I'm sure they've tipped off the British police about this Iraqi in London who arranged the kidnapping of Karim and then sent his goons after us, and they won't want to risk letting that become public knowledge. Beyond that, I don't know. As far as I'm concerned, seeing Delkin is an opportunity to find out once and for all what really happened to Colonel Jalloul.'

'You're going through all this just to satisfy Hamadi?'

'I suppose there's a bit more to it than that,' he said.

He had wondered about that as well, back in the van that had brought him here. It was curiosity more than anything that drove him on now, he had concluded, a simple need to see things through to their conclusion. In the nine days since he had had that conversation with Hamadi in his garden in Kuwait, this project had taken over his life. Until it was over with he could think of almost nothing else.

They went on waiting for nearly an hour, which seemed to confirm the impression that Yekta and his colleagues had been anxious above all to get them out of Istanbul. Then the door opened and another young *Jandarma* officer came in. He said he would be escorting them on the flight, and he led them out through the concourse to a door opening on to the apron. Soldiers were formed up in three long lines and were boarding through the rear doors of the planes, but Dale and Jack were taken to a gangway that led up to a forward crew door. Just behind the cockpit was an area curtained off from the main cabin, where they were invited to take two of the eight or nine seats. The aircraft had turned out to be an ageing American Hercules; its fittings were utilitarian but the seating was comfortable enough, and Jack wasn't surprised when the other seats in what passed for first class were taken by senior officers. A glance back through a gap in the curtain showed the young Turkish soldiers being packed like sardines into the cabin.

It was another twenty minutes, a little after one o'clock in the morning, before the doors were finally closed and the four big engines roared into life. The plane rolled on to the runway and paused for a moment, then trundled forward, gathered speed and lumbered heavily into the night sky.

For nearly three hours the Hercules droned above the plains of Anatolia. Jack and Dale both got some fitful sleep but were awake for the last fifteen minutes of the journey, looking down on the black expanse of Lake Van as the plane descended towards the glow of the town on its eastern shore.

It made a bumpy landing in the dark and taxied to a point well away from the terminal. In spite of that it was obvious that the place was just as busy as Eskisehir had been. The two other Hercules had already landed, several more planes were parked some distance away and endless convoys of trucks were waiting to receive soldiers and cargo.

Jack and Dale were escorted down the gangway ahead of anyone else. There was a sharp chill in the air, reminding them that they were deep in the interior of western Asia now, nearly a thousand kilometres from balmy Istanbul. As the young officer led them round past the nose of the Hercules they made a more surprising discovery. A big helicopter painted in military camouflage was parked twenty metres ahead of them, with its doors open and its navigation lights winking.

'We're going in that?' Dale exclaimed.

'Unless you want to ride for four hours in a truck?' the officer said drily. 'I think the general expects you sooner than that.'

By the light from the perimeter lamps Jack could see that it was no ordinary helicopter. There were two doors on its left side; one gave access to the cockpit and the other, just behind it, had been slid back to reveal the snout of a large-calibre machine-gun poking out through the opening. On either side of the aircraft, just above the skids, pods holding clusters of rockets were mounted. Three crewmen in dark flying suits were lounging beside it.

'That's a gunship, isn't it?' Jack said.

'Agusta two-oh-four,' one of the crewmen confirmed with a grin. 'It's the only way to travel around here.'

'Are you expecting trouble?' Dale asked.

'This is Kurdistan, my friends. But the Kurds have their own problems at the moment and shouldn't bother us. Are you ready?'

They clambered awkwardly aboard through the opening where the machine-gun was mounted, ducking beneath the door arch and the low cabin roof and taking the seats they were shown just behind those of the pilot and one of his crewmen. Their luggage was stowed under the seats. The third man moved aft to occupy a swivel chair behind the machine-gun.

The one who spoke English was the pilot. Fitting on a white helmet, he jerked a thumb at the open doorway. 'You'll find it noisy and a little windy,' he said, 'but it's only for an hour. Strap yourselves in, please.'

While they fastened their seat belts the pilot spoke briefly on his radio to the control tower. He went through a complicated ritual of checking and turning on overhead switches, then started his engines. A low rumble grew into a piercing whine as the rotor blades began to spin and then picked up speed. The gunship shuddered and strained, rose slowly from the apron and then executed a swift banking turn. Cold air from its slipstream whipped in through the doorway. Dale was exhilarated, smiling at Jack and turning to stare out through a porthole. It struck him that there were many things he still didn't know about her, including the possibility that she was turned on by danger.

Day was just breaking, a paleness in the sky against a high, jagged line of mountains to the east. They were gaining altitude steadily and within a few minutes the level ground below them had turned from black to misty grey. To the south loomed another forbidding wall of mountains, and they were heading straight towards them.

When the sun came up it revealed peaks smothered in snow, deep gorges and eroded valleys with faint tracks winding through them. Below the snow line the land was rocky and almost bone-dry, with little vegetation and only scattered signs of human settlement. These were the mountains of the southern Taurus that Zakarios had talked about, a bolt-hole for Kurdish guerrillas and a gateway to refugees and smugglers from Iraq, a yellow-grey wilderness that it was hard to imagine anyone choosing to inhabit.

The helicopter was contour-flying, skimming past the peaks and hopping from one pass to the next, so it was only occasionally that they got a wider view, now and then glimpsing the road to the east that wound laboriously up from Van. The cold was numbing and the air had grown thin, making it hard to breathe until Jack and Dale strapped on the oxygen masks they were shown. The crew remained alert but casual in a studied way, the pilot holding crackling conversations on the radio and occasionally shouting descriptions of landmarks to his passengers over the howl of the turbojet engines. Down in that gorge was the Botan River, a tributary of the Tigris. Over there was Cilo Dag, at over four thousand metres one of the highest mountains in Turkey.

When they had been flying for forty minutes he called over his shoulder: 'We have a little time to spare. You want to see our most spectacular sight?' Without waiting for an answer he spoke a few words into his radio and altered course slightly to the west.

The landscape remained much the same for the next few kilometres. Then a valley appeared ahead, opening up between the flanks of the mountains to become wider than the others they had seen. The gunship descended into it, following the southward course of a narrow river swollen by melting snow and tumbling over rocks. There was suddenly a stark little village on its left bank, and a short way further on was a narrow road, clogged by a long, stationary line of civilian trucks. They were all facing to the west, all heavily laden with people or baggage, and were apparently blocked by one that had broken down. The helicopter was past the spot in a flash, still heading on down the river. Puzzled, Jack tried to ask the pilot what they were supposed to be looking for but he shook his head and raised a hand in a gesture that said: wait and see.

The valley continued to widen out. The river had grown broader too, and shallower, and the gunship was flying low enough to churn up the water with the downdraft from its blades. A short way ahead the river turned to the east, into a defile where the mountainsides became suddenly steeper. The pilot followed it, edging over to the left bank as they rounded the bend.

And then they did see.

The whole side of the mountain that rose from the right bank was smothered by people and their possessions. From the river's edge up to a height of several hundred metres the bare slopes were covered by a great mass of humanity, moving and standing and sitting among a litter of tents, blankets, sacks, cardboard boxes and sheets of polythene formed into makeshift shelters. The smoke from hundreds of small fires hung over them, blending with the morning mist off the water and drifting across it to where the Turkish soldiers stood on the opposite bank, on guard against any attempt to cross the river.

The sight was not what the pilot had called it, spectacular; it was chaotic, grotesque, almost unbelievable. There must have been tens of thousands of people just here who had spent the night in the open; others, the luckier ones, were no doubt inside the shelters, and more could be glimpsed beyond the next bend in the river, an entire nation uprooted and set down on this unwelcoming frontier. Drab grey and brown clothing was relieved by the outlandish pinks and blues of women's dresses and headgear. The ground beneath them was churned into mud and what few trees there were had been stripped down to their trunks for firewood; it was as though the refugees had taken over a Great War battlefield.

The pilot had reduced his speed and was flying low, close enough for the Kurds to be seen no longer as a blur but as individuals. Their faces were turned up to the helicopter, most of them looking indifferent but some shaking their fists at it. Mingled smells of woodsmoke, cooking and excrement wafted in through the gun door.

What must once have been an unmarked frontier was now defined by new, shining coils of barbed wire on this side of the river. A road ran parallel to it, choked with a mixture of military and civilian vehicles. A kilometre or so further on it reached a junction giving access to a low concrete bridge, and the pilot gained some height and went into hover above it for a minute. There was a semblance of a border post here, with a small customs building and a striped boom across the road on the Turkish side, but clearly all civil functions had been taken over by the army. An open truck laden with bulging sacks had just crossed the bridge and was slithering up the muddy slope, chased by a swarm of refugees. Some tried to clamber onto it and were fended off with the rifle butts of Turkish soldiers sitting on the cargo. When it finally stopped, the troops began opening the sacks and throwing flat loaves of unleavened bread into the crowd, who scrambled and fought over them like animals.

'We do what we can for them,' the pilot shouted at his passengers. 'We try to feed them, but there's never enough.'

Dale was shaken by what she was seeing, no longer getting a charge out of the experience. 'Why can't you let

347

them in?' she demanded. 'Give them temporary shelter, at least?'

'Many thousands have already come in. Then we had to close the border. They say there may be a million of them in these mountains. How can we take them all?'

The road on the Iraqi side was also jammed with cars and trucks. Some were being allowed across the bridge; others had been turned back, several of them getting stuck in the mud beside the road while trying to reverse, adding to the confusion.

The gunship surged forward and continued its journey. It banked away from the river and gained more height, returning to flit among the icy peaks which now seemed tranquil and almost welcoming. After a few minutes Hakkari came into view, a jumble of low buildings perched on a rocky plateau. Although the sun was well up now, the town still lay in the shadow of the Cilo Dag mountain. The military base took shape as a rectangle of high metal fencing enclosing ramshackle barracks and rows of tents, set up no doubt as emergency quarters for the extra troops that had been drafted in.

Half a dozen helicopters were parked on a paved square marked out with white circles. The gunship hovered above one of these, eased itself down and settled on its skids. The pilot disengaged the rotor and cut his engines; suddenly the unearthly scream that Jack and Dale had somehow got used to was gone, replaced by the whip of the decelerating blades and beyond it the eerie silence of the mountains.

Clambering out of the helicopter, stiff and cold, they found another officer of the *Jandarma* waiting to meet them. He was a young captain who introduced himself as Brigadier-General Delkin's aide-de-camp. The notion that they were still prisoners seemed to have been forgotten, for he gave them a smart salute and shook their hands before helping them with their luggage and leading them off to meet the general.

# 30

He didn't look the way Jack had imagined he would. For one thing his appearance, like that of a small minority of Turks, was more European than Middle Eastern; for another, it wasn't soldierly. He had a pale, chubby, clean-shaven face and black hair edged with grey, and he wore glasses with old-fashioned Buddy Holly frames. Beneath the quilted combat jacket and thick khaki pullover, his body looked soft and paunchy. If anything, the uniform emphasized the want of a military bearing; General Delkin might have been an out-of-shape businessman paying to take part in some weekend war game.

Nevertheless, to have reached such a rank at his age, which was the early forties, he must have some outstanding quality. At a guess, it was his intelligence. His English was excellent, and for half-past five in the morning his manner was energetic by anyone's standards.

Once he had greeted them at the door of his office the first thing he said was: 'Have you been given breakfast?'

When they said no, he called in an orderly and gave some brisk instructions. He invited Jack and Dale to sit down and apologized for the spartan nature of the office. It was separate from the main barracks, in a tacky prefabricated building that was meant to be temporary, he said, and so had no heating. That explained the general's warm clothing but wasn't helping Jack and Dale to thaw out after the freezing helicopter ride. The main feature of the office was a large-scale map of south-eastern Turkey fixed to one wall, with the meandering borders of Iraq and Iran heavily outlined in purple. The rest was government-issue furniture, the desk piled with papers but also accommodating two surprisingly modern digital key telephones. The window looked out towards the mountains in the south.

Back in his own seat, Delkin joined his fingertips and said: 'I'm sure you would like to rest, but there are some important things we should clear up first. I gather you've been given a look at the problem we have to deal with here, so you'll understand what pressure I am under.'

'What I don't understand,' Dale said sharply, 'is why you can't give those people temporary refuge on this side of the border. They're freezing and starving on those mountains. The help that is reaching them is obviously inadequate.'

'Miss Griggs, I have every personal sympathy with the Kurds. But politically such a thing is impossible. Temporary arrangements have a way of becoming permanent. Any one of those people who set foot on Turkish soil would gain the status of a political refugee and become our responsibility. Yes, we would get help from the United Nations and from other countries, but in the end we would be left with a million or more people on our hands. Homeless, destitute, discontented people: another Palestinian problem. And, frankly, we have enough trouble with the Kurds who live under our jurisdiction as it is.'

'You're letting some of them in,' Dale said. 'We saw trucks full of people being allowed across the bridge.'

'The frontier remains open at its official crossing points,' Delkin said, 'and people whose papers are in order are naturally free to enter. Those you saw were probably Kurds with Turkish nationality, of whom there are many in Iraq. They've been hiring trucks to bring them out. The ones on the mountainsides are Saddam Hussein's own citizens, whether they like it or not. But let us talk of more immediate things. Do you have any idea why you were asked to come here?'

'We weren't exactly asked,' Jack couldn't help pointing out.

'Ah. No. I must apologize for that as well. It was something of a ploy, frankly. I couldn't be sure that you would agree to speak to me voluntarily, so I arranged to have you brought here, where you would be . . . less subject to outside pressures, shall we say? But since your interests and mine seem to coincide, perhaps you will forgive my presumption.'

So he'd been right about the Turks trying to keep them under wraps, Jack thought. 'We *wanted* to talk to you,' he said. 'It was the only reason we came to Turkey.'

'But things have changed since you arrived. What happened at Yildiz Fort yesterday has given all of us the answers to some questions. You know that those men were trying to kill you, and I . . . well, I know why they were trying.' The general looked at them significantly. 'I have a particular interest in this matter, and, of course, I have read transcripts of your interrogations yesterday. From those, and from the questioning of this man Issa Shakir, it is clear that these people think you know more than you actually do. I would like them to go on thinking that.'

'Why?'

'Let's take it one step at a time. Do you have the documents with you that were examined by Captain Yekta? They are probably clearer than the copies that were sent to me.'

Jack opened his briefcase and handed over his sets of papers. Delkin searched quickly through them, removed one page and pushed it back across the desk. It was one of the photocopies Jack had obtained from Zunckel, containing the picture and passport details of one of the six mysterious Iraqi clients for whom he had opened bank accounts. It was the man who went by the name of Sharif Hayawi. Jack recalled that his assets at the Handelsbank

Bauer were in the region of two and three-quarter million dollars.

'You said to Captain Yekta that this name was an alias?' Delkin asked. 'And that the man who used it is now dead?'

'That's what was reported to me. But why single him out? He was only one of half a dozen, and not the most important one.'

'Because in his case at least you may have been misinformed. That is to say, as far as his death is concerned. He was alive and well less than forty-eight hours ago.'

Delkin spoke matter-of-factly. Jack stared at him.

'One of the things we established from the questioning of Issa Shakir was the identity of his superior in London. The man who planned the abduction and murder of Abdel Karim, and who sent Issa and Ali to kill you. They knew him only by the title of Mudeer, an Arabic word meaning 'boss' or 'director'. However, Issa was, of course, able to recognize him by his photograph.' Delkin held up the blurred picture. 'This is him.'

Jack said blankly: 'He's in London? But that can't be! I was told—'

'I know. You were told that he was killed in Kuwait during Desert Storm at the end of February, along with General Malik and the four other Iraqis who had all that money in Zurich. But by Issa's account he has been in England since last December. And if Hayawi is still alive . . .?' Delkin raised his eyebrows rhetorically, like a schoolmaster.

'Then so are the others?'

'How can they not be?'

There was a knock on the door and the orderly came in with their breakfast: a pot of coffee and baskets full of croissants and cheese-filled pastries. Jack and Dale began tucking in hungrily while Delkin poured coffee for all three of them and produced a bottle of Scotch from a drawer of his desk.

'Something to keep out the cold,' he said, splashing whisky into their cups. He was smiling, still enjoying their surprise. 'I thought it wise to order Yekta not to tell you any of this. I wanted you here first, safe from the possibility that any leaks might occur.'

'Are you saying these six Iraqis faked their own deaths? Jack said through a mouthful of croissant.

'I have no proof of it, but consider the circumstances. They were supposed to have been among a dozen men in a truck that was hit by a phosphorus bomb. Your source in Kuwait confirmed what I had already heard from my own informants, that all the bodies were charred beyond recognition. However, papers identifying them as Malik and the others were conveniently found in the cab. Perhaps your researches have taught you enough to know that these people are able to step in and out of new identities almost whenever they please. I'm sure this particular little group wouldn't have found it difficult to arrange a thing like that. In fact, I doubt if any of them got close to any real fighting.'

'But why do it?'

'Because they were in the process of making a new future for themselves,' Delkin said. 'It was something they had been planning for years. Not the kind of future that my friend Ibrahim Jalloul was seeking, and not for the same reasons. They were the secret police, the iron fist of the regime and also its pampered favourites. They had access to luxuries, hard currency, foreign travel, the proceeds of corruption, all the benefits that were denied to ordinary Iraqis. And they knew better than anyone that it couldn't last. One day Saddam Hussein and his friends would fall from power, and with them would go the *Mukhabarat* that had propped them up. Hence the foreign bank accounts, the secret investments, the new identities. Poor devoted little fools like those Shakir brothers weren't working for the cause they imagined they were; they were slaving to line their masters' pockets.

'When Saddam invaded Kuwait these people sensed trouble ahead; when the Allies drove him out, his downfall must have seemed imminent. What better time to make their move? And what better opportunity to discard their old selves than to die in the Mother of All Battles?'

'Except,' said Jack, 'that those bank accounts and investments haven't been touched. Not since before the invasion.'

'That's because they've been lying low. Because they don't want to risk losing an even bigger prize.'

Dale paused with her coffee cup halfway to her mouth. 'The gold?'

'Exactly. The gold. Forty million dollars' worth of it, more than the value of all their present investments put together. It's strange how wealth makes people greedy for more. It's their greed that is going to destroy them, Miss Griggs. I'm going to see to that. It's what I promised my friend Ibrahim I would do.'

Delkin said this in such a quiet, measured way that its effect was all the more startling. Jack and Dale looked at each other. Jack said: 'Did you make that promise when he phoned you from Amman? Last August, when he was arranging to get Noura Hamadi out of Kuwait?'

The general nodded in confirmation. 'You'll gather that this is a personal thing for me. We had been close friends for ten years, ever since we met at Camberley. We trusted each other totally. That was the last time we spoke, and he told me about the deal he was making with Hamadi. And more. He told me how the gold might cost him his life; and how, if it did, I should use it to avenge his death. The time for that may now be approaching. And I want you to help me.'

This was getting more bizarre by the minute. 'You're saying you actually know that Jalloul is dead?' Jack asked.

'I have positive proof of it,' said Delkin calmly. 'And you have provided it. More exactly, you have, Miss Griggs.'

'Me? I didn't know a damn thing about this until Jack—'

The general silenced her with a look. 'One thing Jalloul did not tell me was the alias he would use, or even that he would have an alias, when he took Noura Hamadi out of Kuwait. It was the simple fact that you overheard that name, Mohamed Ghani, that made all the difference. Until last night I had never heard the name. When I received the transcripts of your interrogations I initiated a search of all the Iraqi public documents that our intelligence services had been gathering since the invasion of Kuwait. They came up with just one thing.'

He tugged a slip of paper out of the pile on his desk. 'A single sentence on an inside page of the government newspaper, *Al-Jumhuriyah*, dated the eighth of September last year. Buried among a lot of official announcements about price controls and import regulations. Since you do not read Arabic, I will translate: "The Revolutionary Command Council announces that the economic traitor Mohamed Ghani was executed on the fourth of September".'

Delkin pushed the paper aside. 'No details of where, how, why: just another piece of business news. No trial is mentioned, which means it was a summary execution by the *Mukhabarat*. Take note that the name Ghani is used, not Jalloul, and that he is described as an "economic traitor". That explains a lot in itself.'

'You didn't know until last night,' Jack said, 'but you suspected? Is that what you were trying to tell Nadine Schuster when you visited her in March?'

'For as long as the Gulf crisis lasted, I thought there was some slender hope that Jalloul might have been imprisoned rather than killed. Once the war was over and there was still no word of him, I was fairly sure that he was dead. I tried to prepare poor Nadine for it without actually giving her any facts. I let her think the idea was her own. Now I will have to break the news to her, but only once all this is over.'

'And what exactly is all this?' Dale asked.

'Between what I know and you have learned, we have almost the whole picture now. You need to understand that the *Mukhabarat* not only distrusted people like Jalloul, they also feared them. Men like him, honest and honourable men who refuse to accept the cult of Saddam Hussein, will one day gather the strength to overthrow him. The secret police do everything they can to discredit such people, but they must also move cautiously. Hence the spies in his office, the constant search for evidence of his disloyalty.

'When your Dr Hamadi approached Dr Zunckel, the lawyer in Zurich, asking him to find Jalloul, Zunckel naturally went to the best contact he had in Iraq: the businessman Mohamed Ghani, who also happened to be General Malik. And Malik jumped at the chance to perform this favour. Neither of these foreigners could know that he saw it as an opportunity to destroy Jalloul.

'He had a particular reason for wanting to do so just at that time. A few days earlier, immediately after the invasion of Kuwait, when they were beginning to have serious worries about their futures, Malik and his group had stolen some of the gold they had removed from the Central Bank. I suppose it was just irresistible. They had hidden it and were making plans to remove it to somewhere safer, but they knew that Jalloul suspected them of the theft. He had been involved in the transport arrangements and he might even have some documentary evidence of what they had done. He had turned the tables on them; perhaps he could send *them* before a firing squad. This wasn't just a case of a petty kickback, it was stealing assets directly from the state.

'But now there was a chance to redeem the situation. Malik and his people knew nothing about this job that Jalloul was to carry out. But they did have ways of keeping track of him, working out roughly what was involved and turning it to their own advantage.

'As Abdel Karim told you, there is a sort of pool of false

identities available to members of all the Iraqi intelligence services but the *Mukhabarat* has ultimate control of it. A touch of irony here: from what you have learned it is obvious that Malik arranged for Jalloul to be given the papers of the fictitious businessman named Mohamed Ghani, an alias that Malik had already used for himself. Why? Because that way he could, almost literally, kill two birds with one stone. Once Jalloul was eliminated, unable to speak for himself, the evidence of his crimes could be revealed to those in power in Baghdad. That economic treachery that Malik himself had committed under the name of Ghani. Including the theft of the gold.'

Delkin sat back with satisfaction. Astonished, Jack said: 'That was what it was all about? Pinning the blame on Jalloul for the disappearance of the gold?'

'Pinning it on a man called Ghani, and proving that Ghani was really Jalloul. They knew that sooner or later, once the discrepancies in the figures were found, somebody would have to take the blame; why not the very man who might expose them as the culprits? That way they could throw in a string of past crimes as well, and a conspiracy involving the daughter of a rich Kuwaiti businessman. Dictators love to believe in conspiracies, to see traitors unmasked, and they don't look too hard at the facts; their secret police feed them a steady diet of such things. In his official report, Malik no doubt explained how he had traced the theft of the gold to Jalloul, how his vigilant men had stopped the criminal as he was about to leave Kuwait, and how he tried to resist arrest and was shot. Regrettably, they had been just too late to prevent the disappearance of the gold itself. This was an embarrassing detail. Hence, no triumphant headlines, just that one sentence in *Al-Jumhuriyah*.

'I can't tell you exactly what happened that night, but I can make a reasonable guess. On the phone from Amman, Jalloul told me he thought Malik might have learned of his plans to bring a plane in from Baghdad to fly Noura Hamadi out. It would make sense to stop him at the airport; it would add conviction to the story about his trying to flee. Any witnesses to what actually took place could conveniently be eliminated there and then. In view of something else I found out, it seems likely that Malik and his men used that same plane to remove the gold from Kuwait.'

General Delkin stood up and walked to the map on the wall. 'You will recall,' he said, 'that we and our American allies were engaged in intensive aerial, satellite and electronic surveillance of Iraq and Kuwait at that time. I requested the intelligence reports for the morning of the fourth of September, and I learned that an SR-Seventy-One spy plane flying from the American base at Incirlik here in Turkey had picked up the radar and radio signals from an aircraft that took off from Kuwait City at about two-thirty. It flew north-north-west for eight hundred kilometres, landing at around daybreak near a place called Zibar, in Iraqi Kurdistan.' He pointed to a spot in the bottom right-hand corner of the map, a short way below the purple line marking the Iraqi frontier. 'It's a place of no significance, but it was once the base of a German company with a contract for constructing hydro-electric dams on the Great Zab River, and they built an airstrip there.

'The plane stayed on the ground for two hours. Aerial photographs taken in daylight identified it as a small commercial jet, a Piaggio capable of carrying a payload of, would you believe, just over three thousand kilos? A further sequence of pictures from a number of overflights showed its cargo being offloaded into a truck, which was then driven north along this track into the mountains.'

Delkin's finger followed a tracery of tiny red dots that wandered among densely packed contour lines. 'All this was routinely recorded, along with hundreds of other ground and air movements. Since these ones obviously had no military significance the Americans weren't interested in them. But of course I was. We in the *Jandarma* have mapped that area very carefully because of its potential use as a refuge for Kurdish terrorists. That track was built by the German company as well, and it leads nowhere except to an old construction camp, abandoned for many years and quite cut off from the world.' He turned and looked out of the window. 'It's only ten kilometres from the border. You could almost see it from here if it weren't for a few peaks in between.'

'And that's where you think the gold is?' Jack asked.'

'Unless they have shifted it since. But my feeling is that they planned to leave it there, buried perhaps, and no doubt discreetly guarded, until the time came to move it into Turkey. The end of the Gulf War would have been the right moment, but then came the Kurdish insurrection, turning that area into hostile territory for members of the *Mukhabarat*.' Deklin paused. 'When you spoke to Zakarios, the old smuggler, he suggested a route that these people might take. Along the old Silk Road to the Mediterranean coast?'

'That's right.'

'There is a ship that arrived unladen four days ago at Iskenderun and is still there, waiting for a cargo. A small freighter, registered in Panama, that sails frequently between the eastern Mediterranean and Bombay. It may have no connection with this business, and its captain and its agent would probably not be involved in any case. We have not questioned them for fear of scaring off the conspirators, but we have kept the vessel under observation. It may have been chartered by Malik and his friends as soon as it became clear that the rebellion of the Kurds was going to be crushed. The idea presumably would be to smuggle the gold into Turkey, perhaps already broken down into smaller quantities, and transport it by road to Iskenderun: a journey of twelve hours or so. At that time nobody could have foreseen the situation that you witnessed along the frontier this morning. If you were Malik, what would you do in these circumstances?'

'Keep lying low, I suppose,' Jack said. 'Wait until things on the border quietened down.'

'And cancel the charter of the ship? It can't stay in Iskenderun indefinitely. And it might be weeks, or months, before another one could be arranged.'

'Presumably Malik has plenty of time.'

'Not necessarily. Remember that his ultimate purpose is to disappear. Presumably in due course he intends to resurface in Switzerland, still using the name of Ghani to claim his wealth from the bank and add to it whatever the sale of the gold has brought him. Nobody in Zurich knows or cares that someone called Ghani has been executed in Iraq. Then Malik vanishes again, perhaps emerging elsewhere under yet another name. His fellow-crooks follow a similar course. But in the meantime this operation is too important for them not to want to be in charge of it themselves. That means they are in Iraq now. And in view of what has happened over the past few days, they are vulnerable to exposure. Which means, perhaps, that we can panic them.'

'We?' said Jack.

'This time I mean just you, Mr Rushton. But I gathered from what you said after your arrest that you weren't likely to co-operate unless Miss Griggs was a party to the arrangement.' Delkin smiled and poured more whisky into their cups. 'That's why I brought you here. These Iraqis know of your involvement, but they've got a distorted picture of it. One phone call from you, Mr Rushton, could bring them across the border. With the gold. Into a trap.'

Jack still wasn't sure if the soldier was serious. 'Who am I supposed to call?'

'There is one person among all those you have met who actually has a means of making contact with Malik himself. I refer to Dr Zunckel, the lawyer in Zurich. Remember what you told Captain Yekta about the phone number Zunckel had in Baghdad? The one he could use in an emergency to reach his client Ghani? I want you to provide him with a reason for calling that number.'

'I don't know that that arrangement still exists. Zunckel said he hadn't used it for months.'

'What you said was that he hadn't *tried* to use it. With good reason. His last conversation with the man he knew as Ghani had been soon after the invasion of Kuwait, and Ghani had been talking about a mysterious deal involving a lot of gold. It frightened Zunckel off. But think about it. Even if he can no longer reach that number, a man like Zunckel will have other resources. He's had good connections in Iraq for twenty years or more. He will find a way of contacting Malik if you can convince him that it's in his interests to do so.'

'How do I do that?'

'By frightening him again,' Delkin said easily. 'With certain significant omissions, you can tell him the truth. Then it will be for him to decide which of his clients he is more afraid of.'

The general glanced at his watch. 'His office will be open in four hours' time. In the meantime I suggest you get some rest.'

# 31

They were given a room to share in the officers' quarters in the main barracks building. It was just as austere as General Delkin's office but it was blessed with central heating. The warmth made them feel drowsy, and as soon as they lay down on the hard twin beds they fell asleep.

Just before ten o'clock they were roused by Delkin's aide-de-camp, reviving them with more coffee and then leading them back through the crisp mountain air to the prefab. Alone with them in his office, the general dialled the Zurich number Jack gave him and then silently handed over the receiver.

The secretary answered, sounding a long way off and nervous at the sound of his voice. She asked him to wait, and a good minute went by before Zunckel came on the line.

'Yes?' The tone still aggrieved, but also wary.

'Dr Zunckel, I'm calling you from Turkey. I want you to know that I've found proof that your client Jalloul is dead. I assume this means that the contract with Dr Hamadi can now be cancelled and the account at the Handelsbank closed.'

'If your proof is satisfactory, then of course.' Even Zunckel couldn't resist being curious. 'How did you find it? And what's taken you to Turkey?'

'It's too complicated to explain in any detail. Briefly, it involves those other clients of yours, Ghani and the rest. I don't know that I owe you any favours, Doctor, but I thought I should give you a friendly warning that I'm going to have to tell the whole story to Dr Hamadi. I've established that Ghani is really an Iraqi secret police officer named General Omar Hassan Malik. He and the five others were responsible for murdering Jalloul. They have also tried to kill me.'

There was a long pause. 'Tried to *kill* you? How? Why?'

'They seemed to think I was getting too close to them. Apparently they believe I know more than I do. I've had a hard time convincing the Turkish police that I'm not somehow involved with them myself. They held me for questioning for a time.'

'And you say Hamadi doesn't know about this yet?'

'No. But I'll have to explain it to him.'

'You did give me an undertaking of confidentiality.'

'I know. But there's more involved now than a simple financial transaction. And you and I both have a duty to Dr Hamadi. Malik's criminal activities are the whole reason for Hamadi's problems. I imagine he'll find some way of getting his own back. You know what resources he has. His *wasta* extends all over the Middle East. He'll find a way of letting the authorities in Baghdad know what Malik has been up to.'

Another pause. 'Mr Rushton . . . I've no doubt that Dr Hamadi will be happy to have this matter cleared up. You know that my role in it has been entirely incidental. Does your report have to mention my connection with this Malik and the others?'

'I'm not sure it can be avoided. I assume you're still representing them, which means you do have a certain responsibility for what's happened.'

Jack could almost hear Zunckel sweating. 'I am grateful for your warning, Mr Rushton. If I were able to terminate my relationship with these clients within twenty-four hours, say, do you suppose it could be overlooked? And if there's anything I can do by way of compensating you for the difficulties you've been through, you need only say so.'

'I'm not looking for a bribe, Dr Zunckel. But let me think it over.'

'You'll give me twenty-four hours? Where can I reach you?'

'You can't at the moment. I'm on my way back to London. But I'll call you again at this time tomorrow.'

Jack put down the phone. Delkin gave him a satisfied look and said: 'Very good. Zunckel now gets in touch with Malik, repeats what you have said and tells him they are no longer in business together. Malik realizes his cover is blown and that he has to leave Iraq. But since you didn't mention the gold he thinks his plans for that are still safe. The trap is baited; it remains to be seen if it will be sprung. You are free to go now if you wish. But perhaps you would like to stay and see the outcome?'

Jack glanced at Dale again. What he saw in her eyes answered the question for him.

The rest of the day stretched emptily before them. Dale went for a run around the perimeter of the base, and later Delkin's aide took them for lunch at a restaurant in Hakkari. The place was swarming with soldiers, a garrison town in what had come to feel like occupied territory. Afterwards the gendarme took them out to see what few local sights there were. He was in civilian clothes and he drove his own car, explaining casually that the Turkish army wasn't exactly popular among the local Kurdish population and he didn't want to risk making a target for a sniper. He showed them the spectacular gorge of the Zab, where bare cliffs tumbled for nearly a thousand metres down to the rushing river, and he took them to see an ancient Nestorian monastery and an encampment of nomads. There were military checkpoints on every road.

Back in Hakkari, they killed more time over a few drinks in a bar crowded with foreign journalists and television crews. English, American and French voices were raised in complaints to each other about the Turkish authorities' slowness in allowing them to get to the frontier.

Jack and Dale had dinner with Delkin in his quarters. He had spent most of the day on the border, and he told them he had spread a number of his own men about among the troops guarding the crossing points, with orders to report directly to him if they observed anything unusual.

'Even if we have succeeded in panicking these Iraqis,' he said, 'they're unlikely to come across without making some preparations beforehand. Somebody will surely meet them on this side. For us, the important thing is to let them think they are safe. Let them get firmly on to Turkish soil, on the road to Iskenderun, and we will have them in our grasp. On charges of smuggling gold in that quantity, they should go to jail for twenty years at least. I only wish we could try them as well for the murder of Jalloul.'

'Can you really be sure they'll come within twenty-four hours?' Dale asked.

'I can't be sure of anything. But that is the time limit that Zunckel should have conveyed to Malik. He in turn will have to weigh the risks of coming out against those of staying in Iraq and having his crimes exposed. There is always a chance that he will simply abandon the gold, but after the time and trouble he has invested in it, I think that is unlikely.'

Delkin plied them with more whisky, before and after dinner. On top of what they had drunk that afternoon, and the exhausting journey of the night before, it made them both slightly plastered. At ten o'clock they lurched back to their room and fell into bed.

Jack felt himself being shaken awake in the dark and was aware that he had a dry mouth and a headache. Delkin's aide-de-camp was in the room, whispering apologetically but urgently.

'Sorry sir. The general asks for you to come at once.'

Jack groaned and heaved himself out of bed. The luminous dial of his watch told him it was half-past three. While the aide went to wait outside, Jack woke

Dale up and they both scrambled into the warmest clothes they had.

Even at this hour the base wasn't at rest. Sentries were on patrol, vehicles were coming and going through the gates and soldiers were moving about among the lines of tents. Delkin had just ended a meeting with a group of officers who were filing out of his room, and Jack wondered when the man ever slept.

'Some news at last!' he said triumphantly. 'Come. We must not waste time.'

Instead of asking them into the office he led them straight back out of the building, round a corner towards the helicopter pad. The same Agusta gunship that had brought Dale and Jack in the morning before was waiting for them again, and they climbed in after the general and strapped themselves into their seats. Delkin sat opposite them, grinning and rubbing his hands in anticipation.

'It seems that your call to Zurich has got things moving in just the way we hoped,' he said. 'Did you see a village close to the frontier yesterday? Some of the guards are billeted in houses there. Last night a group of strangers arrived in two cars and moved into rooms in the local *pansiyon*. They contrived to meet some off-duty soldiers, bought them a great many drinks and eventually offered them a large bribe to let a certain truck across the river unhindered when the border opens this morning. Some of my own men were among the soldiers and they reported the matter straight to me. I gave instructions that the bribe should be accepted. So now we go there and watch the trap being sprung!

'These people are certainly gangsters of the Grey Wolves,' he bawled at them as the chopper's engines started up. 'I could have ordered their arrest, of course, but we don't want to scare off the big fish by netting the little ones.'

The noise drowned out further conversation as the helicopter rose, hovered and banked towards the mountains, and the familiar cold wind came howling through the gun door. They gained height steadily until they were among the peaks of the Taurus again, the snowfields gleaming dimly below them in the starlight.

They followed the course of the river valley and landed in a rectangle of lights that marked the perimeter of a small, well-guarded *Jandarma* station. Its commander was waiting to meet them, and he gave Delkin a report that he relayed to Jack and Dale. The nearby *pansiyon* had been kept discreetly under observation, and within the past half-hour the party of strangers had driven off along the road that skirted the border to the west. They had not been followed for fear of alerting them. In any case, the truck they were expected to meet could cross the river at only one point, the bridge that Jack and Dale had seen from the air.

A jeep was ready to take them to the spot. It bumped along a rough track for a couple of kilometres before meeting the paved road beside the river at the point where it turned to the east, giving them a sudden night view of the scene they had witnessed the day before.

The Turks had set up floodlights on this side of the river to discourage any attempt to cross it under cover of darkness. Beyond the reach of their harsh beams, the mountainside above the far bank was an eerie sight. A thousand small fires flickered against the dark mass of rock and mud, the light they created merging into a vast but subdued glow, as though the mountain itself were luminous. Against this dim light, figures and shadows constantly moved, making the mass of refugees seem like some huge colony of restless insects. Thick smoke and a fetid smell hung in the cold, windless air over the valley.

The jeep halted opposite the bridge, beside the road junction that was turning into a mess of mud-filled potholes under the volume of heavy traffic. Soldiers were everywhere, and half a dozen tents had been pitched behind the crossing to serve as a headquarters for this sector of the border operation. Delkin took Jack and Dale into the largest tent, where he was greeted by salutes from half a dozen officers gathered round a map spread out on a trestle table. Gas pressure lamps hissed and kerosene heaters gave out a stifling warmth, and there was another table to one side where an orderly was in charge of tea and coffee urns and trays of food.

Delkin immediately got involved in a conversation with his subordinates, leaving Jack and Dale to themselves. They accepted cups of coffee, and after a few minutes Jack wandered outside to stare once again at the scene across the river. There was just the barest hint of daylight above the mountain ridges to the east now, slightly dimming the glow from the fires. Without the roar of the jeep's engine to smother them there were noises from across there as well, a fusion of thousands of small rustling sounds overlaid by the murmur of voices, punctuated occasionally, incongruously, by a burst of laughter. The comparison with an insect colony no longer seemed apt; this was what an army camped in the field might have looked and sounded like a long time ago, nervous and sleepless in the hours before a dawn attack. He wondered idly what could stop them if they simply marched *en masse* across the border, wading the river, cutting the wire.

As the light strengthened he could make out the road that led south from the bridge, disappearing between the folds of the mountains on the Iraqi side. A line of vehicles that had arrived during the night stretched into the distance, waiting for the border post to open at six o'clock. Perhaps the truck they were looking for was already there, if it was coming at all.

It was a blue Chevrolet three-tonner, according to what Delkin's informants had been told, ostensibly another hired vehicle carrying Kurds of Turkish nationality fleeing with their belongings from the fighting further south. Unlike the people on the hillsides they would be in possession of precious bits of paper entitling them to enter

Turkey, but were supposedly sensitive about having those belongings searched. Hence the bribe, presented as a cash alternative to surrendering television sets, valuable carpets or jewellery. It was something quite common along this border, Delkin said, where the regular traffic in refugees encouraged desperation on their part and corruption among the low-paid soldiery. As long as Malik and his men did not expect to be singled out for attention, they could be confident of getting through; and once inside Turkey they would no doubt be escorted to their next destination by the Grey Wolves.

And yet to Jack's mind it seemed a little too easy. Even if frightened into hasty action, with forty million dollars at stake would the Iraqis really want to depend on such a patched-together arrangement? A maxim that Colonel Thorpe had quoted popped suddenly into Jack's head. *When capable, pretend to be incapable. When far away, seem near.* Or had it been the other way around?

Delkin seemed sure of what he was doing, anyway, and when Jack returned to the tent he found the general sloshing whisky into Dale's second cup of coffee as well as his own.

'I want both of you to stay in here now,' he said. 'I can't afford to expose you to danger. And when the truck arrives, or if the gangster friends of the Iraqis return, the sight of Westerners will certainly arouse suspicion. The border opens in an hour's time. We facilitate their arrival, we let them get on the road, and we pounce!'

After a while he went off to attend to something else, followed by his retinue of officers, leaving the two of them alone in the tent. Settling down in a camp chair in the warmth, Jack imagined he might catch up on his sleep but soon gave up the idea, knowing he was far too tense.

Feeling more superfluous than ever, they sat in silence as daylight crept slowly through the canvas.

When six o'clock finally came Jack realized Dale had fallen asleep. He went and stood by the front flaps of the tent, taking care not to expose himself to the light from outside.

Thin sunshine was penetrating the mist and smoke that lay across the river. The opening looked across the cratered road junction towards the bridge, about fifty metres away, and almost immediately he saw the boom beside the customs post being raised. No vehicles from the Iraqi side were being allowed through yet; they were made to wait while three trucks crossed in the other direction, piled high with sacks and crates of food. The Kurds had spotted them well in advance and at least a thousand of them were gathered at the far end of the bridge, like animals recognizing their feeding time. They followed the trucks up the slope and there was another degrading scramble as the soldiers threw loaves of bread and bags of rice among them.

When the vehicles had returned to the Turkish side the troops manning the bridge gave their attention to the northbound ones. The first truck had about twenty people packed into the back, and all of them had their papers carefully examined. After much argument four or five of them were turned away to join the wretched crowds on the slopes, while the vehicle with the rest of its passengers was allowed through.

A helicopter went screaming by, following the river towards the west. The noise woke Dale up and she came to join him by the opening. He explained what was happening and they watched the same procedure being followed with the next truck, and the one after that. By half-past six only three of them had been processed. At this rate, even if the Chevrolet was near the front of the queue, it could take half the day to reach the bridge.

Jack noticed one other thing. The refugees were not having their belongings searched, and he guessed this was another ploy to encourage the Iraqis into thinking they were safe.

Delkin confirmed this when he and some of his entourage paid another fleeting visit to the tent a few minutes later. 'It also helps to speed things up,' he said. 'Our friends will be with us in less than an hour.'

'You mean they're actually there?' Jack exclaimed.

'Spotted from a helicopter,' the general announced with a smile. 'They won't have paid that any attention; they expect plenty of military activity, and they have no reason to think we have any special interest in them. You should be able to see them yourselves quite soon. Try using these.' He took a pair of field glasses from an officer beside him and handed them to Jack. Adjusting the focusing rings, he got a foreshortened view of the line of trucks across the river; there was one about ten from the front with a cab that might have been painted light blue, though in the smoky haze it was difficult to be certain about colours.

They were there, though. Delkin had been right, and Jack's earlier vague doubts disappeared. In an hour's time it would all be over, and suddenly there was some irony in the thought that what had begun with the private worries of one rich man should end among the anguish of these thousands of outcasts.

'Remember not to show yourselves,' Delkin reminded them before disappearing again. 'We are preparing a roadblock two kilometres to the west. I'll see you again as soon as we have our catch in the bag.'

Left on their own once more, Jack and Dale took turns with the binoculars. Half a dozen more trucks got across the bridge, but on each one there were several people whose papers were not in order and who were not allowed through. The one Jack had picked out drew closer, and now its colour could be seen as definitely blue, and the distinctive Chevrolet emblem was visible on its grille. Half a dozen people, unidentifiable at this distance, sat or stood on its uncovered cargo deck among a large mound of what looked like nondescript baggage. Three more figures were seated in the cab.

'I suppose you have to admire their nerve,' he said.

'For forty million dollars I guess I'd take a few risks myself,' Dale said, peering through the binoculars. 'Uh-oh, another hold-up.'

Two more trucks packed with food supplies had arrived. The boom was lowered behind them and the traffic coming this way was halted for ten minutes while they crossed the bridge and distributed their load to the usual frenzied mob. Jack wondered if the same people got their hands on the food every time.

Dale still had the glasses. 'Hey, things are moving faster!' she said.

She handed him the binoculars, but he didn't need them to understand what had happened. The soldiers at the bridge must have realized, or been told, that they didn't have to stop work every time the traffic was held up. They had used the interval to work back along the queue and process the people on board the waiting trucks. Three of them now lumbered in succession across the bridge, and the blue Chevrolet was next in line.

Jack held his breath, watching as three or four gendarmes surrounded the truck, examining the documents handed down to them by the passengers in the cab and in the rear. An agony of time seemed to go by while an officer spoke in a casual way to the driver; either he was putting on an act or he was ignorant of the vehicle's importance. But none of its occupants were being ordered off, and their baggage was being ignored.

The papers were given back. The officer waved at the driver. The striped boom was raised and the Chevrolet drove into Turkey.

It approached the junction, passing within twenty metres of where Jack and Dale were concealed. Straining to identify any of its passengers, Jack caught only blurred features that would hardly have been recognizable at that distance anyway, even if he'd had something better than indifferent photographs to go by. They were all men, though, all convincingly dressed as Kurds, some in baggy trousers and two or three with turbans.

They were jolted about as the truck rocked over the potholes at the junction and then turned left, on to the westbound road that led eventually to Iskenderun and the sea. It gathered speed quickly and in a few moments had disappeared.

Jack turned to Dale, seeing the same mixture of suspense and relief on her face that must have been apparent on his own. The thing was over but not quite done with. Malik and his men were on Turkish soil and couldn't now escape. But the final act was being played offstage, down the road. Jack found himself half-awaiting the sound of shooting from that direction as the desperate *Mukhabarat* tried to fight their way out of the trap.

The warmth in the tent suddenly seemed overwhelming. He took a step outside and felt Dale pluck at his arm.

'Hey, we're supposed to stay in here.'

'It can't matter now.'

'What if those Grey Wolf guys come back this way?'

'They won't. Their business is in the same direction as Malik's.'

She followed him outside, a bit dubiously but grateful for the fresh air as well. They walked to the junction and stood looking across the river. The sunshine had given a counterfeit gaiety to the scene on the mountainside, picking out the bright colours of the women's dresses and the green and orange sheets of plastic that the Kurds had used to make their pathetic shelters.

Another food convoy was approaching and they stepped off the road to let it pass. One more truck had made it across the bridge as well, down on its springs and sagging heavily into the potholes at the junction as it waited for the food lorries to get round the turning. Jack's gaze was still fixed on the mountainside, so it was something entirely outside his consciousness that drew his mind back to the truck. Even then he wasn't paying it any real attention, he was merely aware of its bringing something into focus, some inconsistency in his memory of recent events.

Then he knew what it was. Why hadn't the Chevrolet been moving in the heavy way that this vehicle was? The Chevrolet was supposed to be loaded with three tons of gold, yet it had bounced over the potholes as though it was carrying hardly any weight at all.

He looked up at this truck. Still rather absently, he saw that it was a cream-coloured Dodge, spattered with mud.

Through the side window of the cab he saw the face of General Malik.

It was unmistakable, in spite of the limitations imposed by comparing it with that single fuzzy photograph. The heavy jowls, the frowning brow, the dark pouches under the eyes. At the same moment Jack was aware of Malik staring at him, looking him over, noticing the injured arm in its sling. Whether there was actual recognition hardly mattered; his presence here, with Dale beside him, was a giveaway in itself. Malik knew that something was out of place, but then he must have thought it would be.

*When near, you should seem to be far away.*

Malik had second-guessed his enemies. Delkin's trap had been set for the wrong people.

As if confirmation of this were needed, the truck lurched out into the junction, and instead of turning left, towards the west, it headed in the other direction.

# 32

Dale had seen him staring, had gathered that something was wrong, but didn't know what. The whole episode had taken only a couple of seconds and now Jack, speechless with astonishment, was pointing with his good arm at the Dodge as it drove off to the east.

'Malik!' he blurted out at last.

'Malik is on that truck? Jesus, let's do something!'

But for another few seconds they did nothing. Immobilized by their surprise, they watched the truck moving away from them along the narrow road, ponderously at first and then picking up speed. It had high ground clearance and there was a canvas canopy over the back, open to the rear and showing the figures of three men squatting among a heap of bundles and boxes.

Not enough weight there to put the truck so far down on its springs.

Three men in the back and two in the cab made five. Malik and four of his henchmen from the *Mukhabarat*; the fifth, Hayawi, still in London. Three tons of gold hidden somewhere beneath that other cargo. And, unbelievably, they were getting away with it.

The truck vanished around a bend two hundred metres away. Recollecting themselves, Jack and Dale sprinted to the tents.

The biggest one was empty, they knew, Delkin away uselessly stopping and searching the wrong vehicle. They pushed their way into the one beside it and found a single young soldier sitting at a table, manning a crackling radio transceiver. Their arrival alarmed him and he made startled negative gestures as they tried to explain what was needed.

'General Delkin,' Dale said. 'We have to speak to General Delkin.' She pointed at the radio. 'Can you call him on that?'

She tried French and Arabic as well. The boy replied in Turkish and went on waving his hands in front of him until, with relief, he saw someone else enter the tent behind him. This was a junior officer, but he too spoke only Turkish and seemed to have even more trouble trying to understand them.

'There's a man called Malik who has come into Turkey,' Jack enunciated carefully, supplementing his words with sign language. 'Malik, an Iraqi, whom General Delkin wants to arrest. We must speak to General Delkin about this Iraqi.'

'Iraq?' The officer had caught only one word of this speech. He pointed out of the tent, towards the border, and gave them a questioning look.

Jack made signs mimicking a conversation on the radio, but to no avail. He glanced at Dale in despair. These were regular army men, without the red armbands of the *Jandarma*, and obviously for reasons of security they had not been told the purpose of Delkin's operation. Nobody but the general and his immediate staff was going to know what these two foreigners were talking about. It seemed impossible that they should be standing here in his headquarters, with instant communication to hand, and knowing that because they could not make themselves understood Malik was slipping away through their fingers.

'I'll go find Delkin,' Dale said decisively.

'But—'

'He's the only one we can deal with. He's two kilometres away, right? I can make it in six minutes. Maybe seven, in these.' She pointed down at the flat-heeled boots she was wearing, with the corduroy jeans she had put on for warmth tucked into them. 'You stay right here in case I miss him.'

With the two Turks gaping at her she pulled off her sweater, revealing the white T-shirt she wore beneath

376

it, and without another word she turned and left. Jack followed her to the front of the tent and saw her set off at a steady run down the road to the west.

It seemed he could do nothing but wait. Then he remembered the map that was spread out in the other tent and he went and studied it. The road that ran eastwards from here was marked out as a solid red line for about twenty kilometres. Then it degenerated into a faint track twisting into the mountains to the north. This, however, met up eventually with another road he remembered old Zakarios mentioning, the one that travelled from a point north of Hakkari to the Iranian border.

Could that be Malik's destination, Iran? Or did he have a plan for hiding the gold once again among these wild mountains? Or even, as Zakarios had suggested, breaking it down into smaller quantities and smuggling it piecemeal out of Turkey? Whatever his intentions, he had neatly circumvented Delkin's trap. The arrival of the Grey Wolves in the area last night, the story about the blue Chevrolet truck, had clearly been a blind. Perhaps the ship waiting at Iskenderun was part of it, too, suggesting that Malik had made his plans much further in advance than Delkin imagined. Instead of being scared off by the situation on the border, he had turned its confusion to his advantage.

The manoeuvre was as bold as it was risky. And if Delkin didn't get after him soon there seemed every chance that he would get away with it.

Jack went on staring at the map for a while. The orderly who had been in the tent earlier had left, but there was still hot coffee in the urn and he helped himself to some and went and stood at the entrance, gazing across the river again. Ten minutes had gone by when he heard the howl of a helicopter approaching, and a few moments later it came in from his right, another gunship or perhaps the same one that had brought them here, flying very fast towards the east. There was no way of knowing whether it was responding to an emergency or not.

The latest food convoy was making its way back across the bridge after again being besieged by the mob. Trucks were still coming across in this direction as though nothing untoward had happened. Then there was a roar of motors from the right and Delkin's jeep swung in off the road, followed by another one crammed with his officers. Dale was sitting in the rear of the leading vehicle beside the general, and she gave Jack a thumbs-up sign as the jeeps slid to a halt next to the tents. A troop carrier drew up behind them, and soldiers piled out and ran to take up crouching positions along either side of the road, rifles and carbines held ready.

Delkin remained in the jeep, talking urgently into a radio handset. Dale hopped to the ground, showing not a trace of exhaustion after her run. Jack gave her a hug, but before either of them could speak the sound of shooting came from the east, two or three deep-throated bursts from a machine-gun, and then the whine of the helicopter was audible again, growing gradually louder.

Dale explained quickly what had happened: 'I got to Delkin in time for him to order a roadblock set up about fifteen kilometres from here. The Iraqis turned the truck around when they saw it and they're coming back this way. And now the helicopter has caught up with them.'

Delkin was still muttering into his radio. Beneath that and the rising scream of the turbojet engines the whole valley seemed to have fallen silent. Even the Kurds on the mountainside had ceased their restlessness, gazing downriver like everyone else as though they sensed some high drama being enacted on the opposite bank.

The gunship finally came into view, flying very low above the road from the east. Then, a minute later, the Dodge truck lurched around the nearest bend with dust billowing up around it. The helicopter was right over it, its skids just a metre or two above the cab, like a bird of prey waiting for its moment to pounce. If it had been going to attack, though, it would have done so before now. Jack realized that the shots they had heard had been warning bursts from the helicopter's gun door. Delkin still wanted the Iraqis alive if possible, and short of strafing the vehicle and killing its occupants the gunship could do nothing to control its movements.

As it approached the junction along the straight stretch of road the truck showed no sign of stopping. If anything, it was picking up speed. Delkin made a decision and barked an order into his radio. A second later it was relayed to the troops beside the road, and a rattle of small-arms fire broke out.

What they hit, if anything, was impossible to see, for the helicopter raised such a storm of dust as it passed them by that it almost obliterated the target. But as the truck reached the junction it veered heavily to the left, hitting the side of the troop carrier and swerving almost out of control before the driver straightened it and set it on a shaky course towards the bridge.

A kind of collective gasp went up from the group in front of the tents as they realized what was happening. Malik was trying to re-cross the river. Taking the gold with him, preferring to chance his survival back in Iraq.

If he got back there he would be out of reach for ever.

The soldiers had scrambled to their feet and were firing at the rear of the truck. None of the *Mukhabarat* was visible beneath the canopy, presumably having dropped behind the tailboard to protect themselves. The helicopter had overshot the junction and was now circling to get back above its target. And the Dodge, although peppered with bullet holes, was still moving. It was rolling on to the bridge.

It hit the metal boom at speed, buckling it and knocking it aside. Now the road ahead was clear, with the vehicles on the Iraqi side halted short of the approach to the bridge. There was nothing there to stop it.

Except the Kurds.

There was no way of gauging how much they understood of what going on. They had seen the helicopter shadowing the truck and they had heard the shooting; but the fact that must have been uppermost in their hunger-conscious minds was that the only vehicles that crossed into Iraq at present were food trucks. Within a matter of seconds, it seemed, hundreds of them had materialized from nowhere to gather in a tight, expectant knot at the far end of the bridge. If they noticed that there were no Turkish soldiers on the truck it probably only heightened their anticipation. What they didn't notice until it was too late was that the Dodge wasn't slowing down.

It charged straight towards them. It was being chased by the helicopter now, which had levelled out about twenty metres above and behind it and would probably have opened fire but for the certainty of killing Kurds as well as Iraqis. The crowd broke and ran, scattering in all directions as the truck bore down on them, but for a few trapped in the centre it was too late. Frozen with horror, Jack and the others by the tents saw figures knocked down and thrown into the air, and heard the sickening bump of wheels going over bodies and the screams of panic that echoed across the river.

Perhaps the driver finally lost his nerve, or perhaps the sheer resistance of the bodies that he ploughed into halted his progress. Either way, what they saw from the Turkish side was the truck slewing off the road and halting, jammed in the mud that coated the hillside. Five or six people lay flat on the ground around it. And now the rest of the Kurds, who had spread out in a wide circle, began to converge on it with a great roar of anger.

Jack started forward. Dale followed him and then Delkin and his officers joined them in a scramble towards the bridge. As they ran, they saw the crowd enveloping the truck, piling on to it like a pack of animals. This time it wasn't food they were after, it was vengeance. The doors of the cab were wrenched open and its occupants were dragged out. To the rear, a dozen men hoisted themselves over the tailboard. An Iraqi leaped out past them and was immediately seized by the mob. A raised knife blade flashed in the sunshine as he was brought down.

Hundreds more people were running from the mountainside to swell the mob. Reaching the end of the bridge, Jack and Dale were jammed in among them. Turkish soldiers, swinging their rifle butts, were trying to clear a path but making no progress.

Somehow the Kurds had identified their enemies. If there was one group of people they had more cause to hate than any other, it was the *Mukhabarat*. Catching hold of the name, they began repeating it in a rhythmic, angry chant as General Malik and his comrades were carried head-high among them, their limbs flailing. Then they were overwhelmed, swallowed up. Fists clutching knives, stones and sticks rose and fell around them. The Kurds who had boarded the truck from the rear had already thrown the two remaining Iraqis to the crowd and were flinging out the boxes and bundles they found there, pots and pans and other household goods bursting out of their flimsy wrappings of blankets and sheets. All the Kurds' frustration and rage was boiling over in this reckless surge of looting and violence.

Now those on the truck had found something else. They had lowered the tailboard and were tossing slabs of dull yellow metal to the ground. Too heavy for the upraised hands to grasp, the bars of gold were snatched up from the mud and carried clumsily off, each one cheered on its way and surrounded by an eager section of the crowd. From somewhere came a few bursts of shots as soldiers fired over their heads, but it made no difference. Thousands of people were surrounding the truck now and the bars were being slid out three and four at a time, all being grabbed and vanishing as quickly as they appeared.

General Malik's stolen wealth was being redistributed.

Apart from relatives gathered round the bodies of those who had been run over, the mood of the crowd was suddenly gleeful. There was no fighting over the gold, just an eager scrum of people wanting to claim a stake in every bar as it was whisked off up the mountainside. The mob was thinning out but those at the rear were still pressing anxiously forward. Jack and Dale, clinging to each other, were thrust towards the centre, and now they could see the gold, spread out in a single, rapidly diminishing layer on the cargo deck of the truck. The Kurds were hiding the bars in their clothing as they ran off, or wrapping them in layers of paper or cloth. There was no possibility that any would ever be recovered.

The people run over by the truck were being carried away but the Iraqis were forgotten, their bodies being trampled into the muck. Jack stumbled over one of them, lying on its back and already half buried, and saw that it was Malik. Blood leaking from a dozen stab wounds in his torso was being soaked up by the mud. His face was swollen and bruised from beating but he was still recognizable, an expression of horror frozen on his surly features.

The last bar of gold disappeared from the truck and the crowd began to disperse.

The Kurds were light-headed, laughing almost hysterically as they headed back to their encampment.

They had snatched a kind of victory out of their despair. They would go on being cold and hungry until the world took more notice of them, but a collective windfall of forty million dollars would go a long way towards rebuilding their lives.

It was a thought that would have pleased Abdel Karim.

General Delkin flew back with them to Istanbul that afternoon and they spent the night in his house at Yildiz Fort. The next morning Jack made a long phone call to Dr Hamadi.

He had put considerable thought into what he was going to say, not only because he owed Hamadi a full account of

382

what had happened but because it affected the futures of several people.

Hamadi's secret would be safe, and he could go on making his millions with as little embarrassment as before. He was grateful enough to be responsive to all Jack's suggestions.

Of the two million dollars that he had agreed to pay Jalloul, the first half would probably stay where it was indefinitely, in a ghost account at the Handelsbank Bauer with no-one willing or able to claim a title to it. The second million would be returned to Hamadi once he had wound up his legal covenant with Zunckel. Since he had been willing to write off this amount and more, if necessary, he was agreeable to paying half of it to Nadine Schuster to be held in trust for her son, Etienne, and to making the other half available to Jack.

As another favour, he would also make a private recommendation to Major Al-Shaheb that the charges against Lieutenant Fadel be dropped. No such intercession was likely on behalf of Sharif Hayawi, who had been arrested in London and would be tried for the kidnapping and murder of Abdel Karim.

Jack would be going back to Banstead, but only for long enough to put a proposal to Alison. He didn't have to accept the half-million dollars from Hamadi, which, as things stood, would have to be split between them under the terms of the divorce settlement. He would take the money, and use it to set up an investment fund that would benefit the two of them and the twins equally, only on condition that they had joint custody of the girls and equal access to them. Otherwise he would turn the payment down.

She would tell him he was mad but he did not expect her to refuse.

Hamadi said: 'You're forgetting one other small thing. I owe you fifty thousand dollars, the second half of your original fee. I'll let you have it at once if you'll tell me where to send it.'

Jack put his hand over the receiver and looked at Dale. 'Where are we going to be living?' he said.

'I don't know. I guess we could start at the Henderson Hotel.'

**THE END**